QUEEN'S CATACOMBS

JORDAN H. BARTLETT

The Frean Chronicles

The golden crown casts deadly shadows.

CamCat Books

CamCat Publishing, LLC
Brentwood, Tennessee 37027
camcatpublishing.com

Hardcover ISBN 9780744307764
Paperback ISBN 9780744307788
Large-Print Paperback ISBN 9780744307986
eBook ISBN 9780744307818
Audiobook ISBN 9780744307863

Library of Congress Control Number: 2022915043

Book and cover design by Maryann Appel
Map illustration by Andrew Martin

5 3 1 2 4

In memory of Nana Jill,

for showing me the true power of a matriarch.

You had all the time in the world for me,

I wish I had a little more time with you.

The Queendom of
NYSA
The Queendom of
FREA
Terrelle
Parima
Luxlow
Hesperida
Brinora
Newfrea
Court's
Mountain
Springbank
Thealis
Catacombs
of Lethe
Basileia
Reed
Bregend
SouthGate
South
Battlement
Bridgeport
Salmyre
The Salt Pits
Hendrick's
Dam
Abysterra

Azulon Sea
N
The Kingdom of
AUSTER
Griffin's Peak
Wrenstrom
Everden
Llynhaven
Jacs' Farm
Sennuik
Oldfrean Bastion
Nadir
Fenlea

1

PLANNING THE GAMBIT

"Tell me where you're keeping them."

Jacs balled her fists, manicured fingernails digging into her palms. She swept her cloak behind her. It was a rich, deep blue velvet edged with silver ermine and a gold embroidered trim. A true vestment of state, one she could not have dreamed of setting eyes on three months ago, let alone wearing.

The good it did her now.

She stood in the center of the Council of Four's chamber. The chamber's floor sank in the middle like a caldera and four sets of three steps rose away from it, marking the points of a compass. At the top of each set of steps sat a member of the Council. Their chairs were as close to throne-like as was allowed. The entitled self-indulgence of the Councilors dripped from every aspect of this chamber's decor. Jacs glared up at each smug countenance and tried not to act like the petulant child they thought her to be.

She could not believe her predecessor, Queen Ariel, had been oblivious to the terrifying power the Four wielded. Maybe she had known but, like Jacs, lacked the ability to do anything but stomp her feet and dance to their tune.

"My dear, repetition of this request will not change the answer," Cllr. Gretchen Dilmont drawled. She sat at the north point of the room's compass. Her short, white-blonde hair stood on end and her red-lipped mouth curled up in one corner as she spoke. She did not deign to look at her Queen and instead examined the large gold ring on her index finger.

"Indeed, it's repetition of an action with an expectation of a different outcome that is the very definition of insanity. Are you quite well, child?" Cllr. Rosalind Perda added. She sat directly opposite Cllr. Dilmont. Jacs had to spin around to face her. Cllr. Perda's dark, pinched features sharpened into a smile. Jacs imagined herself to be a mouse under the gaze of a hawk, the Councilor's sharp eyes taking in every out-of-place auburn hair on Jacs's head. Her own black hair was slicked back and secured with a jeweled hair comb. Blood-red rubies surrounded a tear-shaped onyx stone. It almost looked like a crown. Almost.

"Yes, should we call Master Epione? She may have a tincture for you." Cllr. Beatrice Fengar piped up from Cllr. Perda's left. She appeared to be enjoying the banter and, in Jacs's experience, never tended to add anything of substance to an interaction. Her thick brown hair was piled high on top of her head in a swirling bun, loose waves framing her high cheekbones. She fiddled with the silver fringe of her sleeve and smiled at Jacs.

Though her smile lacked the coldness that emanated from the first two Councilors, Jacs still clenched her teeth. She felt like a ball of yarn being batted about by three smug cats.

"Now Councilors, have a heart. It can be frightening when a girl loses her mother." Cllr. Portia Stewart's wispy voice came from the equally wispy woman directly opposite Cllr. Fengar. Again, Jacs was forced to spin around. Cllr. Stewart's brow was creased with concern. She looked about the room at each of her colleagues and pursed her lips slightly. She was perched on the edge of her seat with the look of a bird ready to take flight. Her pure white hair floated around her like a cloud.

Jacs glared at her and retorted hotly, "I haven't *lost* her; I know you have her. Likely the same place you have Master Leschi. Now, where are they?" Her stomach tightened. She had last seen her mother, battered and beaten on the floor of a prison cell, moments before the Prince proclaimed Jacs as the Queen. As for Master Leschi, Jacs hadn't seen her since they'd launched their final hot-air balloon; her mentor's face had been bright with hope, excitement, and pride as Jacs drifted farther and farther into the sky. Recalling her mother's bruised and bloodied face, she dreaded the thought of what Master Leschi might look like now.

What she would give to see her again. Her mentor had always known what the next steps should be, and how to get Jacs there. After the purple-hooded assassins shot Queen Ariel from their clocktower, it had been Master Leschi who suggested Jacs compete to win the crown for their people. But what kind of queen was Jacs shaping up to be if she couldn't even free the two most important women in her life? She could stare their captors in the face with a crown on her head and an ermine cloak around her shoulders yet enact absolutely no change.

It was clear from the moment they discovered her Lowrian heritage that the Councilors disapproved of her winning the crown, but over the last three months it became obvious that they were actively working against her. Their withholding of Master Leschi and Maria Tabart was one of the many ways they ensured Jacs knew who was really in control of the Queendom.

She turned back to Cllr. Fengar, who piped up redundantly. "Maybe a glass of warm milk to settle the nerves?"

Jacs said nothing. She was used to being ignored by Cllr. Perda and Cllr. Dilmont, but being ignored by Cllr. Fengar felt like hitting a new low.

"And let's acknowledge the hard work our little queen is putting into fulfilling our requests. Surely that's worth a treat?" Cllr. Perda said.

Jacs set her jaw and waited. Rotating her healed wrist, she felt a ripple of satisfying pops. It had never quite been the same since she had broken it climbing Court's Mountain in the first task. While Master Epione had mended it as well as she could, that little melody of pops remained, as a permanent souvenir from the Contest.

"You're right, but what to give a girl who has everything?" Cllr. Dilmont said sardonically, still not looking up from her ring.

Jacs took a breath and forced her voice to remain level. "You *know* what I want," she said. "Let my mother go. Tell me where Master Leschi is. Or at least let me see them. It's been three months. I've done all you've asked. Let them go." Jacs bit her tongue to hold back the *please* that almost burst from her lips. She would not beg. A queen did not beg.

The Councilors looked at one another.

"Oh, poppet, no. That we cannot do," Cllr. Stewart said. She actually looked contrite.

Jacs wasn't surprised, but somehow the answer still hurt. She looked up into each of the four Councilors' eyes in turn, trying to find some warmth, some shred of compassion.

"However," Cllr. Perda said after a time, "we do have some correspondence from your mother that was delivered to us."

Jacs's heart skipped a beat, but she forced her face to remain impassive.

Cllr. Perda continued. "Unfortunately, we cannot share it unless a certain document is signed by the hand of the Queen."

Jacs almost rolled her eyes, but again restrained herself. It would be easier if they just stated what they required of her at the beginning of each meeting. Instead, Jacs had to follow the steps of their specific dance, only learning each new step right before her foot touched the ground.

"What document is this?" she asked.

Cllr. Perda inclined her head toward Cllr. Fengar, who pulled a piece of parchment from a small side table by her elbow. Holding it delicately, she read its contents.

Jacs listened carefully, knowing that she did not have much of a choice in whether she signed it or not. Through the lengthy jargon, Jacs determined it was a document that called to shift the border between Lord Witbron's and Lord Claustrom's lands. Apparently, Lord Witbron of Luxlow was bequeathing 10 percent of her lands to Lord Claustrom of Hesperida voluntarily. However, as it was land initially gifted by the crown, Jacs needed to sign off on its transfer.

Jacs walked up the few steps to retrieve the parchment from Cllr. Fengar. Moving over to a small desk in the northeast corner of her sunken dais, she bent over the paper, dipped her quill in the provided inkwell, and was poised to sign. Melted wax pooled in a small dish above a candle to the right of her hand, ready to be poured for her seal.

". . . Lord Hera Claustrom is eager to put this new land to better use and bids to thank the Queen for her blessing in this matter," Cllr. Fengar finished.

Jacs jerked upright with a start, her quill dripping a dollop of ink on the line for her signature. "Who?" Jacs asked.

"Lord Hera Claustrom," Cllr. Fengar repeated.

"No," Jacs said, "you mean *Dame* Hera Claustrom?" Although still new to the hierarchy and politics of the Upper Realm, Jacs knew Dame Hera Claustrom. Hera, a contestant beaten by Jacs in the Contest of Queens. The current Dame who actively spoke against Jacs at every opportunity in the embarrassment that was the public throne-room audience. Her mother was Lord Sybil Claustrom. Very wealthy, very influential, and very much in control of most of the Lords in the Upper Realm.

"No, Councilor Fengar did not misspeak." Jacs turned to face Cllr. Perda. "You must have been visiting Newfrea when the announcement was made. Dame Hera Claustrom has inherited her mother's title of lord, as the now Lady Sybil Claustrom wishes to spend her remaining years in a little more peace. Given her many contributions to our Queendom throughout her reign, she has certainly earned some time to reap the fruits of her labor." Cllr. Perda's sharp eyes narrowed slightly, but her remaining features depicted humble reverence.

Jacs's thoughts reeled, and her heart sank. *More good news,* she thought glumly.

Almost apologetically, Cllr. Stewart cut across her musing. "You have yet to sign, dear."

Jacs looked down, her hand hovering over the parchment. The blot sat defiantly at the beginning of her line. Looking up, she said, "Let me see the letter you have from my mother first."

Cllr. Perda clicked her tongue. "So distrusting."

Jacs waited.

"Here," Cllr. Perda said finally, pulling a grubby scrap of parchment from a pocket within her bell sleeve.

Jacs's heart jumped to her throat. She swallowed, bent, and signed the document. Without looking at any of them, she poured the thimble-sized ball of wax onto the bottom, removed her signet ring that held the royal sigil, and pressed it down. Rich molten wax pillowed around the edges of the ring. Methodically, she dusted and blew on the ink, peeled her ring out of the wax, leaving the ornate Frean *F* behind, rolled up the document, and walked up to stand in front of Cllr. Perda.

Cllr. Perda slowly extended her hand to receive the parchment. Jacs held hers out expectantly in return. There was a moment of tension. Neither woman yielded. Each waited to feel the weight of the other's paper in her palm before relinquishing her own. Jacs made the first move, extending her wrist a fraction, and the document landed home. Once Cllr. Perda's fingers snapped shut, Jacs snatched her mother's letter and clutched it to her heart. Cllr. Perda's eyes sparkled in victory, and the corners of her mouth twitched up slightly in a smirk. Jacs didn't care. She walked back down to her dais, the note still at her breast, and inclined her head slightly to each Councilor in turn.

"If that is all, I must attend to this in my study." She fought to remain composed, the facade of a queen a mere glimmer on her countenance. The Councilors said nothing to detain her, and she turned toward the door at the southwest corner of the room. She passed between Cllr. Perda and Cllr. Fengar, determined to avoid eye contact with both of them.

The heavy door closed behind Jacs, and she took a breath to steady herself. Flanking the doorway stood Chivilras Amber Everstar and Andromeda Turner, her friends and knights of the Queensguard. Both wore the lightweight leather armor and sheathed short sword that befitted a knight of the realm.

It was said that knights did not need a weapon at all: Their training and teamwork took them to the height of physical lethality, and their sheathed swords were mere symbols of that. Jacs had watched them train. It was an awe-inspiring sight watching two women moving and striking as one unit.

Amber's crooked grin turned into a frown at the look of distress on Jacs's face. She stood at ease, chin naturally jutting forward—likely from a life lived as the shortest woman in most rooms—brown eyes alert and bright. A long coil of dark brown hair hung in a sleek tail down her back. Andromeda, in contrast, stood over a head taller than her partner. She was a woman of sharp angles and cold calculations, yet her dark eyes were always soft and her tone never barbed with anything harsher than sarcasm. Her ash blonde hair was restrained in a fishtail plait swept over one shoulder. They made an odd set of bookends, and despite the disparity, Amber's presence always seemed more imposing than her partner's. The personification of a rock and a hard place.

Amber nodded pointedly to Andromeda, who stepped out in front, leading the way. Placing a hand on the small of Jacs's back, Amber whispered in her ear, "We're almost clear, Jacqueline."

With the warmth of Amber's hand, Jacs stood up straighter and walked silently through the corridors. Thankfully, they did not meet anyone of note along the way. Jacs did not quite know where they were taking her, but she knew enough to trust Amber's direction. She clung to the small piece of paper and placed one foot in front of the other until she found herself outside in the palace gardens.

Corridors, tapestries, and torches were replaced with cobbles, hedges, and the sweet scent of spring flowers. They crossed a checkered lawn often used for large games of chess and came across Connor, sitting at a desk that had most likely been moved outside at his request. Papers littered the surface, and two guardpairs stood to attention around the perimeter of the makeshift outdoor study.

Connor, Royal Advisor to the Queen, formally Cornelius Frean, looked up as Jacs approached and smiled. He stood to greet her. His brown hair was tousled from the breeze, and he wore the Royal Advisor's seal pinned over his heart. A golden ring encircling a crossed sword and feather.

Jacs ran to him. She caught a glimpse of his smile furrowing in concern before her arms were around his neck and her head was burrowed in his chest. She was aware of Amber's muttered comment to Andromeda, aware of the guardpairs' instructed aversion of gaze, aware even that the gardeners they passed earlier would now be privy to this impulsive action of their Queen. But for now, it was enough to feel Connor's hand on her hair, to hear his murmured "hey," and to count his heartbeats against her cheek.

It was enough.

"Come, sit with me," he said after her breathing had slowed. She nodded and allowed him to lead her to one of the stone benches at the edge of the small courtyard he had adopted for his study. The guard-pairs shifted to accommodate this change in position without being told, and without looking directly at the Queen and her Advisor. Jacs and Connor settled on the herb-flanked bench. Jacs noted the scents of rosemary and lavender and smiled sadly. The smell sparked a memory of Master Leschi's cluttered workshop.

"Rosemary for memory," she said.

Connor, whose arm was around her shoulders, gave her a squeeze. "A scholar's best friend, they say," he replied.

He searched her face for a moment before kissing her chastely on the cheek.

"We'll find them," he said.

Jacs saw hope glitter in his blue eyes and felt the cold hands around her heart loosen. She sighed. "I mean, we at least know who knows where they are. Getting them to talk is the next step." She wrinkled her nose in frustration.

She didn't know what was worse, having no leads at all, or their only lead being a dead end.

"Well," he said tentatively, "we don't know that for sure."

Jacs decided not to have this discussion again and instead pulled out her mother's letter. "They gave me this today," she said quietly.

Connor made a motion to take it, changed his mind, and cocked his head.

She ran her finger over the broad-stroked *J* on the front. Looking at the letter in the light she noticed it was grubbier than she had initially thought. The paper was folded in half and its edges were frayed. The *J* was written with a shaking hand. Black ink splatters and blotches of a dark rust color peppered the page. Jacs held it closer, gasped, and recoiled. Eyes wide, she looked at Connor. He must have realized at the same time, because he asked very quietly, "Is that . . .? It's not . . . That looks like . . ."

Dried blood.

Hardly daring to breathe, she unfolded the paper and saw the same shaking and splotchy writing inside. Over top of her mother's writing, sections had been painted over with black ink. A neat script had been added to the bottom of the letter in a different hand:

Certain sections have been omitted due to their lack of relevance to the Queen's needs.

Eyes darting back to her mother's writing, she forced the bile rising in her throat down and read:

Plum,
Am well. Can't say where, ————————. It's dark all the time and I can hear ————————. I miss you. Please ————————.
I love you.

Connor read the short message over her shoulder, snapped his fingers, and ordered: "A goblet of wine for Her Majesty. She is not feeling well." At once, a pair of guards bowed and started toward the castle. Amber and Andromeda smoothly took their positions, hands clasped in front.

Jacs's composure, which had been slipping all afternoon, finally cracked. She felt heat flare in her cheeks and her brow darkened. She wanted to scream, to throw something, but knew the Council had eyes everywhere. Any perceived loss of control would paint her as weak and unfit to rule. She thought of her mother, holed up who knew where, hopeful that her note would reach sympathetic eyes. Each letter laboriously traced on parchment, only to be blacked out by an unfeeling brute.

"Connor," Jacs breathed. She felt as though a griffin were sitting on her chest. "I need you to distract me. Right now. I don't want to think about this here. *Please*." She held his gaze to keep from drowning.

"Okay, sure. Okay."

Connor looked about him hurriedly, arm still tight around her. With the other hand, he took the note, put it carefully in his breast pocket, and took her hand in his.

"Well, how about I tell you what I've been working on. Okay? Okay. I've been looking at our gold stores." As Connor spoke, he rubbed the back of Jacs's hand with his thumb, his tone low and soothing. "It's a bit of a head scratcher, actually. Every year we get a documented amount of eggshells from the Court, and every year the treasury's books document a significantly larger deposit. I'm not sure if I would consider that a problem. In fact, it really is the opposite of a problem. I definitely wouldn't complain, it's just I can't find any reason why we would be so much better off with each hatching than we should be."

Jacs took quick, shallow breaths and listened intently. She nodded for him to continue.

"And if it's the case that all the golden eggs from the Court are accounted for appropriately, then where would we be getting all the extra eggshells? It would be different if it were an extra shell every so often, but it's almost half the Court's amount every hatching." Connor paused for a moment and gave her hand a squeeze. "It really just doesn't make sense," he finished.

Jacs's breathing slowed. She stared at the ring on her pinkie finger, Connor's fingers wrapped around hers. The ring was smaller than her royal seal. It was her first gift from Connor, even though they had not yet met when she received it. She remembered the little boat that had sailed down the waterfall and washed up at the base of the Cliff separating their two realms.

Their two worlds.

To think, a little ring could lead to all this. She had worn it these last five years, although when she was younger it had hung from a cord, then a chain around her neck; now it sat proudly on her finger.

Shining in the sunlight, the tiny, engraved Griffin pranced above golden clouds. The Court of Griffins were the Queendom's only source of gold. Their golden eggshells had supplied the two realms ever since people had formed an alliance with them. Connor was right: for the Queendom to consistently have more than what the Court provided didn't make sense.

"Who is in charge of tallying the gold shells?" Jacs asked.

"The Council of Four. I believe Cllr. Fengar is normally in charge of the gold income. From there, some is transferred to the gold merchants, a portion of it goes to the Lower Realm during Trading Week, and the rest is divvied up to pay debts, to fund the military, to subsidize various guilds and so on," Connor replied. He ticked off the items on his fingers.

Jacs, whose experience with the Councilor still rang in her ears, asked sharply, "Why does Cllr. Fengar have that role?"

Connor raised an eyebrow. "Because it's one of the highest honors to bestow on a person and the Four are second only to the Queen. The Queen doesn't do it herself because she has too many other important duties to oversee, and the task may put her life at risk."

He pulled back a little and searched her face again. He frowned.

"Jacs," he said in a low voice, "I know your dealings with the Four have been rocky, and I know you think they're behind what's happening to your mother—"

"I *know* they're behind what's—"

"But—" he pressed firmly, pausing for a moment as he searched for his next words. "You have to understand, they are core pillars to our way of life. Not just for the Upperites but the Lowrians too. This is so much bigger than a personal dispute. They are the cogs that keep the Queendom's machine running. Maybe if you saw them as less of an enemy . . . maybe if you tried . . . you could start working on the same side?"

Jacs felt as though she had been slapped. She looked around to see if anyone was listening and hissed so only Connor could hear: "Connor, they have my mother and Master Leschi Alti-knows-where. They keep using them to blackmail me into doing whatever they want. From their standpoint, they don't *need* to play nice, they don't *need* to play fair, they don't *even need to* pretend to collaborate. I. Am. A. Pawn." Her voice wavered and she took a breath. "And they'll never see me as anything other than a Lowrian who flew too close to the sun."

"Jacs," he said softly, "you may not feel like it now, but you *are* our Queen. The contest picked you. The people chose you. You, above all others. Somehow it will all work out. It has to."

Jacs thought about the bloodstained parchment and a knot formed in her stomach. *But how long will that take?* she thought. *And how long can they hold on for?*

The wine was delivered, and sips were taken. Connor rubbed the pad of his thumb across the back of her hand, and she watched the rhythmic movement absently. *It will all work out*, Connor had said. She felt her heart rate slow and her mind detach from the pain she felt there.

Suddenly she was back in the sunlit second-story mess of Master Leschi's workshop. Phillip was humming to himself downstairs, and Master Leschi was unfurling the plans for their latest project.

"Something is wrong with the fulcrum," Master Leschi was saying. As she spoke, she weighted down each corner of the plans with an odd assortment of paperweights. "The effort needed to lift the load is too high given the amount of effort we hypothesized using. It's not efficient. So"—she looked up from the plans and fixed Jacs with a piercing gaze, a twinkle of excitement glittering in her eye and dancing at the corners of her mouth—"how do we fix it?"

Sitting with Connor now, Jacs felt her mentor's gaze on her once more. Master Leschi had always taught her that every question craved an answer. Nothing had changed, she had simply forgotten her training for a moment. Hers was another problem in need of a solution. She just needed to figure it out. *So*, she thought, *how do I fix it?*

"Connor," she began, "did your mother keep a journal? A personal journal, something she would have written her thoughts in?"

"A journal?" Connor thought for a moment. "The biographers collected most of her public writings shortly after . . ." He trailed off and picked up a different thread. "But as for something personal, I'm not sure. I could send a message to Father to see if he remembers." Absently, he touched the Royal Advisor's pin with his fingertips. It had belonged to the King.

The dowager King had left Basileia to stay in the coastal city of Terrelle shortly after Jacs had been crowned. He had shaken Jacs's hand before leaving. His bony fingers were the texture of parchment, and his spine was stooped as though the world hung around his neck. "The sea air will do him good," Connor said, but the crease of worry at his brow had only deepened the longer his father stayed away.

Jacs nodded. "Yes, write to him when you can, and send a messenger you trust." She took another sip of wine and swirled the crimson liquid around the goblet. "I'll meet with Lena and Anya for lunch today," she said and looked over at his desk littered with parchment. "Can you join us?"

He smiled and kissed her. She felt the knot loosen in her chest ever so slightly, but the thought of her mother's note carved deep creases between her brows.

"I wish I could, but I have a meeting," he said.

"What meeting?"

Connor's eyes shifted from hers to his table of parchment, "Just a meeting about, uh, this egg situation. I want to get a better understanding of it."

Jacs paused, then said, "Shouldn't I be a part of that meeting too?"

"No, no. It's not one I'd trouble you with," Connor said quickly.

"Oh," Jacs said quietly.

"I will tell you every boring detail tonight if you like." Connor clasped her hands in his and kissed her knuckles.

She felt the corners of her mouth lift and pushed her doubts aside. "Deal," she said.

2

THE COUNSEL OF THE FOUR

Connor watched Jacs's figure retreat across the lawn, flanked by Chiv. Everstar and Chiv. Turner. She seemed to have left in slightly higher spirits than she had arrived, but fear and grief had lingered around her eyes as she turned to leave. Sighing, he pulled the scrap of parchment out of his pocket and studied it. Despite what he had said to Jacs, seeing the tidy edits in Cllr. Perda's handwriting had caused him to doubt. He knew the Council was loyal to the Queen, it would be unthinkable if they were working against her. He had grown up seeing the way they supported his mother, but what if Jacs was right? She had no reason to lie. What if they had a hand in her mother's disappearance? What if they were using Ms. Tabart as leverage over the new Queen? He simply could not believe that the Council of Four would allow this to happen. They were not his favorite, but his mother had trusted them. His father had trusted them. Despite not always seeing eye to eye, he knew they had the Queendom's best interest at heart. They may have been distrusting of a Lowrian becoming Queen at the start, but they would not be so petty as to jeopardize the Queendom's well-being for the sake of personal prejudice. There had to be an explanation.

And if Jacs is right? he asked himself, but the implications were horrifying, and he quickly rejected the thought. No, there had to be an explanation.

Tucking the parchment back into his pocket, he stood and gathered a few important documents he had been working on, including the annual egg tally and treasury reports. Motioning to one of his attendants, he instructed them to clear his things and return them and the desk back to his study. Throwing the rest of his wine back, he grimaced, put the goblet down, and gestured to his guardpair to accompany him. Following Jacs's steps, he returned to the palace.

He paused just in front of the Council of Four's chamber door. There was a soft murmuring inside, but the door was thick enough that not much sound made it through. He took a breath, lifted his fist, and knocked loudly. Silence. The moments trickled by. Then the door opened and Cllr. Stewart's soft features appeared.

"Prince—I apologize—Advisor Cornelius, what a pleasant surprise!" she exclaimed. "Come in, come in, dear. We were just about to have tea; would you like a cup?"

"Good afternoon, Councilor Stewart," he said cheerily. "That sounds wonderful. I hope I'm not disturbing you; I just had a few questions I was hoping you or one of the other Councilors could help me with."

"Of course, Your Grace. Please, do come in," she said, stepping back and beckoning him to follow. He indicated for his guardpair to remain outside and strode through the doorway. The door closed with a hollow thud behind him.

The Four had descended from their perches to meet with him in the depressed center of the room. With inviting gestures, they led him to where tea was served in a small alcove off to the side between and below Cllr. Dilmont and Cllr. Stewart's seats. Connor exchanged the necessary pleasantries before setting his cup down, leaning forward in a way reminiscent of his father, and saying, "Your Eminences, I need you to help me understand."

The Councilors looked at one another and back at Connor. Suddenly he was ten again, sitting in on his mother's council meeting and being scolded for slouching in his seat. Clearing his throat, he pressed on, "Help me understand the meaning of this." With a flourish, he withdrew Maria Tabart's letter and thrust it toward them on the table.

Silence followed. The Councilors first looked at it with interest, then shifted their eyes, almost pretending not to see it. Finally, Cllr. Perda delicately drew the parchment toward her with the tip of a pointed finger and said, "Yes, it's a terrible business. We've been trying to reason with them, but the more we press, the more power they feel they hold, and then they send us bread crumbs like this to spark hope in our poor, dear Queen. Never have we had a Queen so at the mercy of radicals."

The other three women nodded gravely. Connor sat back and scratched the back of his neck. "What do you mean?" he said.

"The radicals who have the mother of the Queen captive. They refuse to give an inch in our negotiations," Cllr. Perda said silkily.

"But"—Connor paused, searching for the right words—"but I thought *you* were holding Ms. Tabart? Look, you've even edited her note." He pointed to the black ink strokes as he spoke.

The Councilors looked at one another incredulously. Cllr. Perda delicately touched a hand to her heart. "Us? Keep the Queen's mother captive? Why on earth would we do that? That is the highest treason," she said.

"But the edits," he insisted.

"Were to protect Her Majesty. She is already under enough strain as the new ruler of a Queendom she barely knows. The words we omitted were heartbreaking for us. I cannot imagine what they would do to our poor Queen. It is our duty to protect her, after all." Again, the women nodded in grave agreement.

"Whatever gave you the idea we could do such a monstrous thing?" Cllr. Fengar said softly.

"Well, what did they say?" he asked.

Cllr. Perda shook her head sadly. "I'm sorry, Your Grace, I cannot remember. But trust us when we say it was for the Queen's well-being that we omitted those lines."

Connor scratched the back of his neck again, momentarily at a loss for words. Jacs had been so adamant, but she must have been mistaken. It would be treason for the Four to enact any form of harm on a member of the royal family.

"I . . ." he began without knowing where his sentence would lead him, "I suppose it just seemed"—he looked about him—"but of course it would be unheard of. I must have been mistaken. I apologize for the accusation, of course I could never believe a member of the Council could do such a thing."

Cllr. Perda nodded slowly. Looking hesitant, she leaned forward and said in a low voice, "I wonder, Your Grace, if our young Queen told you we were responsible?" She held up her hand to prevent his answering and continued. "Regardless, I wonder if the pressure of this position is already too much for her. Of course, she is our rightful Queen, but such a change from rags to riches is immense for anyone to go through, let alone a poor Lowrian. Did you know her little farm was on the brink of ruin before she took the throne? Realm difference aside, that is a huge leap for anyone to make."

She reached out and placed her hand gently on his. He felt the back of her ring scrape against his knuckle. She smiled sadly and said, "Your Grace, for the safety of our Queen, and for the good of the

Queendom, you must keep an eye on any bouts of paranoia you observe. In my experience, they will only get worse, and she does her Queendom no good if she is unwell."

Connor sat back in shock; his hand slipped from hers. He had known Jacs had been under a lot of stress, but never could he have dreamed the toll that stress might have on her mind.

"What . . . what can I do? I'm her Chief Advisor now, I can't believe I didn't realize the impact this would have on her! How do you think I should help the Queen?" Connor pleaded, his eyes wide.

One corner of Cllr. Dilmont's lips lifted, and she shifted in her seat. Cllr. Perda considered for a moment, then said, "Keep an eye on her, Your Grace. You two already share such a special bond. You are in the perfect position to observe and note any variances in her demeanor. Keep us informed of any changes; it is important her Council is prepared for any major shifts in temperament Her Majesty may experience."

"It might be helpful, Your Grace," Cllr. Stewart piped up, "to divert her in some way. She is dealing with the fate of the Queendom as well as the disappearance of her mother; it is likely she needs some enjoyment in her life."

Cllr. Perda shot her a look, then nodded and glanced back at Connor. "You are such a source of comfort for her in this trying time, Prince Cornelius, we rely on your support and judgment in this matter," she said.

Connor nodded and stood abruptly. "Thank you, Councilors. I will do what I can to support our Queen, and I can most certainly keep you informed of her condition. I'm sure she will be fine. Every new ruler has their growing pains?" His last statement landed as a question. He suddenly felt nervous. It was his tasks and his contest that had chosen Jacs as Queen.

She had to succeed, for both their sakes.

"Of course!" Cllr. Fengar simpered.

"Although, this is the first Queen we have had who is so much a fish out of water," Cllr. Dilmont supplied in a neutral tone. "Now more than ever, we must do what is best for our Queendom."

Cllr. Perda shot her a look harsher than the one she had given Cllr. Stewart and finished: "And we are here to provide whatever support our young Queen may need in the months to come. We will continue to put pressure on these radicals." She paused for a moment and then added, "But it is advisable that your knowledge of them remains private. In the ripples of our late Queen Ariel's assassination, Goddess rest her"—the other Councilors echoed this last line—"we want to avoid giving these radicals more power than they already have by giving them notice." With a swift motion, she whisked the parchment into the folds of her bell sleeve.

Connor nodded in earnest; his right hand floated up to the left side of his chest to absently rub a slightly worn patch of fabric there. "Of course, and I thank you all for your counsel. I will do what I can."

They all stood and bowed their heads toward him. He rose and did the same, then with the appropriate farewells, made his leave. As the door closed behind him, he ran his fingers through his hair in agitation. He had been Royal Advisor for three months and already he was quite blind to the needs of his Queen, of Jacs, who he thought he knew very well. He realized he had a lot to learn and almost buckled under the weight of it. So many tasks ahead of him. As though facing an immeasurable staircase, he vowed to at least take the first step. Forcing a breath, he straightened and with shoulders back marched toward where he knew Edith would be at this time of day. If it was a distraction his Queen needed, a distraction he would provide. He had a lot to do and knew he could not do it alone.

3

A SAFE SPACE

Despite her frame of mind, Jacs adored this room. With the white marble pillars wrapped in deep green ivy surrounding the central courtyard, a modest fountain trickling at the north wall, glass windows lining the others, and a vaulted ceiling topped with a domed glass roof high above her, she felt as though she had stepped into the clouds. Master Leschi would faint to see the blueprints of the ceiling alone. For this to be her casual luncheon space was a thing of dreams. The conservatory also housed a collection of exotic flowers, and their delicate scents filled the air.

Jacs, Courtierdame Lena Glowra, daughter of Lord Ava Glowra of Terrelle, and Courtier Anya Bishop sat around a table spread for twelve and set for five. Both Lena and Anya had been named Courtiers during the Contest of Queens after they had ridden with a Griffin of the Court in the first task. To Jacs's knowledge, the three of them were the only people to have ridden with the Court in decades.

Lena's smooth black hair was tied up in an intricate twist, a few pearls nestled prettily in the folds. Her fawn nose was dotted with freckles, and her hazel eyes were rimmed with dark lashes. Anya stood a head taller, with thick, curly black hair smoothly braided against her skull and left free to tickle the warm ochre skin at the nape of her slender neck. She wore a delicate golden ear cuff that twined around the edge of one ear like ivy. Jacs beckoned Amber and Andromeda over from their posts.

The two guards looked at each other, scanned the perimeter, noted the two entrances as viable weak points, and set their chairs to face them. They appeared to relax only a little, and Jacs noted Andromeda's gaze kept flashing to the door.

"So," Jacs began, the shred of the Queen-like facade falling away, "how are you all?"

Anya helped herself to a tartlet and settled into the chair. "Well, you know," she said, "same old." Amber barked a laugh.

The rest of the table smiled. The corners of their mouths shattered something as they lifted and soon, they were inconsolable. Jacs was short of breath and wiping her eyes. Lena beamed and held tight to Anya's hand. Amber's laugh rang around the peaceful courtyard, and even Andromeda was heard to blow air forcefully out her nose a few times in her version of a chuckle.

Jacs felt the knot in her chest loosen, and she settled into her chair more comfortably. "What a . . . I was going to say *year*, but it's only been a few months," she said. The others nodded.

Lena leaned forward and patted Jacs's knee comfortingly. "How are you holding up?" she asked.

Jacs tried to fix a look of bravado on her face but felt it slip. Sighing, she shook her head.

"It's been hard," she said simply.

Amber set her lips in a line and frowned. "Well, it'd be easier if those old bats stopped messing with you," she growled.

Andromeda cleared her throat and shifted uncomfortably in her seat, eyes now fixed on the door.

"Come on Turner, you know it's true," Amber said.

"No, no, I know. It's just, they're still the most powerful women in the Queendom." Andromeda fiddled with the pommel of her sword. "Some respect wouldn't hurt."

Amber rolled her eyes good-naturedly and amended, "You're right. The *Esteemed* old bats."

Andromeda wrinkled her nose. "Better," she said gruffly.

Amber helped herself to a chocolate-dipped strawberry and bit down, the crunch of the chocolate shell punctuating Andromeda's comment.

Jacs sighed and stopped herself the moment before wiping her face. As Queen she wore powders and creams she often found herself smudging. Instead, she twirled a loose strand of hair around her finger.

"The meeting with the Council went"—Amber searched for the word—"poorly today," she explained to the others.

Jacs nodded and added, "At first they were just cold, and now they're cold, cruel, and most definitely enjoying themselves."

"You need leverage," Amber said. "Right now, they hold all the cards."

"Do we have any dirt on the Council?" Anya asked.

"Or is there any way you can gain their respect so they stop torturing you?" Lena added.

Jacs shook her head, "No, and I doubt it. They are pretty good at keeping their records clean. They only seem to show their colors when I'm alone with them, and they can talk their way out of pretty much anything when confronted. Plus, I have a feeling they keep anyone who would benefit their cause well paid. Connor just told me Cllr. Fengar oversees the golden eggshell documentation and acquisition."

Lena shared a knowing look with Anya at the intimate nickname. Jacs pretended not to see. "They are literally the Queendom's treasury, security, military, and policy. How do you compete with that?"

The others sat in silence, thinking.

"And it's not just that," Jacs continued. "I mean, it's bad enough they have Master Leschi and Mum, it's bad enough that they're using them to pull on my strings like a puppet, but it's worse that I haven't been able to do a single thing about the Lower Realm. I haven't yet been able to visit—something the new Queen does within the first month of rule. Trade Week is almost an entire year away, so that's no help. And besides my scry crystal recall, I haven't been able to enact any major law or policy to benefit them. I haven't even been able to get news on how they're doing. The whole point was to give my people a voice, and I just feel so useless."

Lena refilled Jacs's teacup. "Well, you know you have us to help you. No matter what," she said simply.

Jacs smiled gratefully as the others added their words of support. "Lucky you mentioned it," Jacs said after taking a sip, "because I have a plan."

Anya flashed her crooked grin and said, "Yes! There's our Jacqueline!"

They all leaned forward eagerly as Jacs began to outline her idea. "The issue is twofold. Fold one, my mum and Master Leschi: If I find them, that breaks the Council's control over me, and I can start putting through policies I believe in and can maybe make some progress. Fold two, the Lower Realm: I need to know my crowning as a result of their voting hasn't worsened things for them down there—and things were already pretty bad." She took a breath. She hadn't mentioned the nightmare of trying to get the respect from the Lords and Genteels, but a bridge was for climbing when one came to it, not before.

"The Council would likely limit how many people know where my family is. I suspect they deal with them directly. So, if we follow the Council, we find where they're keeping Mum and Master Leschi." Jacs pulled a small wrapped bundle out of her skirt pocket and cleared a space on the table. The others leaned forward with interest. Gently, she unwrapped the cloth and revealed a scry crystal. It glowed with a soft purple that seemed to absorb the surrounding light rather than illuminate the cloth it was nestled in. As soon as the others had seen what it was, she covered it back up.

"Where did you get that?" Amber whispered.

"Weren't they all destroyed after the contest?" Lena whispered too. Although the crystals could only transmit visuals, everyone now spoke as if it could hear them as well.

"Yes," Jacs replied.

As well as clearing both her name and her pseudonym from the scry crystal's memory bank, she had made sure the crystals in both the Upper and Lower Realms had been rounded up and destroyed within the first month of becoming Queen. After witnessing firsthand how they were used to spy on and keep track of citizens in the Lower Realm, she had decided it was not worth her people's privacy and freedom to keep them, even if it did make sharing entertainment events easier. She still had nightmares about rooms and caves filled with that ominous purple glow. At her insistence, scry crystal mining had also ceased, and she was in the process of shutting down the mines altogether. Why mine for a resource that the Queendom didn't intend on using anymore?

"But I kept a few, locked up and covered of course." At Lena's raised eyebrow, Jacs explained, "I wanted to find out how they worked. Anyway," she continued, "what if I took small pieces of the crystal and turned them into, I don't know, a broach or a necklace and gave one to each of the Councilors? Then I just say either Mum or Master Leschi's name into a mirror until something shows up. If they're in range of the crystal, I'll be able to see, and maybe find out where one or both are." Jacs finished and looked at her friends eagerly.

Lena chewed her lower lip, and Anya looked concerned. Andromeda was the first to speak. "You want to spy on the Council of Four with crystals they took pains to distribute across the Queendom?" she said.

"Well . . . yes," Jacs replied.

"Jacqueline, I mean, it could work, but . . ." Lena trailed off.

"What if they find out?" Anya asked. "It's not as if these things are subtle; they glow."

"Yeah, but they'll be small," Jacs said.

"I think it's a great idea!" said Amber. "Beat them with their own stick!"

"Jacqueline," Lena said gently, "just consider what they would do to your mother and Master Leschi if they discovered your plan before you could get any information. Anya's right: They glow, and they do not look like any rock or gem we have in the Upper Realm. Besides, would they still work the same at a fraction of the size?"

"And, Your Highness, the Councilors have shown you nothing but undeserved hostility and disdain. Don't you think they'll be at least a little suspicious if suddenly you're presenting them with jewelry?" Andromeda said.

Jacs felt deflated. Looking at the cloth parcel in her lap, she had to accept the logic of her friends' arguments. "Well," she said awkwardly, "it was just an idea. But maybe there are a few kinks to press out. I'll think about it some more."

The others nodded. Amber opened her mouth to say something but took a swig of tea instead. "So, how's your Prince? Sorry, Royal Advisor?" she said as the silence stretched thin.

Jacs felt her cheeks flush and tucked the strand of hair she had been fiddling with behind her ear. "You saw him earlier; you know he's doing well," she said.

Amber grinned, "I know, but I knew Lena was curious, and I wanted to see your face change color," she said with a laugh. Jacs tried and failed to suppress a grin and playfully threw a grape at the knight. Amber caught it deftly and popped it in her mouth.

"He's wonderful," Jacs said softly. "I don't know what I'd do without him."

The others beamed.

"So when do we get to call him your King?" Amber asked slyly. A sound from the doorway saved Jacs from answering. Andromeda sprang to her feet and rested a hand on the pommel of her sword, stepping between the Queen and the newcomer.

"Speaking of . . ." Amber muttered and stood with a smirk beside Andromeda. The knights parted so that Jacs could see Connor coming to greet her. A guardpair followed a few steps behind him and stood flanking the door. Jacs rose and hurriedly brushed the crumbs from her skirts.

"Good afternoon, Your Highness." Connor beamed, strode toward her, and swept her fingers into his, kissing the back of her hand. Jacs, aware of her friends' eyes on her, tried to adopt an air of nonchalance but felt her traitorous cheeks burn. He turned and performed a short bow to the table. "Ladies," he said, "I apologize for my intrusion, but I was hoping to steal your host from you." Turning back to Jacs, he said, "Lord Claustrom and the Council of Four are requesting an audience and are waiting for you in the Councilors' chamber."

Jacs felt her heart sink as imaginary strings tightened around her wrists and ankles.

Lena narrowed her eyes slightly and said, "Your Highness, you are looking a touch chilled. From my recollection, the Councilors' chamber is quite drafty, and it would do you no good to catch a cold. Would it not be better for Your Majesty's health to move the meeting to a warmer, more comfortable room?" Meeting Jacs's eye, Lena winked.

"Wonderful idea, Dame Glowra," Jacs said with a nod. "Cornelius, let's send a message for them to meet me in the throne room. It is much warmer, and I'm sure we will all be more comfortable there."

A serving boy was brought in to send the message.

Connor held out his arm for Jacs to take. "May I escort you to the throne room, Your Highness?"

"Of course. I'll see you both tomorrow." Jacs bid farewell to Lena and Anya, hugging the former a moment longer to whisper a thank-you in her ear. Chiv. Everstar and Chiv. Turner stood to attention, and Jacs accepted Connor's arm warmly. Two by two, the group left the peaceful conservatory.

4

AN OLD WOUND

The door closed with a soft click. Queen Jacqueline and her entourage were muted behind solid oak. All that was heard for a time was the fountain's gentle trickling. Sunlight warmed the room and the air hung heavy with the scent of lilacs. Blossoms stood in vases around the fountain's pool.

"I'm worried about her," Lena said quietly, arms folded gently. She moved to stand next to the fountain and watched a flower swirl in a sudden eddy.

"I know," Anya said. She wrapped her arms around Lena from behind and rested her cheek on the top of her head. Lena closed her eyes for a moment and melted into the embrace.

"I am too. She was so pale today, and I don't think she's eating much," Anya said.

Lena could feel the words reverberate down her back. She sighed and said, "But she knows we are on her side, and most importantly, she knows we're going to be honest with her. We're people she can trust in a court full of liars and fools. That must be a small comfort." Lena thought about the look of disappointment on Jacqueline's face at the reactions to the idea of giving the Councilors the crystal pieces. "It's better to hear hard truths than be misled by pretty lies," she said, more to appease her own guilt than anything.

Lena felt Anya nod. "So, we need to consider what will happen when we leave."

Anya stiffened. "What do you mean, when we leave?"

"Well, right now we're here at Jacqueline's request and will likely be needed for a few more months, but we can't stay in Basileia forever. I will need to return to Terrelle at some point to help Mother, and I couldn't bear it if you didn't come with me, so that point is nonnegotiable. I suspect there will be some discussions with Mother about my taking on her title at some point. I heard Dame Claustrom has already claimed her mother's title. That will cause a trend among the lesser Lords, no doubt, to abdicate earlier. Mother will be less likely to want to relinquish the reins so soon, but she may see fit to intensify my training in the meantime. Plus, Mother left so quickly after the contest that we really didn't have time to introduce ourselves as a couple. I know that will take some adjustment; I think she still holds hope that I will give Lord Lemmington's daughter another chance because of their connections with—"

Anya spun Lena to face her with a quick twist and caught her next words against her lips. Lena felt her smile. "It's a busy world in that mind of yours," Anya said.

"Not always," Lena replied coyly and wrapped her arms around Anya's neck. She had to stand on her tiptoes to reach. Anya bent slightly on instinct. Their eyes met, and Lena felt a warmth envelop her. She cupped Anya's cheek in her hand and drew her in once more.

Anya slipped her hands from her mid back to her waist. In a flash, the heat evaporated, and Lena froze. Her hands began to tremble. Her knees buckled, and Anya's arms tightened around her to stop her falling. Too tight, they held her.

Her breathing was short and sharp.

"Just breathe."

In.

Out.

"Good. Again."

In.

Out.

"I'm here, Lee. You're okay."

Lena was sitting on the edge of the fountain, Anya at her side rubbing her back. Slowly, Anya shifted to kneel in front of her and peered into eyes still struggling to focus.

"There we go. I'm just going to get you some water."

Anya shifted Lena's hands to her knees in a braced position, paused for a moment to make sure she could sit on her own, then moved over to the lunch table. Returning quickly, she pressed a cool glass into Lena's hand and helped her take a sip.

Anya smiled sadly. "Are you all right?"

Lena, confused and embarrassed, took another sip of water and nodded. She felt tears burn in the corners of her eyes. "I'm fine," she said hurriedly. "Anya, I'm sorry—"

Anya held up her hand and shook her head. "Don't, you have nothing to be sorry about. I didn't mean to . . ." she looked down awkwardly and seemed to not know how to finish her sentence. "Lee, I would never . . . I could never . . . you know I'd never do anything to hurt you."

"I know! Oh, Anya, you did nothing wrong. I—" The lump in her throat cut off her next words.

"Do you want to talk about it?"

"No," Lena said sharply, then softened. "No, not right now. It's honestly nothing. It's just hot in here. I felt faint for a moment. I'm all right."

Anya looked at her doubtfully and did not press the matter. They sat quietly on the edge of the fountain. The moment lay shattered at their feet.

Finally, Anya cleared her throat and said, "I guess before we leave it would make sense to give Jacqueline as many insider tips to dealing with the Lords as you know. I don't have a lot of experience in that area, but I do know what it's like being on the outside. The Lords definitely have their own language."

Lena nodded. Placing the glass beside her on the stone, she clasped her hands in her lap. She took a few deep breaths in through her nose, and the trembling quieted. Looking down at her thumbs, she said, "That's true. She needs as much information as I can give her. I wouldn't send anyone to that wolf den without a few tricks up their sleeves."

"Lee, are you sure you're okay?" Anya asked tentatively.

"I'm fine."

"Because this isn't the first—"

"I said I'm fine, Anya. I just need some air." Lena stood abruptly, straightened her gown, and looked at Anya. Smiling, she held out her hand. "Will you walk with me? We could go see the lily pond?"

Anya looked up at her, then at the offered hand. Concern creased her brow, but she took it, stood, and followed Lena out the door.

Together, they stepped into the fresh air, both blinking in the sunlight.

5

THE FISSURE

If Lord Hera Claustrom or the Council of Four were annoyed by the change of venue, they hid their displeasure well. All smiles and simpers, neither of which quite reached their eyes. Jacs supposed she had Connor's presence to thank for that. He stood at her side, one step down from her perch. Sitting above them on the dais in the Griffin-shaped throne, Jacs felt a little foolish but had to admit it was much better than standing in the middle of the Council's four-pointed cauldron, unsure who she should be facing.

The open-walled, open-floored turret set in the ceiling above them was empty. Typically, that was the seat of the Court of Griffins, but they only tended to oversee throne-room meetings that carried weight and consequence. Squabbles like this wouldn't need their witness. Although Jacs did wish she had the support their presence brought. They, unlike the Council, agreed with her appointment as Queen. They had even vouched for her during the third task.

Jacs turned her attention to where the Council of Four stood with Hera at the base of the dais. "Dame Claustrom, I heard of your new title this morning, so I welcome you now as Lord Claustrom," she said.

Hera bowed, and Jacs noticed her knee did not quite connect with the floor as was proper before she rose back to standing. Her golden hair was arranged half in a plaited knot on the top of her head, and the rest flowed down her shoulders. She wore a blue lace bodice with capped sleeves. Her silk skirts cascaded away from the edges of her bodice and pooled around her feet. She wore the old style with a defiant tilt of her chin. Jacs noted the display of royal colors but said nothing. She did not *own* the color blue, but she did suspect Hera's choice of donning the royal colors was intentional.

"You honor me, Your Majesty, in seeing me at such short notice," Hera said.

Jacs nodded and waited for her to continue.

"And I thank you in your signing over the portion of Lord Witbron's lands to Hesperida. I look forward to being able to make a greater contribution to our Queendom with what we are able to do with that land."

Jacs remained silent. She had found that others tended to get to the point quicker when they felt the need to fill these silences, especially if they wanted something from her.

Hera pressed on. "However, as our boundary has shifted and more people are included under my county, the taxes have increased. While I completely agree these taxes are important to support the Queendom's economy, it does not make sense that my region must now pay more taxes than smaller regions like Terrelle. We may very well go bankrupt as our coffers empty, and my citizens find themselves unable to purchase even a loaf of bread. I request that you decrease the percentage of taxes Hesperida need pay."

Jacs considered this. "Lord Claustrom, were you aware of how the tax percentage would affect your lands when you adopted Luxlow acres into your region?"

Hera pursed her lips. "Yes, Your Majesty."

"I see. And you desire to pay less taxes even though more land, more people, more workers, and more businesses will likely increase your county's profits?"

"Well, that's not a certainty, Your Highness," Hera said, her cheeks coloring.

"No, you are right." Jacs thought for a moment.

Cllr. Perda stepped forward. "Your Highness poses important questions, and the altering of taxes for one Lord over others may appear as favoritism. I commend you for deeply considering the matter."

Jacs tried not to appear like a child receiving praise from a strict schoolteacher, but she couldn't help sitting a little straighter. "Lord Claustrom, as this land acquisition is new, I'm sure there are a few things to be worked out before everything is settled." Jacs tried to make her words sound regal instead of vague, but realized she lacked the jargon and felt her point flutter uselessly around the room.

To her relief, Connor stepped toward her and whispered, "It might make sense to ask Lord Claustrom to share her county's ledgers with the Queen after a six-month period so that we can see how the taxes are affecting the financial well-being of her people?"

Jacs smiled at him and repeated his suggestion to the room. The Council beamed, and even Hera looked satisfied.

"A fair and just suggestion, Your Highness and Your Grace." Hera bowed again and smiled sweetly up at Connor. Jacs bristled. She began to feel unnerved by the whole exchange. She was not used to conversations with the Council or this particular Lord going so smoothly and amicably. While she was ashamed of the suspicion that crept into her mind, she couldn't seem to shake it. Determined to believe the best in the situation, she swallowed her doubts and smiled down at Hera.

"You must be eager to return to Hesperida to get settled into your duties as Lord. I wonder when you are planning to return home?" Jacs asked pointedly.

Hera's dimples deepened. "I am, Your Majesty, very eager. While these next few months will be agony to be separated from my county, I do have several policies and requests to make of the crown, as well as a few more items of transition to wrap up with the Council before I can return home."

Jacs's heart sank, but she kept her expression clear. "Of course. The palace will be a brighter place for your presence."

Cllr. Perda stepped forward. "If that is all, Your Highness, Lord Claustrom needs escorting. I wonder if His Grace wouldn't mind seeing her out as there is one small matter the Council and I would like to discuss with you."

Jacs felt the knot in her chest tighten but agreed. Connor squeezed her hand and bounded down the steps to meet Lord Claustrom. She radiated gratitude, and with a half bow to the Queen, took Connor's arm and walked with him down the length of the hall. Jacs watched them go. Saw Hera shift her weight into Connor. Heard her laugh at something Jacs did not hear and heard him chuckle in return. She found herself glaring at Hera's retreating figure.

Alarmed at this sudden surge of jealousy, she turned her attention to the Council.

Cllr. Perda had followed her gaze and remarked neutrally, "A handsome pair indeed."

Cllr. Dilmont and Cllr. Fengar both turned to look and nodded. Jacs remained silent. The women waited a few beats as the sounds of Connor and Hera faded. Jacs began to fidget and said, "You had another matter to discuss with me, Councilors?" They turned back to look at her.

Cllr. Perda smiled slowly. From within her sleeve she withdrew the blood- and ink-stained parchment. "It has come to our attention that you are being careless with information shared in confidence."

Jacs felt cold sweat bead her forehead as her heart leaped to quiver in her throat. "Where did you—" she all but whispered.

"Oh, my dear, we have eyes everywhere. Surely you are aware of this by now?" Cllr. Dilmont said in a low voice. Her red lips savored each word.

"I—I must have dropped it," Jacs stammered. She thought back to where she had last seen it. Had she left it outside when she had shown it to Connor?

Cllr. Perda made a tsking noise. "Do not lie. Your conversation with the Prince was reported to us. We are very disappointed at your lack of discretion, and quite frankly, your choice of confidant. Misplaced trust is a foe's best weapon. The danger this information could pose. What would your mother think?"

Jacs felt her breath catch.

"Trust is very important to us, Jacqueline," Cllr. Dilmont said.

"I know, and I would never . . ." Jacs bit back the bile rising in her throat, her eyes filled with images of her mother's dried blood.

"Good." Cllr. Perda walked up the steps of the dais and reached over Jacs on the throne to where a short candle flickered in a ceramic holder, a small pool of sweet-smelling oils in a basin above the flame. Jacs tried not to flinch, but she felt herself instinctively move away from the Councilor, bunching up in her chair. The scent of Cllr. Perda's rosewater-and-citrus perfume stung her nose.

Cllr. Perda tickled the corner of her mother's note in the flame until it caught. She did not look at the little flame; instead, she stared straight at Jacs. She held the parchment for a moment as the fire stretched along the edges, then just as it neared her fingertips, dropped it on the marble floor of the dais. Jacs sat very still, her hands balled into fists, her pulse beating a war cry in her veins, and did nothing.

Smiling, Cllr. Perda inclined her head and stepped leisurely down to join the others. Jacs watched tendrils of flame consume the words *I love you*, and the paper fell to ash.

"Thank you for your time, Your Majesty," Cllr. Stewart said. Her brow creased slightly, and a tinge of sadness colored her tone.

Jacs turned to face them all. "You may go," she said flatly. The Councilors faltered, looked to Cllr. Perda, then followed her lead as she again inclined her head and turned to walk out of the room.

Jacs heard Cllr. Stewart whisper, "I fear you push too hard, Rosalind," but she did not catch the reply.

She looked down at the black and smoking remains of her mother's letter and willed herself to be strong. It was just a piece of paper after all. She sifted through the ashes and retrieved the largest salvageable scrap. *Plum* could be discerned from the soot. Gently, she placed the piece in a pocket in her bodice.

Taking a few deep breaths, she dusted her hands and stepped down from the dais. The great marble pillars flanking the rich navy-and-gold rug that spanned from throne to door were her only company as she walked the length of the room. Her cloak billowed slightly behind her as she hastened her steps. Her skirts were split down the center—as was the new fashion—and she strode forward, unencumbered, with purpose.

This is all just an elaborate puzzle I need to figure out, she thought grimly to herself. Logic would keep her sane. Reason would keep her moving forward. Indulging in emotion and feeling would do nothing but send her into a numb oblivion. She had been there before, and she would not descend again. Her father's words rang in her ears, *Despair is a pit that goes nowhere.* She would not succumb. She was strong, and she could do this.

Head high, she pushed open the doors of the throne room to hear a giggle quickly stifled. Hera and Conner were locked in some sort of embrace. Hera had her back to Connor, hands lifting her hair up to expose the nape of her neck. He was standing close behind her, head bent, fingertips raised to her neckline.

"What?" Jacs couldn't think of anything else to say.

Connor dropped his hands and spun around. He smiled upon hearing her voice, but it quickly disappeared when he saw the look on her face. Before he could say anything, Hera stammered, "Oh my, Your Majesty, I—" A hand flying to her throat, she flinched slightly as though she had been caught in a compromising position.

Jacs held up a hand to silence her. "You may go," she said coldly, echoing her parting words to the Council.

"Oh dear, I truly am so embarr—"

"Leave."

Hera paled, and her simper vanished. Bowing low, she turned and left without another word. Connor looked at Jacs, a confused expression on his face. She felt cold. Her mind was trying to understand what she had seen.

"What," she faltered and tried again. "What were you doing?"

Connor shifted uncomfortably under her gaze. "Jacs, she needed help with her necklace clasp. I don't know why she carried on like that."

Relief flooded her heart, but pride refused to let it go. "And she couldn't figure it out on her own?"

He eyed her warily. "Jacs—"

"Forget it." She hated the words as soon as they had left her lips, and she wished to pull them back. "I'm sorry, I'm just tired." She looked down to avoid his gaze.

He sighed and stepped slowly toward her. She tensed, but he gathered her gently into an embrace. Resting her head on his chest, feeling his hand caress her hair, she softened. Eyes closed, she clung to him, her arms encircling his waist.

"Jacs," he said simply. "I have always been *yours*."

She pulled back and searched his eyes. She saw a ghost of herself reflected in his blue irises and wondered for a moment how he saw her.

Swift enough to make her blink, he playfully pecked her on the nose. His eyes crinkled as he smiled. Doubts vanished as suddenly as they had risen, and she felt her heart glow. Grinning shyly, she kissed his nose in return. Mischief flashed across his features. He brought both palms below her ears, fingers entwined at the base of her head. Holding her firmly, he brought her cheek to his mouth and licked from her jaw to her cheek bone.

Jacs squealed and tried to pull away, but he held her fast. She swatted at his chest, and he struggled to bring her other cheek closer to his mouth. Laughing and squirming, she braced herself against him like a cat avoiding a bath, while he craned his neck to get closer.

"No!" she shrieked. "I am your Queen!" She broke off in a fit of giggles and said, "This is disgusting!"

"Aha!" he cried, triumphant. "There it is! My Queen, I feared your radiant smile had been extinguished, but it has returned more brilliant than before." In the brief moment that she relaxed her grip against him, he pulled her close and kissed her. Like recalling a half-forgotten melody, all the notes fell into place and the fragment became a composition, its dissonance smoothing to harmony. She leaned closer into him. Her palms rested lightly on his chest, fingertips gathering the fabric of his tunic. His forefinger cupped her chin, then moved to tangle in her hair, while the other hand slipped to her waist. Her mind went deliciously blank. Suspended there, Jacs felt her heart quicken and time slow. They lingered in the quiet space between them. When they broke apart, both slightly out of breath, Jacs's cheeks felt hot, and Connor's eyes shone.

The spell was broken by a soft cough near the edge of the entrance hall. Connor's gaze darted over Jacs's shoulder, and his grin widened.

"Edith! Perfect timing." Then he whispered to Jacs: "I have a surprise for you." He took her hand and led her to where Edith—Connor's valet, childhood friend, and most recently, Jacs's liberator—stood.

She carried herself with the pride of station, her hair tucked neatly into a tight bun, and each seam of her uniform firmly pressed. She had a round face and deep dimples, with an overall air of professionalism and a perpetual sparkle of mischief in her hazel eyes. Jacs felt she was still figuring Edith out.

Jacs greeted her warmly. Edith bowed, and in a business-like tone, said, "Now, Your Highness, please close your eyes and do not be afraid."

"Why would I be af—hey!" Jacs's question was cut off as a length of heavy fabric was placed over her eyes. "What are you doing?"

"Well, it wouldn't be much of a surprise if you knew the answer to that, so hold tight to my hand, and listen carefully." Connor's voice shifted from her right to left ear as he took up a position beside her. She lifted her hand toward him, he entwined their forearms, bent their elbows, and held her hand in his.

He whispered something to Edith. Jacs heard the shifting of fabric, a soft clinking, and Connor adjusting something on his other side. Standing quietly, she awaited her fate. Excitement bubbled within her, and she fought a smile.

"Okay, ready?" Connor asked.

She nodded.

"Careful now, let's go."

The next several minutes were a mixture of stumbles and giggles. Jacs attempted to keep track of where they were headed, but she suspected Connor of misleading her on purpose. More than once, she was sure he had spun her around only to head back the way they had come. Her footsteps echoed in some rooms and were muffled in others. She could tell when they were passing through a room with windows when she felt the sun on her face, and when a room was lit with candles and lamps.

Finally, Connor said, "All right, now watch your head here, just duck a little and stop. Reach out in front. Feel that? Now the other hand, got it? Okay, now I'm right behind you, hand over hand, make your way up the ladder."

She turned to where his voice came from and raised her eyebrows. She felt a soft kiss on her wrinkled brow and Connor's hand on the small of her back, pushing her forward.

"As your Royal Advisor, I advise you to trust me," he said.

"Sound advice, Your Grace." She scoffed, gripped the rungs, and pulled herself up. The wood was worn beneath her palms. Feeling her way up the ladder, she was comforted by the steady weight of Connor's hand on her back as he climbed up behind her.

Just as the ladder ran out, and Jacs felt a floor of a room extend away from her, Connor said, "Now, watch your head. That's it. Last rung. Crawl forward a little and wait for me there."

Jacs felt the closeness of the walls and imagined herself in a burrow. This place felt quiet. Secret. Sitting obediently, she hugged her knees and rested her chin on them. Eyes open or closed, she saw nothing because of the blindfold. The sound of Connor hoisting himself from the ladder to join her made her smile. She hoped her landing had been a little more graceful than his sounded.

"Okay, ready?" he asked. He sat directly in front of her, and she felt his breath on her face. She nodded and unclasped her knees, giving Connor her hands so he could pull her to her feet. Gently, he reached behind her head and untied the blindfold. The fabric fell away, and she blinked in the gloom.

They were in a loft of sorts, and despite the low ceiling, she could stand comfortably. In the room sat a low workbench-like table with a few cushions placed around it. A bouquet of lilies, which perfumed the room, and a tray of fruit tarts and cheeses decorated the cloth-covered table. A bottle of wine and two glasses accompanied the spread. On the far wall was a round stained-glass window. The image of a Griffin prancing above the clouds mosaicked its pane. With the proud head, wings, and front talons of an eagle and the back haunches and tail of a lion, it reared against the blue sky beyond the window. Jacs gasped and held her hand with Connor's Griffin ring up to the light, then up to him excitedly. It was the same image. He smiled as her eyes grew wider. The walls were lined with wooden shelves, one shelf in the corner coming only to waist height. On top sat a pitcher and water basin and above it hung a circular mirror. Jacs noticed that two of the shelves contained rows of leather-bound books, some woodworking tools, and paints, but the rest held a few wooden boats and dozens of small, neatly folded hot-air balloons.

With her mouth open slightly, she placed a hand on her heart and moved to inspect the nearest boat. The hull, painted with a light stain, had a secret compartment that opened to reveal a shallow recess down its center. Just big enough to fit a tightly rolled letter. She clutched it to her chest, and her eyes wandered along the shelf. Her fingers brushed the waxed canvas of one of her successful hot-air balloons. The cords were folded neatly, and the candle still had a little wax left to burn. Boat in hand, she spun to face Connor. He stood apprehensively by the ladder.

"Connor," she breathed. "This place. This is . . . it's us."

He beamed.

"This is where it all started," she said in wonder. "Without your little boat, none of this would have been possible."

He crossed the room and swept her hand up in his. One palm cradling her cheek, he said, "Without *you*, none of this would have been possible. I was just a little boy with a toy boat hoping to find adventure. You were the girl who could fly."

The boat in Jacs's hands fell to the floor as she closed the distance between them. A soft *thud* sounded near her feet as the boat hit the rug. She glimpsed his smile just before catching it on her lips. He ran his fingers down her spine to rest on her hips. Her breath hitched. A soap bubble of bliss rose somewhere around her navel and quivered near her heart. Pulse quickened. The sensation was familiar and still so thrillingly new. She pulled him closer. To think that her hot-air balloons would lead her to this life, this boy . . . His thumb brushed her cheek while his other hand encircled her waist. In Connor she had found what she knew others spent decades searching for.

His breath tickled her ear and sent a shiver through her core. She gripped the fabric of his tunic and entwined her fingers in his hair. Eyes closed, she softened under his touch. The tension in her shoulders melted away. She drew his lips to hers again. Craving closeness, she felt a delicious ache thrum through her. A modulation. But too fast. Free-falling, she scrambled for purchase in this new territory.

With a shuddering breath, she drew back. Needing a moment to recalibrate, a moment for her heart to settle, she rested her forehead on his, fingers clasped around his neck. He opened his eyes and searched her gaze with breath as ragged as her own. Its warmth tickled her lips and the tip of her nose.

As though reading something behind her irises, he stilled. Slowly, he dropped his fingertips from where they had been exploring the borders between skin and bodice and instead traced his palms from her elbows to shoulders, wrapping his arms around her. She hadn't realized how much she needed the comfort of his embrace until he held her tight. A gear clicked into place. Her frenzied thoughts subsided. For a moment, the weight of the Queendom was lifted off her shoulders.

"Jacs," he murmured, holding her close, "things will get easier, you'll see."

To avoid answering, she kissed his cheek lightly and curled into him. With her cheek on his chest, she felt the metronome of his breaths and focused on matching hers to his rhythm. The soft pressure of his chin on the top of her head became her anchor. Absently, he began stroking her hair and she felt a few of the more elaborate plaits come loose as he worked his fingers through them. She closed her eyes to the sensation.

"Hungry?" he asked brightly, making her smile.

"Always."

The sun hovered low on the horizon; its last rays shone gold through the Griffin's wings. Jacs was still getting used to how long the daylight hours were in the Upper Realm. If she were back home, the shadows from the surrounding mountains would have long since swallowed her farm. Here, it felt like the days stretched luxurious arms around the realm. Unhurried and reluctant to let them go into night's embrace.

At Connor's gesture, they both lowered themselves to the pillows surrounding the little table, and Jacs plucked a raspberry off the nearest tart and popped it into her mouth. With a flourish, he withdrew a corkscrew from a pouch at his belt, uncorked the bottle of wine, and poured them each a glass. Jacs accepted hers gratefully. Their glasses chimed together before each took a sip.

In this moment of quiet, Jacs let herself breathe. The stillness, the calm, and Connor's gentle presence slowed the war drum within her. Connor watched her from across the table, and she kept catching his eye. The fleeting glance summoned a smile each time. Her fingers found reason to brush his as she reached for her glass, and the pressure of his knee against hers sent tickles of electricity up her spine. Surrendering to the gravity of his pull, she set her glass down, wiped her fingers on a linen napkin and shifted around the table to sit within the circle of his embrace.

Enveloped in Connor's arms, she looked around the room. Her eyes scanned the shelves and took in each balloon. Each one was its own success story.

She thought back to all the launches she had performed, all the trials and failed attempts, all the rainy days she had sat looking out the window glumly, waiting for a clear sky to try again. She looked at each little boat, so lovingly carved. Each one painted, each compartment waterproofed. Both balloon and boat defied the odds to find their destinations.

"Did you really make every boat you sent down?" Jacs asked.

"Well, Heph helped with the big cutting, but I finished them," Connor said proudly.

"Heph?"

"Oh, you've probably not met him yet. Master Aestos, he's the head goldsmith, but he does a lot of other work with wood and metal as well. Luckily for me, he never asked too many questions about my fascination with wooden boats." Connor paused and took a sip, thinking. "I thought I was so clever back then. As a boy, I thought I was the only one who knew about this place; I thought of it as my secret workshop." Jacs could feel the words rumble in Connor's chest as he spoke. "It took me years to question why it was always immaculate when I arrived, where the fresh snacks would come from, and why the coat of arms I imagined for myself appeared as a stained-glass window after a trip to the outer counties." He shrugged. "But even so, it's always felt like my private sanctuary."

"I guess privacy is more an illusion when you're royalty," Jacs said softly. She thought of her breakdown earlier in the gardens. The guards, knights, and attending servants had averted their gaze, but they had seen.

"I guess, but it's not so bad," Connor said, giving her shoulder a wiggle and making her smile. "Anyway," he said, changing the subject. "I want you to pick one."

"Pick one?" She shifted to look up at him.

"A boat."

"A boat?"

He laughed. "Yes, a boat. Pick a boat, because you're going to write a letter and send it to someone in your village. Now, they may not receive it, and if they do, they most likely won't have brains like yours to send a reply, but I know you've been worried that you haven't communicated with the Lower Realm, and I know you're upset that you haven't been able to visit them yet, so I thought this might be something that can . . . you know . . . feel like you're doing something at least." He tapered off.

She smiled and kissed his cheek. "That's a sweet idea. Thank you."

He studied her expression for a moment and said seriously, "Listen, I know it's been hard, and I know the palace can feel a bit like a cage. Why do you think I sent those boats off the Cliff in the first place? But we'll get there. It'll take time, but soon this will feel like home, and you'll get the hang of working with the Council. They mean well, and they really are trying their best."

Jacs frowned but quickly turned to the shelves to hide her displeasure. Scanning the different boats, she looked at the one that had fallen from her hands earlier and picked it up, turning the little vessel over between her palms.

"This really is a lovely idea, Connor." She ran her finger over the smooth green hull. "You are a saint."

"Just an Advisor, I'm afraid," he said cheekily. "And my advice? Let's fix your hair. You, my Queen, are a mess."

She poked her tongue out at him, the culprit responsible, and let him lead her over to the water basin in the corner. A small mirror hung above it.

She raised an eyebrow.

"What? I was making boats in assumed secrecy; you think I was going to show up to meet my father covered in sawdust and paint? No, a prince must always look his best."

She chuckled. "I would love to see you spend a day on my farm."

Catching her reflection in the mirror, she realized that *mess* had been an exaggeration, but she wasn't going to decline his offer. He came to stand behind her and began working out a tangle with his fingers.

"So, who do you think you'll write to?" Connor asked lightly.

Jacs considered, wincing as his finger snagged in a knot.

"Sorry," he said.

"Probably my friend Phillip. He's most likely worried about me and is definitely worried sick about his mum. I'll be able to tell him I'm looking for her at least." With deft fingers, he arranged her hair loosely around her shoulders, salvaged some of the braids and twisted them into a half updo. She closed her eyes, enjoying the sensation.

"Phillip . . . Leschi? Master Leschi's son? Whoa." Connor cut off and Jacs opened her eyes.

The mirror above the basin had turned opaque for a moment, their reflections having vanished. Jacs stopped breathing. She stared at the fogged surface, willing it to change. The seconds ticked by. Finally, the glass cleared, and Phillip's likeness replaced Jacs's own. She gasped.

He walked with a limp, shoulders hunched, down what Jacs recognized as the main street in her hometown, Bridgeport. His clothing was worn, his features dull, and he looked as though he had aged several years in the few months she had been gone. He had even grown a beard. She reached out and touched the surface of the glass.

"Phillip?"

A guardpair walked past him, and she saw him shrink into himself. She felt something inside her break to see her bear-sized lamb, her gentle giant, cower in the street. A thousand questions ran through her mind, but she stalled on the *how*. How was this possible?

"Connor, I thought they had collected all the scry crystals from the Lower Realm. I *ordered* them to be removed. But look!" She gestured at the mirror. Phillip had passed several shops and was now heading toward the town square. "We've watched him walk down the whole block, there must be crystals on every storefront for that to be possible!"

Connor's mouth had fallen open, but no sound came out. Jacs watched now as Phillip turned the corner to enter the town square. She saw the ruins of the clocktower. The town had not been allowed to rebuild it after Queen Ariel's murder. It stood as a constant reminder of her death and the horror of the massacre that followed. Here, Jacs saw two more guardpairs cut across Phillip's path. Again, he shrunk into himself, eyes down, hands in his pockets, shuffling despite the limp.

Realization hit Jacs like a blow to the stomach. This had been the one thing she had been able to do for the Lower Realm. Remove the crystals, return their privacy. The one thing she had signed her name to that she had written herself. The one shred of good she felt she had made. And it was a lie. It was a joke. She imagined the Councilors laughing at her. Their little puppet Queen: happy with the one crumb of hope they had given her.

Rage swelled in her heart and took root. She felt it constrict her breathing and curl her hands into fists. Two useless fists a realm away.

"Jacs." Connor had found his voice and looked at her changed expression with alarm. "Jacs, there will be an explanation for this."

Jacs watched another guardpair march in and out of view of the crystal's target. That was four in the short amount of time they had been watching Phillip's progress through town. That was already more than she would have expected. What had happened? They had increased the crystals *and* the patrols? How could she have let this happen? She felt a pit open up beneath her feet. Weightless and powerless, she plummeted. A rushing filled her ears, and still she watched Phillip, her Phillip, now the shadow of the man he had once been, shuffling around his hometown like a whipped dog.

Connor was speaking, but his voice sounded as if it was far away. "It's likely they're still taking them down or . . . maybe some towns were stripped of crystals before others. The Council will likely know and will be able to explain it all."

"The Council," she said through gritted teeth, "is the cause of this. They are the poison within the Queendom, and they are the wall in the way of progress." She turned to face him. "Why can't you see that? Why do you defend them? They have the power to change this, and they *don't*. Instead, they make it worse."

"Jacs, I know you're stressed, but you can't just pick someone to blame. The Council is not what's wrong with the Queendom. They have spent their lives in service to both Realms. The longer you paint them as the enemy, the more you stand in your own way, and in the Queendom's," Connor said with forced patience.

She reeled. "You think *I'm* the problem?"

"That's not what I said," Connor said quickly.

"But it's what you meant. Connor, I can't keep having this argument with you. Either you believe me, or you don't. Pick a side," she said, crossing her arms.

"Jacs, we are on the same side. The Council is here to *help you*. Everything they do is to help the Queen. *You* are their Queen. Their loyalty is to you," he snapped, running his hands roughly through his hair.

"How can you think that, when they have my mother captive?"

"For the last time, they do *not* have your mother captive," he said, his voice rising.

"Yes, they do. Why would I make that up?" She kept her voice level. She felt the muted sting of her fingernails in her palm, but she did not let her composure crumble.

He crossed his arms. "I should go, this is getting us nowhere."

An ill-fitting cog stalled the mechanism, and Jacs felt something seize inside her chest. Before she could stop herself, she fired back, "Sure, go. You don't like the conversation? Disappear. For a year maybe? That wouldn't be anything new." Suddenly the pain of his abandonment after Queen Ariel's death surfaced and threatened to smother her. Here he was, leaving her to fight this alone, leaving her because he didn't like what she had to say. At her words, he froze and looked at her as though he had been struck. A clock ticked somewhere, marking the space stretching between them.

"That's not . . ." His eyes narrowed, and he swore under his breath. Shaking his head, he exploded, "For Queen's sake, think! I'm here. I'm trying to help you. *They're* trying to help you! They're the ones trying to *free* your mother."

"What do you mean?"

"They're trying to make a deal with the radicals who kidnapped her. Why would they commit treason just to piss you off?"

Running his fingers through his hair again, he turned away but not soon enough to hide the flicker of fire behind his eyes.

"How do you know that?" Jacs said in a low voice.

"I . . ." Connor took a few steadying breaths and looked suddenly unsure. "I confronted them today. They told me the truth."

"You confronted them?" Jacs's thoughts were spinning. "What did you tell them?"

"I asked them." He hesitated, a hand on one of the shelves, and did not look at her. "I asked them to explain the letter."

Understanding flooded through her. Cllr. Perda's words fluttered into her mind, *Misplaced trust is a foe's best weapon.* She had been talking about Connor. He was theirs.

"I was trying to help, Jacs. I didn't know what to do. I see you're hurting; every day I see it. And it kills me. And if they were responsible, I had to know for sure. But they're not. Jacs they're honestly not." Whatever fire had been in him before smoldered now. He tentatively clasped her hands in his, his blue eyes pleading.

Jacs fought back the panic swirling within her and met his gaze levelly. She could not convince him, not while the Council had him. That much she knew for certain. They had wound their threads around him, but she could not blame him for that. She would solve nothing by ranting and raving. If anything, that would prove their claim that she wasn't fit for the crown. Connor would see the truth with enough evidence. *He has to,* she thought fiercely. Until then, she would just have to play their game.

Play along, learn the rules, then learn how to beat them. Steeling her resolve, she forced a look of contrition to her features.

"You're right," she said.

"I'm—"

"You're absolutely right. I've been so caught up in my own head, I've been blind to reason. Thank you for helping me see that," she said as she hugged him, burrowing her face in his chest to avoid meeting his gaze. She felt a fissure form between them as he held her close. "Thank you for this wonderful night, but I have a long day tomorrow," she said with forced nonchalance.

Connor stiffened and broke from her. Responding to the dismissal in her voice, he hesitated a moment longer, eyes searching hers, before gathering their things and assisting her down the ladder. At the bottom, she smiled up at him, fixing this new mask in place, and saw his concern fade a little.

Walking back to her chambers, she intentionally slowed her strides to a relaxed pace. Fragments of conversation passed between them but both minds were elsewhere, and the words disappeared like icing sugar on water.

At her chamber door, she said, "I will sleep alone tonight," and he did not ask why. With a lingering glance, he handed her the little boat, kissed her cheek, and turned from her. She held the vessel to her chest and felt the warmth of his lips glow there like a match flaring, then fade. The mask settled comfortably into her skin, and she wondered idly when she would next be free to remove it.

6

EVENING TEA

Connor paced and rang for Edith. His room was much the same from when he was a boy—the desk in front of the large bay windows, bookshelves lining the walls, his four-poster bed in the center and a fireplace along one wall. The only changes were in the now much more serious book titles and the reduction of childish knickknacks lying about, like spyglasses and handmade treasure maps. Once he had dreamed of being an explorer like Amelia the Daring; now he was a Royal Advisor like his father.

The argument rang in his ears, and his neck grew hot each time he remembered how his voice had risen, how his hands had clenched into fists, and how his vision had blurred just for a moment. As royalty, he believed he was above base impulses, but apparently not always. And she had looked at him with such disappointment.

He ran his fingers through his hair in agitation.

Just a stupid boy who can't control his temper, he thought viciously.

Why did Jacs's view of the Council upset him so much? Why couldn't she just believe him? She was so stubbornly against them and—

"Your Grace?" Edith said as she opened the door to his chamber, cutting off his train of thought.

"Edith, fantastic," he said curtly. She had brought a tray of tea and biscuits with her. He smiled as he noticed the second cup and gestured to one of the two chairs in front of the fire. Edith took his cue, placed the tray on a side table, poured the tea, and sat. As if sensing his mood, she did not press him into conversation. Instead, she blew on her tea and scanned the room.

"I'll send someone to clean those windows tomorrow, Your Grace. You may want to move any important documents from your desk tonight."

"Fine, fine," he said absently, fingering the rim of his own cup.

A pause.

"Your Grace, with all due respect, I did not expect you to need me this evening." The implication hung for a moment before she pressed on. "While I am happy to keep you company, I wonder if everything is all right? How did the Queen like her surprise?" Edith's words were tentative, but not fearful. Connor knew her well enough to know she was not being nosy, and that her questions came from a place of care. But it did not stop them from stirring up the shame where it lay like sludge in his mind.

He looked away into the fire. The flames danced and flickered in the grate.

Unable to answer her question, he instead asked, "Edith, how do you know you're doing the right thing?"

"Your Grace, that is quite the question. I suppose I trust that I know the right thing when given the choice," she said simply.

"Yes, but what if two people think they're doing the right thing but the things they're doing are in opposition to one another?" he asked, still watching the flames.

"I think that's how most wars start, Your Grace," she replied with a smile.

"I'm serious," he said softly, finally looking at her. She straightened and looked at him questioningly. "I fought with Jacqueline earlier. I'm worried about her," he explained.

"You fought? Your Grace, I thought the point of your afternoon was to help her relax. Weren't you supposed to take her mind off of . . . everything?" she asked.

Connor didn't reply. Edith tsked and set her cup down.

"Okay, I may have made things worse," he said after a time.

Edith frowned. "I know you would not have meant to. If you fought, try to understand where she was coming from. No one sets out to be wrong, so if you have different views, something must have broken down somewhere," she said kindly.

"She's just so convinced they're out to get her," he said.

"Who?"

"The Council, mostly. Now me, I think," he said quietly. Edith raised her eyebrow slightly at his last comment.

"Your Grace, consider for a moment," she said. Her words were slow and low; with each sentence Connor found himself relaxing. "She is a long way from everything that is familiar to her. She most likely needs to feel safe. It's hard to do that when everything and everyone is foreign. Give her time and seek to listen first. She does not strike me as someone who imagines enemies out of shadows," she replied with the conviction of someone advising how to get a wine stain out of silk.

"No, you're right." He scratched his jaw with his knuckles and took a sip of tea.

"So," Edith began when he did not elaborate, "did she like the surprise at least?"

Smiling a little at the memory of Jacs's face when the blindfold came off, and reddening at the thought of her touch, her kiss afterward, he said, "Yes."

Edith hid her smile in her cup and said nothing.

Turning to her, Connor said, "Thank you, for the advice. You have a way of making things make sense."

"The world for you; you know this," she replied.

Long after Edith had cleared the tea tray and bid him good night, Connor found himself beside his desk in front of the window. He stood still, alone in the dark. The only light he had not extinguished in the room behind him flickered from the dying fire. He peered into the depths of the night sky beyond the window's glass. As his eyes adjusted, the pinpricks of stars began to shine brighter until he could discern their patterns.

Mind quiet, he sought out familiar constellations. He spotted the mighty huntress, Orion, and the vain Queen, Cassiopeia. The sight of the eagle, Aquila, made him think of his father, as it was an eagle that adorned the dowager King's crest. King Aren had made the role of Royal Advisor look so easy, always booming a laugh and ready to get his hands dirty when situations became serious.

I could really use your help, Father, he thought sadly. But no, the man had decided to abandon his son in favor of the seaside.

His eyes slid past the eagle to rest on Leo, the lioness. His mother. He swallowed the lump that rose in his throat. What he would give to hear her voice one more time. With her, the world had made sense. Whether praising or scolding him, her kindness had been a constant. Her lessons came with laughter, and each moment with her was embedded in his mind like a jewel. All but the last. He absently rubbed at the space to the left of his sternum. The last moment was a rusty nail driven into his mind. But she had been forced to leave. That had not been her choice.

Pinching the bridge of his nose, he scanned the bookshelf to distract himself from thoughts that threatened to spiral. His well-worn copies of Amelia the Daring's adventures beckoned, but his headspace turned the promise of their comforting tales sour. *All the good stories are about women*, he thought bitterly, *so where do I fit in?*

With a sigh of resignation, he propelled himself into action. Focusing on his desk, he gathered the documents he'd been reviewing, thinking to clear the surface as Edith had recommended. Tables and tallies dating back decades consistently showed a disconnect between the eggshells gifted by the Court and the amount of gold distributed into the treasury each year. The reason behind the extra eggshell count continued to elude him. He paused a moment with the documents still in his hands and felt the draw of the puzzle, the promise of distraction.

Lighting the candles, he sat down and flipped open his notebook to a fresh page. *Where are the eggshells coming from?* he wrote.

7

MIRRORS IN THE MOONLIGHT

It had been a long day. Jacs knew she should call Adaine to help her undress, but she couldn't bring herself to talk to anyone. Encased in her gown, she wanted to shrink within herself. To shrink and shrink until her crown tumbled to the floor and she was too small for anyone to find. But she hadn't worked so hard to earn the blasted thing to run away now.

Absently, she walked over to the semicircle of windows that spanned half her room and drew the curtains across them. In the daylight, the view was breathtaking. If she stood close to the glass, she could imagine she was flying, soaring high above the palace grounds. The gardens and ponds stretched out before her. Then her breath would fog the glass, her view would blur, and she would feel like a fish in a bowl.

Walking over to her vanity, she retrieved a gold-backed looking glass. Its handle was beautifully formed with swirls like waves or gusts of air. Her reflection gazed back at her with a knotted brow, and she paused to smooth it. Carrying the mirror over to the chaise lounge near the fireplace, she sat on the edge of the chair, and with a tight chest breathed the words, "Maria Tabart."

Nothing. She waited desperately for what could have been hours or mere minutes. Taking another breath, she tried again. "Bruna Leschi."

The mirror's surface remained on her reflection. Her heart shuddered in her chest.

She hesitated, then said, "Phillip Leschi."

As it had in Connor's secret room, the surface of the mirror clouded for several heartbeats, then Phillip's silhouette appeared. It was different than it had been during the twilight hours. Now in the dark, the crystal picked up only his glowing outline. In the absence of light, every person appeared with a purple-tinged light surrounding them. Objects and buildings had a much fainter glow. It was enough to see if someone was inside or outside, but not often enough to determine exactly where inside they were.

As Jacs watched, she saw Phillip shrug into a cloak, hunch his shoulders, and leave an interior to step out onto the street. His image disappeared for a moment, only to reappear at intervals as he walked down the road heading away from what Jacs guessed was his home. As he lived a few blocks away from the main street, it made sense that the crystals were sparser in this area. No one else appeared along the stretch he skulked down, and for that Jacs was thankful. It was well past curfew, and the guards were notoriously brutal to anyone caught breaking it. She noticed he was doing his best not to be seen. He paused at intersections, kept his head down, and ducked down alleys, disappearing from the mirror's view for minutes at a time before reemerging and hurrying on. For a long time, this was all Jacs saw.

Finally, he stopped and leaned casually against a building at the entrance of an alley. He would have disappeared from the crystal's gaze again, but for an elbow that poked out from behind the wall. Jacs stared at the fragment, willing the man attached to it to go home. What was he doing out after curfew? With the number of guardpairs she had seen roaming the streets during the day, it was a miracle he hadn't been caught already.

Five minutes passed. Then ten. Jacs was about to say someone else's name into the mirror when she noticed another hunched figure come into view. This person too acted like they did not want to be observed and quickly ducked down the alley to join Phillip. The second figure wore a hooded cloak. Jacs strained her eyes to see more than just the fragment of elbow and the hooded figure's right arm.

What were they doing? What were they talking about? Why would Phillip risk breaking curfew to meet someone in an alley halfway across town?

Jacs felt a tightening in her chest and gripped the mirror harder. With rising panic, she saw the elbow shift and vanish, and with it, the scene. Her breath fogged the mirror and she waited, but Phillip did not reappear. She simply hoped that he had headed further down the alley and took a route home that did not pass by any crystals. That somehow the conversation was no more dangerous than asking to borrow a cup of sugar from a neighbor. But her thoughts plummeted down a hole full of terrible alternatives.

To ease her mind, she decided to check on someone else. Looking around the room, despite knowing it to be empty, she whispered, "Breville Grimsby." Mr. Grimsby had always had time for Jacs, having taught her how to weave flax into fishing traps and even how to dance. He himself had two left feet, but he had proved to be a very competent teacher. He and his wife Merope were old friends of her parents and had been exceptionally kind to her family when her father had passed.

The mirror clouded once more and cleared to reveal a well-lit room, sparsely but lovingly furnished. Mr. Grimsby was sitting very still on a stool in his kitchen while Merope stood in front of him with a bowl of water and a cloth. She was dabbing at a split lip and a bloodied eye. He winced. At first glance, his onyx skin hid the bruises Jacs now noticed purpled around his eye, nose, and jaw. He spoke, and they both laughed, but sadness hung around their eyes like spider webs.

The fact that she could see the couple at all filled her with dread.

The crystals are still in people's homes, she thought sadly.

Jacs bit her lip and said a different name. "Mallard Wetler." Mallard had tormented Jacs growing up. Since the Queen's death, they had built a tentative bridge over their pasts' troubled waters. His father had disappeared on the day of the assassination, and the guards had punished his family for the assumed connection with the Levelist assassins in purple cloaks.

The scene in the Grimsbys' household faded, clouded, and was replaced with another scene like Phillip's: dark with purple glowing outlines. All Jacs could see was a single figure in a hooded cloak. It hurried down a road, looking neither left nor right, and did not meet anyone in its path. With no one else in the frame, Jacs had to assume this was Mal. *But where was he going?* she wondered. The consistency of his image began to break up more and more frequently as he moved away from the center of town. Finally, his image disappeared altogether. She was left with only her reflection and an empty feeling in her stomach. None of the visions had brought her a sliver of peace.

With shaking hands, she set the mirror facedown on a side table. Staring into the fire, she perched on the edge of her seat in a gown of blue and gold. Phillip's hunched outline, glowing images of hooded figures skulking in the dark, and poor Merope tending to her husband's wounds. What kind of life were her people suffering through? While she sat encased in gold thread, what horrors did each day bring them? She couldn't just sit there looking pretty and dance to the

Council's endless tune. She couldn't do nothing while her mother bled the words, *I love you* on parchment. Pulling the scrap of singed paper from her bodice, she brushed her fingertip over the word *Plum*, a shudder rippling through her.

For a moment, the fire flared, sinking its teeth into a dry section of wood. The light glanced off the mirror's handle in a flash. Suddenly, Jacs's mind was transported back to Connor's secret room, back to the soft pillows, his steady breathing, and the light shining through the glass wings of the Griffin. The Griffin, with wings outstretched, claiming the skies for their own. Head held high; talons curled. So similar to the Griffin she had ridden with months ago. She remembered the feeling as the ground slipped away beneath her, the air shaping itself around her, the sky opening up above her. Freedom. Control. Power. A thought struck her. Her brow furrowed and she ran her finger across the shining mirror handle absently as the thought became a plan.

It had been a long day, just like the day before, and just as tomorrow would be. There would be no reason to rouse suspicion in those who watched her, and no need to cause alarm in those who cared for her. She would survive another long day as Queen, and come nightfall she would act. With the setting of the sun, she would rise. She was the rightful Queen. She had been chosen to protect her people. She was worthy of the crown, and tomorrow she would prove it.

8

FLIRTING WITH FIRE

"Get up." Amber paced around the crumpled body of her Queen impatiently.

Boots scrunched on sand; her hand gripped the leather hilt of a dagger. With a flick of her wrist, she threw it, blade down, into the sand by the Queen's curled fist.

"Get up!" she said again.

Jacqueline groaned and pushed herself up to her knees. She reluctantly retrieved the dagger.

"A Queen does not kneel before her knights. Now stand up and try again," Amber snarled. Positive reinforcement had never been her style, and tough love had churned out enough capable fighters that she didn't feel the need to adapt her methods. When they had initially started, Amber had been nervous about harming the Queen, even if it was for the sake of training. Those feelings had long since vanished as she now saw that any pain inflicted in the ring was pain avoided outside of it. The Queen had improved rapidly since her coronation, but still had a long way to go to be considered any form of a threat. Like a newborn foal, Jacqueline got shakily to her feet. Her hands adjusted their grip around the dagger, and she stood to face Amber.

The knight smiled. "Good," she said curtly. "Again."

Jacqueline shifted her dagger between her hands and rolled her shoulders back. With a swift motion, she slid the blade into a sheath strapped to her forearm.

The Queen had similar sheaths strapped to her inner thigh, left hip, and concealed within her calf-high boot. In the real world, these would be covered by whatever gown or tunic she would be wearing. For training, they were exposed for ease of access. She wore dark leggings and a close-fitting tunic, her hair tied in a simple tail down her back.

Repositioning her feet, Jacqueline settled into her stance and waited. The two women stood in the center of the training ring. Guardpairs and knights trained alongside the Queen but were careful to give her a wide berth. The ring was filled with sand, the ceiling open to the scorching midmorning sun, and a few Lordsons lounged in the surrounding stands watching, like lovesick puppies, the women training. Amber could hear them boasting loudly, reacting to the blows in the ring with the exaggeration of one wanting to draw attention. It was well known the Lords brought their sons to the palace to catch the eye of the Queen, or at the very least, one of the Dames flitting about her for favor.

Jacqueline kept her eyes on the circling knight, and Amber was pleased to see her ignoring the sounds coming from the surrounding combat. Self-consciousness had long since been beaten out of her, any sideways glance or turn of the head had been seized as openings and optimized. She was learning to focus. Amber circled her once, twice, then lunged toward her. It took three heartbeats for Jacqueline to slip her forearm dagger into her waiting palm and thrust it at the knight. It took Amber only two to trip her, strike her chest, and send her sprawling on her back. Sand streaked the Queen's arms and outlined the trickles of sweat running down her brow. A cry of disappointment came from the stands. Amber ignored it and stood above her student.

"Faster. Light contact until the blade's in your palm, then grip and strike. Water becoming ice. Fluid to solid. Lighter on your toes. Don't let me throw your balance. Get up," she said.

They had been at it for hours. Amber could see Jacqueline's fatigue, could see her pain, and more important, could see the frustration building behind her eyes. She had been cultivating this moment, pushing her harder, forcing her closer to her breaking point.

"Again!" she barked. Finally, eyes burning, Jacqueline pushed herself back to her knees, launched herself at the knight with a scream of fury, and Amber pounced. In a fluid motion, she sidestepped around the Queen and clasped her wrist, twisting it behind her back and wrenching upward. Jacqueline cried out and bowed forward, struggling uselessly against Amber's grip. Taking a knee behind her, Amber brought her lips to her ear and said, "Anger will blind you; the fire will consume you, and when it does, you will lose. Every time. You're not some weak little boy, a slave to his tantrums. Any woman worth her mettle remains in control even in the direst of battles. A fire will flare for a moment. A flash and it's gone. Wild and unpredictable. But the ocean will drown any that oppose it. Its depths are a constant and deadly force. Be that force. Never lose control."

Jacqueline was breathing hard. She had stopped attempting to twist free and Amber felt the tension in her limbs dissipate. Felt her breathing slow. Still on her knees, Jacqueline melted into Amber's grip, then suddenly slammed the knight backward into the sand. With a twist, Jacqueline was now on top of her, her knee on her chest and a dagger at her throat.

The Queen grinned. The fire in her eyes that had flashed moments before had vanished, now clear and calm. The Lordsons in the stand cheered.

Panting slightly, Jacqueline tucked the dagger back in its sheath, pushed herself off Amber and said, "Let's run that again."

When the sun hung directly overhead, Amber called a halt to their training. Like a puppet with its strings cut, Jacqueline collapsed, breathing heavily. Amber hadn't realized how hard the Queen had been hanging on by sheer force of will alone. She lay on the sand of the training arena with her knees bent and a hand over her eyes, a satisfied smirk on her face. Amber gave her a moment, eyes scanning the stands. She noticed Lena and Anya sitting with Andromeda on the nearby benches and waved.

"The Courtiers are here," Amber said, walking over to where Jacqueline lay. At her words, the Queen opened her eyes, found the pair, and waved at them too. With a grunt, Amber hoisted Jacqueline to her feet. Her palms were slick and covered in grit.

They collected their things and made their way to the side of the ring. While they were still well beyond earshot, Jacqueline's fingers closed around her wrist, forcing her pace to slow. The seriousness in her gaze piqued Amber's curiosity, and she leaned toward Jacqueline instinctively.

"I need you to help me with something this evening," Jacqueline said softly. "Don't ask questions, and don't breathe a word to anyone. You and Andromeda are to meet me in the stables at midnight. We will be going for a ride, so pack a day's worth of supplies. No one must see you, and no one"—she emphasized the last words, her eyes flicking toward where Lena and Anya sat—"*no one* must know what we are doing. I'll explain more tonight." She waited a beat for Amber's swift nod, and in the next instant, Jacqueline let go, her face cleared, and she walked to greet the Courtiers at the edge of the ring.

Amber followed slowly and scratched the back of her neck. The Queen's intensity had thrown her. Frowning a little, she rolled her shoulders and wondered idly what it was Jacqueline would need help with at that hour. Whatever it was, it was important enough to keep secret, even from Lena. That indicated it was either dangerous or unlawful. Or both.

She groaned internally when she remembered the evening's plans she would now have to cancel. Given that this was the third cancellation in a row, she doubted her latest beau would be sticking around much longer. *A pity,* she thought, *I was actually starting to like this one.* Being a knight, especially one as decorated as herself, definitely helped attract beaus, but it did nothing to help keep them. The excitement of being courted by a woman in armor wore off quickly when she was never around.

Especially when guards also get armor and have better hours, Amber thought grimly. However, her mindset was not severe. She would have traded her left arm for the opportunity to serve the Queen. And being a knight in her Queensguard? That was a dream come true.

Maybe she could buy him a box of pastries or chocolates as an apology. It's definitely harder to be mad when your belly is full. Luckily, she would have some time this afternoon to patch things up. Content with her plan, she joined Jacqueline and the others, sharing a few subtle gestures with Andromeda. They would talk after their shift.

As if on cue, she saw her replacements walking toward the Queen, who was chatting with her friends. There was Masterchiv Cassida Rathbone, head of the Queensguard and Chiv.—no, that wasn't a knight with her, that was a guard. In the place of a knight's short sword, a guard's dagger and leather restraining strap hung at her hip. Amber raised an eyebrow in surprise. Before Queen Ariel's assassination, the Queensguard had always been a collection of the Queen's most trusted guards and knights led by a Master. After her death, it had been decided that only the finest knights of the realm could be trusted to protect the Queen, and guards were excluded from the honor of serving. Now, even within the palace, the Queen was always escorted by at least two knights.

To see a mere guard accompanying Masterchiv Rathbone was unexpected. She could not imagine what a guard could have done to have deserved such an honor.

Masterchiv Rathbone strode purposefully in their direction, gray eyes ceaselessly scanning her surroundings. Her blonde hair was wound in a tight braided bun at the base of her skull with a few escaped tendrils of hair around her temples. She wore the golden cloak of her station, and a sword swung at her hip. As always, it had been polished to a high shine, the face of a roaring lion on its pommel. It was the mark of her skills as a fighter that the sword had only ever been unsheathed in battle twice.

As the newcomers approached, Andromeda rose from the bench. Mirroring her partner, Amber stood to attention after hurriedly wiping at the grit from her own sword's pommel. She was suddenly aware of how dusty she was. Shoulders back, the two knights tapped their crossed wrists together twice, fists closed, in salute. Masterchiv Rathbone inclined her head, but the guard returned the gesture. The latter held Amber's gaze for just a moment too long, her eyes flicking to appraise her with a slight smile playing in the corners of her mouth. Amber felt the back of her neck grow hot.

Out of the corner of her eye, Amber saw Jacqueline greet her new guard. The Queen's demeanor shifted from casual to formal in the time it took Masterchiv Rathbone to look her way.

"Masterchiv Rathbone," the Queen said by way of greeting. "And this is?"

"Dyna Flent, Your Majesty, a guard. She is the niece of Cllr. Fengar and is filling in for Chiv. Ryder today," Masterchiv Rathbone replied with a meaningful look at Jacqueline. If Jacqueline had an opinion on the change, it was impossible to tell. At the very most, the information may have bored her.

Cllr. Fengar's niece, Amber thought as she shared a wry smile with Andromeda. *That explains it.*

The guard shifted nervously as the Queen's gaze fell upon her. Amber was impressed that, despite her apparent discomfort, Flent did not look away. Her dark umber skin blanched a little under the Queen's steady gaze, but otherwise she stood proud. Hands clasped behind her back, feet hip distance, and with her chin jutting forward slightly, she radiated an eager determination. The midday sun played with the warm tones in her thick black hair. She wore her uniform in perfect accordance with regulations, with the personal touch of a thin fabric band nestled in her tight curls and tied at the nape of her neck, keeping the hair from her pale green-gray eyes.

"It is an honor to serve, Your Majesty," she said with a voice of honey. She took a knee with a dancer's grace, and Amber felt a blush creep up her neck. Hurriedly, she looked away, chiding herself. *Not an option.*

Jacqueline smiled. "Rise. Thank you, Flent. You and Masterchiv Rathbone are in for a perilous shift. I hope you're up for it," she said with mock seriousness.

The young guard stood to attention and nodded adamantly, missing the Queen's attempt at humor. "I'm up for anything, Your Majesty."

"Perfect. I will bathe, change, and then Courtiers Glowra and Bishop will be teaching me etiquette."

The guard's face fell slightly.

After a quick debrief, Amber and Andromeda were dismissed. Amber watched Jacqueline walk in the direction of the bathhouse, then her gaze shifted to the departing figure of Flent.

Andromeda watched her with crossed arms and followed her gaze. She scoffed.

"What?" Amber asked innocently, turning to face her partner.

"You're unbelievable," she said.

"I don't know what you're talking about," Amber replied, crossing her arms to mirror Andromeda.

"How're things going with, what was his name? Niqo?"

"Fine," she said shortly.

The sounds from the training grounds floated between them, grunts and scuffles painting a picture of the thrusts and blocks in the ring. Every so often, the Lordsons punctuated the sounds with a groan or a cheer.

"We don't court guards," Andromeda reminded her.

Amber felt the heat rush to her face and fought the wave of indignation that followed. "I know," she said stiffly, playing with the pommel of her sword. With forced bravado, she winked at her partner. "A girl can look though, can't she?"

Andromeda shook her head. "You're ridiculous," she said, not unkindly.

Grinning now, Amber playfully shoved her elbow. "You love it. Anyway, we have a mission. I hope you didn't have plans tonight." In a low tone, Amber filled her in on what Jacqueline had said. Leaving the training grounds, they took the long way through the gardens. Amber was careful to keep her voice quiet. Even outside it was never safe to assume others weren't listening. Andromeda looked just as perplexed as Amber had been.

They split at the barracks to go to their respective quarters, each with a list of preparations to make, and Amber with her evening plans to break.

9

DANCE LESSONS

The Queen emerged from the bathhouse in much less time than Lena had been expecting. She guessed it was the farm-girl upbringing, but Jacqueline hadn't yet mastered the art of how to sit still, much less relax. No matter; that just meant more time for teaching. It did feel wonderful to be useful. Having just spent the better part of the week focusing on table etiquette, Lena had decided they needed a change of pace. The Queen had a lifetime's worth of Upperite manners, customs, and behaviors to learn as quickly as possible—not that her Lowrian customs were wrong by any means, but they were more . . . rugged than those of the Upper Realm. For a Queen to be taken seriously, she had to know how to act.

Lena was thankful now for her mother's strict lessons all those years ago, painful though her methods had sometimes been. Despite the residual scars across the backs of her thighs, Lena was the perfect example of Upperite etiquette and could now pass these skills onto the new Queen. Luckily, Jacqueline was an eager and capable student, so Lena's methods could be much gentler than her mother's had been.

"Anya, let Jacqueline lead." Lena paused as the dancers readjusted, then said, "Again! One and two, three and four, switch, five and six, right foot forward and!" Lena counted, clapping out the rhythm. Jacqueline led Anya in a dance around the stone floor of the expansive circle balcony. Split skirts twirling, they spun around each other.

That is, until: "Ow!"

"Sorry," Jacqueline said automatically as Anya winced at another trodden-upon toe.

"Spin and spin, step together! One and two . . ."

"Sorry."

"Three and four . . ."

"Sorry!"

Lena cut off as the two on the makeshift dance floor broke into giggles. She felt a wry smile creep across her face but forced it down. "This is serious!" she insisted, only making them laugh harder. "Ladies, stop, we can't have a Queen with two left feet!"

"I won't have any feet left at the rate Her Majesty's going," Anya quipped, holding Jacqueline at arm's length and repositioning her grip. "On the four, I'll be coming forward and you have to step back. Here, if you hold my waist here you have more control over where I go."

Jacqueline readjusted and tried again, head down to keep track of her feet. Lena looked out over the castle grounds. It was a clear day. Gardeners spotted the hedges and flowerbeds, stooping and weeding in the sun. There were a few Dames strolling along the paths, and other nobles had found shady benches on which to read or gossip. The Queensguard stood at ease by the balcony doorway. Lena could see the bored look on Masterchiv Rathbone's features mirrored in Dyna

Flent's. The latter fidgeted first with her hair, then her belt, then the hilt of her dagger. She had obviously expected a more thrilling charge.

"All right, from the top!" Lena announced, turning back to face the pair.

"Lena, I think I could benefit from a demonstration," Jacqueline said innocently with a glance at Anya. "Could you and Anya show me?"

Despite it being posed as a question, Jacqueline had already dropped her hand from Anya's waist and stepped back with a beckoning gesture. She backed away to sit on the balcony banister. Lena felt a blush creep up her cheeks and met Anya's eyes with a smile.

"Okay," she said.

Suddenly she was thirteen again, standing in her mother's empty ballroom asking a young Anya, flower crown on her head, to dance with her. Anya had been reluctant then, arms crossed, eyes worried. "Someone will see, and I'll get in trouble," she had said. "Servants can't dance with Dames."

Now, Lena held out her hand and Anya stepped forward eagerly. The two women met in the center of the balcony, hovered for a moment, then touched palms with their eyes locked, and the dance swept them away. Lena felt her world reduce to the light pressure at her waist, the slight shift as she spun, and the warmth of Anya's deep brown eyes. Like petals in the breeze, they floated around each other. Time seemed to slow. But then their feet stilled, and suddenly it was over. With a lingering look, they stepped apart. Lena could hear Jacqueline clapping. She felt her cheeks burning, her heart hammering, and she grinned up at Anya. With a grin to match, Anya gave her hand a squeeze before letting go.

"Much better," Jacqueline said as she approached from the banister. "Now I get it. I think I was lacking . . . passion?" she teased.

Lena tapped her chin in mock serious consideration and said, "Well, we could always call for His Grace? I'm sure he could inspire something of the sort in you."

Rather than cheer her, her words seemed to still something in Jacqueline. Her shoulders sank ever so slightly, and the corners of her mouth followed suit. Like a flower wilting, Jacqueline appeared to droop. "Maybe," was all she said.

Lena exchanged a worried look with Anya, who simply shrugged.

"Actually, I have a question," Jacqueline said, changing the subject. With a tilt of the head, she beckoned them to follow and walked back to where she had been sitting at the edge of the balcony. Resting her left palm lightly on the banister, she pointed vaguely with her right at a point in the garden.

"What tree is that?" she asked.

Lena looked to where she was pointing. There were several different trees and bushes in the area, and all were hard to discern from their vantage point.

"Which one?"

"That one, see? With the flowers?"

"You mean the cherry blossom?" Anya asked, stepping closer on her right, trying to follow her finger.

"No, that one."

Lena stepped closer on Jacqueline's left, her hand resting on the banister as she leaned forward. As soon as her hand touched the stone, she felt the dry edge of parchment prickle her pinky finger. Looking down, she saw Jacqueline pass her a small, folded note. The words *Open if I'm missing tomorrow evening* were scrawled in the Queen's hand on the front. She quickly covered the note with her hand and looked up at Jacqueline, who did not shift her gaze from the tree in the grounds. However, Lena noticed a subtle nod as she palmed the note.

"Oh, do you mean the magnolia?" she asked.

"Yes! That's the one, magnolia. Beautiful tree," Jacqueline said, looking relieved.

"Beautiful and hardy," Anya said, oblivious to what had transpired. "Did you know it represents long life, endurance, and eternity?

It's exceptionally good at adapting to changes in climate and geography and is able to survive hard conditions. Plus, it's resistant to most pests and diseases. Pretty to look at, hard to kill."

"My kind of flower," Jacqueline said quietly as Anya finished.

The three women stood for a moment enjoying the view of the gardens. Chickadees and fantails chirped happily in spurts, and the buzz of bees made the air feel warm and lazy. Lena spotted Cornelius walking in the gardens with Cllr. Perda, Cllr. Dilmont, and Lord Claustrom. The quartet was paired; the Councilors walked together behind the Royal Advisor and Lord. The latter two appeared deep in conversation, and Lord Claustrom took Cornelius's arm to avoid an uneven cobblestone. Cornelius was quick to drop the embrace once the path became level again, but Lena felt Jacqueline bristle beside her.

Mood suddenly somber, the Queen pushed away from the stone railing. By the time they turned back to the balcony, Lena had hidden the note in the cuff of her dress. Neither Masterchiv Rathbone nor Dyna Flent showed any sign of having seen anything unusual. Regardless, Lena felt it burn at her wrist for the remainder of the afternoon like a brand.

Why would Jacqueline think she might be missing tomorrow evening?

10

HEAT SENSITIVE

Dusk had been a long time coming, but finally, Jacs was able to excuse herself from the evening meal and leave for bed early, complaining of a headache. Closing her chamber's doors behind her, she exhaled. One of the serving boys had gotten her room ready for her. A fire crackled merrily in the hearth. The corner of her duvet had been turned down, and she knew without looking that a heating pot filled with boiling water would have been placed between her sheets. The air felt warm and cozy. A tray of tea and biscuits had been laid out for her by the fire.

Jacs surveyed this with the gaze of a stranger in a foreign land and took several deep breaths to collect her thoughts. It would be a few hours before she could meet Amber and Andromeda, but she needed time to think. Walking over to her desk, she picked up a piece of parchment and a pen and began writing. She was not sure how successful her endeavor would be, or how long she would be away if she was at any point detained, so she had to write to Connor. Let him know where she had gone and why. And likely beg his forgiveness for not telling him, for not inviting him along. Someone needed to lead in her stead, and the Council could not be trusted alone.

Finishing the first letter and storing it safely away, she began the second. Hunched over her work and deep in thought she did not hear the gentle knock at her door, did not hear her name called, did not hear the soft footfalls across the rugs, and only realized she was not alone in her rooms when she felt a light touch on her shoulder.

Startled, she spun around and hurriedly covered the parchment.

It was Connor.

"Don't do that!" she said stupidly, willing her heart rate to slow.

"Sorry, I came to see how you were feeling. I knocked and . . ." He gestured at the door and trailed off, his gaze darting to the parchment half concealed under Jacs's palm. "What are you writing?" he asked.

"It's nothing," she said hurriedly. "Just jotting some ideas down. Do you, um, do you want a cup of tea?" Jacs asked, standing and pulling Connor away from her desk. He lingered, eyes still on the parchment, then turned to Jacs curiously.

"That's addressed to me," he said. It wasn't a question.

Jacs hesitated for a moment before admitting, "Yes."

"What does it say?" he asked. Jacs noticed he made no attempt to take it from where it lay on her desk, and no attempt to read it from where it was partially concealed. He met her eyes and waited; hand still loosely clasped in hers. Jacs bit the inside of her lip and fought the urge to look away. If she told him now, he would surely try to stop her, or try to come along, or at the very least be a knowing bystander to what was to follow. She did not want any of those outcomes. It was better if he did not know.

But I can't lie to him, she thought.

"If I asked you to wait to find out, would you?" she said quietly.

"Yes," he said after a slight pause, perceptible only to Jacs in the slight shift of his feet.

"Thank you," she said. "It's something I can't tell you yet, and something you are better off not knowing now."

Searching her face, he reluctantly nodded. Hurt flickered behind his eyes. It was to his credit that he did not look toward the desk again.

Jacs felt the fissure between them widen as they made their way over to the couch by the fire. While she settled on the cushions, he poured them both cups and brought one over to her. Watching his concentration to avoid spilling a slightly overfilled cup made her smile, but when he looked up briefly, he did not smile back. His eyes had a tightness around them, with dark shadows beneath. He looked exhausted.

They sat in an awkward silence punctuated only by the crackle of the fire and the clink of cup on saucer. Jacs debated her decision not to tell Connor. Although she hadn't yet said it out loud, she loved him. You weren't supposed to keep secrets from the person you loved. Besides, he might have insight that she could use. Resolved, she opened her mouth to explain her plan, but Connor beat her to it, and she closed it again.

"Jacs, I sent a letter to Father," he said in a hollow voice, "asking about Mother's journal. We should hopefully hear back next week if the messenger is fast. In the meantime, though, I found this while looking through the drawers in Mother's study—well, your study now—pushed way at the back of one of them, and I thought it might be useful." He handed her a small, blue leather-bound notebook. It felt warm to the touch and was no longer than Jacs's palm. With careful fingers, she pried the small cover open. The pages were sewn together with gold thread and made of a rich cream parchment. Due to its size and the thickness of the parchment, the book only held about fifteen pages in total. Each page was filled with a tight, neat hand in black ink.

Scanning the entries, Jacs realized quickly that each line had a name, an age, a date, and a location. Assuming that the unigender names denoted boys, all names were male.

She looked up at Connor in confusion. He scratched the back of his head and said uncomfortably, "That's definitely her handwriting, and look." He leaned over, took the book, pressed down hard and dragged the pad of his thumb across the cover page. The word *Missing* trailed behind the path his thumb made before vanishing again.

In response to her unasked question, he said, "Heat-sensitive ink. Mother used to write me coded messages and treasure maps with it when I was a boy. It responds to body heat and anything hotter just makes the words stay longer before they fade."

Nodding, Jacs inspected the little book again. "Missing . . ." she mused out loud. Flicking through the pages of names, she said, "Do you think this is a list of missing people?"

Connor shrugged but said, "It looks like it. Which raises a host of questions. Namely, why was my mother recording them? Was she looking for them? How did she know about them? I know I had never heard about anything like this. And why are they only boys? Look, it lists mostly places from the Lower Realm. And look at the dates." He shifted closer to her on the couch so they could both squint at the tiny print on the pages as he pointed. "This spans decades. Are they birth dates? Death dates? The dates they went missing? The dates they were found?" He was speaking low and very quickly. Running his fingers through his hair, he finished: "And if all these boys are missing, who's taking them? Where? Why? And why isn't this talked about?"

Sliding her gaze down each row, she spotted the name of her hometown: Bridgeport. Tracing the line back, she saw that the name Gadwall Wetler was dated twelve years earlier. Gadwall Wetler, Mallard's older brother.

A memory sparked in her. He had disappeared when she had been about five, but she had heard the story years after. They said he had fallen into the river one morning and drowned. It was during the rainy season, and they had never found his body. Even years afterward, children had not been allowed to go down to the river alone because of it. Mallard, seven at the time, had told anyone who would listen that Gad hadn't drowned, that he had run away with a visiting group of traveling players. The players had stayed at the inn long after Gadwall's funeral, and no one had believed the grieving child. By the time Jacs started attending school with him, he had stopped telling that story and refused to speak about his brother at all.

Closing the book, she passed her thumb across the title as Connor had and watched the word appear and disappear in an instant. Sighing, she said, "I don't know what this means yet, but thank you for showing me. May I keep it?"

"Of course," he said stiffly.

"And have you shown anyone else this? Have you mentioned it to anyone?" Jacs spoke without thinking, her mind ticking off facts needed without considering the tact or sensitivity required in the question's delivery. The image of him strolling the grounds earlier that day with Hera and the two Councilors swam to her mind's eye.

Connor frowned. "No," he said, shifting away from her a fraction, his body rigid, tone frosty.

Jacs looked up and saw a hardness in his eyes as he set his jaw. She sighed, "I didn't mean . . ." She did not want to argue with him. Not tonight.

"I know what you meant," he said coldly, then, seeing the look on her face, he softened. "Listen, Jacs, I promise you, I'm yours. If you don't believe me now"—his eyes flicked for a moment to her desk, then back to her—"I'll spend the rest of my days proving it. I'm here, by your side, I won't leave you." He left *again* unsaid, but they both felt it. "Jacs," he clasped her hands in his, "we won't work if we don't trust each other. Not as leaders, not as friends, and not as . . ." He stalled, not quite able to shape the words.

The idea danced between them, making them both look away. It seemed almost silly to Jacs; they had known each other for almost five years, been friends for five years. They shared their lives with each other, shared their dreams with each other, but still, still, she could not make a vow of love. And he hadn't either; he wouldn't until she did. They had said everything else, but Jacs couldn't bring herself to say those words, could not bring herself to change what they had. She supposed it was because for her to admit that she loved him meant the next step, toward marriage.

She couldn't do that without Master Leschi to guide her, without her mother beside her. She loved him with all her heart, and in her heart that knowledge stayed.

Jacs squeezed his hand and said, "Connor, I know I haven't been the easiest person to understand lately, but you need to know that I am trying my best to be a Queen worthy of the crown. If that means concealing things from people until they are ready to hear them, then that is what I have to do." *Especially if those people meet with Councilors and Lords behind my back*, she thought sadly.

Connor frowned. "You don't have to do this alone."

"I know, but—"

"How am I supposed to advise you when I don't know half of what's going on with you?" he asked, irritation flaring.

Jacs narrowed her eyes. "You could start by trusting me."

Connor scoffed. "Like you obviously trust me? It goes both ways, Jacs."

"Connor I—"

"You know what? Forget it. Keep your secrets. If you want to do this without my help, be my guest," he said, pushing to his feet.

"Connor, wait—" Jacs grasped for his hand, but he brushed her away.

"You know where to find me when you change your mind," he said bitterly and strode from the room.

The door shut with a snap. Jacs sat, conflicted, where Connor had left her. He would forgive her. When he realized what it was all for, he had to forgive her, she tried to convince herself. With a sigh, she shook her head and made to follow him.

The clock on her mantel chimed.

Jacs cursed, she was going to be late. She didn't have time to patch up this mess. Changing her mind again, she retrieved the pack from under her bed, and exchanged her evening's outfit for a pair of dark leggings, a navy blue tunic, and gray traveling cloak. She selected her most understated crown, a simple band of gold, and slipped it in her pack. It looked out of place next to the assortment of items including food, her waterskin, a change of clothes, a stack of signed and sealed parchment, pen, ink, a bar of soap, and a comb. As she slipped into a pair of warm socks and leather travel boots, her eyes landed on the tea tray, and as an afterthought, she palmed a couple of sugar cubes.

Hesitating, she debated telling Connor. It was a short distance to his room; she could still make things right. Her stomach clenched at the thought of leaving things the way they were. Torn, she bit the skin around her thumbnail. She didn't have time. Moving to her desk, she retrieved the letter, signed and sealed it, and placed it on her pillow. He would forgive her.

She eased the door open a crack and stepped out into the passage. Connor was nowhere in sight. Carefully, she closed the door behind her.

11

EARLY-MORNING RIDE

"I got held up. Connor came to visit," Jacs said by way of explanation as soon as the waiting knights came within earshot in the stable courtyard. Andromeda's face remained impassive, but Amber flashed her lopsided grin and arched an eyebrow.

Jacs ignored her assumption, instead saying, "If we're stopped, we're simply going for a midnight ride. But it's better if no one spots us. The horses are waiting for us, let's get them and get out. I'll explain more once we're beyond the palace walls."

The knights nodded and fell into step behind Jacs. Each had a small pack with them, and both wore the dark uniform of the evening watch, a choice much better suited for stealth. Jacs smiled grimly.

It was half past midnight, and the stables were empty except for the horses. Jacs had paid the stable boy with three silver scyphs to make sure he was visiting the tack house between the hours of twelve and one, and to also make sure three horses were fed, watered, and saddled. Pointed ears pricked forward at the creak of the stable door, and the three women stole across the floor like shadows. The only sounds were the occasional huffing from velvet muzzles and the chirp of crickets from beyond the doors.

The requested horses were waiting patiently in their stalls. Peggy, Jacs's mare, sniffed her hands eagerly when she reached for her lead rope. Jacs chuckled and withdrew the lumps of sugar from her pocket, delighting in the soft nibbling against her palm as Peggy ensured she claimed every sugar crystal. Eagerly, she sniffed Jacs's hands for more and snorted to find them empty.

"Sorry, girl," Jacs said fondly, stroking her mane. Gesturing for quiet, Jacs began leading them out through the stable, across the stable yard, and through the servants' entrance, heart in her throat. Horseshoes rang on stone like a blacksmith's hammer. Each swish of a tail or snort sounded like a trumpeter's blast, and Jacs held her breath for fear of adding to the cacophony. Luckily, they met no one. A voice in the back of Jacs's head marveled at the lack of security around the servants' quarters and servants' entrance. Something she would have to address once she returned.

If you return, a voice whispered in her mind. Frowning, she pushed the thought away. Of course she would return.

Once clear of the palace walls, they mounted their horses and made faster progress. The cool night air kissed Jacs's cheeks. She felt buoyed up and let her hood fall back, her hair streaming behind her as they pushed their mounts to a trot, a gallop, then a canter, racing across the fields beyond the palace.

Jacs heard Amber whoop and even caught Andromeda's decisive, "Ha!" as they sped through the tall grasses. They slowed to a walk, then stopped on the banks of the river. The same river that Connor had sailed his first boat down all those years earlier.

It flowed thick and shining in the moonlight, looking more like tar than water. The surrounding fields became forest away to her right, toward the Lower Realm, and rose into mountains to her left. Court's Mountain. Windswept and exhilarated, Jacs turned her back to the river to face the others.

"Your Majesty, with all due respect, what are we doing out here?" Andromeda asked.

"We are going up Court's Mountain," Jacs said simply. The knights gaped at her.

Amber's gaze followed a line up the looming shadow before them. "What?" she asked incredulously.

"We're going up Court's Mountain," Jacs repeated.

"Sorry, wrong question. Why?" Amber asked, still in disbelief.

"Because." Jacs took a deep breath. "Because I'm going to ride with the Court down to the Lower Realm to see what I can do to help the situation in Bridgeport."

The stunned silence was fractured by the rushing river at Jacs's back.

"You're going to . . ." Andromeda said, appearing to process Jacs's words as she repeated them.

"Ride with the Court to the Lower Realm. Now, neither of you will be expected to accompany me once we reach the top of the mountain. That will be your choice. But I felt it would be a reckless act as Queen to ride up the mountain at night alone. . ."

"Yeah, wouldn't want to do anything reckless," Amber said sardonically.

Jacs shot her a look but saw that Amber was smiling.

"You mean to say you would go to the Lower Realm without proper guard?" Andromeda said, scandalized.

"Well . . . I couldn't force you to ride with the Court."

"Of course we will go with you! A Queen without her guard, and in the Lower Realm, no less. That's ridiculous." Andromeda, rarely ruffled, looked shocked at the thought.

"Yup, and I go where she goes, so it looks like we're all in," Amber said cheerfully.

Relief rushed over Jacs, and she could have hugged them both had they not been on horseback.

"Plus, I've always wanted to see the land below the clouds. Growing up here, you hear some weird stories about Lowrians. I mean, you're all right," Amber added with a nod to Jacs, "but who knows what the rest of them are like? Do they eat normal food down there? Do they have ten fingers like we do? How many fingers do you have again, Jacqueline?"

"Eleven, why?" Jacs said casually.

"Wait, what? Really?"

Jacs laughed. "No. Ten fingers, eight toes, just like every other Frean."

For confirmation, Amber looked at Andromeda, who shook her head.

Applying gentle pressure through her thighs, Jacs spun Peggy toward the mountain, following the river. Bodies moving with the horses' hoofbeats, each woman fell into a fluid rhythm.

Gradually, the horses picked up speed. Jacs heard the wind rushing around her and saw the bridge ahead. Padding on dirt changed to a clatter on wood, then they were across it and heading up the trail to Court's Mountain. The path rose steadily and soon their pace had slowed to a walk. The horses were happy to press on but reluctant to do so any faster. Jacs was glad for it. While the road had been well maintained, few ventured up this mountain path and it was littered with loose rocks, debris, and the odd gnarled tree root. Luckily, the moon was bright, and the sky was clear, so Jacs was able to scan the ground, alert for hazards that might trip the horses. The odd gopher hole threatened to twist an ankle.

Navigating the ascent was more laborious than Jacs remembered from the descent after the first task. Although, she reflected, back then she gave Peggy free rein, and much of the trip was passed in semi-consciousness. Now, every fiber of Jacs's being felt alert. Her mind kept imagining how the Council would react to what she was about to do. Swallowing, she ignored the panic that threatened to consume her. Reason took over: She had never been banned from seeking the Court's services. It had never been forbidden for her to visit the Lower Realm. Surely, they can't punish her for something she, technically, was not aware was off-limits. She was Queen after all; with that came a certain level of command. She was not some child awaiting instructions. She was the ruler of their two realms.

It's better to beg forgiveness than ask permission, Master Leschi's words came to her mind in a flash, and she smiled. Suddenly, she was back with her mentor, working through the night in her mother's barn on their last hot-air balloon. The balloon that eventually transported her to the Upper Realm. Eyes strained in the lamplight; ears pricked for any sound of an unwelcome approach. Her mother stood watch at the barn door with the gray cat Ranger curled at her feet. The memory faded, leaving an ache in Jacs's chest.

Hours trickled by and still the horses climbed. They stopped once to stretch their limbs while Amber picked a stone from her mount's hoof. Any moment of pause felt like a moment of darkness lost and a moment closer to discovery. Jacs marveled at the distance. The contestants of the Contest of Queens had not been allowed to use the road; their path up the mountain had been treacherous and uncertain. Now, even with the road making the trail easier, the distance was immense.

"Can you believe we climbed up this mountain with eggs hanging from our necks?" Jacs called over her shoulder.

"And without water," Amber called. "Bloody Prince, I bet he didn't test out his tasks before setting them."

Jacs's laugh was whisked away behind her. Knowing Connor, it was very likely he'd never personally attempted his tasks. Although she knew they would have been meticulously planned out and researched.

"At least you two didn't get lost and have to do half of it twice," Andromeda remarked from the rear.

"Hey, I had to do the top bit twice!" Jacs said with mock indignation.

"That was a choice, not a blunder," Amber retorted.

"Not a blunder, just . . . reduced terrain awareness." Andromeda's grumble barely made it up to Jacs at the front of the line.

They pressed on.

As the predawn glow began to edge the surrounding valleys and distant mountains, the party cleared the false summit. The rest of the peak stood before them like a natural cathedral. As though the mountain had formed its own monument at its crown, it was a mixture of natural and hewn structure. No woman could have created such an edifice. The elegant arches, vaulted ceilings, and flying buttresses appeared as though poured into a Goddess-forged mold. The entrance, a vast hollow wide enough to fit ten women across, loomed before them. Darkness lay beyond.

Jacs swung down from her saddle, staggering slightly as her feet touched the earth, and her legs forgot how to work for a moment. The others joined her and stretched out the kinks they had accumulated from riding. Jacs shouldered her pack and watched Amber do the same.

"Ready?" Jacs asked. Amber had set her jaw, and Andromeda, rolling her shoulders, collected her pack with a determined nod.

"What about the horses?" Amber asked.

"Peggy knows the way home," Jacs said confidently. "Don't you, girl?" She reached out and stroked her nose. The mare's soft eye regarded Jacs levelly and she whickered. "That's right, you got me back safely once, now take these two with you. Take them home," she said softly, indicating the other horses. After a final sniff at Jacs's pockets revealed no further sugar cubes, Peggy nuzzled Jacs's chest and blew out sharply through her nose, then turned to the other two horses. With a flick of her tail, a pitch in her ears, and a soft whinny, she began the slow walk down the mountain. When she had walked several meters ahead of the other, unmoving horses, she called to them with a longer, drawn-out whinny. They responded with whinnies of their own and lurched into motion to follow the mare. For a moment, the three women watched the retreating forms of the horses disappear below the ridge of the mountain.

The knights looked from the horses to Jacs in astonishment.

"Told you," she said with a smile.

Heart aflutter, she turned to face the cavern opening. Since meeting the Court for the first time earlier that year, Jacs had brushed up on the proper Court etiquette. She now knew the appropriate way to greet a member of the Court, but her education had not covered how to approach the Court in the early hours of the morning. She looked from Amber's determined grimace to Andromeda's stone-faced resolve and took a deep, settling breath. With her left foot, she stepped forward. Her right moved her closer still, and soon she was inside the cavern. The instant she crossed the threshold, fire flared into life in a cascading ring around the entrance chamber. Torches set in sconces on the walls flickered, casting distorted shadows on the floor.

Not wanting to cause alarm, Jacs called out, "Esteemed members of the Court, Your Alti, I, Courtierqueen Jacqueline, beg an audience."

A sourceless breeze caused the torches to flicker again, and Jacs heard a rushing in her ears. A clatter sounded from overhead, and Jacs looked up quickly. Two large Griffins appeared from alcoves at the top of the vaulted ceiling and launched themselves into the air. They descended at an alarming speed toward the ground. Jacs braced herself for a crash that never came. The creatures unfurled their wings at the last minute and caught the air gracefully, hovering above the ground for a moment before touching down with the lightness of a feather on glass.

The Griffins stood proudly before them. Each sleek feathered head, wings, and talons of an eagle merged seamlessly with the silky haunches and tail of a lion. The first, Altus Thenya, Jacs recognized as the Griffin who had greeted the contestants at the end of the first task. It had white feathers and cream haunches, while the other, Altus Hermes, had gray feathers and tawny haunches. Jacs had ridden with Altus Hermes to find her friends on the mountainside and the Griffin had then flown Anya and Lena to safety.

Jacs heard Amber's sharp intake of breath behind her but did not turn around. Slowly, and gesturing for the knights to do the same, she sunk into a deep and reverential bow. Chin tucked, she heard one of the Griffins step toward her. Razor-sharp talons and snow-white down entered her visual field. Its claws clicked slightly on the stone floor as it approached. Jacs held perfectly still while Altus Thenya preened her. The sharp beak was surprisingly gentle as it ran through her hair. It wasn't until both knights had been preened and Altus Thenya had returned to its place beside Altus Hermes, beckoning with a swift motion of its head and a click of its beak, that first Jacs, then the knights, rose to standing.

Both Griffins looked at Jacs expectantly. Their gaze held the heavy solemnity of those who have seen Queendoms rise and fall and the quiet assurance of those who know they will witness countless more. Suddenly, Jacs was struck with how trivial it all was in the eyes of these ancient creatures.

She thought of her squabbles with the Council, their petty vendettas, her arguments with Connor, even the feud between the two realms, and realized that it all must look the same from high on this mountain. As quickly as this thought entered her mind, a stronger thought squashed it. *It is not trivial to those who are living it.*

Rolling her shoulders back, she stood up straighter and said, "Your Alti, please forgive the hour, I did not come with the knowing support of many within the palace, and discretion was necessary."

Altus Thenya inclined its head as if to bid her to continue, and Jacs hurried to make her case.

"As you know, I am Lowrian born. Yesterday evening I was able to see how the living conditions in Bridgeport, and likely many other areas of the Lower Realm, have worsened since my coronation. I beseech you to help me right a wrong that is within my power to correct. I humbly ask that I and my two knights ride with you to Bridgeport. I vouch for these women as I vouched for Courtierdame Lena Glowra and Courtier Anya Bishop all those months ago. They are my guard and council. We would only need a day there." She finished and clasped her hands behind her back, feet slightly apart. Altus Hermes cocked its head and looked at the white Griffin, who studied Jacs intently.

Jacs did not drop her gaze. Altus Thenya approached her as it had before, and as it had upon their first meeting, placed the dorsal portion of its beak firmly into Jacs's chest. Jacs closed her eyes and braced herself for what came next. The moment lingered, carving out the space between heartbeats. Then a wave of thoughts, memories, and emotions slammed into Jacs. If the Griffin's beak had not been anchoring her in place, she would have crumpled.

Her whole life, all she'd seen, all she'd done, all she'd felt, rushed through her mind. Who she was, who she wanted to be, and the lies she told herself swirled in a kaleidoscope of images and sensations. Pain shot through her heart like an ice splinter, then warmth filled in its place like a flower in bloom. The flower withered and died, and the ice returned. Caught in this eternal cycle, she fell deep within her mind.

She was a little girl again, crouched on the pebbled edge of a deep, dark pool. In wonder, she saw her father's face rise from the depths. It was blurred around the edges in uncertain memory, the eyes shifting from blue to green to gray and back again. The smile she remembered so well spread across his cheeks, then froze. His eyes grew wide, fear flooding the irises that were suddenly too blue. A frozen blue. Frost began to spread from his icy gaze across his face. His lips turned purple, and bubbles erupted from his mouth. They froze the instant they left his lips, crowding the pool with opaque spheres and obscuring his image as he sank below the ice now forming on the surface.

The ice became a mirror reflecting nothing, then cracks splintered like veins from the center, and Master Leschi's kind and gentle face broke through. It hovered for a moment, her usual assortment of writing utensils and tools protruding from her messy black-and-gray bun. The dried ink at the tip of each pen shifted from black to a rich, wet crimson. The utensils glittered wickedly and began sinking into Master Leschi's skull. Her face transformed into a mask of horror. A shadow consumed her, and she sank a moment later into the pool.

Her mother's face now floated up from the depths. Black hair wafted around her smiling visage. Jacs saw her mother mouth the words, "Hello, Plum," before bruises blossomed across her skin. Blood trickled from her nose and the inner corners of her eyes. Thick and so dark it was almost black, it dripped from her open mouth like molasses. Teeth fell from her gums like snowflakes, and her face sank slowly below the surface of the water, bloody tendrils trailing from her now slightly distorted features. A silent scream sent ripples across the surface of the pool.

When the waters cleared, Connor's face gazed back at Jacs. His eyes, full of love, crinkled softly in the corners. Like the snuffing of a candle, his expression changed. A look of disgust contorted his handsome features. Jacs heard his voice echo in her mind: *I was never yours,* his words dripped venom. He turned away and Hera's face replaced his. Her cruel blue eyes stared with haughty derision, her red lips curled in a sinister grin, and a golden crown sat on her golden hair. Behind her, the Council of Four nodded in approval, faces plastered with satisfied smirks.

From a far-off place deep within her mind, Jacs heard herself scream. With the rushing sensation of being simultaneously sucked into and wrenched out of herself, she felt her knees buckle and collide with the cold stone floor. The anchoring pressure of the Griffin's beak vanished from her chest, and she lurched forward, her palms hitting the ground reflexively.

The Griffin stepped back and allowed Jacs to compose herself without judgment. Gasping and retching, crouched on all fours, Jacs closed her eyes and waited for the visions to subside, but they didn't disappear. They clung to her mind as shrouded afterimages. It had been worse this time, much worse. She began to tremble and wrapped her arms around herself. Huddled in a tight ball, eyes squeezed shut, she fought against the visions that still plagued her.

"Jacqueline!" Amber cried out, alarmed.

Andromeda demanded, "What have you done to her?"

Jacs heard their tentative footsteps as the knights decided their Queen's safety trumped Griffin decorum. Before they had moved more than two steps, a vicious snarl made them stop dead. The room hung suspended in time. All eyes rested on the Queen's crumpled form.

A part of Jacs wanted to remain within, to live with the ghosts, as frightening as they had been. But she couldn't help anybody while staying still. She felt her heart rate slow and blinked her eyes open. With shaking hands, she wiped at the tears from where they had run freely down her cheeks. She took first one, then two shuddering breaths, and rose to a kneeling position.

Altus Thenya cooed in approval, the low, rippling sound breaking the held-breath silence.

Sitting back on her heels, Jacs asked in a wavering voice, "What was that? Why did I see those . . . those horrible things? That was not"—she cleared her throat, willing strength into her next words—"that was not like last time."

There was a pause. The Griffins regarded her coolly. Altus Hermes clicked its beak and Altus Thenya growled deep in its throat. It seemed to be considering. It stepped forward again and gently touched its beak to Jacs's temple. Another storm of images entered her mind, but these did not come from her. These had a controlled power to them. A deep resonance. She clearly saw the image of a caterpillar inching its way across a leaf in the sunshine. The image shifted, and the caterpillar hung from the leaf, weaving a chrysalis around itself. As Jacs watched, she saw the chrysalis shudder as the caterpillar within fought to emerge. There, the vision ended, and the Griffin stepped back. Jacs was left feeling like a child whose mother had to explain a very simple concept to her, one that she still could not grasp.

Uncertain what to do next, Jacs slowly got to her feet and waited. For one dreadful moment, she was sure she had somehow failed their test. Sure that the Griffins would refuse her request and she would no longer be accepted to ride with the Court. She heard one of the knights shift her weight behind her.

Finally, Altus Thenya bowed its head, and Altus Hermes followed suit. The white Griffin arched its neck and called up into the high ceiling. The cry was a perfect blend of eagle cry and lion roar; it crashed around the room like thunder and resounded in Jacs's heart. After a brief pause, Jacs saw a third Griffin launch itself into the air and descend to where they stood below. This Griffin's white feathers were flecked through with brown, and its haunches were a glossy caramel. It landed more heavily than the first two had and flicked its tail eagerly as it regarded Altus Thenya. Jacs recognized this Griffin as Novice Nemea. It was comparatively quite young within the Court, only around fifty seasons old, and had recently been transitioned from the status of fledgling to novice. Regardless of rank within the Court, all Griffins were referred to by humans as, "Your Altus," or "Your Alti" if referring to multiple members at once.

Altus Thenya inclined its head to the novice, repeated the gesture to Jacs and her knights, and took flight, returning the way it had come. Altus Hermes touched its beak against the young Griffin's, and they shared a few moments in this position. Jacs hoped the images they shared with one another were more pleasant than the ones she had had to endure. She turned to the others while the Griffins conversed.

Careful not to turn her back on the Griffins, Jacs came to stand between the knights. Amber touched her lightly on the shoulder and handed her a kerchief without comment. Jacs accepted it gratefully and wiped her eyes in swift, businesslike strokes.

Andromeda asked quietly, "Your Highness, are you okay?"

"What did you see? You're as white as a ghost," Amber said.

"They didn't . . . hurt you, did they?" Andromeda added in an undertone.

She shook her head. "Later," she murmured.

Andromeda squeezed her hand and said nothing.

They turned back to see the Griffins moving apart and beckoning the women to follow them toward the entrance. Suddenly what they were about to do became real. Jacs saw the others come to the same realization moments later. Jacs noticed Amber had a spring in her step, and Andromeda had paled. Her own heart began to beat faster as she recalled the last time she had flown with the Court.

Shoulders back, they approached the two Griffins at the edge of the mountain. The sun rose above the distant peaks far off to the east and bathed the Realms in a soft golden glow. Lakes and rivers blushed pink and sparkled in the new dawn. Altus Hermes beckoned to Jacs solemnly, and Altus Nemea, much less solemn and with an air of excitement that matched Amber's, beckoned to the knights.

Jacs thought she heard Andromeda mutter anxiously, "Great, we get the greenbeak."

Altus Hermes bent its foreleg and allowed Jacs to climb on its back in front of its wing joints. Its feathers slipped through her fingers like water, and she was careful not to pluck any by accident. This left her with very few handholds, and she tried to remember how she had stayed on last time.

Amber passed her pack up for Jacs to hold for the flight. She strapped it to her front without a word and watched Andromeda settle on Altus Nemea's back first, then pull Amber up in front of her. Amber smirked as Andromeda immediately clutched her tightly around her waist and said, "Let a knight breathe, Turner." But Jacs noticed Amber pat Andromeda's hand reassuringly as they both readied themselves on the Griffin.

All too soon, the Griffins stepped to the edge of the mountain. Jacs felt Altus Hermes crouch for just a moment, then launch into the air. The ground rushed away beneath them, and screams, hers or her knights', rang in her ears.

12

CONNOR ALONE

Connor paced his room angrily. Fire flickered in his chest and pressure pounded between his temples. He kicked at a footstool as he strode past it. She didn't trust him. Was keeping secrets from him like he was some child, some stranger. As if everything he'd done wasn't to help her.

She probably told Dame Glowra though, he thought with another rough kick at the footstool. Holed up in their etiquette lessons every day, she probably told her everything. Probably even told her knights. She'd only known them for three months but apparently that was more important than the five years she'd known Connor. He thought he was her person, but it turned out she had a lot of those. A wave of loneliness swept over him unbidden, and he pushed it away. He needed to calm down.

He threw himself into his chair by the fire and glared at the empty grate. He thought of the stricken expression on Jacs's face as he left her rooms. Edith's chat from the night before came back to him and something his mother had told him once rose to the forefront of his mind: *Never go to sleep angry. The dawn should bring a new day, not yesterday's storm.*

He sighed and felt the tension seep from his shoulders. Scrubbing his face roughly, he got to his feet. He'd solve nothing by sulking in his room. Why did she have to make it so difficult? But he'd be a useless Advisor if he ran away every time they had a disagreement.

Taking his time to set the footstool right, aligning it with the corner of the rug, he adjusted his tunic and forced himself to return to Jacs's rooms. He knocked gently on the door and waited. No answer. Pinching the bridge of his nose, he knocked louder and let himself in.

"Jacs, listen, we should—" he cut off as he entered her room and found it empty. "Jacs?" he called.

Nothing.

He checked her bathing room and closet. They were also empty. Everything was as he'd left it not even half an hour ago, except Jacs was nowhere to be found. His eyes scanned the room. Where would she have gone?

Spotting a square of white on her pillow, he walked over to her bed and picked up a letter. It was addressed to him. In Jacs's hand he read: *Connor. Read when you're alone. Show no one.* He looked around for good measure.

Shaking his head, he broke the seal and moved to sit by the fire to read it.

Connor,

I've taken Chiv. Everstar and Chiv. Turner with me out of the palace. I will be safe in their care. We will be away all day tomorrow and will hopefully return in the evening. For now, it's better if all you know is that it is for the good of the Queendom that I do this. I understand that my absence will be noticed. I need your help stalling the search parties until I return. I do not want to arouse panic or suspicion. Please find a way to account for my absence. It could be that I am still sick from my "headache" this evening and cannot be disturbed. Whatever you do, do not let the Council think anything is amiss. You may be right about them, but if I'm right, then giving them this knowledge puts me in danger.

If I do not return by tomorrow evening, find the next letter in a place only you would know to look.

I hope to be able to share everything with you soon. Until then, know that I am forever and always,

Yours,

Jacs

Connor let the hand with the letter fall limply into his lap. A flash of anger was quickly smothered by a deeper sense of loss. The metallic taste of betrayal crept up the back of his throat. He read the letter through again, then once more. She had left. They had fought and she had left him with nothing but a note. She had left, and there was a chance she wouldn't come back. Other than that, the letter held so little information.

Yet the message that bled through each line and seeped from the spaces between words was *I have left you. I don't need you.*

He had abandoned her once and had the written proof of the pain he had caused her. He never wanted to put her through that again. Not by choice. After so many years separated by the Cliff, it was a miracle they were united at all, so why would they be apart from one another if they didn't have to be?

But now . . .

She made the choice for you. She left you, an oily voice whispered in his mind. He shook his head. He was being dramatic. It was only for a day; it was probably nothing.

Then why didn't she tell you? the voice whispered again.

"Because she doesn't trust me," he breathed aloud. He read the words again, lingering on the last line. Ignoring the tightness in his chest, he brushed his thumb over her name and sighed. His eyes swept the room, then he sat up straighter. Trust was earned. Not demanded. He wouldn't earn it by moping around here.

In three strides he was at the foot of her four-poster bed. With a few swift jerks, he settled the curtains to shield it from view. Satisfied, he looked over the letter again and with a pang of regret, pushed it into the embers of the fire. It flared, edges curling in on themselves. He watched it crumble to ash. Standing, he strode out into the hall, closing the door behind him. A wave of exhaustion held him in front of the door. He leaned his head against it and fought the urge to sink to the floor. First, he needed sleep.

Tomorrow he would find Edith.

Splinters of early-morning sunlight were refracted by the patterned crystal windows of his bedchamber. Springing awake—not that he had slept well anyway—he dressed and strode across the room. The soft carpets muted his footfalls and took the edge out of his strides. With a hearty tug, he rang the call bell and spun on his heel to cross the room again. Hands clasped behind his back, he stood at his window looking out at the grounds. A gentle rock brought him between heel and toe as he shifted his weight. It wasn't long before a rap at the door brought him from his musings and he called, "Enter," without turning around.

"Good morning, Your Grace. I brought you some tea," Edith said, and Connor turned to face her. One look at his bloodshot eyes and disheveled hair caused her brows to furrow, and she said seriously, "What's happened?"

"Jacs is gone."

Edith balked and shook her head. "Gone? She can't be—"

Connor nodded and stepped toward her, not quite sure what to do with his limbs. "She said she would be back and not to worry, but Edith, what if she's done something dangerous? I mean, she flew up here on a balloon, for Altus's sake! We fought before she left." He ran his fingers through his hair.

"You fought?"

"And now she's gone."

Edith placed the tea tray down and looked thoughtful. "How do you know she's gone and not just out for a morning stroll?"

"She left a letter," Connor said distractedly.

Edith nodded. "Did she leave any instructions?"

"Yes."

"What were they?" The businesslike clip in Edith's tone was calming the whirling in Connor's mind, and he felt his shoulders melt down his back.

"She needed me to cover for her. Buy her time and make sure the Council doesn't find out she's gone. She suggested we claim she's still ill from last night."

Edith nodded again. "Then that's what we'll do. Your Grace, we have to trust she knows what she's doing, and this is something we can help with in the meantime."

Connor scoffed. "Trust her." Edith raised an eyebrow and looked at him severely. Connor dropped his hands to his sides, feeling lost. In an embarrassingly small voice he asked, "Edith, why didn't she tell me where she was going?"

Edith's features softened. "That I don't know, but she has her reasons. She has entrusted you with a task, Your Grace, let's see it's done properly."

The plan was set in motion in a matter of minutes. Edith planned to discuss the Queen's sudden illness with Master Epione ("no need to see her, she has only just managed to fall back asleep and I would hate to disturb her"), arranged to fetch a number of herbal remedies from the kitchens that she would personally deliver ("it's better if only myself and His Grace visit her for now, we don't want to overwhelm her while she's recovering"), and Connor was left to tell the Council the Queen was taking the day to rest.

He and Edith parted ways near the servants' stairwell. His mind was now calmer with a plan to occupy it, and he headed toward the Council of Four's chambers. It was still early, but he might catch them before breakfast. He loped down the wide marble staircase and stopped to turn toward a voice floating up from below him.

"Oh, good morning, Your Grace!"

Hera.

Connor slowed his pace to walk the rest of the way down the steps. "Good morning, Lord Claustrom. What has you up this early?"

"I could ask the same question, it seems," she said sweetly, a coy smile pricking the corners of her lips.

Connor found himself smiling in return. "So you could. I am off to speak with the Council of Four."

"Ah, so business, then?" she said lightly.

Connor nodded. "Unfortunately. And you?"

Hera cocked her head to the side. "I just love the quiet the morning brings. I wonder if I could ask you to accompany me for a walk in the gardens. It's such a clear day, and the walk is much nicer with company."

Connor looked down the corridor that led to the Councilors' chambers and back at Hera. Her eyes shone, and the sunlight from the window behind her played in her blonde curls. It was a clear day, he thought to himself, and a walk might do him some good. His mind flickered to Jacs's words curling in the fire and he shook his head. "Unfortunately, I need to attend to this matter first."

"Of course, Your Grace. Will your morning permit you to join me afterward?" she asked sweetly. "Or will you be spending the day with the Queen?" Hera looked around as if trying to locate her.

Connor shook his head again. “No, the Queen is unwell today.” He considered for a moment, then ventured: “I suppose I can meet you for a walk after I speak with the Councilors.”

“Wonderful!” Hera said brightly. “I will wait for you in the lily garden in half an hour. See you soon.” She bowed deeply and left before he had a chance to change his mind.

Connor watched her disappear down the corridor and frowned, unsure why he suddenly felt so uneasy. Pushing those thoughts away, he continued toward the Councilors’ chambers and knocked on the door.

No answer.

He raised his knuckles to knock again, then saw the door had shifted slightly inward under the weight of his first attempt. Cllr. Perda’s voice drifted through the opening, harsh and urgent. “By trading with Nysa, we cut out the need for the Lower altogether, and strengthen the relationship between Queendoms.”

“But Rosalind, the Lowrians are predictable; we know what we’re getting with them,” Cllr. Dilmont reasoned.

“And containable,” quipped Cllr. Fengar.

“Less and less, I fear, especially with the sense of entitlement a Lowrian Queen has given them.” Cllr. Perda sighed.

“But the damage that fallout would cause . . .” Cllr. Stewart’s voice was barely a whisper.

Connor leaned closer to avoid missing her next words, but his movement against the door caused it to shift on its hinges. A loud creak silenced the voices within. Inwardly cursing himself, he attempted to salvage the situation by knocking loudly and saying, “Councilors? Ah!” He swung the door open and beamed upon seeing them. “Good morning! I hoped to find you all here. I trust you slept well?”

The Councilors were seated around the small table laden with breakfast items and hurried to stand up as Connor entered the room. Apart from the slight widening of the eyes, Cllr. Perda did not otherwise appear surprised at the Royal Advisor's entrance and inclined her head with the others.

"Good morning, Your Grace," she said smoothly. "To what do we owe the pleasure?"

Connor, still unsure how to process the information he just heard, stuck to his first objective. "I have news of the Queen. She is still unwell and requests not to be disturbed today."

Cllr. Stewart delicately placed a hand to her chest. "Oh dear, should we send for someone?"

Connor shook his head. "I have Edith attending to her personally, Master Epione has already been consulted, and remedies recommended. It sounds like all she needs now is rest and quiet."

The Councilors nodded slowly and glanced at one another.

"Is there anything we can do?" Cllr. Stewart said with genuine concern. Looking pointedly at Cllr. Perda, she said, "Our Queen has been through so much recently."

Cllr. Perda studied Connor for a moment with narrowed eyes. Connor felt suddenly exposed, as though she were able to read his thoughts. He tried to look sincere but felt he had forgotten where his tongue usually sat in his mouth. Finally, she smiled tightly and shook her head. "I'm sure Master Epione knows what is best. If our young Queen needs rest, then rest she should get. I do wonder if there is a way we can raise her spirits once she returns to us in better health?"

"Raise her spirits?" Cllr. Dilmont asked, incredulous.

"Of course! It's as Portia said, the poor dear has been through so much recently, it's no wonder her health is failing her. I wonder if we should host a gala in her honor?" Cllr. Perda's tone was light, but her gaze held steel as it flicked across the other Councilors.

"A gala?" Connor repeated. "That is actually a great idea! Just what she needs to get her mind off"—his thoughts jumped to Jacs's reaction to seeing Phillip in the mirror—"everything."

Cllr. Perda beamed. "Yes, and I know Lady Sybil Claustrom mentioned the Sons of Celos are making their rounds this time of year. They never fail to entertain. Beatrice." Cllr. Perda spun to face Cllr. Fengar, the latter having paused with a grape midway to her mouth. "I trust you can see to booking the Sons of Celos to attend a gala next week?"

Cllr. Fengar nodded and said, "Of course, I will send a messenger after breakfast," before popping the grape into her mouth.

"Well, Your Grace, it appears we have a gala to organize, and you have a Queen to tend to. Thank you for sharing this saddening news, and for giving us an opportunity to be useful to her." Cllr. Dilmont stepped forward as she spoke, a dismissal in her tone.

Connor inclined his head and backed toward the door. "I'll leave it in your hands, Councilors. Let me know if I can be of assistance." His mind filled with the excitement of the gala. He had only seen the Sons of Celos once before, but he remembered their acrobatic skills and was eager to see them again. That was something Jacs would like; she had never attended a gala, and the troupe was one of the best. If anything could distract her from her worries, the Sons of Celos would.

Passing a grandmother clock in the corridor, he checked the time. Hera would be waiting for him. He quickened his pace. Maybe she would have some insight into arrangements for the gala. His gut clenched and he scratched the back of his neck. *This is good. Something to cheer her up when she comes back*, he thought. He ignored the tiny voice that whispered, *If.*

13

AMONG LILIES AND HEDGEROWS

"That's twice in two days they've walked in the gardens together; you'd think Lord Claustrom would get sick of the pansies at some point." Anya's tone was conversational but worry laced her comment and caught Lena's ear. With her arm looped in Anya's, she swiveled them both around to better see the pair strolling a few yards ahead.

Lena frowned. News of Jacqueline's illness had spread quickly that morning. Many had seen her leave dinner early the night before and rumors were already circulating about what ailment she was suffering from. Edith had not allowed her or Anya to check in on her, saying she was resting.

But the folded slip of parchment with the words *Open if I'm missing tomorrow evening* scrawled on the front burned in Lena's pocket with the promise of another story. Jacqueline must have her reasons for not sharing her plans with Lena just yet. All the same, it was a lesson in restraint to leave the letter sealed.

"What do you make of them?" Anya asked.

Lena watched Lord Claustrom bend to smell one of the lilies along the path. She held her golden curls away from her face and smiled becomingly as she inhaled. An act presumably for the Advisor's benefit as even Lena knew that type of lily had no scent. Cornelius stopped to wait, his gaze darting over the other blooms in the garden. Lena grinned to see Hera's disappointment. The Lord was accustomed to being admired, and it appeared the Advisor had other matters on his mind.

Keeping her voice low and slowing their pace, Lena replied, "I'm not sure. I mean, I know what to make of her, she takes what she wants. She's been like that since we were girls; do you remember that summer she visited with her mother and wouldn't eat a bite until my mother sold her our prized mare?"

"You think she wants His Grace?" Anya asked softly.

"No, I think she wants the crown," Lena replied with certainty. "But as for what Cornelius wants . . ." She trailed off only to pick back up: "Boys are fickle, but he is good to Jacqueline."

As if aware of their comments, Cornelius turned to see them following. He beamed and waved them over. Hera straightened with a crease between her brows.

The four exchanged pleasantries when within earshot, and at Lena's question, Cornelius assured them all that the Queen was not in any immediate danger.

"She simply needs rest and quiet," he said confidently.

"It must be so luxurious to be able to take a day off like that," Hera commented. "I don't know how she can rest, knowing the Queendom sails on without her at the helm! She's lucky to have such a competent Advisor to take the wheel in her stead."

Cornelius shifted his weight, looking uncomfortable. "I assure you she is still hard at work despite her illness," he said. Lena felt a fondness for the Royal Advisor flair in her chest.

"And we can't always be working," Lena said sweetly. "Sometimes we have to take time to smell the lilies."

Hera's cheeks flushed slightly at the comment, but she held her tongue and simply smiled.

"It's actually fortunate we ran into you," Cornelius said. "I was just telling Lord Claustrom that the Councilors will be hosting a gala for the Queen next week. If you have any suggestions of what we could include in the festivities, I'd love to hear them." He looked from Lena to Anya hopefully.

"Oh, what is the occasion?" Lena asked.

The corners of his mouth dipped down a fraction, and he absentmindedly brought his knuckles to rub a spot near his breastbone. "To, ah, cheer her. She has been in need of some levity after working so hard for the sake of our Queendom."

Hera drew her lips into a thin line as she nodded in agreement.

"We can certainly think on it, Your Grace," Lena responded.

"I can speak with the palace florist. I know Her Majesty's favorites, and flowers have a way of brightening any room," Anya suggested.

"That would be wonderful," the Advisor said appreciatively.

"And we can check in with Chivilras Everstar and Turner; they spend much of their days with Her Majesty and will likely have some ideas too. Actually"—Lena turned to Anya—"let's go find them now, I have another matter I need to discuss with Chiv. Everstar."

"You won't find them today," Cornelius said quickly.

Lena looked at him, surprised. "No? Where are they?"

"They've, I mean, I was informed that they have both left on official business just for the day, so you likely won't find them in the palace," he said, stumbling through his explanation.

Hera's eyebrow arched in intrigue.

"The Queen's most trusted knights have both abandoned her in her hour of need? How curious."

Lena saw the color splotches on Cornelius's cheeks and thought again of her concealed note. "Oh Hera," she said dismissively, "I hardly think a day of bedrest requires the attendance of two of the highest-ranking knights in the realm, one of whom holds the Soterian Medal. It makes sense that they would take this time to complete important business elsewhere." She noticed Cornelius nod slightly in thanks. "But Courtier Bishop and I must leave you in the lily patch, I'm afraid. We will think more on ideas for the gala and let you know." She looped her arm through Anya's and both women dropped into a bow before the Royal Advisor and inclined their heads in Hera's direction.

Cornelius and Hera bid them farewell, and Anya added as they turned to leave, "And I will chat with the palace florist—what is their name?"

Cornelius thought for a moment, "The palace head gardener is Master Borage; he's the one to talk to about the gardens and greenhouses. As for the palace florist, I believe her name is Master Caldriene."

Anya thanked him, and together, she and Lena ambled down the garden path. Once out of earshot, Anya whispered, "Lee . . . it *is* odd Jacqueline's two most trusted knights are out of town while she's sick. Surely, they should be with her today? Especially since she's too sick to even see us?"

Lena made a sound of agreement. "I think there's more to this, for sure. Yesterday, during our dance lesson, she slipped me a note to read only if she is missing this evening."

"She what?" Anya drew up short to look at her.

Lena glanced around to ensure they were alone and withdrew the note from a concealed pocket in her sleeve.

Anya looked from her to the note. "Have you read it?"

"No, of course not. Not yet," Lena said quietly, slipping it back in her sleeve.

Anya bit her lip. "Shouldn't we read it? It might be important now."

Lena considered. A large part of her agreed and was sorely tempted, but she knew her instructions. "I think," she hesitated, "whatever it is, Jacqueline would have her reasons to keep us in the dark for the moment." Anya opened her mouth as if to refute, but Lena said quickly, "and knowledge can be dangerous. If it is something we could be implicated in, I'm guessing she wants to keep us out of the know until absolutely necessary. I can't see another reason as to why the time limit."

Anya looked apprehensive. "But Lee, you're going to find out what's in there eventually, and what if we can help her now?"

"She said to wait."

"She might need us."

"But it's a direct order from the Queen!"

"But she's our friend, and she might be in trouble."

After a moment's hesitation, Lena reluctantly agreed. They stepped off the garden path into an alcove in the hedges. The space was small, and Lena was suddenly aware of how close they both were. Anya shifted further in, and Lena heard the soft snap of twigs and brush of leaves as she moved. All other sounds of the garden seemed muffled here. Forgetting herself for a moment, she looked up and smiled to see Anya watching her. Her brown eyes were creased with worry.

Lena shifted closer and, standing on tiptoe, kissed her cheek.

Anya's frown evaporated and she pulled Lena into a one-armed embrace as Lena retrieved the letter from her sleeve again. Head resting against Anya's chest, the sound of her heartbeat in her ears, Lena unfolded the paper and they both read:

Dear Lena,

If you're reading this, I haven't returned in time. Or Anya convinced you to read it early. Either way, you're likely worried about me and for that I am sorry. I didn't tell you sooner because it's safer the less you know, especially if the Council decides to question you. So, what you need to know is this: Amber and Andromeda are with me, and we have ridden with the Court to the Lower Realm. I need to right a wrong and this was the only way I could think of where I would actually get anything of substance done. If I haven't returned, it may be that my task has taken longer than expected.

In that case, I need you to cover for my absence. Connor and likely Edith will be following my instructions, but they may need help with the ruse. If you speak with either of them, do not let them know that I have gone to the Lower Realm until Connor has read his second letter. He knows less than you, for his and my safety.

The Lower Realm is overrun with scry crystals, so I have registered myself under the name Jacs Frean. If you need to check in on me, use this name only if you are sure you are completely alone. If the Council finds out, speak with Perkins. He will erase my name from the crystal's memory bank and keep them from spying on me.

I've included a written command with my seal for you and you alone to send an expedition down to the Lower Realm if needed. This decree grants you power to act as Queen in my stead while I am absent and should be enough to outmaneuver any opposition the Council may pose. I don't think you will need to use it as I doubt I will be in any danger, but I would much rather have someone I trust calling the shots in what might follow.

Your discretion is key, and your help is invaluable.

Thank you for everything,

Jacqueline

Lena and Anya exchanged looks of concern.

Shaking her head, Anya whispered, "I can't believe she'd fly with the Court with only a pair of knights."

Lena was at a loss for words. She chewed the inside of her cheek thoughtfully. No wonder Jacqueline had been subdued the day before, she had been planning to fly off the Cliff. Lena felt something like fear take root in her navel. She exhaled slowly. Jacqueline was with Amber and Andromeda, two of the best knights in the realm, there was no reason to believe her plan wouldn't go smoothly and Lena could pretend she never had to open the letter. No reason to believe they wouldn't return safe and sound with a story of success. Right? And yet her brow furrowed, and her mind spun with the what-ifs that stood in the way.

As if reading her thoughts, Anya added, "Lee, I'm sure they'll be fine. If anything, this might ease Jacqueline's mind. We were just saying how worried she's been. If . . . no, when she comes back, she'll return with a new zeal. I'm sure of it." Anya bent slightly to position her face in front of where Lena's was still buried in the letter. Lena looked up and Anya planted a quick kiss on her nose.

Pulling apart and studying the letter again, Anya threaded her arm around Lena's waist.

"You know what I'm worried about though," Anya said in a low voice that added melody to the shifting leaves behind her, "is all this stuff she's saying about her safety and keeping Cornelius out of the loop. It almost sounds like she's protecting herself *from* him as much as she's protecting him. Do you think they're doing okay? Did you know they were having any issues?"

Lena reread the related section again. "No," she said with mild surprise. "I had no idea. They seemed fine when he came to escort her to the throne room the other day." Lena cocked her head slightly to think. "Although, Jacqueline did see Cornelius and Hera walking in the gardens yesterday and seemed a bit prickly about it."

"Well, Lord Claustrom does have a way of making others feel prickly," Anya muttered.

“I’m sure Hera’s just stirring the pot; there’s no way Cornelius would act on anything she presents him with.” The silence following Lena’s words undercut their certainty.

“And all we can really do is trust Cornelius knows better and wait for the evening,” Anya said finally.

Folding the letter up carefully, Lena slipped it back into her sleeve and rested her head lightly on Anya’s chest. Her palms slipped around her waist to rest on her lower back. Anya encircled her with her arms and rested her chin on the top of Lena’s head. Wrapped up in each other, the world became smaller just for a moment. A water droplet suspended from a leaf before joining the awaiting pond beneath.

14

WELCOME HOME

The flight from Court's Mountain to the Cliff wore out the night's darkness. As the two Griffins reached the Cliff—Upper Realm stretching endlessly behind them, Lower Realm contained in the vast basin before them—the sun stretched its rays across the sky in welcome. Radiant dawn light glittered on the gold-dusted feathers adorning the Alti.

Replacing the evening's stars, the two Griffins and the women they rode with soared along the border between the realms for a moment, before Altus Hermes shook its head back, roared, and dove into the Lower Realm. Altus Nemea followed suit with two much less resonant—but much more enthusiastic—calls into the fading night.

The wind rushed at Jacs and filled her ears. Squinting so as not to miss a thing, she felt her heart glow. Eyes streaming, teeth cold from the wind in a smiling mouth, she whooped as the Griffins angled themselves toward the ground. As though turning back time, they moved from the new dawn of the Upper Realm to the predawn twilight of the Lower Realm. The colors that had been ignited by the rising sun were now muted and merged. Almost-greens and not-quite-blues lay in wait for the sun to grace them with its presence. As they flew lower and lower, Jacs started recognizing landmarks and found her farm just outside Bridgeport. Suddenly apprehensive, she pointed to it and Altus Hermes shifted its course to accommodate.

In no time at all, the two esteemed members of the Court landed gracefully in front of her modest farmhouse. Jacs slipped off Altus Hermes's back and glanced around. Everything was so quiet. No sounds at all came from the barn. Her grumpy cow, Brindle, had been sold for money for her to take to the Upper Realm. Delilah, her horse, had been sold years ago to pay taxes. The fields were filled with weeds and in desperate need of attention.

A soft *mrrroww* brought Jacs from her solemn reverie and she saw the mangy gray cat, Ranger, bound toward her. With a laugh of relief, she caught him up in her arms and scratched behind his ears.

"Cute cat," Amber's voice came from behind her. She had helped a very windswept Andromeda down from Altus Nemea and both knights stood to attention, eyes scanning the perimeter.

"Where are we?" a green-faced Andromeda asked. Her voice lacked its usual depth.

Jacs looked around her childhood home now through the eyes of her knights and felt heat flush her cheeks. It was certainly no palace.

"My home," she said simply, watching her friends' faces change in response. Amber's jaw dropped and she looked around her now with vested interest, while Andromeda set her features in an unreadable mask, one eyebrow arched ever so slightly.

"I thought we could regroup here, make a plan for our entrance, and if anything, just wait for the sun to reach us," Jacs continued.

"The sun to reach? How long does that take?" Amber asked.

Jacs thought for a moment. "We probably have another hour or so. The town will be up and bustling, but I think it better we wait for the sun. I have a few things I need to pick up from my room. Would either of you like a cup of tea?"

The knights looked at each other, still processing their new environment, and nodded. Jacs let Ranger jump down from her arms, and his kinked tail flicked in satisfaction. The Griffins made themselves comfortable on the lawn beneath the large apple tree. Altus Nemea plucked an overripe apple from the branches and crunched away happily. With a skip in her step, she let herself into the kitchen.

A wall of stale air met Jacs as she opened the white wooden door. Dust motes swirled in the door's wake, and a loud clattering made Jacs jump. A stack of pots and pans arranged in front of the door tumbled to the floor and announced her presence. Not quite registering what that might mean, Jacs stepped into the kitchen without thinking. A sharp tug on her tunic brought her back outside as Amber deftly switched places with her. Not quick enough for Jacs to miss seeing the state of her kitchen. *Mess* was an understatement. It had been ransacked. Cupboards had been emptied on every surface and sifted through. Pots, pans, and utensils littered the earthen floor like confetti.

With growing apprehension, Jacs swallowed and watched Amber and Andromeda take up formation as they entered the building. Quietly, they made their way through the mess, Jacs following at a distance, reminding herself to breathe. At Amber's questioning look, Jacs pointed at her bedroom door. Andromeda took the left side, Amber the right, but before either of them could reach for the handle, the door burst open.

"Stay back!" a familiar voice roared and a large man with a smithing hammer barreled into the room swinging. In three swift movements, Amber and Andromeda had disarmed him, tripped him, and clasped his hands behind his back. He growled with his cheek pressed into the packed earth floor and struggled against Amber's weight on his back.

It all happened in the span of four heartbeats. On the fifth, Jacs called out, "Wait! I know him, let him up! Phillip, it's Jacqueline."

There was a pause as Amber and Andromeda hesitated before releasing him, a pause as the man on the floor focused his eyes on Jacs, a pause before recognition filled them and Jacs saw the raw hurt and rage bleed through. A pause, a moment, then his eyes lit up and something close to a smile transformed his features.

"Jacqueline?" he asked, tentative, pushing himself up to his knees.

Jacs nodded, tears pricking the corners of her eyes.

"Jacqueline!" Hysterical relief filled his tone, and they ran to embrace each other. The knights kept a wary eye on Phillip's hulking figure, and Amber slid the forgotten hammer well out of reach.

Jacs held her friend close, hardly daring to let go in case this was all a cruel trick. Phillip was here, he was safe, and she could help him.

"How are you here?" Phillip asked eagerly. He took a step back and held her by the shoulders to study her face. "Why are you here?" his second question came out harsher, more wary.

"I'm here to help and—" Jacs, now able to see his face more clearly, froze. Although she had seen his battered appearance in the mirror, her heart ached to see how much worse he looked in person. He had a few new wounds now, a graze on his chin and a bruise near his left temple. "Phillip, what's happened to you?"

Phillip shrugged and looked away, eyeing the knights warily.

"Sorry," Jacs said quickly. "Hold on, Phillip these are my knights of the Queensguard, Chivilras Amber Everstar and Andromeda Turner, and this is Phillip Leschi, Master Leschi's son." The two knights nodded in greeting. Phillip's eyes grew wide as he regarded Jacs and, realizing his mistake, hurriedly dropped to his knees. "Your M-majesty," he stuttered.

Jacs felt her face grow hot. "Oh, Phillip, please get up. Okay, this is a lot. I'm going to make tea. I think we've got a lot to talk about. How about for now you go outside with Chiv. Everstar and meet the Griffins?"

"Meet the what!"

After both knights had conducted a swift search of the house to make sure no one else was lurking in the shadows, Amber placed her hand on the small of Phillip's back and guided him out the door while Jacs hunted for the kettle. She found it lying near an overturned chair with a large crack down the side. Sighing, she turned to see Andromeda holding four mismatched cups in her hands. Jacs smiled grimly, picking through the tatters of her mother's kitchen, and hunted in the back corner of a lower cabinet for the bottle of apple cider she knew would be there.

Before leaving the kitchen, she ventured into her bedroom. It was in a similar state to the kitchen—if not worse—and she took a deep breath before stepping over the threshold. Her balloon prototypes, her collection of wooden boats, her half-finished and proudly completed projects lay scattered around the bed. *It's only stuff*, she thought firmly, but couldn't stop the small sob that escaped her lips to see her father's fiddle, usually carefully perched on a stand near her door, smashed to pieces. The strings had been snapped, neck splintered, and bow broken clean in two. Her fingers closed around a fragment of the polished wood, and she tucked it into her pocket. Next, she moved over to her desk and sifted through the mess of papers and notebooks. Somehow, Connor's Griffin quill remained intact, not a feather vane out of place. She tucked that away in her pack. With one last glance around her room, she retrieved the bottle of cider she had left by the door, nodded briskly to Andromeda, who stood hovering nearby, and they both made their way outside.

Out in the garden, Phillip was still marveling at the Griffins. Jacs had heard his exclamations from inside the house and came out to find him staring at them from a distance. Walking up beside Amber, the knight muttered to her, "He won't get any closer."

Placing a cup in everyone's hand and pouring a measure of the dark yellow liquid into each, they all found a place to sit near (but not too near) where the Griffins were lounging beneath the apple tree.

"It's so good to see you're okay, Phillip," Jacs said softly. He tore his gaze away from the Alti to look at her.

"I mean, I've been better. . ." he said, running his fingers through his hair distractedly. "Jacqueline, it's so good to see you. Have you seen Ma?" he asked eagerly, cupping his hands around his drink as if it were the promised mug of hot tea.

Jacs hesitated. "No."

"No? But she was taken up the Cliff," he said slowly.

"I know."

"You know? You're the Queen, how have you not seen her? Do you even know if she's okay?"

"No, but—"

"What do you mean, no? Have you even tried looking for her? How can you not know? Or are you too hopped up on that throne of yours to even care?" His voice had risen.

Jacs couldn't remember ever hearing him raise his voice to anyone before, and never to her.

"Phillip—" she began, trying to remain calm, but guilt caught in her throat and made her breathing hitch. She noticed Andromeda stiffen nearby, and Amber placed her cup on an overturned flowerpot carefully, eyes locked on Phillip.

"I mean how hard is it to check in on someone who pretty well raised you? You're the Queen, Jacqueline! I thought she was safe up there with you! Now you're telling me you don't even know where she is." He stood up, cider spilling over the rim of his cup as he pointed his finger at her. "So, then what have you been doing all this time? Playing ruler with all the Lordsons? Did you get bored? Decide to just float down here to see how the commoners are doing?" He took a step toward her. A fire flickered behind his eyes.

Amber and Andromeda rose as one, but Jacs held up a hand for them to stand down. Slowly, she got to her feet.

"You have no *idea* what you're talking about, Phillip," she said, her voice deadly. He continued to glare at her, but she noticed a shadow of doubt pass across his features. "Master Leschi and my mother are both being held prisoner by my own Councilors so they can blackmail me into doing whatever they want. I have spent the months since my coronation trying to find them. I will not stop until I do, but it is a nightmare trying to make any progress in the maze of politics and loyalties and secrets up there. I have tried my best but haven't been able to do a thing despite this crown on my head." She was breathing heavily now but kept her voice steady.

"I came down here as soon as I discovered the scry crystals were still being used. I figured this was something I could actually do right. I had to sneak out of the palace in the middle of the night to do this! Me! The Queen! So don't you dare say I'm not trying," Jacs finished, matching Phillip's glare. The sound of the kitchen door creaking in the breeze was all that was heard until Phillip finally looked away and sighed. He rubbed his face with a free hand, wincing a little. Jacs glared at him, arms crossed.

"Sorry," he said gruffly.

"S'all right," Jacs said.

Amber cleared her throat and both Jacs and Phillip lowered themselves back to their seats, neither able to look at the other at first.

"So then, Phillip, what were you doing in Her Majesty's house?" Andromeda asked neutrally.

Jacs looked up, suddenly curious. Phillip fidgeted where he sat, uncomfortable.

"It's, um . . . well, it's been pretty bad down here. Jacqueline, you remember the curfews? Well, they were only getting warmed up with those. Town feels like a prison yard. I've got a bigger target on my back than most, what with Ma getting arrested and all. Living in the middle of it was too much, and well, no one comes out here, so I decided to see if it was any safer staying here. Out of sight, out of mind, you know? And I was hoping to find"—he caught Jacs's eye and cut off, face flushing a deep red—"but it doesn't matter now, I found you instead. Or, I guess, you found me." He laughed nervously and took a swallow of cider.

"I'm glad you could find some peace here," Jacs said. He nodded, his lips a thin line. Jacs studied him thoughtfully, noted his hunched shoulders, his flushed face, and eyes that darted around beneath his drawn brows. She had known him for well over five years, and so she knew without a shadow of a doubt that he was hiding something from her. Her mind fluttered to the mirror's reflection of him skulking around the alleyways late at night and she frowned.

"How's everyone else doing? The Grimsbys? The Severins? What about Master Tremain and"—she faltered—"how's Mal? Mallard Wetler?" Jacs asked.

Phillip seemed to deflate. "I mean the Grimsbys are fine, I still have my job with the Severins and the shop's doing okay, I don't see Master Tremain much. But . . . Mal's gone missing."

"What?" Jacs felt her stomach drop.

"Yeah."

"What do you mean, missing?"

"Just missing. No one knows where he went. Some people say he ran off, but there was no note or anything, no sign of struggle or any evidence that he was taken. Just up and vanished. He's the fourth in the last few months."

"The fourth?"

"Yeah, from here anyway. Not sure if it's happening in other towns. At first people thought the guards were keeping them in for questioning, but Cadence—you know Cadence Fentree? She drops special meals off at the prison once a week or so and she didn't see any of them there either." Phillip shrugged and looked off toward the town, before finishing in a low voice, "Everyone has their own theories, but this only started happening after you became Queen. People are connecting the dots and drawing their own conclusions."

Jacs stared at him open-mouthed. "They think *I* have something to do with this?" she asked incredulously.

Phillip just shrugged again and looked at his hands.

"Who are the others?" she asked.

Phillip scratched his knuckles along the ungrazed portion of his chin and counted them off, "Well, Mal, Bentin, Farrow, and Lynn."

Jacs recognized the names, they had all been boys above and below her in age when she went to school. She hadn't seen much of them after she had stopped attending classes, but Farrow was always kind to her on market days, adding an extra plum to her basket with a wink, and Lynn had played the fiddle with her one year at the Trade Week festival. Bentin, she had only seen a handful of times when she had visited the clocktower during construction.

Mal, Bentin, Farrow, and Lynn. All missing. Her mind fluttered to Queen Ariel's little book tucked in her pack. Could it be connected?

Briefly, she told Phillip about the list of names. His mouth opened in disbelief. "All those boys . . . for years . . . just disappearing," he said quietly. "It's like the attercoppe stories, but now people actually believe them."

Jacs released a breath. She knew about the attercoppe, of course. It was a fairy tale parents used to tell their sons to keep the fire of their tempers in check. "If you keep yelling like that, the attercoppe will take you away in the night"; "Don't scream at your father, that'll attract the attercoppe." Master Leschi hadn't been the type to threaten her son with that kind of nonsense, and Jacs didn't have brothers, so she and Phillip had never taken the stories seriously growing up. Some of her peers had though.

Unsure what to do, she looked up to the mountaintops the sun rose over every day and saw the golden halo that preceded the Lowrian dawn. She drained her cup, stood, and announced, "We can deal with that when I have more information, but we'll stick to the first task." Shaken but attempting optimism, she said, "It's actually lucky we found you, I need your help."

"Yeah? With what?" Phillip said.

"Our mission is to remove the scry crystals from Bridgeport. First, we will need to gather the guards. I can give them instructions on the collection of the crystals. I'll also need to send guards to towns farther out with a similar message. But I am very aware that I've come here with minimal fanfare. So, what I'll have you and Chivilras Everstar and Turner do is walk with Altus Nemea into town, calling everyone's attention as you go. I'll ride in with Altus Hermes once you reach the town square. That way, hopefully, we get everyone's attention and make sure everyone shows up."

"Fanfare?" Amber asked. "Like banging on pots and pans or something? Aren't we supposed to be incognito?"

Jacs winked at her. "We're here. The Council can't reach us now even if they find out what we've done. Feel free to use your imagination."

With the plan in motion, Jacs had a moment of peace high up on Altus Hermes's back. She could see the little parade, far below: Three walking figures and the faint golden shine of Altus Nemea bringing up the rear. Like children's toys, marching down a pretend road. Everything seemed so much simpler from a viewpoint above it all. She had thought seeing Phillip again would be all excitement, but apprehension filled her mind, and she couldn't shake the feeling that he was hiding something from her. What was so big that he couldn't tell her about it? Especially when she might be able to help? And the missing boys: How had nothing been done? She thought of her vision of Mal in the mirror; he must have disappeared no more than a day ago.

She exhaled sharply through her nose and pushed the thoughts away. She couldn't help everyone at once, and she was the last person who had the right to get upset with people for hiding things from her. Her thoughts shifted briefly to Connor, and she swallowed, pushing her guilt down before it could take root in her mind. She knew the importance of secrets—at least, these past few months had hammered that particular lesson into her.

Closing her eyes for a moment, she let herself enjoy the sensation as the wind whipped around her. Altus Hermes was flying low and at a relaxed pace, carving luxurious sweeping lines in the sky. Their fly speed was much faster than the walking speed of her friends, and Jacs had the feeling the Griffin was enjoying the loping movements as much as she was.

All too soon, they reached the edge of town. The moment the party below crossed the edge of the first property, Altus Nemea let loose with a loud, booming cry that cut the silent morning like thunder. It reverberated around the buildings and caused anyone nearby to stop what they were doing and spill out into the street. Altus Nemea roared again and again, steady as a beating drum and with the power of an explosion. Amber, Andromeda, and Phillip were calling out to the people they passed, but from Jacs's vantage point, all she could hear were the rolling roars.

The town square filled with villagers and guardpairs quickly. Altus Nemea and her escort of three positioned themselves in the center, near the base of the still ruined clocktower. *In the spot the King had announced the contest over a year ago*, Jacs thought with a pang.

When most were settled around the Griffin, Altus Nemea fell silent and looked skyward. At the signal, Altus Hermes let out an echoing, ear-splitting screech. All eyes turned toward them as one and watched in awe as Jacs and Altus Hermes circled in a slow, sweeping spiral toward them, finally landing in front of the group.

Jacs dismounted to complete silence and stood before the dumbstruck crowd. She felt a flutter of panic in her chest as she saw how so many familiar faces had changed in the last few months. With eyes filled with mistrust and lips drawn tight, they waited for her to speak.

She took a breath, cleared her throat, and said, "Thank you all for coming at such short notice. I . . ." She faltered; that didn't seem like the right way to start at all. She tried again. "It is so wonderful to see you all again." She hesitated. That sentiment felt superficial, why was it so hard to speak to her own people? She felt the breath of Altus Hermes at her back and drew strength from its presence. Shoulders dropping, she said, "I know things here have not gotten any easier since I became Queen."

A low murmur of agreement rippled through the crowd.

"The Bridgeport of my childhood was a bright and lively place. To see it now so altered, and to see that things have only gotten worse since I ascended the throne is . . ." She searched for the right word and gestured around at the charred clocktower, the boarded-up windows along the main street, and the dozens of scry crystals dotting the buildings and lanes. "It's not what I want, and it's not what you deserve. For that I am sorry, and believe me when I say I have been trying. Big changes take dozens of small steps, and I came here today to take the first of many. When I became Queen, I passed a law to ban scry crystals and I'm here to make sure that law is carried out. Guards!" she called across the sea of townsfolk to the perimeter of guardpairs. All stood to attention at the address. "By royal decree, all scry crystals shall be removed from public and private dwellings. All citizens are by law required to turn in their crystal, and all crystals in public spaces are to be henceforth removed. These devices are a gross breach of individual privacy and have no place in this fair Queendom."

A stunned silence lasted only a moment before the crowd began cheering, tentatively at first, then with gusto.

Jacs smiled and held a hand up for silence. "Wagons will be placed in the center of town to receive disposed crystals, and guards will accompany these wagons up the Bridge. Furthermore, guardpairs will be sent to all Lowrian towns with copies of this decree and similar removal protocols will be followed, to be completed within the month." Jacs paused, waiting for quiet before continuing. "And finally, guardpair numbers shall be reevaluated, and Lowrian women shall be trained to fill at least fifty percent of these positions. We are all working toward a united Queendom and cannot do so without trusting those in positions of authority. We also can't do so when we don't see *ourselves* represented in those positions of authority."

The crowd yelled their agreement.

"I was born here; I grew up as one of you. Believe me when I say the Upperites are more similar to us than they are different. We need to remember we are all on the same side. I will do all I can to honor and speak for all people within Frea, and I will try to be the Queen you all deserve. It will be a long road, but I promise it will be worthwhile." Another cheer erupted from the crowd, faces that had at first seemed too fearful to hope split into wide grins.

The rest of the day was filled with instruction, direction, and reunion. Wagons were located and quickly filled with personal and public crystals. Old friends came one after another to wring her hands in greeting and thanks. Guardpairs received written copies of her decree to deliver to villages and towns all over the Lower Realm, and Jacs appointed General Hawkins, as well as Lowrian Mayor Odette Linheir, to make sure Bridgeport appropriately complied with the new law.

Around noon, Jacs detached herself from her meeting with Mayor Linheir and found Ms. and Mr. Grimsby waiting outside for her with a linen-wrapped sandwich and flagon of liquid covered with condensation. "We thought you might be hungry, Your Majesty,"

Mr. Grimsby said. Jacs drew him up from an attempted bow and hugged them both.

"It's so wonderful to see you!" She beamed. "You look—" she cut off, suddenly serious, as she took in the state of Mr. Grimsby's face. "Who did that to you?" she said, indicating his blackened eye.

Mr. Grimsby looked nervously at his wife, and she shook her head. "Let's find a quiet place to have lunch," she said, looking around warily.

Jacs allowed them to lead her to a quiet courtyard surrounded by low hedges and dotted with stone benches. Amber and Andromeda followed a few paces behind and stationed themselves on either side of the courtyard entrance. At ease, but alert.

Jacs was confused as to why they were meeting outside, but Ms. Grimsby commented: "Our crystals are still up, and this is more private by far."

Sitting on the benches, Jacs accepted a poured glass of ale and unwrapped her sandwich on her lap. "So, what happened?"

Mr. Grimsby took a swig from his glass and said quietly, "It was my fault really, I went putting my nose where it shouldn't be. I'm not sure if you've heard, but a few of our boys have gone missing. About one every month since you became Queen." There was no accusation in his voice, but Jacs's heart sank. "We just found out last night that the Wetler boy's missing now too."

"I heard. It's awful," Jacs said softly.

Mr. Grimsby took a bite of his sandwich. "Well, a few nights ago, I was out in my garden, couldn't sleep. It was well past midnight, and I saw this person hurrying down the lane behind my house. Something about how they were moving didn't sit right and I had a feeling."

"And his feelings are usually worth a faering," Ms. Grimsby piped up.

Mr. Grimsby looked at her fondly and continued: "They had their hood up and were trying their best to dodge the crystals, so I followed them. I'm pretty light on my feet. I went undetected for a while. They were doing the strangest thing. Maybe one in every ten houses they came to, they marked the side of the door with this glowing white paint."

"Glowing?" Jacs asked.

"Yeah, but it wasn't bright. Actually, if you didn't know to look for it, you'd probably miss it. Small little spot, it was. You could mistake it for a weird trick of the moonlight. They marked a couple houses while I was watching, the Wetlers' being one of them."

"So this person marking the doors, they did that to you?" Jacs asked, indicating his bruises.

"What, this? No, that came next. I followed this person around the back of the clocktower and when I rounded the corner, they vanished. Poof! One minute I was hot on their tail, the next they're nowhere to be seen. So now I'm in the middle of town well past curfew. I turn back to go home, and that's when my luck runs out. Two guardpairs picked me up, didn't ask many questions, just came to their own conclusions." Ms. Grimsby busied herself refilling everyone's glasses. Jacs could see red splotches on her cheeks.

Jacs remained silent for a moment, thinking. "Could you identify the guards for me?" she said.

Mr. Grimsby looked at her sharply. He considered her words, and two emotions warred across his face. Fear and hope, but to Jacs's dismay, fear seemed to prevail, and he looked at his hands, replying, "No, no I don't think I remember what they looked like. It was dark, and I didn't see their faces."

"Are you sure? They can't be allowed to get away with this. They are meant to protect, not bully."

Mr. Grimsby now looked very uncomfortable. "Yes, I'm quite sure. They all dress the same anyway, I wouldn't be confident I could pick them out of a lineup."

A familiar helpless feeling stole through Jacs's chest, turning all it found there to lead. She felt both restless and paralyzed, rooted to the spot when she just wanted to do something, anything that might have an impact. Instead, she reached into the coin purse in her pack and drew out a handful of gold faerings.

As if she had shouted at them, the Grimsbys drew back from her offered hand, eyes wide. It was more than either of them would make in a year. Jacs hated the cold weight in her palm. Hated that, deep down, she felt she was bribing her own guilt away.

"I'd like to at least cover any medical costs that came from that night," she insisted.

"Y-your Majesty, that's far too generous—" Ms. Grimsby said.

"Please," she said firmly. "It's one of the few things I can do."

Her old friends looked at each other and back to her.

At last, Mr. Grimsby shook his head and said kindly, "Jacqueline. You are one of the few people I know who will take on every problem within this Queendom as a personal project." He held her gaze and lowered himself to one knee in front of her, a comforting hand on her shoulder. "But you'll have to forgive yourself for the problems you can't solve. No one can solve them all, and no one should try." He inspected the faerings in her palm, withdrew two with a nod of thanks, and closed her fingers over the rest. "You already do more than what most people can only dream of attempting. You always give more than you get. For these reasons alone I know you're gonna make a brilliant Queen, one we can all be proud of, but promise this old man one thing."

Jacs nodded, not trusting herself to speak past the lump in her throat.

"Promise me you won't lose yourself along the way."

Feeling like a little girl again, she clutched the coins tightly in her fist until they pinched her skin, and she embraced Mr. Grimsby.

In a flash, she recalled the man hunkering down next to her on his haunches to show her the correct way to weave a flax basket.

Not too tight, and not too loose, you want to tuck these ends under, see? You're in control of the tension, so keep a firm hand.

That seemed like a lifetime ago.

She withdrew, eyes swimming, and smiled at the two of them. "I've missed you both," she said with a shaky laugh.

Ms. Grimsby smiled and said, "You know where to find us. We may be a realm away, but just remember: We're rooting for you down here."

As the sun began to set and the extended twilight of the Lower Realm prepared to settle in, Jacs reviewed all that had been accomplished to make sure she hadn't forgotten anything. The missing boys still plagued her thoughts, but she knew she needed more information, and more time. Not only that, but her letters to Connor and Lena were still in motion and she felt the urgency to return increase with every passing minute.

It was time for her to go back to the palace.

She found Phillip helping dismantle a particularly stubborn crystal on a lamppost and drew him aside.

"Come with me," she said. It wasn't an order.

"What? Where?" he asked.

"To the palace. You'll be closer to those who have the answers about Master Leschi, and you can help me in the search." She watched hope then doubt flash across his face.

"But I can't just leave," he said tentatively.

"Sure, you can, it won't be forever. You can return whenever you want, I just . . ." She thought again of his dark-alley encounter, his anger at the farm, and the missing boys. "I'm worried about you. It might not be safe here and I can't"—she struggled to find the words—"I can't lose you too."

He looked away as he considered it. Scratching his chin absently, he asked, "But my work is here, what will I do up there?"

Jacs thought for a moment. “You could always work with Master Aestos, the palace goldsmith. Consider it an extension of your training. I bet you don’t get too much experience working with gold down here.” She meant the comment to lighten his mood, but noticed his brow darken.

“We do all right down here, Your Majesty,” he said stiffly.

Jacs sighed inwardly. “I know, I didn’t mean . . . listen, it’s an option, it’s up to you, so please think it over, but I would breathe easier knowing you were safe. And I’d love your help finding our mums.” She touched his upper arm. “You don’t have to decide right away, there will be convoys of crystal wagons going up the Bridge, I’ll let General Hawkins know you must be granted passage with them if you so choose.”

Phillip nodded and turned back to the crystal he had been dismantling. Jacs studied his half-turned-away face for a moment. His eyes were cold. His countenance unreadable. She said her good-byes and left him to his task, unsettled. Phillip had always been an open book with her, an older brother with a Jacs-shaped soft spot.

This was a new Phillip, a hurt Phillip. Whatever had hurt him, and she could take several guesses as to who and what were the culprits, had left its mark. His stress, his loss, his pain was warping the gentlehearted man she had known.

Now she just hoped he hadn’t lost that kind part of himself completely.

With so much on her mind, it was a relief that the return flight passed without much excitement. Weary and worried but proud of her accomplishments, Jacs let her mind go deliciously blank as she enjoyed the airborne freedom. Andromeda had been much less nervous about remounting Altus Nemea.

Amber called her a natural, and Jacs noticed Andromeda's proud smile before she restrained it behind her usual composure.

As an extreme kindness, the Alti decided to fly them to the throne room, rather than dropping them off at the top of Court's Mountain. As the last of the day's sunlight guttered and died, snuffed out behind the western mountain range, the two Griffins landed on the rooftop near the pillared and roofed belvedere.

Jacs had only seen this structure from below and was shocked at how large it was up close. With twelve pillars evenly spaced around its perimeter, it could accommodate a dozen Griffins, and allowed them to peer into the throne room through the oculus with ease. The roof extended past the edge of the pillars to allow the Court some protection from weather under its eaves. Both Griffins walked to the edge of the oculus and gracefully dropped into the throne room. Jacs felt like a pebble being thrown into a well.

Wings unfurled the moment before landing, and both Griffins touched down with the lightness of a feather. Dismounting, Jacs bowed deeply to Altus Hermes and watched her knights do the same out of the corner of her eye. Altus Hermes ran its beak through her hair before taking flight and disappearing the way it had come with Altus Nemea close behind.

In the sudden silence that followed, Jacs grinned at Amber and Andromeda. The knights beamed back. All looked considerably more windswept and hopeful than they had that morning. That is until a voice coming from the throne made Jacs spin around, her smile slipping from her face.

"Welcome back, Your Majesty." Cllr. Perda stood on the dais in front of the throne. Jacs felt a jolt of satisfaction that the Councilor's insolence didn't extend so far as to seat herself on the throne. As usual, her hair was slicked back into a severe knot on the top of her head, a jeweled hairpin holding it in place. Her floor-length gown was steel gray with a heavily beaded neckline and long bell sleeves. Likely in defiance of the new style Jacs had introduced at court, the skirts were full and were not split down the middle.

"I'm so glad to see you have made a full recovery," the Councilor said in a neutral tone, her eyes glittering.

Jacs felt the color rush to her cheeks. After all the change she had affected in a matter of hours, she still felt like a child caught with her hand in a cookie jar.

Clearing her throat, she drew herself up and said, "Good evening, Councilor. I've just returned from the Lower Realm. I'm sure you will be pleased to hear that the law I passed months ago, the law that had not been upheld due to a communication error no doubt, has now been set right. We shall expect all scry crystals to be returned to us within the month."

The Councilor fought to keep her expression clear. "Well," she said softly, inclining her head, "all hail the Queen." Her gaze darted to where the Griffins had disappeared through the hole in the ceiling and swept over the knights. "It appears we can add two new names to our list of Courtiers," she noted. "Soon that title will be as common as muck; hopefully it holds its magnitude."

Jacs, after a long day of negotiations and preparations, found the length of her fuse to be lacking. "Come now, Councilor. Surely you can't mean to imply that a title decreases in importance the more there are who hold it? With that logic, would a Lord feel any less inferior knowing she is one of twelve in the Queendom? Or a knight's achievement be any less impressive given the dozens of others who hold the same title? The title holds weight regardless of how many there are to claim it."

The Chivilras shared a look, and Amber hid a smirk. Cllr. Perda's eyes narrowed minutely, but it could have been a trick of the shadows playing across her face.

"May we escort you to your chambers, Your Highness?" Amber asked, turning her back to Cllr. Perda.

"Yes," Jacs said, "it has been a long day. If you'll excuse me, Councilor."

With steps ringing out in victory, the three women left the Councilor alone in the dwindling light.

Once they were out of earshot, Andromeda cleared her throat and said firmly, "Your Majesty, we were your guests with the Court. We did not have to undergo the same ordeal to be deemed worthy. With all due respect, it would not feel right to adopt the same title."

Amber nodded, adding, "Besides, the only title I'm interested in adding to my extensive list of honors is Master. Don't want to muddy the waters. *Courtier* Masterchiv Amber Everstar, Soterian knight, head of the Queensguard is a bit of a mouthful."

Andromeda raised an eyebrow. "*Head* of the Queensguard?"

"It'll happen."

Jacs skipped the next few steps, her heart lighter than it had been in weeks. "Whatever you prefer."

15

REFRESHMENTS

It was evening, and Jacs hadn't returned. Connor paced the floor before the Queen's fireplace impatiently. A flutter of panic rose within his rib cage, and he took a deep breath to steady himself. His letter had read: *If I do not return by tomorrow evening, then find the next letter in a place only you would know to look.* Was it too soon? The sun had only just set; maybe he should wait a few more minutes. But it was technically evening.

Surely, it wouldn't hurt to at least *find* the letter. If it was multiple pages, then he could get started sooner, and if it was only a short letter, he would have extra time to read it through more than once. Either way, it wouldn't be against her wishes to find it now. He already knew where it would be: the little green boat perched on her writing desk had sat mocking him all day.

He approached the desk, then turned away abruptly. A part of him was apprehensive about what the letter held. Spinning on his heel when he got to the fireplace, he returned to the desk. Hesitating a moment, he reached for the boat, withdrew his hand as though from a flame. Then he changed his mind again and picked it up.

It was warm from sitting in the sun all day. Carefully, he slid open the compartment and was unsurprised to see the folded parchment. With a slight tremor in his fingers, he withdrew the letter and replaced the boat. Moving to his seat by the fireplace, he lowered himself into it and slowly unfolded the paper.

He read the words:

Dear Connor,

If you're reading this, I haven't returned and I want to start by apologizing for any worry I'm causing you. I promise it's—

"Connor!" He cut off reading as the sounds of a door opening and Jacs's voice interrupted the room's solemn silence.

"Jacs!" he said, relief flooding him. She stood, looking tired but triumphant, in the door frame. Her hair was windswept and tangled around her simple gold crown. Casting the letter aside, he rose and ran to her, sweeping her into his arms, and holding her close. Her familiar weight against his chest eased the tension in his heart.

"I was so worried, I was just about to read your second letter, I'm so glad you're okay! Where did you go? What did you . . . " He stopped as Jacs placed a finger on his lips and kissed him.

"It's kind of a long story, and I'm in desperate need of a bath. Would you accompany me to the pools?" she asked with mischief in her eyes.

He looked at her incredulously. Suddenly all his fear and worry rose in his throat like bile. "You need a bath?" he repeated softly, trying to contain the poison hovering behind his molars.

"And I haven't eaten. Let's call for a platter of something, maybe some cheeses? Bread for sure, and do you think the kitchen has dates?" Jacs asked happily.

"You disappear for an entire day with nothing but a letter full of empty words, and you're asking about dates?" He backed away from her, thumb brushing the side of his mouth. "You knew you were leaving. When I came to visit, you knew you were leaving. I saw you writing my letter."

Her smile faded. "Connor—"

A serpent reared within his chest and sunk its fangs deep into his heart. Venom flooded his next words. "No! Jacs, this is pitmuck. I've been worried sick. I came back to your rooms not twenty minutes after our fight and you weren't there. You left! You left after a fight! What's worse is you knew you were leaving and let me walk off . . . What if something had happened to you, and that was the last thing I'd said to you? I couldn't live with myself for that. Couldn't forgive myself for that. And you just left!"

"Connor, I'm sorry—"

"Oh, you're sorry! That makes it all better. Asking about dates. No, I can't . . . I can't be around you right now."

She crossed her arms. "So, what, you're going to storm out again?"

Connor glared at her and took a breath. "Yes, you can't just waltz back in like everything's rosy . . . I need a minute . . . before I say something stupid. Just"—he forced an exhale and waved a hand angrily—"give me, give me an hour, and I'll meet you in the pools."

"Connor . . ."

"And don't you dare disappear again!" he called over his shoulder, yanking hard on the door handle.

"Connor!"

"Welcome back," Connor said as the door shut behind him.

Desperate for a task to clear his head, he consulted a passing servant and made a beeline for the laundry, where he was told Adaine would be. Adaine Concorde was a shorter woman with a long, thin nose and high cheekbones. She wore her blue-and-gold livery proudly and had added the personal touch of a poppy-shaped pin to her lapel. While she was still getting used to her new role as Queen's valet, she was a quick learner and a fast walker, which made her efficient, with an air of eagerness that was incredibly endearing.

If she was alarmed by Connor's mood, she didn't comment on it. For that, he was grateful. "Adaine, do we have dates?" Connor asked bluntly.

"Dates, Your Grace? For what? I can check the calendar," she said quickly, placing a pile of folded linens on a shelf. Connor chided himself. He knew from experience that she had a very literal way of thinking. Backtracking, he said, "No, edible dates. The Queen is feeling better and has requested a platter of cheeses, fruits, and a bottle of wine in the pools. Not *in* the pools. To be delivered to a table in the bathing-pool room," he clarified. The last thing he wanted was soggy cheese. He was satisfied to see her quick nod of understanding before she disappeared to complete her task.

That done, Connor took a moment to breathe. He was happy Jacs was safe. He was glad she'd come back. But she could be so . . . I mean *dates?* Honestly? And the thoughts that circled in his mind like vultures, swooping low when he let his guard down for a moment, were that she had not wanted him beside her in this. She trusted her knights, but not him. She left without a good-bye, and worse, she left him when they were angry. If she hadn't come back, if his last words to her had been so callous . . .

He remembered his last words to his mother. Empty, frivolous things. He had made a comment about a woman's hat. It was an odd shape, a kind of question mark curve with a live bird perched on top. Then in a matter of seconds he had been kneeling over his mother's body, pleading with her empty shell. The spark that was *her* had vanished in an instant. If he had known then, he would have said something more profound than *Look at its feathers*.

It no doubt meant nothing to the departed what people said to them before they disappeared, but it meant everything to those left behind. He shook himself and stomped heavily down the hallway. A satisfying electric jolt shot up his calf with each footfall. She was safe. She had come back. They had time to talk.

He took the long way round to the pools.

"And you did all that today?" Connor asked. Despite his prickly mood, he couldn't keep the wonder from his voice. He joined her as he said he would. The platter and wine had arrived before he got there, but he noticed Jacs hadn't touched it. While she had initially looked relieved to see him, now she couldn't quite meet his gaze. Conversation flowed in fits and starts. Neither wanted to be the first to apologize, but both sought resolution, so instead they floated next to each other in the warm water, awkwardly patching the tear between them.

They sat, submerged to their necks in steaming water, on marble benches in one of the smaller pools. The air was filled with a faint floral scent, the walls and alcoves were lined with candles, and the sounds of waterfalls that connected the three main pools echoed around the open-air chamber.

Upon his arrival, the Queen had ordered the room cleared, except for Adaine, who stood just inside the door, and a knight pair of the Queensguard who waited outside—Chivilras Lerin Pamheir and Claudia Fayworth. Amber and Andromeda had been given the evening off after such an eventful day.

Jacs ran her fingers through the water, watching the ripples swirl into the pool's current, all tension gone from her face. She replied without looking at him. "It felt so good to actually be doing something. It really highlighted that old saying 'If you want something done right, you have to do it yourself.'" Her shoulders dropped and she tentatively met Connor's gaze. "It was hard seeing how bad things had gotten up close. And it was different: It was like I wasn't quite one of them anymore. Even Phillip was different toward me, calling me Your Majesty . . ." She trailed off.

"But Jacs, that's only proper. I'm sure he was just trying to navigate your new station," Connor said helpfully, his inflection forming a question rather than a statement.

Jacs was silent, then said quietly, "I suppose. I guess I just wasn't prepared for how much things had changed."

Connor noticed her mood shift and reached for her hands in the water. Holding them just below the surface, he gave them a squeeze. "Jacs, change isn't always easy, but if you've taught me anything, it's that it's necessary to move forward. What you're doing is so important. What you *did* is so important. If it makes a few past relationships awkward, then I'm afraid that's just the way it has to be. I'm sure you'll both get used to it eventually. Maybe Phillip calling you Your Majesty won't feel so weird next time you visit Bridgeport."

Jacs squeezed his fingers in response. "Yeah, that's true." Her face lit up as an idea struck her. "And I might not even have to wait that long, I invited him to stay at the palace and gave him permission to travel the Bridge when he makes his decision. So, I might see him within the month!"

Connor's mouth fell open in shock, but he was quick to close it. "You invited him here?" he asked, his mind playing catch up with this new information. He couldn't explain it, but the idea of Phillip living in the palace struck a chord of unease inside him. Was it dread he was feeling? Or maybe just protectiveness over Jacs. That was probably it.

"Yes," Jacs replied, not noticing his reaction. "It'll be great, you can finally meet him!"

"Of course," Connor agreed, still reeling, "but are you sure that was . . . wise?"

Jacs frowned. "What do you mean?"

"I don't know, it's just, you know how much you have to deal with as a Lowrian and you're the Queen. Are you sure you're not . . . inviting a lamb into a lioness's den?"

"I didn't even think of that," she said softly.

"I'm sure it'll be fine!"

"No, but you're right. I was so worried about the dangers of him staying in the Lower Realm. Connor, you should have seen him. He looked so . . . broken. But I never stopped to consider that there would be different dangers up here." She bit at the corner of her lip. Shrugging her shoulders, she said, "But it's done now. He might not even accept—he seemed unconvinced when I left him. And if he does come to stay, we'll just have to keep an eye on him. Maybe I can assign him a guardpair. He might not like that, actually . . . but I'll think of something. I offered him a position with Master Aestos. So maybe he'll sneak under the radar if we put him straight to work in the workshop. No one really needs to know where he came from . . . But he likely won't like having to hide who he is. I know better than most that trying to hide it is fruitless. It comes out in the end." She sighed, then realized what she had said. "But he shouldn't have to hide where he's from in the first place! Being Lowrian born doesn't make you a second-class citizen." She scrubbed her face, annoyed with herself.

Connor shifted closer to her in the water, not quite knowing what to say. "Well," he ventured finally, "we can always scale that bridge when we come to it. I'm guessing that just the offer would have given him something to hope for. Whether he takes it or not will be up to him, but a situation always seems easier when you have an out."

She nodded but still looked troubled.

Connor rubbed his thumb across her knuckles gently. "How bad was it down there?" he asked softly.

She was quiet for a moment. All he could hear was the gentle trickling of water, and the occasional hiss as condensation fell into a candle's flame.

"It was much worse," she said, "and I know I didn't see the half of it. There were so many guardpairs, they stood around the outside of the town square while I made my speech and I swear they were almost shoulder to shoulder. And my people," she struggled to find the words, "they just looked so hollow. It's only been three months since I last saw them—three months, and some of them have aged years."

"And Connor, four more boys have gone missing," she added in a low voice.

"What? And no one's—"

"No one has any idea where they've gone. One of them I scryed in the mirror probably the day before he disappeared. He was running out of town in a cloak in the middle of the night. That's all I could make out."

"What do you think that means?" Connor asked.

"I think it could mean anything, did he run away? Apparently, there was no note or anything. Was he taken in the night? Possibly, but why? He's the baker's son and quite a big guy, it would take a guardpair or more to take him down. And if it is the guards, that still doesn't answer why the secrecy. Apparently, none of the missing boys have shown up in the town's prison. Surely if you wanted to make an example of a rebellious citizen you would let the town know you had them locked up? Mr. Grimsby mentioned that a hooded figure was marking door frames and Mal's was one of them. Does that mean he was targeted? It doesn't make sense."

"And like you say, if it's not the guards, who else would kidnap men?" Connor added. "And where have they taken them?"

Jacs, still troubled, shook her head. Wanting to take her mind elsewhere, she eagerly changed the subject. "So what did you do today?"

Connor cocked an eyebrow and lifted his shoulders. "Worried about you."

She held tight to his hand under the water. "Connor, I'm sorry. I should have told you."

"You should have," he said evenly.

"And I definitely shouldn't have left without saying good-bye."

"Also correct."

"Are you mad at me?"

Connor met her gaze. "Yes." Her face fell, and he continued. "But I'm also so proud of you, Jacs. What you did was incredible. I just . . . I hope you know that I want to be by your side for these things."

"I know," she said softly.

A few stitches pulled the frayed fabric of their relationship together. Connor cleared his throat.

"Other than that, I actually had a pretty productive day. I met with the Council in the morning like you suggested. They were all shades of concern and even decided to throw a gala in your honor—to cheer you up after being bedridden."

Jacs looked at him warily. "They want to throw a gala for me?"

"That they do. They tasked me with sourcing some ideas for it too, because apparently, I'm the Queendom's best and only hope when it comes to bringing forth Her Majesty's smile."

"Is that so?" Jacs replied skeptically, and Connor noticed the corners of her mouth struggle to remain level.

"It's not a task for the faint of heart." He wagged a finger at her, suddenly serious. "Legend has it her smile can light up a room in a way that puts the sun's golden rays to shame. Her lips are a crimson that makes the reddest rose hide its petals. In fact, one flash of her radiant smile is said to warm the hearts of a thousand women and bring peace between realms," Connor said passionately.

Jacs rolled her eyes, lips still fighting a grin, as Connor slid closer to her in the water.

"How do you bear such a burden?" she asked.

"Gladly," he said with a wink and drew her hands up from the water, pausing with her knuckles millimeters from his lips. She leaned in, eyes shining. "Plus, they offered to pay me handsomely so . . ." He cut off with a laugh as Jacs's expression shifted to one of mock indignation. She ripped her hands from his grasp and, with still dripping fingers, flicked droplets of water at him. A traitorous smile lit up on her face as she attempted to dodge his retaliation.

"Ha! There it is!" Connor proclaimed before Jacs sent a larger splash his way, making him splutter as she laughed in triumph.

Soon they were in the middle of a full-out water war. Jacs's squeals reverberated around the open-air chamber, and Connor's laugh entwined with them joyfully. Adaine was pointedly looking away from the Queen and her Advisor, but the corner of her mouth betrayed the ghost of a grin.

Drenched and spluttering, Connor emerged from the water holding his hands up in truce.

"Do you yield?" Jacs, poised for another wave-based assault, grinned as Connor nodded.

"I yield," he said in mock anguish.

"Smart," she said slyly.

Water still in his eyes, Connor pushed his hair from his face and felt Jacs's hand press lightly against his chest. Moving backward slowly with her in the water, he felt the lip of the marble pool against his back, the edge of the bench against his calves. Sinking onto it, he opened his eyes to see Jacs, strands of auburn hair clinging to her face and around her shoulders, floating to straddle him on the bench. He could count the water droplets on her eyelashes. His breath caught. Hands found hips. She cupped his neck with one hand, the other still resting lightly on his chest, and kissed him softly along his jawline, hovering a moment before kissing his lips.

"And now?" she breathed, shifting her weight against him.

"Oh, I yield."

Connor noticed Adaine quietly slipping out into the hall. The soft thud of the closing door was barely perceptible, even if he had been listening for it.

16

THE ART OF MEASURING UP

A few days had passed since her trip to the Lower Realm, and Jacs was beginning to believe it had all been a dream. Not that life as the Queen was ever monotonous, but there was a steady rhythm to it that had enveloped her from the moment she woke up the morning after her flight. Waking, breaking her fast, meeting with the Council—she was convinced they preferred to see her still half asleep—training with Amber, studying with Lena, having lunch with Connor, and taking care of throne-room duties until supper.

The Council had been unusually sweet with her since her brief meeting with Cllr. Perda in the throne room. Rather than displease them, her actions in the Lower Realm had caused them to regard her with a newfound respect. In the first meeting after her return, she had received applause upon entering their chambers.

"Incredible girl!"

"Such mettle!"

"What a resourceful young Queen we have!"

"It appears we underestimated your abilities, Your Majesty."

Jacs had faltered at the threshold and had not known what to say.

"Oh, and of course she's speechless—you must be so tired, dear, come sit. We had some refreshments prepared for you." Cllr. Stewart beamed and indicated a plush chair that had been brought in especially for her.

She had never had a place to sit in the Council of Four's chamber before. Lowering herself into the red velvet, she felt awkward and unsure, as though she had forgotten where her legs should go when seated.

The Council members had abandoned their four-pointed-perches and sat on the sunken dais with her. Their chairs were slightly more elaborate, but not by much. The morning had passed pleasantly: The Council asked details about her adventure, marveled at her ability to navigate the Lowrian mob, and commended her for following up on the law that had, evidently, been ignored by the powers below. By the end of their meeting, Jacs had even found herself smiling.

Before she rose to take her leave, Jacs asked, "And do you have any news of my mother?"

The Councilors looked at one another and Cllr. Fengar responded, "No, pet. But we have located Master Bruna Leschi and await more information."

Jacs, confused, pressed them. "But you *knew* her location. You *know* her location."

"We do *now*," said Cllr. Dilmont. "It has taken a lot of sleuthing, but as we all know, all shadows are brought to light in the end."

"And my mother?"

"Oh, my dear, you must be exhausted! And you have training this morning, no doubt. Such vigor—to be young again! We have some matters to attend to and won't keep you any longer, but congratulations, Your Majesty. Yours was a true triumph."

With a quick succession of movements, Jacs found herself on the other side of their chamber door, disoriented and confused but hopeful. She was almost ashamed of herself, not realizing until that moment how much she had craved their approval. A small voice in her head warned her that it was likely just another trick, *but surely they wouldn't just pretend to be nice to me. I must have actually impressed them,* a louder voice insisted.

The Council's change of tune had persisted over the days that followed and gave her no reason to doubt their intentions.

She poked absently at a bruise above her elbow, fresh from her spar with Amber three days after their return, and gazed longingly out the window. Today she was in the library, a room that still filled her with wonder, studying Queendom history with Lena. It was incredible the amount of information the Lower Realm curriculum omitted. Or, more likely, was not permitted to share.

The library was every bit as impressive as Connor had promised the day they met. It felt more like a cathedral, with a high, domed roof and a myriad of lofts, balconies, and alcoves around its perimeter. In each corner, a steep spiraling staircase took the reader to a second or third gallery lined with books. The shelving system alone was mind boggling, and Jacs felt lucky that reshelving books was left to the librarian, Master Nicola Eyren.

With its bright white walls, gold trim, intricate mosaic floor, and more books than Jacs could read in a lifetime, the library made her heart sing. Learning the history of court intrigue and past policies, however, was not her favorite subject.

". . . so, after his outburst, it was decided that the passions of men were too unpredictable and the male seat in the Council of Four was eliminated," Lena was saying, to which Jacs perked up and rejoined her lesson. "As the saying goes, 'Man's fire fells the empire.'"

"There used to be a man on the Council of Four?" she asked, intrigued. There was an idea. A man on the Council could act as a valid representative for half the Queendom's people. Now that she thought about it, it was ridiculous that a group of women were trusted to make policies that affected the lives of men without gathering any input from them. They might have it all wrong and never know.

"Yes. Men, actually. Centuries ago, the Council had consisted of two women and two men, but over the years that tradition was replaced with the one we have now. Genteel Patrick Wenthrope's famous outburst was the last nail in that coffin. For a few decades after, the slang for throwing a tantrum was 'throwing a Wenthrope' or 'wenthropping.' It comes in and out of fashion, but that's mostly died out now, I think." Lena looked thoughtful. "Or, actually my old cook used to say it, so maybe it just depends on who you talk to.

"Now the most male representation the Queendom will have is if there is a King—depending on how much sway he has with the Queen—and if the Royal Advisor is male. While both are often considered to be no more than figureheads, there have been a number of influential Kings and a few Royal Advisors throughout history who are of note. It's also important to look at *why* these men were as successful as they were. Most analysts believe it is due to the quality of their relationship with the Queen . . ."

The lesson continued for over an hour. They meandered through the predecessors and heirs of each of the Queendom's twelve Lords and dawdled through various dates when Councilors were appointed and when they resigned before settling on the topic of the Frean lineage.

As the crown was only sometimes passed along a familial line, the last name, Frean, was instead given to each new Queen and her descendants. Jacs, who had only just started getting used to Daidala, now had to remember she was a Frean. This surname made it easier to name the present royalty and harder to list the lineage.

"Poor Queen Frea," Jacs giggled, "walking around with a name like "Frea Frean the third, no less!"

Lena seemed to struggle against a traitorous smile, but said sternly, "Jacqueline. Queen Frea the third was an extremely influential monarch." She paused and allowed the corner of her lip to quirk. "But I doubt her parents expected her to become Queen when they named her."

"Hello, hello, what is Her Majesty giggling about?" Anya said as she approached their table. She carried the fragrance of the greenhouses with her, and the tips of her fingers were tinged green from working with flower stems. "I can't imagine anything funny about royal history."

Jacs shook her head. "I've gone loopy with all these names. I'm afraid Frea Frean set me off."

Anya grinned. "Well for the sake of your sanity, it sounds like I'm just in time. I've come to let you know Master Moira has arrived to measure you for the gala."

Standing too eagerly and shooting an apologetic look at Lena's arched eyebrow, she said, "Perfect, let's finish this discussion tomorrow?"

"Of course, Your Majesty. That will give you a whole evening to study," Lena said with a wink and began collecting the books they had been referencing.

"Where is Master Moira now?" Jacs asked Anya.

"She said she'd await you in the conservatory. Apparently the natural light is best there at this time of day."

"Ah, well I shouldn't keep her waiting."

Lena nodded hurriedly in agreement, having a much more intimate knowledge of the seamstress and her quirks. The three women quickly headed for the conservatory, discussing what kind of dress the seamstress might have in mind for this particular occasion.

"Oh, hang on, I've left my quill. You two go ahead and let Master Moira know I'm coming; I'll see you in a moment," Jacs said, realizing she had left Connor's stardust quill in the library. Lena and Anya agreed and continued on without her.

Jacs quickened her pace and retraced her steps. Leaving her knights to wait for her in the hall, she reentered the library and easily found her quill where she had left it on the table. The gold-dusted edges shimmered in the light coming in from the nearby window. Picking it up, she ran it through her fingers and placed it carefully in a deep pocket in her split skirts. She headed out the way she had come but noticed a head of golden curls bent over a table. Jacs was almost able to leave unobserved when, as if sensing her gaze, Hera lifted her head and caught her eye. In the fleeting moment before intention could catch up with expression, Jacs noted Hera's knotted brow and red rimmed eyes.

In a blink the moment passed, and a haughty expression consumed Hera's features once more.

"Good afternoon, Your Majesty," she said softly.

"Lord Claustrom, lovely to see you," Jacs replied, compelled now to step closer.

"I overheard some of your lessons with Dame Glowra," Hera commented after a pause.

"Yes, I'm afraid I now have a host of different names running around inside my head."

Hera inclined her head stiffly and said, "Well, from where I'm sitting you actually seemed to have a knack for learning them. I know I always had trouble untangling all of our twisted family trees as a girl."

Jacs, startled at what was unmistakably a compliment, didn't know how to respond. Hera attempted to subtly wipe away a tear that had slipped free from her lashes.

"Lord Claustrom," Jacs said tentatively, "are you all right?"

"Of course. I'm simply sensitive to dust."

Jacs didn't want to press her and instead looked at the length of parchment Hera had been writing on for a change of subject.

"What are you working on?"

Hera looked down and instinctively covered the papers with her hand. "Oh, I was . . . I was writing a letter to my mother."

"I hope she is well?"

"She is, thank you."

"Please send her my regards."

"I will."

"Wonderful." There was a painful silence.

"Well—" Hera began.

"Well, I will leave you to it," Jacs said.

"Your Majesty," Hera said, bowing her head in farewell.

Jacs left the library.

"Oh, my *dear!* If someone were to have told me four months ago that I would save the future Queen of Frea from a bare-ankled wardrobe *disaster* and that she would be wearing my designs *exclusively*, well I would have called them mad! Now here we are, and your calves will forever be in safe hands while under my careful stitches. By Alti they will."

Master Moira spoke without pause for breath or thought.

"No longer a Daidala but a Frean! When you stood upon that footstool in the Griffin's Den, I simply *sensed* the greatness in you, my dear. I even said to Juliana—didn't I, Juliana—I said, 'Those are the shoulders of greatness!' Didn't I say just that?" Master Moira's boisterous tones echoed around the ivy and orchids. Her assistant, Juliana, nodded in agreement with her mistress's claims and retrieved a notebook from a skirt pocket. She was a slim woman and wore a neat gray skirt and collared shirt. She hunched protectively forward and nervously gripped her pen in one hand.

Master Moira, in contrast, waved her arms about like an enthusiastic conductor. She carried herself with the grace of a dancer and was larger in size and stature than Phillip. As though waltzing to a melody only she could hear, she moved around Jacs, who stood on a stool with her arms out. She wore a dress of a darker gray than her assistant and with much more flair. The bustle had been gathered above her sacrum to reveal a delicate, shifting, opalescent fabric beneath. Slits in her sleeves also gave way to this ethereal fabric, and overall, the effect reminded Jacs of a geode she had found as a girl. Dark, sturdy rock on the outside, concealing a brilliant treasure within.

"Ah yes, just as I thought, the stress of ruling a Queendom has slimmed the middle, you must eat more, Your Majesty! You'll waste away before our eyes, and the eyes of the people are now fixed upon you! Believe me, dearest, they'll notice, and it will become a trend, and I will be forced to use less fabric and firmer stays and . . . actually that would do rather well for business so, as you were!" She laughed heartily and removed the measuring tape from Jacs's waist.

"It is a good thing we measured, the dress I have in mind will be elegant and it would not *do* if I were even one inch off. Measure twice, cut once, as the adage goes!"

"What did you have in mind?" Jacs asked.

"My dear, you will look as beautiful as the night sky! The jewel to this Queendom's crown! We will of course be incorporating your preference for a split skirt?"

Jacs nodded.

"And would you prefer a central split? Or shall we try something different, something bolder. Maybe asymmetric? Or even two splits, one down either side?" Master Moira's eyes sparkled.

Jacs considered. "Master Moira, I trust you know what will look best and leave that decision in your capable hands."

Measuring tape entwined in her fingers, the seamstress clapped her palms together and beamed. "Such a wise matriarch you are already proving yourself to be! Of course, I shall make sure you *shine*! Juliana! Are we done here? Yes, I have what I need. Farewell, Your

Majesty. I shall have this gown to you in three days, just in time for the gala."

Jacs attempted a dignified good-bye, but Master Moira, her head seemingly filled with patterns, had already bustled out of the room.

The waterfall trickled merrily in the silence that followed. Jacs, eyes slightly wider than usual, saw similar expressions on Lena's and Anya's faces.

"Anyone fancy a drink?" Jacs asked quietly.

Anya laughed. "Yes, I thought it'd be nice to have a break from the flowers, but I definitely need something after that whirlwind."

Lena signaled to a servant stationed near the door who jumped to life and brought over a bottle of wine and three glasses. "I had this brought earlier when I heard we were meeting with Master Moira," Lena said by way of explanation.

With the wine poured, glasses clinked in cheers, and each woman took a moment to breathe. Sitting in cushioned chairs near the waterfall, conversation was slow to start but soon veered to the topic of Master Leschi and Jacs's mother.

"Still no word then?" Anya asked.

"No, it's the wildest thing. It's like the Council has forgotten all they said before that implicated them as the captors. I think back on the conversations and, while they never outright admitted to knowing where they're being held, or to being the ones who held them, it was always heavily implied. Now it's like I've remembered it all wrong. They're shocked whenever I suggest or outright state that they know where they are. They deny being capable of such monstrosities and even go so far as to outline in detail the lengths they're going to find them. The focus has shifted entirely too, we don't talk about my mother unless I bring her up, but they are eager to bring up the progress they are making with finding Master Leschi at every turn." Jacs scratched the back of her neck. "I honestly don't know what to believe. What if I was just overreacting before?"

Lena and Anya shared a look. Lena said softly, "I mean, you obviously proved yourself to them by going to the Lower Realm. That seems to have changed their attitudes significantly."

"Maybe they really don't know where your mother is, and were just using your conviction to their advantage," Anya supplied.

"Then why the switch now?" Jacs asked.

"Because you showed you are more than they assumed you were," Lena suggested.

"Maybe." Doubt flecked Jacs's reply.

"Have you asked them at all about the missing boys?" Anya asked.

Jacs sighed and withdrew the little book from a pocket within her skirts. She had added the names of the four boys Phillip mentioned to the list. Absently, she ran her thumb over the cover and watched "Missing" appear and disappear. "No, not yet. I probably should . . . but if anything, I want them to focus on the two missing women in my life first. I still don't know enough about why these boys are missing to start announcing it to everyone."

"Did you get any leads from people you spoke to in Bridgeport?" Lena asked.

"No, not really, but it was a very busy day."

Lena reached over and patted the back of Jacs's hand. "All you can do is take on each problem as it comes. Although I will say that it is bizarre how many of your problems involve missing people," Lena mused lightly.

Jacs nodded in agreement. "Very bizarre."

"Maybe they'll turn up in the same place," Anya said optimistically.

"Maybe . . . hang on . . . that might actually make sense," Jacs said, her mind beginning to spin through the possibilities. "What if it's the same culprit? If they're in the business of abducting people, two more wouldn't be too difficult. And"—she brandished the book—"they must have a location big enough to hide this many people undetected." Jacs looked at the other two excitedly.

"It would make things simpler," Lena agreed.

"And Master Leschi always said it's the simple solutions that usually solve the problem. Reality is rarely overcomplicated," Jacs said.

"So, we're looking for someone—" Lena began.

"Or a group of someones," Anya interjected.

"Right, or a group of someones who abduct people?" Lena finished.

"Would there really be a market for making people disappear?" Jacs asked, looking at Lena.

"You'd be surprised. The Lords can get quite brutal, and politics always brings out the worst in people. It's possible. It would have to be very hush-hush though."

"It seems pretty far-fetched," Anya said doubtfully.

Jacs sighed and swirled her wine around her glass. "Agreed. Especially because, while I have a strong suspicion the Council might still be behind my mother and Master Leschi's disappearance, what on Frea would they need all these boys for?"

Lena lifted her hands, palms up, and Anya shrugged.

"But we won't rule it out just yet. Besides, it will save us a lot of trouble if we end up only needing to find one secret people-hiding place," Jacs said frankly.

To keep her mind on the facts helped her skirt around the ache in her chest. It had been so long since she had seen her mother, battered and bloodied in the prison cell. Months since she had promised to return, only to find she was too late. A dangerous thought struck her, *What if I'm too late now? What if the Council avoided talking about her because she's . . . no.* She shook her head and turned away from the gaping void that threatened to pull her in. No. She would keep looking.

17

A BARD'S LAMENT

Amber had a reputation. She was the youngest woman to earn her knighthood since Chiv. Strellen, the youngest knight to be appointed to the Queensguard, and one of the handful of women awarded the Soterian Medal in this century. She was used to impressing people.

She was used to being admired.

She was not used to rejection.

The late afternoon found her training with Andromeda, having just heard from Niqo that his tiny brain couldn't navigate dating a woman with such a "busy" schedule. She was in desperate need of something to punch.

"Everstar, you sure you're all right?" Andromeda asked, massaging her jaw and pushing herself up off the sandy floor.

"Just fine. Let's run that one again, I think I put too much weight on my front foot," she replied, panting a little as she helped Andromeda to her feet.

"Okay, but I'm going to get some pads. At this rate, I'll be a kaleidoscope by the end of the night." Andromeda walked over to the equipment bins, and Amber rolled out her shoulders. She glowered and rewound her hand wraps. Boys were so fickle anyway. Who needed all that drama?

"Ready?" Andromeda asked, a pillow-length pad in her arms.

"Come on, I didn't hit you that hard!"

Andromeda raised her eyebrows. "I know. This is so you can hit harder," she said.

Amber found herself smiling. "Thanks, Turner." She set her stance.

Thirty minutes later, face streaming and feeling much better, she and Andromeda collapsed on one of the benches around the perimeter of the training ring.

"So, what happened?" Andromeda asked, handing Amber a waterskin.

Amber accepted it with a nod of thanks and tossed a towel to her partner, who caught it deftly. "Niqo. He told me he couldn't handle being courted by a woman who was never around. I think our impromptu day in the Lower Realm was the last straw."

"I'm sorry to hear."

"Yeah, it was bound to happen," Amber said with forced bravado. "It's not the end of the world."

"No. But that doesn't stop it from hurting."

"Yeah." Amber took a drink from her waterskin to avoid looking at her.

"Do you want to do something this evening?" Andromeda asked.

"Like what?"

"Anything. I just don't want you sitting alone in the dark wallowing."

"I do not wallow!" Amber said indignantly.

"You definitely wallow," Andromeda replied, not unkindly.

"Well, I *won't* wallow. I just need a distraction," Amber said, forcing a smile to her lips. She wasn't too cut up about Niqo. Not really. The rejection hurt more than the actual loss. Next time she'd have to be quicker on the draw and end it first.

Out of the corner of her eye she spotted Dyna Flent sparring with another guard. Her form was sloppy when blocking low attacks, but otherwise she looked pretty good. *Her fighting*—she caught herself—*her fighting looks pretty good.*

"You could find a new hobby," Andromeda suggested, then, noticing the pull on her attention, added, "We don't court guards."

"What do you—I wasn't thinking that!" Amber said, turning away from Flent to see Andromeda looking severe. "Okay, okay. A new hobby, got it."

"Try sketching, or something."

"Sketching?"

"I don't know, but just . . ." she glanced back at Flent quickly and added, "she's not worth the risk."

"You don't know that," Amber said, suddenly defensive.

"I know that she's the niece of a Councilor, and already flying too far above her station. She'll use you as a stepping stone, and watch you plummet when she's done with you. Mark my words."

Amber scoffed and passed the waterskin back to Andromeda.

"What about you anyway? You've always got an opinion about who I'm courting. Any beau on the horizon?" Amber asked, eager to change the subject.

"No," Andromeda said shortly.

"No? Not even someone you fancy?" Amber asked, mischief shining in her eyes. Andromeda could be infuriatingly stoic, but every once in a while, Amber was able to squeeze a smile out of her.

"No."

Evidently, now was not one of those times. Amber studied her expression but could no more read it than she could an Austerian sonnet. Sighing, she wiped a towel across the back of her neck.

"Okay, well, we're not on duty till nine tomorrow. Let's go to the Gilded Talon. I'm in the mood for some music."

Andromeda considered for a moment then replied, "One condition."

"What?" Amber asked as she rose to her feet.

"We don't end up at the Dipping Wick," Andromeda stipulated, also rising.

"What have you got against the Dipping Wick?" Amber said, chin jutting forward.

"Last time we were there, you broke a man's wrist."

"In an arm wrestle! He should have yielded!"

"No Dipping Wick."

"Fine."

They headed in the direction of the wash house; Amber glanced briefly over her shoulder and caught Flent's eye before averting her gaze and following Andromeda's lead.

Clean, changed, and smelling faintly of sage and sandalwood, Amber and Andromeda walked through the Gilded Talon's double doors into the wall of sound that greeted them. Despite their change of clothes, their posture and in-step strides marked them as military, and women and men eyed them warily as they crossed the threshold. Andromeda signaled to the man behind the counter who nodded in their direction as they sat down at a small table near the far side of the room.

By instinct, they sat with their backs to the wall. The room was dimly lit, and the establishment obviously catered to a more affluent clientele. Dark blue walls were accented with gold, cream velvet chairs circled low wooden tables, and crystal-encased candles studded most surfaces. Women lounged and boasted. Men chittered and flaunted. Each person's peripherals tracked their desire, whether it be realistic or otherwise.

Amber always found it interesting to watch people orbit one another. There was a certain electricity in the ebb and flow between people when the sun went down.

Continuing their conversation from the walk in, Andromeda said, "Her Majesty's asked for a list of potential trainers for the new Lowrian guards. I said we'd get back to her within the week, so let me know if you have any suggestions. Hawkins's most recent report included an estimate of the number of Lowrian women wanting to sign up, and there will be more than enough recruits by the looks of it."

Amber nodded, thoughtful. "She really opened a can of worms with that decree. Hopefully, we can keep on top of it. Though Lowrian guards isn't the worst idea in the world. I mean, it saves us diluting our numbers up here."

Andromeda tilted her head in agreement and they shared a look.

"Is she still insisting on moving forward with recruiting men into the military?" Amber said in a much lower voice, almost conspiratorially.

Andromeda just nodded. A single, crisp motion.

Amber huffed a sigh. "It's crazy. You gotta be able to make life to take life, that's how it's always been."

Arching one eyebrow, Andromeda said evenly, "I'm not so sure. In our last meeting, Her Majesty raised some compelling points. Their strength could be an asset with the proper training. Like she said, if we don't harness it, someone else will, and then we would be on the wrong side of progress. It could cost us in battle."

Amber shifted in her seat uncomfortably. Jutting her chin out, she said, "Well, I'll believe it when I see it."

"Auster's had men in their military for years."

"Oh, so we're taking cues from the backward Kingdom now?" Amber scoffed. "I—we—flattened their forces in Everden, remember? We've only ever needed women in ours, same with Nysa, and it's worked great so far."

Andromeda studied her but said nothing; the ghost of a smile hovered around her lips. Amber bristled, but thankfully, her partner didn't push the matter.

Of course, Amber was loyal to the crown. She agreed with Jacqueline's laws and ideas for change, and had anyone else said what she'd just said to Andromeda, she would likely have challenged them until they stood down.

But she could be honest with Andromeda, and until recently they had always been of the same mind when it came to men joining the military. Apparently not anymore. A slithering coil of unease unfurled in her stomach. It used to be so clear cut. Now she didn't know what to think.

Interrupting her thoughts, the bartender, a well-built older man with a salt-and-pepper beard and tight-fitting tunic with sleeves rolled to the elbows approached and asked, "Can I get you anything this evening?"

"Yes, two ciders," Andromeda said, placing four silver scyphs in his palm. He bowed in thanks and hurried to fulfil the order.

"Cider?" Amber asked mildly. "No wine tonight?"

"We work tomorrow. Wine gives you a headache."

Amber shrugged and ran her finger across the crystal fringe on the candle holder. It refracted the light prettily as each crystal settled back into place.

A man stood on a small circular stage in the middle of the room playing a fiddle. He was dressed well, though the elbows of his tunic were neatly patched, and stood with the air of one accustomed to being heard. Next to him, a woman in flowing skirts of shining copper played a lute. She played with eyes closed as the lilting melody washed over her. The man danced about much more ostentatiously, winking at the women who caught his eye as he wove around the stage.

The music was lively, and several couples had taken to the dance floor, with many other revelers content to stamp their feet and clap in time to the beat.

Andromeda eyed the couples warily. “You’re not in a dancing mood tonight, are you?” she asked Amber. It was clear she dreaded the possibility of a yes.

Amber feigned surprise. “Chivilra Turner, are you, per chance, asking me to dance with you?”

“No! No, no, I was just checking in,” she hurried to correct herself.

“Are you sure? That sounded awfully close to a dance proposal,” Amber teased.

“No, definitely not. Forget it,” Andromeda said.

Amber chuckled and let it be. Andromeda was a “single clap after each song” kind of partygoer, and it didn’t pay to push her too far outside her comfort zone.

The drinks arrived. There was a crisp clink as glass hit glass and a rounded thunk as glass tapped wood, the dissonant notes adding to the tavern’s ambiance as the knights toasted. The players started up a new song, and Andromeda asked, “Not that it’s my business, but why don’t you take some time out of the courting game?”

Amber drew her eyes away from the dancers. “What do you mean?”

“Just take some time not worrying about a beau. It might do your head some good.” She took a sip, watching Amber’s reaction.

To buy herself some time to respond, Amber mirrored her sip but spluttered as she struggled with an overly large mouthful. “You might be right.” She coughed. Wiping her mouth with the back of her sleeve, she said, “You know, it can be infuriating how often your advice tends to pan out.”

“When you decide to take it,” Andromeda remarked.

"When I decide to take it," Amber agreed with a smirk.

The singer's chorus rose to a volume that made talking impossible for the moment. The crowd sang along and clapped in a rehearsed manner. This was obviously a popular ditty. Amber hadn't heard it before and turned to listen.

The smile that played on her lips froze, then vanished in an instant as she made out the words:

And we'll send her nether [clap clap clap]
Send her nether once more!
Though she rose from the gutter,
Oh, nether once more!

Amber looked to Andromeda, whose jaw had dropped.

"That's not about . . ." she began.

"They wouldn't dare," Andromeda replied. "That's treason."

The singers launched into the next verse. Bar patrons laughed, some sang along, and all but a few joined in clapping.

Now the basemutt was cunning,
With a mind full of plot.
So, she found her a boy
Whose heart she could besot.
He discovered too late,
From the nether she came,
Placed a crown on her head
And our throne she did claim.

And we'll send her nether [clap clap clap]
Send her nether once more!
Throw her back where she came from,
Oh, nether once more!

"We have to do something," Amber whispered furiously near Andromeda's ear. "They're not even being clever; this is blatantly about Jacqueline."

"If we cause a scene, we only work to strengthen their message," Andromeda retorted.

"So, what should we do?"

"I don't—"

Oh, nether once more!

"I won't stand for this," Amber muttered and clambered up on top of their table, spilling Andromeda's drink and knocking the candle to the floor.

Its flame spluttered and went out.

"Oi!" she shouted over the din.

The people nearest her turned to look, but the players remained oblivious.

"OI!" she roared, smashing her glass on the floor. Her shout and the shatter caused more people to turn to her.

The players, finally noticing, stuttered into silence.

"Some respect for the crown is in order, bard," she yelled from her perch.

Murmurs of dissent rippled around the room.

"Who are you to dictate my set list?" the player called back, feigning amusement over the fire that had flared in his eyes.

"Chivilra Everstar of the Queensguard."

"Queensguard . . ." the player repeated softly, face falling.

"And it's my night off, so be a good lad and play something with a little less treason in it, hey?"

The player started to say something, but Amber jumped down from her table and cut him off. Waving a pointed forefinger around her head she said, "Barkeep! Next round is a gift from our fair Queen; put it on my tab along with the glass." She gestured to the shattered remains on the floor. "And if this worm," she jabbed her finger at the now beet-red player, "spouts any more treason, a gold faering to the woman who shuts him up."

With the promise of a free drink, and the potential to make a faering, the frowns and glares from the crowd quickly smoothed.

"To the Queen!" Andromeda moved to stand beside Amber and held her glass aloft.

"To the Queen!" came a disjointed echo.

A small number still eyed Amber warily, but more joined in the cheer and moved to the bar to claim their pints. The players looked at one another and back to Amber, who stood at ease, chin tilted, eyes fixed. They strummed a few tentative notes, then began a jovial tune about a woman chasing boys from her apple tree. Amber nodded her approval and returned to her seat, Andromeda following close behind.

"That . . ." Andromeda started to say, then shook her head. "That actually went better than expected."

Amber forced a laugh, felt the flush in her cheeks subside and her rapid pulse slow. "You can say that again," she said. "But now I have to cover one basemutt of a tab."

"For the Queen," Andromeda said, tilting the remains of her cider toward Amber.

"For the Queen," Amber sighed. She couldn't stay glum for too long, however, as her announcement had dislodged some fans from the audience who approached her now.

"Chivilra Everstar? Can we buy your next drink?"

"Would you sign my kerchief?"

"You were wonderful in Everden!"

"Can we see your medal?"

Amber leaned back in her chair and accepted a fresh cider gladly. She ignored the amused look Andromeda gave her and reached for the offered quill.

18

SPECIAL DELIVERY

Twilight gathered around the palace gardens like a shawl settling over a woman's shoulders. It had been a warm day and a heady aroma wafted through the hedgerows and hallways. The spicy twang of rosemary cut through the rounded scent of the calendula. Twilight's host of birds bid farewell to their sun-loving sisters and awaited their moon-kissed kin. They bandied their soft songs back and forth between boughs and bushes.

Jacs walked alone—this evening's guardpair consisting of Masterchiv Rathbone and Chiv. Fayworth, who walked five paces behind her—savoring this rare moment to herself. Her soft footfalls alerted her to the shift from gravel path to cobblestones and she followed her feet toward the palace's main courtyard. At this time of evening, most areas of the palace, even the entrance, were relatively peaceful.

However, as Jacs approached, a cacophony of voices rushed toward her. She turned to her guardpair, eyebrows raised.

"Did either of you hear about any visitors to the palace this evening?" she asked.

Both knights shook their heads and moved to walk in front of their Queen as the small group went to investigate.

The courtyard was in an uproar. Four wagons full to bursting with covered cargo lined the circular perimeter. Guardpairs argued with palace staff, each side trying to speak louder and with wilder hand gestures than the other.

"What's all this?" Jacs asked a nearby palace serving boy. His eyes widened when he saw who was addressing him, giving him the appearance of a startled squirrel.

"Y-your Majesty," he stammered, stopping dead in his tracks and dropping to his knees.

Jacs fought the bloom of impatience and asked again, "Do you know what's going on here?"

"Wagons, Your Majesty. Wagons full of crystals from the Lower Realm."

Realization dawned and Jacs thanked the boy, sending him off to finish his task.

"The first delivery of scry crystals," Jacs said. She turned to her guardpair. Masterchiv Rathbone and Chiv. Fayworth both eyed the scene astutely. "I didn't think they'd come this soon."

"What would you have us do, Your Majesty?" Masterchiv Rathbone asked.

Jacs took in the frustrated Lowrian-come guardpairs, the exasperated palace staff, and the hostile palace guardpairs. She clicked her fingers at three members of the palace staff and gathered a small task force.

Speaking quickly, Jacs began to delegate. "The guardpairs have had a long journey up the Cliff. They'll need lodgings and food. We need to send a message to the kitchens to prepare a hot meal and some refreshments. You." She pointed at a serving woman with a button nose and a fidgety air. "Inform Master Marmaduke of our guests and find help to bring trays of refreshments on your way back out. Once you've distributed those, have the guardpairs from the Lower Realm follow you into the dining hall, where they will be given supper." The woman bobbed in understanding and hurried off.

"You." She pointed to the next member of the palace staff, a man roughly her own age with a brown- and blond-flecked goatee. "Go find Master Boreas and whoever else is needed to help, lead the horses and wagons into the stable yard, and tend to the horses." He bowed low and strode away briskly.

"And Alastor." Jacs rounded on the last staff member, an older man she recognized as a past favorite of the dowager King's. "Please find the Council of Four and summon them to the throne room. I will need to speak with them about what is to be done with these crystals." Alastor bowed slowly and returned to the palace.

Spinning to face her knights, she said, "Masterchiv Rathbone, we need to make sure these wagons and their contents are well guarded and that no scry crystal is removed. Can I trust you to organize the palace guardpairs for this task?"

"Of course, Your Majesty. May I recommend, for your safety, that Chiv. Fayworth escort you directly to the throne room?" Masterchiv Rathbone appeared uneasy about the direction to separate the Queen's guard, and Jacs thought this was a reasonable compromise.

"Great idea."

Masterchiv Rathbone shared a knight's salute with Chiv. Fayworth before departing. Both women tapped their wrists together, palms upturned. With a bow for her Queen, she spun on her heel and began organizing a guard escort for the crystals.

Chiv. Fayworth gestured for Jacs to lead the way into the palace when a familiar voice made her turn.

"Jacqueline!"

It was Phillip.

A relief she did not realize she had been hoping for washed over her. He rushed up the few steps to meet her on the threshold of the palace. She would have ignored decorum and embraced him, had a wall of guards not risen between them and swiftly detained him.

"Stop! Stand down!" Jacs commanded.

Phillip, flat on his stomach, face pressed into the cobbles with hands twisted behind his back, muttered through the side of his mouth, "We have to stop meeting like this, Your Majesty."

Jacs laughed gratefully at his attempt to ease the sudden tension and signaled for the guards to help him up and dust him off.

"You came," she said happily, looping her arm through his and leading them into the palace. Phillip's head turned toward the wagons.

"But my things . . ."

"Molly," Jacs addressed a passing serving woman, "have Phillip's things brought to one of the rooms in the contestants' wing. One with a view is preferable. Then ask Master Marmaduke to make an extra plate and send it up to my rooms. He'll be dining with me this evening." She turned her attention back to Phillip. "So, what changed your mind?"

Phillip smiled. "You've always been the brains, it felt silly to not take your advice."

Jacs nudged him playfully. "Smart man. How was the ride up?"

"Terrifying. I don't know how you did that in a balloon."

"I avoided looking down," she said simply, causing him to smile.

"That would have helped. Luckily, they let me sit on one of the wagons. My legs turned to jelly after we made it up the first elevator."

Jacs thought of the zig-zagging constructions of suspended platforms that made up the Bridge. Over a dozen elevators marked the switchbacks along the route. It was not for the faint of heart.

"I can imagine."

Phillip didn't reply, they had stepped into the entrance hall and all attempts at conversation had fled. Mouth open, eyes wide, he took in the white marble pillars, the golden inlays and sconces, the dual sweeping staircases, and the frescoed ceiling. The juxtaposition of having her childhood friend, a boy who only knew her as the farmgirl and aspiring inventor, in her palace tangled her tongue and she struggled to know what to say next.

"So, this is . . . welcome to the palace," she said awkwardly.

"This is where you live now?" he whispered.

"Yes, and I'll be able to give you the grand tour, but you must be hungry and exhausted, and I have to meet with the Councilors about the crystals," she paused to look him over and wrinkled her nose. "Plus . . . you need a bath. Want to start there?"

Phillip drew his eyes away from the ceiling and made a face at her. "Royal smartarse. But that would actually be great."

"I figured."

"Jacqueline! What—" Connor appeared at the top of the stairs and jogged to meet them on the landing. "What's all the commotion outside? Hello," he said to Phillip when he drew level with them. His gaze flicked over Phillip's travel-stained and windswept appearance and lingered on their linked arms.

Jacs gladly made the introductions. "Cornelius, this is my dear friend Phillip Leschi, Master Leschi's son. Phillip, this is Cornelius Frean, former Prince and now my Royal Advisor. Formally addressed as Your Grace." She muttered the last part for Phillip's benefit.

After the initial greetings, Phillip said, "So, Your Grace, you're the boy with the boats?"

Connor laughed. "That I am, it's great to finally meet you, Phillip, I've heard so much about you from Jacs. It sounds like she helped you out of a rough place down there. I'm glad to see you made it up okay. How was the Bridge?"

Phillip bristled slightly beside Jacs, but his reply was cordial. "Definitely too long for my liking, Your Grace."

Connor nodded. "For mine too."

Jacs interjected, "Phillip arrived with the first load of crystals from the Lower Realm. Actually, Cornelius, I need to go meet with the Council about that. Would you mind showing Phillip to the bathhouse and getting him settled in? I'll meet you all in my chambers afterward. I've requested a meal to be brought there for him."

Connor acceded and gestured for Phillip to accompany him. Before the group parted ways, he kissed Jacs lightly on the cheek and gave her hand a comforting squeeze. "Good luck," he said quietly.

Jacs returned the gesture, shifted her shoulders down her back, and stood a little straighter as she said a quick good-bye. With a spring in her step, she followed the path to the throne room, Chiv. Fayworth close behind.

19

GETTING OFF ON A CERTAIN FOOT

"You look like a new man!" Connor exclaimed as Barlow, the shy serving boy Connor had assigned to Phillip's care, led Phillip into Jacs's chambers. Connor had been reclining in one of her chairs by the fire reading a document containing a not-very-promising lead about eggshell weight calculations and eggshell count disparities. Four pages of tight-script notes had informed him that fertilized eggs tended to have slightly thicker shells than unfertilized which meant heavier eggshells.

Depending on how many fledglings the Court decided to have each year, this could increase the weight-to-quantity ratio, but from what Connor was reading, not by enough to be significant. He happily put the disappointing documents to the side and stood to usher Phillip to the chair opposite.

Phillip, now with damp hair, a clean face, fresh clothes, and the soft fragrance of lavender clinging to him, sat down gratefully. His eyelids carried a post-bath sleepy quality. With a sigh, he sank into the velvet cushions and stretched his legs out in front of him.

"Long day?" Connor asked.

"You have no idea," Phillip said, then, appearing to remember who he was speaking to, sat up straighter and rested his hands on his knees. Phillip glanced at Connor, then his eyes shifted as he took in the splendor.

"And this is Jacqueline's room?" he asked in a muted voice.

"Yes," Connor replied.

"Wow, if you knew her room back home, you'd know how wild this is."

"I think I can guess," Connor said. "I visited Bridgeport over a year ago."

Phillip shot him a look that seemed to weigh his response. Apparently concluding that there had been no offense intended, he visibly relaxed and said, "A lot's changed since then."

A log shifted in the fireplace and both men turned their attention to the flames.

"So," Phillip began awkwardly, "how's she been?"

Connor saw concern flicker across the other man's features. An emotion that hovered between jealousy and pride sparked in his chest. He suddenly felt protective of Jacs, and indignant that this stranger had just waltzed in expecting details on her new life. Connor had Her Majesty's privacy to protect. "In general?" he asked.

Phillip nodded.

"She's doing well. I mean, it's been a steep learning curve, but that comes with any big change," he said confidently.

Phillip eyed him shrewdly. "Really?"

"Yes."

"She's doing well?"

"Yes." Connor felt his confidence slip.

"She's a long way from home, a long way from friends and family who she's not allowed to visit, pushed to hijacking a couple of Griffins in the middle of the night to see us, all the while dealing with the fact that her mother and mine are still missing. And she's doing well?" Phillip leaned forward, forearms on his knees and glared at Connor. All sleepiness now gone, he sat alert with a spark flickering behind his eyes.

"Well . . . she's—"

"Cut the hot air, I've been—we've all been worried sick about her. You're closest to her, I'm assuming, given that cutesy display downstairs. Now tell me honestly, how is she doing?"

Shame replaced whatever emotion had flared in Connor's chest. Cold, clammy shame that dripped down his spine and made his scalp tingle. He clasped his hands loosely and tapped his left thumb on top of his right.

"Okay, you're right. It's . . . it's been tough, tough for her, tough to watch. Although she's been much happier since she flew down to Bridgeport. More hopeful." Connor met Phillip's steady gaze and frowned.

"What I still don't get," Phillip said slowly, "is why she had to sneak down in the first place. She's the Queen. Why didn't she just, I dunno, command a visit?"

Connor sighed. "It's not that simple."

"Why not?" Phillip asked, his tone much more conversational than before.

"It's just a bit more complicated than snapping your fingers and seeing something done. There's the Council to consider." Connor was tired, he really didn't feel in the mood to explain the complexities of palace politics and power hierarchies to a Lowrian blacksmith.

"Shouldn't they work for her?"

"Again, it's not that simple."

"Well, it should be."

"Well, it's not," Connor snapped, then softened. "Especially her being from the Lower Realm, she's had a lot of learning, training, and practicing to do before she could jump into the deep end feetfirst. I think the Council wanted to ease her into the role of Queen and all that came with it. Unfortunately, that's not really Jacs's style. They, er . . . haven't been seeing eye to eye on a lot of matters."

Phillip scoffed mildly and said, "That'll be their loss."

Connor smiled.

"And you care about her?" Phillip asked, extending his left hand on his knee to rest with his right forearm on the other.

"Of course," Connor said immediately. He felt the other man size him up and avoided dropping his gaze.

"And you're willing to fight for her?"

"Naturally." Connor bristled.

"Don't be flippant with me," Phillip said, a knife edge in his voice. His eyes reflected the fire in the hearth. He jabbed a finger at Connor and said, "Listen. I don't care if you're the Prince or Advisor or whatever. Worse they can do to me is send me back to Bridgeport or throw me to the guards. I'm used to both, and the guards I bet I know more intimately than you do." The firelight shifted around his features, and Connor noticed the silvery outline of a scar spanning from cheek to jaw. "I need to know she's got people in her corner who will protect her, look out for her. This Realm is shiny and sparkly, and everyone's got these big stupid grins on their faces, but I know what you people are capable of. If she's in a snake pit, I need you to tell me." A plea lingered in the air, and Phillip, as if to counteract it, lowered his voice to a deadly whisper.

"And if you're planning on hurting her or using her, I swear on my mother's life and my father's grave that I will climb up from whatever pit they throw me into and make sure you feel every drop of pain you inflict on her tenfold."

Connor blanched but did not back down. “Phillip,” he said softly. “I love her.”

“You love her?” Phillip sneered.

“Yes.” Why was it so easy saying it in front of this near stranger when he still couldn’t say it to her?

Phillip was staring at him, eyebrow raised in either question or doubt.

“Have for years,” Connor elaborated. “I will breathe my last breath defending her. I appreciate that you’re worried about her. I am too. But I would also caution you to be careful about what bridges you burn in your desire to protect her. Up here, your allies are few and far between, and many will be looking to your actions to justify their prejudices.” He held up a hand as Phillip opened his mouth to speak. “Don’t forget, you also represent Jacs now. If you go around picking fights with Dames and Lordsons, and . . . Advisors, the Lowrian stain you spread will taint Jacs’s reputation.”

“Lowrian stain?” Phillip said, pushing to his feet.

Connor fought the fire that flared in his chest and took a breath. “Phillip, you are a friend of Jacs’s and that makes you a friend of mine. I’m trying to help, and I’m just being honest. I don’t feel that way, but that is what people up here will think of you. Especially with reactions like that.”

Phillip glared at him for a moment longer, looked down at his hands, and returned to his seat. “Fair point,” he conceded.

Connor relaxed a fist he had unconsciously formed and settled his back deeper into his chair. Neither quite knew what to say next, and luckily the opening of the door broke the silence.

“Good! You’re both here, but the food’s not. Adaine, can you pop to the kitchens and see where it’s got to?” Jacs paused, considered her words, and supplied, “If you find it there, get help to bring it back here, please. Thank you. Hi.” Jacs filled the room like sunlight after a storm. Adaine, who had followed in her wake, bobbed a bow and hurried to do her Queen's bidding. Jacs turned her warmth to the frosty duo by the fire.

Walking by Phillip's chair, she gave his shoulder a familiar squeeze and moved to sit in the chair beside Connor's.

"How did it go with the Council?" he asked.

Jacs leaned back and closed her eyes a moment. "Surprisingly well, actually." Opening them again she said, "They were extremely supportive, had a plan ready for how to dispose of the crystals too. It all felt like a well-designed machine being switched on for the first time."

"You sound surprised?" Phillip commented.

Jacs scratched above her eyebrow. "I've had trouble with the Council ever since I became Queen, but they've been significantly more agreeable since I returned from Bridgeport." She turned to Connor. "Which reminds me, while I was there, I suggested we invite the Court to the gala, it might be a nice thank-you for all they did that day in the Lower Realm."

"That's a great idea, also a reminder for the people that you are their Courtier Queen," Connor commented.

Phillip looked back and forth from Jacs to Connor in confusion. Jacs, noticing, supplied: "The Council is throwing a gala tomorrow evening to celebrate . . . well, me. From what I've heard there will be dancers, a feast, and possibly fireworks?" She looked hopefully at Connor who shook his head with a smile.

"It's supposed to be a surprise, and you won't get any more clues from me!" he said.

She scrunched up her nose playfully at him and continued. "And since I've ridden with the Court, that makes me a *Courtier*, so it's fitting they attend. They've been a huge help in swaying public opinion in my favor."

The last comment faltered and hovered in the air. As if struck by a sudden thought, Jacs sat up straighter and rounded on Phillip. "Oh!

You'll have to attend the gala! We'll get you a suit and you can meet everybody." She smiled hopefully at him.

Connor noticed worry lines form, then dissipate, on Phillip's brow.

"Sure," Phillip said cautiously. "That sounds like fun."

"You'll be fine," Connor said encouragingly. "And if you want, I'll show you the side exits you can slip away through if the whole event becomes too much. I know I always feel better at these kinds of functions if I know where my escape route is."

Some of the tension eased out of Phillip's shoulders, and he nodded toward Connor appreciatively.

Adaine and two other kitchen staff entered the room and laid out several plates on the low table between the group around the fire. Phillip's eyes grew wide as he scanned the selection of meats, cheeses, crusty rolls, dried figs, fresh grapes, and as many jams, spreads, and oils as he had fingers.

Connor saw Jacs smile fondly at Phillip and pushed himself to his feet.

"Well, I was fortunate enough to have Phillip's company all to myself this evening," he said. "It was wonderful to finally meet you, but if you'll both excuse me, I am going to turn in." Jacs stood with him and happily accepted a kiss on the cheek.

"You don't have to go," she said, folding into his embrace.

"I know, but you two have a lot of catching up to do," he said quietly, kissing the tip of her nose. "And I have a few last-minute pieces to place for the gala. Have you seen Courtierdame Glowra and Courtier Bishop this evening?"

"Anya's been in the greenhouses for the past two days, and Lena said she was spending the evening with her—it seemed serious, but she wouldn't tell me when I asked." Jacs shrugged.

Connor nodded. "Okay, I'll speak with Edith. Plus, I can see about getting Phillip's wardrobe sorted."

Phillip chimed in. "I brought clothes."

Connor nodded and replied delicately: "And we can provide whatever else you might need. You'll definitely need something for the gala. Occasions and fashions are slightly different up here, often requiring different garments."

He said his good nights, shared a look of understanding with Phillip, gathered his documents, and left for his own chambers.

In his rooms, Edith was waiting for him with a tea tray and a lit fire.

"Your Grace," she said by way of greeting, but quickly jumped to the point. "The Councilors have sent a few last-minute adjustments and notes for tomorrow's gala. They've left the last-minute pieces for you to straighten out. It's not much, and I got started on all except the line they wrote about the new addition to the guest list. Apparently, Her Majesty informed them this evening that a Phillip Leschi will be in attendance from the Lower Realm?" The last comment rose as a question and Edith waited for confirmation.

Connor removed his boots and warmed his hands by the fire. "Yes, Master Leschi's son, a childhood friend of Her Majesty's, will be staying with us for the foreseeable future at her invitation."

Edith raised an eyebrow and waited for him to elaborate.

"We like him," Connor answered her unasked question. "I'm worried that the chip on his shoulder might get him into trouble, but he has Jacs's best interest at heart and appears to be almost aggressively loyal to her so . . . that's good."

Edith poured the tea and offered him a cup. He gestured for her to take one as well. It was a well-rehearsed ritual, and Edith always brought a second cup with her in anticipation of it.

"Oh, and we'll need to arrange a wardrobe for Phillip that will help him blend in a little more, and an outfit for the gala. What is this?" Connor asked as Edith placed a letter into his hands.

"From the dowager King," she answered, taking a sip of her tea. "It arrived this afternoon."

Connor broke the seal and read its contents. His face fell.

"What is it?" Edith asked

"It ah . . ." Connor cleared his throat. "It appears Father is not returning for the gala. Nor will he be returning in the next few months. The sea air is apparently agreeing with him." He read through the letter again. "He also cannot part with the writings he kept of Mother's just yet but will send some of them along in the next few weeks."

"Queen Ariel's writings?"

"I had asked if he had any. Jacs was looking for information about finding . . ." He glanced up warily.

"Her mother?" Edith finished. Connor nodded, not yet wanting to share details of the little book with names of missing boys.

"And Her Majesty thinks that the late Queen might have known where they would be kept?" Edith asked.

"Sort of. I think she's desperate for any information. I mean, people don't just disappear, especially under the eyes of the Queen."

"Unless you're attercoppe prey, no," Edith said weakly, attempting to lighten his mood.

Connor managed a smile. A creature that stole away badly behaved boys in the night actually fit the description of what they were looking for pretty well. But that was a children's story, and this was real life. The culprits had to be more substantial than an attercoppe.

His mind wandered to the wagonloads of crystals he had seen in the courtyard. "That was the one useful thing about the scry crystals," he said. "Much easier to track people down."

Edith nodded. "And they did make it easier to share information across the Queendom."

"I guess most tools come with a price, along with those who would corrupt their purpose." He rose, retrieved a gilded hand mirror from his dresser, and returned to his seat. "I mean, on the one hand, it would be so easy if Jacs could just say *Maria Tabart* and find out where her mother is." The mirror fogged over in response to his words. He watched the fog swirl for a moment, but no image appeared on its surface. "And we could even use it to track her down. Find Maria Tabart." He said the last words into the mirror.

Again, the mirror fogged over and this time a light spun around the outer rim. This light was supposed to act like a compass and would point in the direction of the crystal nearest to the person named. Without a target though, the light spun around its perimeter three times before fading with the fog.

"But consider, in the wrong hands, someone could just say *Cornelius Frean* and—" Again the mirror fogged over, but this time was replaced with a bird's-eye view of himself, as he was, sitting by the fire holding a mirror in his hands. The image, while distinct, had a shimmering quality on the surface, as if a thin veil were obstructing the picture.

"What in the—"

Edith stood to get a better view of the mirror. Immediately, her eyes lifted to scan the ceiling and the tops of his bookshelves.

"There," she said, pointing to an object set far back on a top shelf. Connor stood to get a better view and saw, next to a line of books he had not touched in years, between a model ship and a portrait of his late uncle, a small lumpy object covered in a deep purple cloth.

His desk chair screeched across the stone floor as he dragged it over to the bookshelf. Stepping onto the chair, he stretched up on the tips of his toes to reach the little object.

The cloth fell open in his hands and he saw what was unmistakably a scry crystal. Half the size of those used in the Contest of Queens tasks, but a scry crystal all the same.

He quickly covered it back up and stuffed it between two couch cushions. Looking up at Edith, he was at a loss.

Edith, meanwhile, seized the mirror from where he had left it on his chair by the fire and said, "Jacqueline Frean." The mirror did not shift from Edith's reflection.

She sighed with relief, but Connor took the mirror from her and said, "Jacqueline Daidala, Jacqueline Tabart, Jacs Tabart, Jacs Frean." After he said the last name, the mirror fogged over before clearing to reveal Connor's own reflection. Nothing more.

They looked at each other, then back to the cushions that concealed the scry crystal. Almost to himself, he said, "Jacs was so careful to erase every name she had registered from these crystals, but I didn't even think to erase mine. Who would be spying on me?" he asked softly.

"And how often does Her Majesty visit your room? Because whoever planted that crystal would have been able to monitor her when she was here," Edith said just as softly. Both spoke as if afraid the crystal could hear them.

Connor felt as though sticky fingers were creeping across his skin. How long had that crystal been there? Who had planted it? And what had they hoped to see? He hated the idea that he had somehow been used to spy on Jacs, and he hated the idea that so many private moments had been broadcast to whomever thought to watch.

Edith watched the emotions flicker across his face and said suddenly, "Leave it to me, Your Grace. I'll dispose of it properly."

And without waiting for confirmation, she wrapped it in a cloth napkin and shoved it deep within her apron pocket.

"Are you all right?" She looked up at him with a crease of concern between her brows.

Connor, still stunned, his skin crawling, simply nodded. She reached up and patted his cheek. "I'll deal with this. You get some rest. And . . ." she hesitated before adding, "I would personally wait until after the gala to share this information with Her Majesty."

"Yeah," Connor said distractedly. "And we'll have to scour the palace to make sure there aren't any more of these hidden around. Or, better yet, let's meet with the palace scryers after the gala and make sure to unregister all names. That would make the crystals useless even if there are thousands hiding around the Queendom." He sighed and scrubbed his face.

Edith helped him change into his bedclothes, collected the tea tray, and departed with a comforting look over her shoulder. She paused at the doorway, tray on her hip, and Connor could see she was trying to find something to say.

"We'll get to the bottom of it, Your Grace," she said finally. "Best not to dwell, worry's only good for grinding teeth and premature balding."

Connor snorted and waved her away. Determined to take her advice, he picked up his copy of *Uncertain Tides* and attempted to distract himself. Stretched on the plush sofa in front of the fire, he quickly became engrossed in the seafaring saga. With a mind much lighter, he felt his eyelids droop and gently close. The book fell from his hands, and the muted thud of spine on carpet reached deaf ears. His last thoughts were tinged with brine and the caw of imagined seagulls. An illusory purple glow lingered softly at the peripheral of his vision.

20

A DEFIANT LITTLE DAISY

"Almost done?" Lena asked softly.

Anya, who had been weaving stems into submission at the base of an elaborate bouquet, gave a start and spun around to where Lena had snuck up behind her. The room smelled amazing, and flowers in dark shades of blues, purples, and bright yellows with bundled sprigs of deep or dusty greenery decorated every available surface. Dahlia, lilies, lavender, and lupine were caught up in gorgeous arrangements or littered the benches and floor.

Bursts of gold shone from ribbons, jewel-studded filigree, and trinkets nestled in the flora. Anya, arms full of blossoms, tucked the final strand of ribbon into the base of the bouquet she had been working on and secured it in place with the two jewel-tipped pins plucked from between her teeth.

"Hi, Lee," she said, sweeping Lena into a one-armed hug. She was careful to hold the still-wet stems out and away from Lena's gown. "Almost. At this point I'm just fluffing." The palace florists hovered over their own bouquets nearby like bumblebees. Some acknowledged Lena's entrance, many were too wrapped up in their blossoms to spare a glance.

"Ever the perfectionist," Lena said fondly, reaching up to kiss her on the cheek. She detached herself and walked about the room, admiring the different displays Anya and the other florists had spent the last two days arranging.

The difficulty with flowers, of course, was they all bloomed at different times and only lasted so long once cut. So big occasions like the Queen's gala required excessive planning, timing, and precision. Wilted blooms were not acceptable; each arrangement had to look fresh. Lena had watched in wonder as bunches of peonies were gently massaged just above the stem and placed in vases of warm water to coax them into opening faster. Tricks of the trade unfolding before her eyes like magic. Apart from their meeting with Master Moira, Lena had barely seen Anya outside the palace greenhouses since the day after Jacqueline returned from the Lower Realm.

"Have you eaten?" Lena asked, inspecting a delicate centerpiece composed of a single sunflower surrounded by tiny white blossoms.

Anya made a noncommittal sound.

"I thought that would be the case." Lena leaned forward to smell a vase bursting with lilac, the sweet fragrance transporting her to a warm summer's day walking through the grounds of her estate. Opening her eyes to the greenhouses, she said, "I have arranged something when you're ready to put the petals down."

Anya shot her a curious glance. "What kind of something?"

"You'll have to wait to find out," Lena said with a coy smile, but apprehension pulled the corners of her lips down, and she turned away quickly before Anya could notice.

Elaborately removing a single stem from the bouquet she had been working on, Anya set the bundle down and presented the lone lily to Lena with a flourish.

"Okay, I'm ready."

Lena happily tucked the lily into the braided coil at the nape of her neck and held out her hand. Anya said her good-nights to the other florists, and the two women exited the greenhouses through the glass double doors.

Lena led the way with determination in each step. They walked away from the greenhouses around the edge of the palace, following garden paths and skirting the lawns until the lights of the main building twinkled behind them. Lena met every question Anya posed with a cryptic answer, if she answered at all. The darkness slowly enveloped the two women and soon the only sounds heard above the natural night orchestra were their soft footfalls.

Arriving at the crest of a hillock, Lena stopped in front of a folly. The ornamental building stood proudly, like a rook on a chessboard. Cylindrical in shape and topped with a crenellated tower, the folly bore spheres of lantern light around the stone battlements. Westly, Lena's most loyal servant, stood to attention at the entrance and gave a little bow as the two women approached.

"Good evening, Your Elegance," he said to Lena.

"Good evening, Westly, I trust everything is in order?" Lena asked, eyeing the candlelit stairway through the open door.

"Everything is as you instructed," he said with a small bow and a fleeting, anxious look toward Anya.

"Excellent. Thank you, Westly."

Anya looked back and forth between the two. "What?" she began, but Lena just pulled her toward the door. The air felt cooler around them as they entered the stone building, but Anya's hand was warm, and the edges of the stairwell were dotted with the cheery glow of tealights.

Step by step, they ascended the spiral staircase. With one hand tracing the outer wall and the other behind her, holding fast to Anya's hand, Lena felt both tethers to be the only things keeping her feet on the ground. Her apprehension was a rising sun inside her chest, guiding her upward inch by inch.

Soon they reached the upper landing. Lena took a breath in front of the wooden ornate door, and gently lifted the latch. The door swung open to reveal a sky full of stars and a balcony full of fairy lights. Lena heard Anya gasp softly behind her and smothered a grin. Evenly spaced crenels encircled the stonework floor at the top of the turret. Each square notch housed a lit candle in a small lantern that cast an ornate shadow on the surrounding stonework. The space was strewn with plush floor cushions and cozy-looking blankets. A low wooden table held a picnic dinner, a bottle of wine, and two glasses. The sea of stars extended miles above their heads.

"What's all this for?" Anya asked softly.

"Do you like it?" Lena spun to see Anya's reaction, beaming.

"It's beautiful. So beautiful, but why . . ."

"Because you've been so busy lately. I decided to make the most of your night off. Plus"—she paused nervously and held Anya's hands in hers—"this way we have a chance to talk."

Anya grinned, candlelight shining in her brown eyes. "Lucky me." Anya moved to embrace her, but Lena pulled away and led her to the table spread with food. Avoiding her eyes, she poured the wine and offered Anya a glass, the moment of recoil vanishing in a blink.

They sat at the low table, and the next few moments passed in relative silence. Silence from Anya, who must have been starving given the rate with which she inhaled her food, and silence from Lena, who was wrestling with the words she knew she had to say. Words written in a sharper hand floated before her eyes and loomed over their pleasant evening.

"How's everything with the flowers going?" Lena finally asked.

Anya leaned back on one hand and sighed contently. "It's . . . it's been incredible. There's so much more variety than what I'm used to back at your manor, and some of the things the palace florists can do with a few stems . . . I'm definitely learning a lot."

Lena played with the rim of her wineglass thoughtfully. "And when this is all over, would you want to stay on with the palace florists?"

Anya looked at her sharply. "Did you hear something?"

"No, I was just asking," Lena said, not looking at her.

"Oh." Anya visibly relaxed and sipped her wine. "I'm not sure, I guess it would depend."

"On?"

"Where you were."

Lena smiled, eyes still on her wineglass. She swirled the contents around slowly, watching the dark liquid leave streaky tears in its wake.

"Where . . ." Anya sat forward, placing her glass on the table. "Where do you want to be?"

Lena looked at her and saw a soft crinkle above her nose. "I, well, I don't have to return to Terrelle anytime soon. Mother sent a message this morning and there was no indication she was thinking of relinquishing her title yet."

"That's a relief," Anya said.

"Yes . . . but she is also not coming for the gala and has refused my request that she visit."

"Well, she's likely busy, I'm sure—"

"Too busy to attend an important gala for the Queen? A gala she was expressly invited to?" Lena cut in.

"She must have her reasons, plus you are technically her represe—"

"It was a purposeful slight, Anya," Lena said with a snap.

"A slight against Jacqueline?"

"Yes . . . and no," Lena said, looking away again.

"I mean, we know she doesn't like Lowrians. It makes sense she found an excuse not to show her support for a Lowrian Queen, and she's likely not alone in that. It's not right, but I don't think it will look too bad, especially with you here." Anya placed a reassuring palm on Lena's knee. She frowned. "But you know all that already. What is it?"

Lena didn't know how to start. Her mother's most recent correspondence danced in her mind's eye, her stern voice whispering over her shoulder. Anya was right, despite Lord Glowra's intended slight, with Lena in attendance, no insult would be perceived. Jacqueline was also still so new to court dynamics and power plays that it would have likely gone unnoticed anyway. That was an issue for another day, and hopefully time would soften her mother's opinion of the new Queen. But it was more than that.

Her mother had refused to see Lena since she had openly started courting Anya. Lord Glowra had left right after the last task of the contest with barely a good-bye, had not even looked at Anya as she waved to her from the family carriage, and each letter Lena received was entirely void of any mention of Anya's existence. Until this last letter.

"Lee, what is it?" Anya repeated, apprehension flecking her cadence.

"Anya . . . there's something you need to know," she began. Just as they had countless times in her childhood, she felt the ghost of her mother's fingers curl over her shoulder. Mild pressure was applied through each fingertip, a warning.

"Lee, what's going on?"

"My mother"—she didn't know how to start—"in her letter, she said that she disapproves of . . . us."

Anya kept her face impassive, but one eyebrow twitched up. "I see. Well, that's nothing new. She's been telling me I would never be good enough for you since the day I first gave you a daisy. I remember. I was six." She picked at a hole in a lace cushion cover as she spoke.

Although her tone was light, Lena caught the downturned corners of her mouth.

Lena bit her lip. "Obviously, she's wrong. But she's threatened to send you away."

"What?" Anya's head shot up.

Lena fought to keep her voice level. "She threatened to transfer you to the Hemlock Estate." At a blank look from Anya, Lena explained quietly: "Where William Hemlock is serving the remainder of his sentence." She hugged her elbows. The implication rippled from her words. William had hung in the stocks under Queen Diana's ruling for the longest stretch of time in Terrelle's recorded history. His victim's identity had, of course, been protected, but the length of his punishment suggested either crimes against multiple survivors, a particularly egregious act, or a highborn survivor. Only a small number of people knew the truth: Lord Glowra, Lordson Hemlock, and Lena.

His name decayed on her tongue. She could not explain the true horror of her mother's threat. As Lena tried to organize the right sequence of words, a glimpse of the past emerged like a figure in her peripheral vision, an unexpected face reflected in a looking glass. The shadow that had haunted her with renewed vigor since the second task. Suddenly a different pair of ghostly hands caressed her. One grasped her wrist, the other circled her neck. The memory of his stale breath as he whispered in her ear sent ice through her veins. Panic burst in her mind like lightning from a storm cloud. She pushed it down, forced it away. It did not serve her. She was done dwelling on a past she had escaped.

His hands loosened and vanished from her wrist and neck.

Anya's face paled in the moonlight, she swallowed, licked her lips, and looked away. "She can't."

"She will try, but—" Lena began, but Anya cut her off.

"So what, I leave you or get shipped to that beast's estate?"

"I won't let that happen, Anya."

"It's not right! I love you, Lee. I mean, I'm a Courtier now! Doesn't that count for anything? It shouldn't matter if . . ." Anya waved her hands vaguely.

Lena steeled herself for what she knew she had to do; a flurry of butterflies swarmed in her chest.

"No it shouldn't matter. It never mattered. It only matters to her and her warped sense of social status. I used to try so hard to please her, to do everything she wanted me to do, to the point where I would try to anticipate what I thought she wanted so she didn't have to waste energy on telling me to do something because it would already be done. Years I've spent trying to please her, and still she would deny me the one thing I've truly wanted. You. You're all I've ever wanted. Anya, I love you." Lena felt momentum build behind her tripping words and forced herself to stop.

To breathe.

"Yeah, but that doesn't seem to be enough for her Lordship. I swear—"

"Anya," Lena said slowly, "I love you."

At her tone, Anya froze and looked up.

"I love you, flower girl. I love how you light up over an unbloomed lily. I love how your hand fits perfectly in mine, and how your nose crinkles when you smile. I love that you cut the frosting off your cake and always give me the bigger piece when we split a scone. I love the way you skip every second step when you climb stairs, unless you're holding my hand because you know I have shorter legs than you. I love you so much it scares me. I don't care what my mother thinks. Not anymore. What I do care about is you, and I know that no life is worth living without you. I can't ask you to entice a Lord's ire unknowingly, so I'm telling you all of this because it is not lightly that I ask you to defy my mother."

"Lee, what are you—" Anya began and gasped as Lena shifted to kneel in front of her. Tears glittered in the corners of her eyes.

From the bodice of her dress, Lena withdrew a small hexagonal velvet box. With shaking fingers, she lifted the latch to reveal a golden ring perched in the middle of a circle of embroidered violets. Three large diamonds sparkled in gold settings.

Anya's hands flew to her mouth, her eyes flicking from the ring to Lena and back.

Fighting the lump in her throat, Lena asked, "Courtier Anya Bishop, I give you my heart, my life, my name. I love you, now and forever. Will you marry me?"

An eternity passed in an instant.

"Yes," Anya whispered. Then louder, "Yes!"

"Yes?"

"Of course! Yes! Yes!" Anya laughed through the tears that flowed freely down her cheeks and pulled Lena into her arms. With excited fumbling, they both slid the ring onto Anya's finger. Shining faces were peppered with tears and kisses, and the evening passed in a joyful blur, the two women shining under the light of a thousand stars. Their wax imitations flickering in lanterns around them.

At one point, Lena lit a tall candle on the edge of the balcony that spluttered with gold sparks, and two minutes later, Westly burst through the door with a bottle of champagne and three crystal flutes. He appeared slightly out of breath and beaming, first wringing Anya's hand.

"Congratulations, dear girl, you take good care of my Lena."

Then he pulled Lena into a delighted embrace.

"Never a doubt, of course she'd say yes."

He popped and poured the stardust libation.

"To many, many years of happiness." He toasted them, eyes brimming with unshed tears.

Long after Westly had excused himself, after the candlewicks dipped low and the wineglasses were emptied, after heartbeats slowed and words subsided, Anya took Lena's hands in hers. Smiling softly, she looked down at her engagement band glittering on her fourth finger and drew Lena's knuckles up to brush her lips.

"When I was six years old," she began in a low voice, "I picked you a daisy and you smiled at me and put it in your hair. I remember thinking even then that you were the most beautiful girl I had ever seen."

Lena blushed and ducked her head.

"When your mother saw, she plucked the flower from your hair and tossed it out the window into the gardens." Lena frowned as Anya continued. "After she'd scolded me, I snuck outside and found the little flower under the windowsill and pressed it between the pages of a book. I don't know why I kept it at the time." Her voice trailed off, and she dropped Lena's hand to search in her pocket for a moment. Withdrawing her closed fist, she continued. "After all these years, I still think you're the most beautiful girl I've ever seen, but now I know that you are so much more than that. You are kind and brave and so generous." She took a shuddering breath. "If I could give you a daisy every day to make you smile, I would." Twisting her fist upward, she slowly uncurled her fingers and held her hand out to Lena.

Sitting in the middle of her palm was a simple gold band with a clear crystal at its center. Lena looked closer and saw, preserved in the stone, a tiny pressed daisy. The petals had been carefully spaced and placed, yet one bore signs of damage. Unlike the others, it was bent at an odd angle and had been torn at the end.

Lena's mouth opened in shock and she met Anya's apprehensive gaze.

"I've been carrying this with me for the past two years. I never dreamed I would be able to give it to you, and I know it's not much," Anya said hurriedly, "but—"

"It's perfect," Lena said, smiling. She eagerly held her left hand out, letting it fall from the wrist, and wiggled her fourth finger. Obliging, Anya slid the ring home. The stone shone in the dying light of the candles.

"Flower girl," Lena said softly, "you have always been enough." She reached up and cupped Anya's cheek with her palm. Anya caught her waist and drew her close.

In the soft glow of candlelight, with a pale moon rising overhead, the two women waltzed to a melody only they could hear. Smiles wide and hearts afire, Anya took the lead and soon Lena was twisting in her arms, dipping low, twirling away, and spinning back in. Bodies aligned. Lips met.

A little voice whispered from Lena's heart to her head. *This is home.*

21

RULES TO KEEP, RULES TO BEND, AND RULES TO BREAK

"You're out late," a voice said from the shadows.

"You are correct," Amber conceded, squinting a little to make out the speaker.

Andromeda had dropped her off at her quarters long after Amber had given up on convincing her partner to cross the threshold of the Dipping Wick. A few minutes sitting in bed had left her restless and needing movement, so Amber had taken to walking around the barracks in the moonlight. The cool night air was a welcome refreshment.

"And you've been drinking." The voice was somewhat familiar, but Amber couldn't place it.

"Two for two. Remedy for a lost beau, I'm afraid. Who are you, oh observant one?" she said with a mock bow. Her smile widened when she saw Dyna Flent step into the light. She wore a loose-fitting tunic and leggings—civilian clothes—and leaned against the wall, arms crossed.

"Ah, Flent," Amber said in acknowledgment, "a pleasure."

"All mine," Flent said smoothly.

Amber cleared her throat. "What are you doing up?"

"Couldn't sleep," Flent said, pushing herself off the wall to approach. Amber took a reflexive step back, causing Flent to raise an eyebrow.

"Do you mind if I walk with you, Chiv. Everstar? I find most nights are better with company."

Amber wished for a witty reply, but the fog between her ears only allowed her to come up with, "Yes. Nights are long."

Flent cocked her head to the side, bemused, and gestured for Amber to lead the way. They walked slowly through the high-walled passageways between the buildings. A strip of stars floated above their heads, and their path was lit from below with the moonlit shine of white marble inlaid in the cobbles at even intervals. At every major junction, a torch cast its warm yellow light against the flickering shadows.

"Are you always this chatty?" Flent asked after several minutes passed in relative silence.

Amber forced a laugh. "It's been a long day, and I wasn't expecting company."

Flent nodded. They turned a corner, following the stone masonry of the barracks. "Sorry to hear about your beau."

Amber cursed her loose tongue and grunted noncommittally.

Flent took a new tack. "I saw you in practice today."

Amber looked up.

"You were amazing," Flent said eagerly.

"Oh," Amber said, "thank you." Why couldn't she think of anything more interesting to say? Her foot caught on an uneven section of stone, and she stumbled slightly. Flent reached out to steady her, and her touch sent a prickle up Amber's arm. She didn't mind the sensation.

Flent let her go and said, "Do you think you could show me some time?"

"Show you?"

"That move you did with Chiv. Turner. She had her pads down low and you swept with one foot and came around with the elbow." Flent attempted to mime a very approximate replication. "And in the blink of an eye, you had her flat on her back."

Amber found herself smiling. "That one works great when you're shorter than your opponent—which I usually am." She gestured to her stature. "Brings them to your level." Flent laughed, and their eyes met. Amber felt a jolt somewhere around her navel and a tingling in her palms. She looked away.

"So, I guess it will work well against me?" Flent said playfully. She stopped in the middle of a courtyard and turned to face Amber, feet shifting easily into a pre-stance, ready.

With a grin, Amber found herself mirroring Flent, sinking low and bringing her hands up. "Let's find out," she said, and pounced.

Flent moved to block half a heartbeat too late and fumbled her footing. Amber shook her head, straightened, and directed, "Shift your weight further forward, and sink more into the hips. They're your powerhouse, so use them."

"Like this?" Flent asked, adjusting her stance and falling just short of where she needed to be.

Amber appraised her attempt and before she realized what she was doing had circled around behind her, aligned her left foot with Flent's back foot as an anchor, and adjusted her hips deeper into the proper stance. She had done this many times when training recruits, but Flent turned her head to look at her. Recruits never did that. And never *like* that. As Flent's curls shifted across her shoulders, Amber caught the soft scent of jasmine. Their eyes met. Amber's hands hesitated on Flent's hips, and she noted with sudden electricity the individual points of contact along their bodies. A new constellation.

Amber's balance shifted unexpectedly, thanks to the Gilded Talon, and she froze, stepped back, and shook her head. "No, no. This," she cleared her throat, "this isn't appropriate. I'm not your partner or your training officer, and I'm not a guard," she said, Andromeda's stern warning sounding in her ears and popping the happy bubble that had risen around her midriff.

"Surely you can bend the rules just a little?" Flent said coyly, dropping her hands to where Amber's had been on her hips a moment before.

Amber flexed her fingers and looked around them. They were alone in a small walled courtyard. "No, I can share the name of the drill with your training officer, but I wouldn't disrespect your progress by interfering."

Flent seemed to deflate somewhat, and Amber fought the urge to bring the smile back to her face. "Thank you for the company, Flent. But I am going to turn in for the night."

"Can I walk you back to your rooms?" Flent asked.

Amber couldn't think of a good enough excuse that didn't include revealing the cause of her sweating palms, so she nodded and began to walk away.

Flent fell into step beside her, some of the swagger gone from her stride.

"Listen," Flent began. "I didn't mean to cause offense. I wasn't trying to overstep."

"No, you're fine," Amber replied. "There's no harm in asking. Your position is an interesting one too, which makes things a little more complicated."

"My position?"

"You know, being a guard working exclusively with knights of the Queensguard. It blurs the lines between ranks a little."

"But not enough to bend the rules?" Flent asked, looking at Amber.

"No."

"Not even the more arbitrary ones?" Flent asked lightly.

"Like?"

"Like *We don't court guards.*" The last words were a rough imitation of Andromeda, and Amber looked up at her with a start. Flent's sage eyes glittered mischievously. "I saw you watching me today in practice, Chiv. Everstar."

Amber felt her mouth go dry. "Observing your form."

"My form?" Flent said, amusement in her voice.

"Not like that. Your fighting form."

"Ah, I see," Flent said. "Any pointers?"

Amber rubbed her knuckles along her jaw. "You tend to leave yourself open to low blows, especially on your left."

"Hmm," Flent mused. "Like from the sweeping maneuver you started to show me?"

Amber could have kicked herself. "Or something similar."

"I see," Flent said and sighed elaborately. "If only I had someone to teach me."

Amber made a noncommittal sound, and Flent let it be. To Amber's annoyance, the saunter returned to Flent's step.

They had reached Amber's door, and she fumbled with her keys, looking anywhere but at the smug guard. She caught the subtle floral scent of her perfume again—there was something else to it, citrus? Not that it mattered—and felt the closeness of their proximity. The key slid home, the door opened, and Amber turned to face her. "Flent," she said by way of dismissal.

"Chivilra Everstar," Flent replied in mock seriousness, reciprocating the proper salute. Leaning forward a little, she added quietly, "Let me know when you decide to break that rule."

She lingered there for just a moment longer, seemingly watching for the knight's reaction. Amber felt her brain stall; all she could manage was a distorted "Yep." Then, with a grin, Flent spun on her heel and returned to her own quarters, leaving the scent of jasmine and orange blossoms in her wake.

22

SONS OF CELOS

The next day passed in a whirlwind of last-minute adjustments, decorations, and revisions. Tensions ran high in everyone involved with preparations, and the servants' smiles were plastered on their faces like war paint. Master Marmaduke sent a cook to the gardens for sprigs of thyme and banished her from the kitchens without another word when the poor cook returned with armfuls of oregano.

Early-morning proaction bled into afternoon frenzy and ended in late afternoon panic as to-do lists were completed and new tasks added at equal speed. Somehow the evening arrived with everything settling into place.

Guests filtered into the expansive throne room, now richly decorated with candles and bouquets of exquisite, exotic flowers of dark blues and bright yellows. The candlelight caught the golden accents and decorations around the room, which from afar was reminiscent of a night sky strewn with gold stars and fireworks.

Connor was in his chamber, dressing for the gala with the help of Edith. He had eaten a quick and early dinner with Jacs and Phillip, and was hopeful that, with their help, Phillip was ready to represent the Lower Realm appropriately.

"I just hope he remembers to watch his tongue," Connor said to Edith.

Edith nodded as she straightened his seams and buttoned his blue velvet jerkin.

"Tonight is an important night for Jacs, and if he chooses it as his moment to . . . I don't know . . . make some political point about the realm divide, it will likely end poorly."

"Close." He closed his eyes at her instruction and stayed still while she carefully outlined them with a thin wet brush dipped in a pot of powdered charcoal. He only ventured to talk again once she had blown twice on each eyelid.

"Not that it isn't an important political point to make," he said, holding out his arms slightly so she could fix his sleeve's cuff. "It's just, there's a time and a place for everything. I hope he recognizes that."

"There you are, Your Grace," Edith said proudly. With hands on her hips, she stepped back and surveyed her handiwork.

He studied himself in the mirror. The blue velvet was embroidered with accents of golden thread and tailored with the superiority of precision only a master could provide. He struck quite an imposing figure.

"Thank you, Edith," he said.

Edith straightened a crease in his cuff and said, "Try not to fret too much, Your Grace. The cards will fall where they may, so best focus on what to do with them when they do, rather than trying to predict the pattern ahead of time."

Connor had to admit she was right.

He bid her farewell and, with one last look in the mirror, strode to the door, pulled it open, and headed toward the throne room. He worried at a spot on the left-hand side of his chest absently and tried to ignore the stone that had formed in the pit of his stomach the moment Phillip's face appeared in the scry glass.

The moon had risen, and the gala was in full swing. Candles flickered in sconces and the room hummed with the sounds of laughter and gossip. A few Griffins had accepted their invitation and sat high above them, observing the evening's entertainment from their tower perch. From below, all that could be seen were their shadowy silhouettes.

Lords and Genteels milled around the marble pillars of the throne room. Dressed to impress, they sparkled with jewels and gold-trimmed garments. Since Jacs's coronation, Connor had noticed a shift in which Dames and Lordsons were invited to join their parents at the palace. When Connor had been the task creator for the Contest of Queens, the palace had been filled with every eligible Dame in the region, all eager to glean information from him. Now that Jacs was Queen and her preference determined, Lords had summoned their sons in droves. Each strutted about like a glittering peacock, with eyes painted, hair coiffed, and outfits in various shades of green (the Queen's reported favorite color). Connor tried not to roll his eyes at their obvious attempts at favor. Luckily, Jacs was never taken in by their vapid flattery.

He searched the room for her now, nodding to Dame Danielle Hart, her blonde hair woven with tiny pearls, who was talking with Dame Fawn Lupine. Last time Connor had seen both had been at the coronation, shortly after the contest. Both had competed for the crown, and both had excused themselves from court for a few months, likely to recover, or in Fawn's case, to lick her wounds. She had been particularly distraught upon hearing of her disqualification in the second task. Luckily, the clump of hair she had pulled out at the time had begun to grow in prettily. She had the shorter tufts of hair pinned back with emerald-studded clips.

Lord Hera Claustrom stood close to the center of the room. Many young Lordsons floated around her like moons, and mooning aptly described their behavior. Her recent elevation and current lack of partner made her jokes exceptionally funny, and her anecdotes particularly profound to those in orbit.

He did not see the Councilors anywhere. This was odd, as they were this evening's hosts. Looking around for them, he spotted Courtierdame Lena Glowra and her fiancé, Courtier Anya Bishop, speaking quietly together near one of the marble pillars that flanked the room. News of their engagement had spread quickly through the palace that morning, and he noted the diamond ring that flashed proudly on the fourth finger of Anya's left hand. Lena had an empty glass of champagne and waved it to punctuate a point, only to snap its stem against the pillar. Giggling, she bent to retrieve it at the same time Anya did. Connor smiled and looked away as they shared a kiss at the bottom of the pillar.

Finally, he spotted Jacs and was relieved to see her looking quite in her element. She wore a dark lapis gown embroidered all over with gold stars. The stars were concentrated across her bodice and spread out from waistline to hem. When she walked, the split down the length of her large skirts allowed a peak at gold leggings that ended in wide bands at the ankles. Her trusted knights, Chiv. Amber Everstar and Chiv. Andromeda Turner, hovered peripherally. Connor noticed they had changed into ceremonial uniforms.

Jacs bent her head to hear a Lordson's comment and laughed openly. A few heads turned, hoping to share in the jest. Any hint of the day's turmoil had been extinguished. Connor caught her eye and smiled, changing his course to approach. She beamed and beckoned him over.

"Lordson Barnaby, is this your accomplice?" Jacs asked the man who had made her laugh and gestured to Connor as he came closer by way of introduction.

Connor held out his hand to accept Lordson Barnaby's and started. "Hector?"

"Your Grace! Wonderful to see you again."

Connor grinned. "Likewise, it's been an age, how are—"

"I've just been telling Her Majesty the trouble we used to get into all those years ago in the palace. Do you remember that time you left me stuck inside a suit of armor down the Falstaff corridor?" Hector's brown eyes sparkled with mirth.

"How could I forget? Or what about the time we let the pigs loose in the squash patch?"

Hector burst into laughter and Connor noticed him touch the Queen lightly on the elbow. "I was always getting into scrapes following this boy's influence, I'd watch out if I were you, Your Majesty," he said good-naturedly. "If a baker's only as good as his bread, an advisor's only as good as his advice!"

Jacs laughed lightly and touched Hector's shoulder. "I'll keep that in mind, Lordson Barnaby."

Connor waited a beat, then said, "It's wonderful to see you, Hector, and I look forward to catching up later this evening, but could I borrow the Queen for a moment? I need a word." He addressed his last comment to Jacs.

She nodded, accepted the formal bow and kiss upon her hand that Lordson Barnaby offered in parting, and turned to face Connor.

"You look lovely, Connor," she said sweetly. He took her hand. He had not quite planned what he wanted to say, just that he didn't want Hector standing so close to her.

"You look, well, you always look beautiful, Your Majesty," he said and saw her blush. "Where's Phillip?" he asked, looking around.

"He was here a moment ago, but I think he went out to get some air. I can't blame him; I haven't had a spare moment since I arrived and I'm guessing it got tedious waiting." Jacs chewed the inside of her cheek and scanned the room.

"Listen," Connor paused until Jacs's attention was focused on his next words, then said in a low tone, "just be on your guard tonight. I will tell you more later, but just keep an eye out."

"Why? Connor, what do you know?" Jacs said, drawing closer to him. Her eyes were serious, calculating.

Edith's warning about waiting was quickly discarded and Connor briefly summarized his discovery of the scry crystal in his room. Jacs paled, but otherwise her face did not betray anything amiss.

"I'll get the name bank erased immediately," she said.

"We can meet with the palace scryers after the gala."

"Good."

"I was thinking, and yes, we should erase the entire bank, but I just wonder if, at least for the moment, we should keep your mother and Master Leschi's names stored. I just think it would be one more way we could find them." Connor searched her face and hurried to add, "But we don't have to if you would prefer them all gone."

Jacs took his hands in hers and kissed him chastely on the cheek, "No. That's a brilliant idea," she whispered in his ear. "That's perfect, thank you. After the gala then, and we'll be on guard in the meantime."

She beckoned Amber and Andromeda closer with a finger and shared the update. The exchange was over in a matter of seconds, but the effect was immediate.

Both knights stood straighter and sent a quick series of hand gestures to nearby guardpairs. While it was kept secret from the public, Connor knew that as part of guard training, recruits also learned a language made entirely of hand gestures. This made communicating across distances simple and served as a code no one without training could decipher. The gestures would have gone unnoticed to any who hadn't been watching for them, but Connor noted the ripple pass through the ranks and saw the formations shift to accommodate the new information.

Jacs turned back to Connor with a tight smile. "Have you seen the Councilors?" she asked, almost by way of distraction. In accordance with custom, they should have arrived before the Queen.

Connor shook his head. "No." He absently scratched his jawline with his knuckles, and the hair on the back of his neck prickled.

Jacs frowned and summoned a nearby attendant. The boy strutted, sternum first, toward them.

"Any news of when the Councilors are to arrive?" she asked him.

"No, Your Majesty, word is they've been detained by another engagement. Perkins was sent not half an hour ago to bring them refreshments in their chambers."

Jacs shared a look of confusion with Connor as she dismissed the boy.

"Your Majesty!" A voice cut across the moment, and the world returned. People laughed, glasses clinked, and the candlelight grew brighter. Jacs's face cleared; a smile bloomed on her cheeks. She squeezed Connor's hands and said lightly, "Let's talk about this later." Then she pulled her hand away from his, and just like that, he had lost her.

Mounting the steps to the dais, she looked every inch a Queen. Chiv. Everstar and Chiv. Turner flanked her on the lowest step. She turned to face the room, eyes flicking across faces in the crowd, and swept her skirts behind her, head high. With a smile that could break a heart, she held up a hand for silence.

"Welcome, Lords, Genteels, Dames, and Lordsons. I thank you all for attending tonight's gala, a treat that I have been promised will be remembered for years to come!"

As she spoke, attendants began working their way from the dais down the long center of the room to the door at the far end. They worked in pairs and gently moved the crowd into the wings of the room, clearing the center carpet to reveal the rich gold-embroidered navy fabric. As they reached the doors, three loud knocks rang through the hall. Excited whispers faded to bated breath. Far overhead, a Griffin stamped its taloned foot in anticipation.

"Enjoy!" She finished, to a round of enthusiastic applause.

Three loud knocks rang again through the hall. This time an attendant opened each of the large doors and stood to the side to reveal a troupe of seven young men: the eldest no older than five and twenty. All were smiling and poised as if in mid dance in the doorway. The crowd cheered and they sprang into action. Their costumes were motley shades of purples and pinks, silks and satins that shone in the candlelight. Two played fiddles, and Connor lifted his gaze to see the Queen's face light up. She began clapping in time to the rhythm.

The troupe members did not appear to spend much time on the ground at all, springing off the floor as soon as they had made contact. Soon the whole hall was clapping and stamping in time to the beat. Stamp, twist, leap. The troupe moved like a flickering flame in an ever-changing breeze. Unpredictable and passionate, they swirled and shifted, never missing a beat. The fiddles played faster, the stamping increased and reached a crescendo, then suddenly—

"Greetings." A deep, velvety voice stopped the players dead in their tracks. They froze, smiles caught in time, the only movement their heaving chests.

The hall erupted in cheers and the man who had spoken opened his arms wide. He had short black hair with the hint of a curl at the base of the neck. His face split in a smile, white teeth gleaming, dark eyes dancing.

He surveyed the crowd. The effect he had on any he made eye contact with was immediate. Dames and Lordsons alike became flustered and looked away under the intensity of his gaze. His eyes finally rested on the Queen, and he sank into a deep, reverential bow. The rest of the troupe followed suit.

As their eyes met, the Queen froze, a blush creeping up her cheeks. The troupe leader smiled wider and did not break eye contact as he rose from the floor. Silence. Everyone looked from the troupe to the Queen expectantly.

"Welcome," Jacqueline said softly. Her voice was able to carry throughout the room in the quiet. Louder, she said, "We look forward to what you have prepared for us this evening."

Again, the crowd cheered. The leader nodded curtly, still with his eyes on the Queen. Connor shifted uneasily. There was hunger in the man's gaze, which he did not like.

The dark-haired man clapped once and boomed, "Your Majesty, my name is Yves, and it gives me great honor to present the Sons of Celos!" At his words, the performers began moving again. The fiddles picked up and a lively tune floated through the hall. The two fiddle players were hoisted on the shoulders of other troupe members, then thrown in the air, the music never wavering or faltering as the players flipped and landed lightly with a flourish. The crowd gasped.

Limbs twirled, smiles flashed, and soon the dancers had brought two of the bolder Dames into the center with them. Dame Fawn Lupine, a fire in her eyes, clasped the arm offered to her and twirled around the room. The couple spun, her split gown whirling around them, then she was airborne. Someone shrieked, the note blending with the fiddles' trill until it was lost. Fawn's hair shook loose and flared around her like a flame. She landed softly in the arms of one of the men, breathing heavily. He spun her once, bowed, and walked her back to the crowd. Her cheeks were flushed, her skirts and hair in disarray.

Dame Shane Adella was next. Her long black hair flicked around her like a blade slicing through the air as she was spun in place. She fixed the dancer with a haughty stare, and he matched her intensity, circling her where she stood for a moment, then catching her waist and dipping her low. Smirking, he pulled her up to face him, and spun her away before she could catch her bearings. The two danced as though exchanging blows—strike, parry, release—neither making contact, but neither gaining ground. With a flourish, Shane was returned to the crowd, sweat beading her brow and a glint in her eyes.

Yves, still watching the Queen, now stepped forward and held out a hand to her. Connor stiffened and his gaze darted to her knights to see their reactions. Chiv. Everstar looked to her for orders, while Chiv. Turner kept her eyes on the crowd. Jacs hesitated, and Connor noted her uncertainty. The crowd had also seen Yves's gesture and began clapping along to the music. The pressure in the room began to build, and soon everyone was watching the Queen.

With a smile, she rose from her throne, and stepped slowly down the dais, aware of the eyes on her and, Connor could tell, feigning confidence.

"Do not worry, Your Majesty." Yves's voice floated above the music. "I will not shift one hair out of place beneath that crown."

Their hands touched. The music changed: slow and sinuous notes weaving through the room. The fiddles played first in harmony, then in dissonance. Connor saw the Queen recoil slightly at the change in tone, but she hid her reaction quickly. She kept her smile in place as the music increased in tempo and accommodated the movements as they became faster and more erratic. They wove in and out, blending, parting, and entwining around each other. The crowd cheered; the tempo increased again. The key changed. Once-defined golden stars on her skirts became a blur. Gold and blue flashed together. Yves never took his eyes off the Queen's face, and Connor saw her meet the dancer's gaze, first shyly, then defiantly.

Connor balled his hands into fists and exhaled slowly through his nose. With a crescendo, the music stopped on one final resounding note. The dancers froze, the audience held their breath, and slowly, Yves let go of the Queen's waist. As if waking from a dream, the crowd began to clap.

Beaming, Jacs allowed Yves to kiss her hand.

Then, several things happened at once.

Yves pulled Jacs into him. Connor watched his lips move close to the Queen's ear and saw her face contort with something between fear and rage. In an instant, Chiv. Everstar and Chiv. Turner sprang from the dais and rushed to the Queen's side. The dancers cried out with palms up as guardpairs materialized to surround them. Several Lordsons screamed. Before the knights could act, before the guardpairs could solidify their formation, Yves lifted his hands in a gesture of surrender, chin tilted upward from the small silver blade aimed at his throat. Jacs pressed the tip of her dagger drawn from somewhere on her person into the flickering pulse on Yves's neck. Two paces behind her, Chiv. Everstar smiled.

"Make your next move carefully, Yves," the Queen said, her voice low and deadly.

The hall had frozen. No one dared to move, and breath came shallow.

"Apologies, my Queen," he said slowly.

Jacs stepped back, blade still in her hand and gestured with the other for her guards to stand by for orders.

"Yves, you and your troupe have put on quite a show. I insist you stay with us the night, and you will dine with me tomorrow morning."

"Of—of course, Your Majesty," Yves said and bowed low.

"I imagine you're tired. You will retire at once. Flent, Chiv. Fayworth," she spoke to the nearest of her Queensguard, "you will escort Yves to his new quarters in the west wing. The rest of your troupe will also be escorted to a different lodging. Ensure they are given separate rooms and refreshments. Place a guard at each door should they require . . . assistance." The plan was in motion before the Queen had time to resheathe her dagger. Connor noticed with a sting of satisfaction that most of the dancers looked relieved at the news, failing to realize their new lodgings were actually glorified prison cells.

Flent and Chiv. Fayworth clasped Yves's upper arms. He inclined his head toward the Queen and said, "Her Majesty is truly too magnanimous." The troupe attempted to retain their dignity while being quickly escorted by guardpairs from the hall. The Queen's knights closed ranks around her, and at a wave of her hand, the musicians that had been playing before the troupe's arrival struck up once more. The congregation took a few moments to move past their confusion, but soon glasses were refilled, and laughter rang through the hall.

Connor reached Jacs two heartbeats after she had sheathed her dagger.

"Are you all right?" he asked in an undertone.

"Yes," she said automatically, then, almost too quiet to hear, she amended, "No."

"What did he say to you? After the dance?"

"He said"—she faltered—"He said, *Hello, Plum.*"

Courtiers Glowra and Bishop came hurrying over. The two knights had resumed scanning the crowd, eyes sharper than the blades at their belts.

"What was that about?" Anya asked when they reached the Queen.

Connor looked around at the crowd surrounding the dais. With the bulk of the guardpairs escorting the Sons of Celos to cells, that left only Chivilras Everstar and Turner and four other guards. *Not enough*, he thought to himself.

"Jacs," he said so only she and her knights could hear, "I think we need to get you out of here, something's off; and there aren't enough guardpairs to protect you."

The knights apparently had the same thought. With a few subtle hand motions, they signaled to the remaining guardpairs to come closer.

"Good idea, maybe it's best I leave first and have you announce my retirement for the evening in a few moments?" Jacs said.

"Of course. And Jacs." He paused, she looked up at him, and his heart ached as time rushed this moment into the next. "Stay safe." He brushed her cheek with a kiss and stepped down from the dais, away from his Queen, to talk with those milling around the base. He forced himself not to turn around as she retreated. Instead, he spoke a little too loudly and gestured a little too grandly in an effort to distract from her disappearing act. He needn't have bothered, the crowd appeared to be more concerned about the disappearing troupe members than where their Queen was going.

23

THE GROWING DARKNESS

Jacs hurried out the small door behind the throne with her knights in front, Lena and Anya close behind, and the guardpair Miera Jaenheir and Faline Cervah bringing up the rear. Leaving only two guards to watch over an entire throne room full of people seemed irresponsible; she just hoped nobody noticed, at least until the reinforcements returned.

"Let's get you back to your chambers. Then we can evaluate the threat, question the troupe, and get some answers," Amber said roughly.

They ran up a set of stairs to the second floor.

"Jacqueline, what's going on?" Lena whispered, holding tight to Anya's hand.

"Not here," Andromeda said bluntly.

They rounded a corner to a darkened hallway, and Amber held up her hand, bringing the group to a sudden halt.

"What is it?" Jacs whispered.

"This hallway isn't usually dark," Amber said.

They peered into the gloom, but the dimly lit interior appeared empty except for the furniture.

"I don't like it," Andromeda said. "Let's go a different way."

The group turned around.

"Wait, where's—" Anya started to say before Amber silenced her with a look. The guardpair that had followed behind were missing. There was no trace of them.

"Come on," Amber said and signaled for Andromeda to take the rear guard. The group chose a different corridor and hurried through the gallery. Large ornate portraits lined one side of the hall, suits of antiquated armor spaced at even intervals beneath, and stone arched windows lined the opposite side. The night was black beyond the windowpanes.

They moved quickly, but the darkness from the hallway behind them grew with each step they took to follow. At first Jacs thought that she was imagining it, but each candle they passed was silently extinguished moments later. Jacs looked back once, and Andromeda shook her head in warning and pushed her to move faster. At a signal Jacs did not hear, Amber broke into a run. The only sound in the long, empty room was the soft thump of boots and slippers on the carpet.

Lena and Anya panted beside her. Amber maintained the lead, her eyes sweeping the path in front constantly. Jacs cast a glance at their reflections in the blackened windows and caught a glimpse of something else—no—some*one* else. A figure standing beside one of the suits of armor. A blink and it was gone. They had almost reached the end of the gallery when Lena's gasp drew Jacs's gaze forward.

Amber threw her arms out and stopped the group in their tracks. The remaining light in the gallery dimmed. Jacs spun around to see the candlelight behind them snuff out. In front, the room beyond the stone archway was plunged into darkness. Now the only source of light was two sconces lining the archway into the next room. Amber and Andromeda closed ranks. Lena and Anya followed suit. Jacs stood in the middle of her friends. All held their breath.

The light did not reach what lay beyond the hall, and Jacs strained her eyes to make out the shapes in the gloom. There was the sound of fabric sweeping across stone. Figures slipped into the room on silent feet. Half a dozen, each wearing a purple hooded cloak. Their faces shrouded in shadow, heads bowed slightly, they approached the group with the slow inevitability of the tide. Jacs felt as if she had stepped off the Cliff. She felt Andromeda's back on hers and craned her neck to see three more emerging from the darkened hallway. They were surrounded.

Lena fumbled for her hand and held it tight. Anya whispered reassurances that were far from confident. Jacs stood tall, knees locked to stop their shaking, her free hand balled into a fist by her side. The hoods that had stood on her clocktower now filled her palace. She would not give them the benefit of seeing her fear, though it rose like a viper within her chest, coils constricting her lungs, fangs poised at her throat.

"You can't run, little Queen. The shadows will always find you," a deep, resonant voice said. Jacs was unsure which hood it came from. The circle of purple drew tighter as each figure stepped forward.

"Cowards," Amber muttered.

"Who among you is the leader?" Jacs asked calmly. "I suspect you have demands."

A ripple traveled through the nine figures. One spoke to Jacs's left. "No demands. Just a warning." The voice was familiar, but Jacs couldn't place it. Like a half-forgotten dream, it skirted the edge of her memory. "The Sons are rising, little Queen. A new dawn to vanquish this corrupt night. You can either embrace the inevitable or perish."

Two more figures emerged from the room beyond and flanked the archway. The hoods took a synchronized step closer.

"You threaten to disrupt the balance within our Queendom," a raspy voice to Jacs's right said. "You have risen, and now must fall." Again, it was unclear which hood the voice came from.

"And order will be restored," a voice near Andromeda said. Jacs felt her head spin. Fear and anger battled inside her. Only one was useful. She felt the fire burn within her and stepped forward to attack. Her fingers twitched, readying themselves to grasp her concealed daggers. Amber shifted, and Jacs paused. The knight's words rushed back to her in an instant. *Any woman worth her mettle remains in control even in the direst of battles.*

Jacs took a breath, then another, her heart rate steadying if only a little. The ring of purple hoods waited silently, like a twisted nightmare.

"So, what is your plan?" she said calmly. "You'll kill me like you did the last Queen? Invoke the outrage of half the Queendom? Then the Contest will begin again, someone new will take my place, and how long before you decide to kill her too? A Queendom cannot thrive without stability, and yet you would disrupt it again. You speak of balance, but how does this course of action create anything remotely resembling balance?"

The hoods remained silent. They could be mistaken for statues if not for the slight movement of their shoulders as they inhaled.

"What do you want?" Jacs asked in a voice far stronger than she felt.

"Justice," the hoods said together. The two figures by the archway reached up and extinguished the torches.

Everything happened at once. Jacs heard Amber yell and Andromeda cry, "Move!" Lena screamed and Anya made a sound as though she had been winded. Jacs felt the women around her suddenly vanish. The air grew colder as they were ripped from her. She drew the small dagger she had used on Yves and spun around. Straining to hear something, anything that would give away the hoods' positions. Her eyes, useless in the darkness, were wide.

A voice drifted toward her with the cold detachment of a cruel soothsayer.

"You are alone, little Queen. Who will you turn to when the darkness consumes you?"

All was still.

All was silent.

All was dark.

With a soft sputter, a lone candle reignited halfway down the hall. Jacs ran to it. Just outside the ring of light, she paused and searched the area, fearing a trap. None came. She inched toward the light and picked it up, holding it high.

The room was empty.

Returning to where she and her friends had been standing, she bent to pick up a small white petal. A flower from Lena's hair. The only proof that she had been with Jacs at all. That, and Jacs's still warm palm. It throbbed slightly and she looked down to see a thin scratch across the center. Lena's fingernail must have grazed her as her hand was ripped away.

Fear threatened to drown her. Gripping the candle tightly, she ran.

Reaching her chambers, she slammed the door and barricaded it behind her.

"Jacqueline?"

It was Phillip. He was hunched over a lower bookshelf beside her bed and straightened quickly as Jacs whipped around to face him. He hurriedly shoved something behind his back.

"Phillip! You're safe! They took them, all of them. We have to find them."

"Who?"

"The hoods. Took my guard, took my friends. Did you see anyone? How did you get here?" she asked, leaning against the door, panting.

"I . . ."

Jacs's mind caught up with the scene before her and she straightened slowly, looking at Phillip in confusion.

"Wait, Phillip, what are you doing in my rooms? What . . ." She paused, noticing the items strewn across her bedspread. "Why aren't you at the gala? Did something happen? Why . . . why are you looking through my things?" Her mind couldn't keep up with the myriad of questions assailing her. She was reminded of her room in Bridgeport, which had been ransacked as though someone had been looking for something there too. That was where she had found Phillip. She stepped closer to the bell pull, eyes hardened, and waited.

"Jacqueline, it's not what it looks like," he said softly, taking a step around the bed, hands still behind his back.

The puzzle pieces flew around her mind. The hoods sneaking into her palace. Phillip sneaking into her rooms. Phillip, the inventor's son, had access to the schematics of the clocktower the hoods climbed to assassinate Queen Ariel. Phillip, snooping around her house in Bridgeport, for what? Phillip coming to the Upper Realm, infiltrating the palace, missing when the troupe distracted the crowd. The troupe that split Jacs's guard, allowing the hoods to isolate and ambush her. It couldn't be a coincidence that he showed up days before the hoods attacked. He had been so angry. How far had he let that anger take him?

"Did you"—her voice broke—"did you bring the hoods here?"

His eyes widened in shock. "The hoods? No! Jacqueline, no, of course not! I didn't mean . . ."

"You didn't mean what, Phillip?" Jacs saw the color drain from his face. "What have you done?" she almost whispered.

"Done? I didn't do anything! I swear," he said, eyes pleading.

He took a step toward her, but she held up a hand, and he froze.

"I promise you, it was the only way, all I gave them was information. I didn't know they meant you any harm." He seemed desperate for her to understand.

"Information? What information?" Jacs demanded. She shifted her feet to steady herself on a floor that was quickly being ripped out from underneath her.

"It was nothing major! Nothing incriminating, just some information about you. But it was nothing that could be used against you."

"What did you think they would use it for?" Jacs asked in disbelief.

Phillip searched for words. "I don't know! I wasn't thinking about that."

"What in Frea was worth the price?"

"They promised—"

But Jacs had stopped listening, a war drum beat in her ears, and she fought to keep calm. "Phillip, you were selling my secrets to the hoods! The same group who murdered Queen Ariel. Why did you think they would want information about me? What did you think they were planning on doing to me?"

He gaped at her, cheeks flushing, and said, "You don't know what it's been like! I didn't have the luxury to think about that. You, safe in your palace, I knew you'd be fine! But I was running out of time, Jacqueline. And no one was gonna help me, so I found someone who would."

"Traitor." She spat the word like a curse. "I don't believe you." Her fingers twitched toward the bell pull. "But as your friend, I will give you one chance to explain yourself before I call the guards," she said.

His eyes studied hers. The corner of his mouth quirked humorlessly. "What guards?" he said softly. "They're all busy with the troupe, the gala, and the hoods, who I believe drew a number of them to the conservatory." He took another step around the bed. "And you seem to have lost your knights, so don't stand there and threaten me, Ms. High and Mighty."

Phillip, her bear-sized lamb, had vanished. Replaced by a cold-eyed stranger she did not recognize. "Why are you doing this?" she whispered.

"It was the only way."

"Help me understand." It was an order, but it entered the room with a whimper. Something flickered in his eyes. Guilt? Fear? She wasn't sure, but whatever it was, it dispelled the coldness slightly.

"At first they came to recruit me to join their organization. I think they'd been approaching a few others in town, promising to take them away to a better life, but I told them I had to stay in Bridgeport in case Ma returned. They promised to help me find her in exchange for information about you. I gave them a bunch of your balloon diagrams, and some journals I found in your room. After your visit, I told them about the book of names you had. That got them interested. Then when I came up here, they promised to take me to her if I found the little book you showed me. That's it. It didn't seem dangerous." He drew his hands from behind his back and displayed one of Jacs's notebooks. It was not the book of names—that she had safely tucked in a pocket in her bodice.

It was a notebook filled with theories and clues she had compiled about the disappearance of her mother and Master Leschi, as well as all she knew about the missing boys.

"Did you ask why they wanted it?"

"Yeah."

"And?"

"They said I didn't need to know."

"And you didn't think, even for a moment, that working for them would put me in danger?" Jacs was trying to hold onto her indignation, her hurt, something. But she knew in her heart that she would have gone to similar lengths to get her own mother back.

"It was a bunch of notebooks and diagrams you weren't even using in exchange for my Ma. I didn't think too much further past that."

Jacs swore. "You're an idiot."

"Likely," he agreed. "But not a traitor."

Jacs raised her eyebrows at him.

"At least not on purpose," he said seriously.

A loud banging at the door made them both jump.

"Jacs, it's me." Connor's voice came from beyond the barred door. Jacs eyed Phillip warily, and he held his hands up as a peace offering.

Jacs unbolted the door and stood back to let Connor in, eyes never leaving Phillip for long.

"Good, you're here, oh, and you're here too, Phillip. The party's getting a little rowdy, but no one seems to have noticed anything's amiss." Connors eyes swept the room and took in Jacs's defensive stance and Phillip's guilty expression. He took a half step back. "Wait, where are your knights? What's happened?"

Jacs motioned for him to close and lock the door and wasted very little time explaining the turn the night had taken since she had left the throne room.

"And Phillip's just told me he has been giving the hoods my notebooks in exchange for his mother's safety," Jacs finished, suppressing the emotions from her report as best she could, still reeling from the series of events that had led her here.

Connor looked from Jacs to Phillip in shock that quickly shifted to something deadly. He rounded on Phillip. "You!" he roared. "You're working with the assassins!" He launched over the bed toward Phillip before Jacs could stop him.

Jacs had never seen either man fight before. They collided like a hammer on a nail, Connor battering into Phillip more with force than technique. As they toppled out of sight, Jacs heard the scuffles and shouts as the two men wrestled on the floor. "Stop!" she yelled, rushing over. "Stop it!"

Despite Phillip being both bigger and stronger than Connor, the latter had obviously learned a few things from the palace knights. He had Phillip pinned to the ground, fist landing a punch to his jaw. Phillip covered his face with his arms as Connor found purchase on any exposed skin he could land a blow on. Jacs dragged him away from Phillip. Realizing who was restraining him, Connor let the fight bleed from his limbs and stood to adjust his doublet.

"You traitor," Connor said with disgust.

Phillip sat up and wiped his mouth with the back of his hand.

"Connor, it's not that simple," Jacs said quietly.

"What are you talking about? Yes, it is. Did he give information about you to the people who murdered my mother, your predecessor? Yes. So, he's a traitor."

"I didn't mean—" Phillip wheezed.

"I don't care what you have to say, basemutt," Connor snarled. Jacs flinched at the slur, but Connor wasn't looking at her.

"Don't call me a—"

"What did I just say!"

"Enough!" Jacs said firmly. Both men paused to look at her. "Connor, I'm not saying what Phillip did was right. It was stupid and reckless, but the intention was not to betray me." She looked at Phillip, crumpled on the floor, dabbing at his split lip, and added, "I have to believe that. The hoods have taken Amber, Andromeda, Anya, Lena, Miera, and Faline, along with who knows who else. Not to mention, we haven't seen the Councilors since before the gala. They might be in danger too." The method clicked into place in her mind. A step-by-step process aligned itself for her to follow. "We need to find out if they're okay. We need to find where the hoods are taking people, and we may just find out if they're the ones taking the boys, and even our mothers." She indicated to Phillip and herself. "They must be the key to all of this. And I don't want to wait around for them to abduct more people I love. We have to find them."

Connor glared at Phillip.

Jacs sighed and said, "Plus, Phillip's been feeding them information about me somehow, it's likely he'll be able to help us find them. Right, Phillip?" she asked hopefully.

Phillip cocked his head to one side, then nodded. "I was supposed to pass on what I found to one of the dancers. Yves?"

"The leader," Connor said. "I knew I didn't like him for a reason. I didn't think they'd be connected to the hoods though."

"They're a front," Phillip said softly. Both Jacs and Connor looked at him sharply. "The dancers go to towns and scope out the place and the people and report back to their hooded friends. They showed up in Bridgeport a week after you were crowned, and we've been losing boys ever since. I didn't make the connection until they approached me a month ago."

"The Sons of Celos are a front?" Jacs repeated quietly, realization dawning on her with a sickening lurch in her stomach. "And the boys, they're not being kidnapped, they're going willingly with these hooded men."

Phillip looked up at them apprehensively. "Listen, I want to do all I can to help. They said they'd take me to my Ma if I gave them the book. Why don't we just stick to that plan?"

Jacs wound a strand of hair around her finger, deep in thought. "If they're honor bound, that could work. But if they're not, then who's to know if they would actually uphold their end of the deal? You may just end up as another entry in Queen Ariel's book." She began pacing the carpet at the end of her bed. "But we have Yves, we have the whole troupe, they might be able to lead us either to our next clue or to the missing people."

The list of names in her mind sent a pain through her chest, and she forced her thoughts back to the plan. How could so many boys choose to follow the hoods? She grasped the bell pull by her door and gave it a hearty yank before continuing. "But if the hoods are lurking around the palace, they might try to liberate the troupe. We need to get to Yves before they do."

There was a businesslike knock at the door and Jacs opened it to reveal Adaine. "Good evening, Your Majesty. How can I help?" she asked as she stepped into the room.

"Adaine, I need you to find the Councilors. Go first to the Council's chamber, then, if you don't find them there, to their individual apartments. When you find them, check that they are safe and well."

"I can confirm that Councilor Stewart has a cold, Your Majesty," Adaine said helpfully.

"Ah, by that I mean I want you to check if they have been hurt or frightened this evening. Once you find them, make sure they have at least one guardpair per Councilor to protect them. Tell them to remain locked in their rooms as I believe they may be in danger."

"Of course, Your Majesty."

"And Adaine," Jacs added, "take a guardpair with you. Keep yourself safe, and if you encounter individuals in purple hooded cloaks, run. They are not our allies."

"Of course, Your Majesty. Anything else?" Adaine's eyes shone with determination.

"No, that's all. When you are done, please return to my rooms and lock yourself in. Only open the door if you recognize the voice of the person knocking." Jacs took her hand briefly and gave it a quick squeeze. Adaine nodded and bowed low over the Queen's hand. A flicker of unease passed across the valet's features but was quickly smothered by a mask of eager professionalism.

Once Adaine had closed the door behind her, Jacs turned to the men. "Let's go. I'll lead, Phillip you walk behind me, and Connor you watch our backs."

In two quick motions, she had unhooked the expansive skirts from around her waist and thrown them on her bed. To ensure ease of movement, she unbuttoned her embroidered sleeves and tossed them on top of the discarded skirts. Now she stood bare-armed in the gold embroidered navy bodice and golden leggings. She exchanged her delicate slippers for knee-high leather boots and slipped a number of daggers in the concealed pockets her outfit offered. The book remained in her bodice. Lastly, she exchanged her crown for a simple gold circlet. In the few moments it took her to dress down, Connor had reluctantly helped Phillip to his feet, still scowling.

With her lips pressed in a thin line, she turned to lead the way. Connor shoved Phillip harder than necessary between the shoulders to fall into step behind her.

24

THE KNIFE EDGE OF SANITY

Time passes differently behind a blindfold. Sensation and sound register sporadically, distorting the metronome. Minutes can stall or sprint, seconds hesitate between breaths. The gentle rocking of boats, hushed voices, and swirling memories blurred the lines between wakefulness and dreaming. Lena fought to remain conscious, pinching at her wrists and biting the inside of her cheek. Control can be so easily lost.

Pressed tightly between two others, Lena had thought of nothing more than the bonds at her wrist from the moment she woke up. She had regained consciousness as they threw her into a boat, but the familiar weight of darkness that pressed down on her told her where she was before she had fully taken stock of the situation. The smothering, twisted cloud stole into her mind like an old friend. It caressed the recesses of her thoughts like a lover and drove the air from her lungs with languid force. Panic welled within her as scenes previously locked in the darkest corners of her brain sprang forward to play in the forefront of her mind.

It was happening again. She couldn't stop it. Helplessness drew itself up around her throat like a heavy woolen blanket. Movement along her back reminded her she was not alone in the boat. Something warm stirred within the cold echoes in her mind. Despair led nowhere. She knew this feeling. She had felt it during the second task, and it had done her no good. She would not waste away, waiting for someone to find her. Not this time.

Sore from whatever journey had led her to this boat, she felt pain splinter down her limbs. Her arms were twisted awkwardly behind her. Numbness frosted a path from elbow to fingertips. She grasped at the sensations around her, the warmth of the woman beside her, the tingling pain in her arms, and steadied herself in the present.

Mind aimed only at the task at hand, she set to work dislodging the small blade she kept in her bodice. Small movements masked by more elaborate squirms wiggled the blade free. Shifting her body with the boat's sway helped conceal her more precise wrist movements while she sawed at the fabric binding her. The importance of her task smothered her rising memories. She didn't have time for a past that would only consume her, so she shoved it away and focused on the present.

Inch by inch, she cut her way through her bonds, her wrists shifting behind her back. Finally, she felt the fabric give way, and her wrists broke free. She palmed the little blade, shifted her position a fraction, and gently clasped the wrist of her neighbor. The blade changed hands, and Lena lay still.

Shadows of the past danced in the periphery of her mind, not yet bold enough to come forward again. She bullied them back. Walls like eyelids fluttered between them and the happy memories she dredged up to take their place. Distraction had always worked best. Here she was, holding her hand out to Anya in her mother's empty ballroom, flowers in her hair. Now they were hiding from the maids, stifling giggles as they feasted on stolen sponge cake. The wind picked up in her mind's eye, and she was riding her first filly, Daisy, around the ring. Anya, face serious, called directions from the center as she shifted from walk to trot. She had always been a patient teacher. Much kinder than the one her mother had hired. Her mother, with eyes of steel and a swift corrective hand, so desperate to shape her into the Lord she would one day become.

Lena knew better. Memories shaped a person. Experiences molded the soul. She was lucky to have Anya in so many of the moments that shaped her heart. *But*—an inky finger crept through her barricades—*what about the rest? Can we pick and choose the memories that make us? And if not, then who could love someone forged by what he did?* Putrid blackness oozed through her walls. Her mind went numb. The flowers wilted.

"Not this time," she whispered to herself. She couldn't control what had happened, but she could control how it shaped her. Each time she bowed to his memories, he won. With every victory, he gained more territory in her mind. He claimed more of her for the void. She could deny him that power. She need not kneel to a phantom. Words only have power if you feel them. Memories only have bite if you live them. Brick by brick, she built her walls higher. For the thoughts she could not lock away, she instead drowned out with her most cherished memories. His residue faded. With fists clenched, she felt her nails bite into flesh and held tight to that sensation. That was real.

As each second trudged by, she could only hope that her blade was circling through the bonds of the other captives. Trusting the knights to have a plan, she waited.

25

INTERROGATION

Jacs and the small party were able to make their way to Yves's confinement chamber without any impediment. Dyna Flent and Chiv. Claudia Fayworth stood alert on either side of the doorway and saluted Jacs as she approached.

"Update," Jacs said in her best imitation of Masterchiv Rathbone.

Flent reported. "He was escorted with no incident, polite and contrite as could be, Your Majesty. We've checked in on him every quarter hour and he has been reading each time. Said he's waiting for you."

Jacs nodded and felt a twist of nerves around her navel. She recalled the effects of his charm on the dance floor and resolved to resist them this time. He was handsome, graceful, and aligned with assassins. She would not allow herself to forget that.

"Your Majesty?" Flent interrupted her thoughts and looked apprehensive.

"Yes, Flent?"

"With all due respect, shouldn't Chiv. Everstar be with you? Where are your knights?" Jacs noticed a flicker of emotion in her eyes, but the rest of her features remained stoic.

"She and Chiv. Turner have been captured, as well as guardpair Miera Jaenheir and Faline Cervah. I suspect others have disappeared this evening, but I'm not sure of numbers yet. Best be on alert: The culprits work in the dark and move as silently as shadows. If you see a purple hood, do not hesitate to bring them down."

Both Flent and Chiv. Fayworth shared a glance and grew pale at the news, but they otherwise did not react beyond showing they understood.

Jacs rolled her shoulders back and approached the door. "Keep your ears keen, I will speak with Yves alone, but don't hesitate to enter if you feel you are needed."

Connor touched her elbow and muttered, low: "Jacs, are you sure you don't want one of us with you?"

She shook her head and replied, "Watch Phillip." In her peripheral vision, Phillip crossed his arms but said nothing.

The door opened. Dark eyes under darker curls looked up from a small leather-bound book and met hers. A slow smile crept over his features, and Yves opened his arms in welcome. The room was small by the palace's standards, and only the higher-than-typical window and heavy locks on the doors would identify it as a cell. This room was used for more esteemed prisoners. Visitors turned villains. Simply furnished, it contained a freshly made narrow bed, two quilted chairs, and a low table. Lanterns lit the small space, and Yves had angled his chair beneath one, the better to read by.

"Hello, Plum," he said smoothly, rising to bow low, eyes locked on hers. "To what do I owe the pleasure?"

Jacs felt her skin prickle. She looked down at him with disdain. "Yves, you will answer my questions truthfully, and I will reconsider your sentence. That is the deal."

Yves raised an eyebrow and made a tsking sound. "But the truth is so subjective, Your Majesty. Words are easily twisted."

"Speak plainly," she said, her heartbeat pounding in her ears, "and I will consider sparing your life."

Yves's smile widened. "You would take my life for what, Your Majesty? Calling you a fruit? That hardly seems a fair punishment. I wonder if it's plums in general that are offensive? Would you have preferred another stone fruit? I confess *Nectarine* doesn't carry the same whimsy. What about *Peach*? Shall I call you my peach?"

Jacs glared at him.

"Or maybe something more elegant: *cherry*, perhaps? Stop me if I'm getting close."

"I know you work with the hoods, Yves," Jacs asserted, ignoring the heat rising in her cheeks. With his dark eyes fixed on her, she felt exposed and entirely out of her depth.

"I work with the troupe, Your Majesty, and you'll notice our capes do not have hoods. We find it blinds the dancers. Much easier to catch someone when you can see them."

"You were awaiting information from someone in the palace," she said.

"Information regarding our next show, our next meals, where we were to sleep. I thank you for supplying the answers to the last two questions," he said easily.

"Information about a book."

"I have one right here." He held up the leather-bound volume in his hands, a finger marking his place between the pages.

Jacs sighed inwardly and chose a different tactic. "I can pay for your cooperation."

"I thought you had it already, Your Majesty."

"Your weight in gold."

His gaze scanned her from head to toe and back again, taking in her gold-embroidered bodice and her golden leggings. She did not like the way his eyes glittered. "Certain golds interest me more than others, Your Majesty."

Her lip curled in disgust at the implication. "I am quite happy to wait. You may call this room your world for however long it takes to loosen your tongue."

She fought to keep her voice level.

"An interesting thought." He paused delicately. "See, I am in no rush. This lodging seems as good a place as any to rest my head, and I do so need a break. But I wonder if your friends have that long? Or"—he cocked his head to the side, innocent except for his eyes—"or a certain inventor who apparently keeps asking about you. I wonder if you're acquainted?"

Jacs felt her heart still. "So you do know," she said quietly.

"Know what?"

"Don't toy with me, Yves."

"But you're so delightful to play with."

She huffed in frustration, only making him smile wider. The door burst open and Connor rushed in.

"Your Majesty, we got one of the other troupe members to talk, we don't need this rat," he said breathlessly.

Jacs turned and smiled at Yves. "Excellent." She clasped her hands in front of her. "Then, Yves, do enjoy your stay in your quarters, I suspect you'll be here quite a while."

She turned to go but slowed her pace at a subtle hand cue from Connor.

"Wait!" Yves called as she reached the threshold.

Jacs stopped but did not turn back around.

"My brothers wouldn't dare betray Celos. You have nothing," he said with much less confidence than before.

Connor took his time answering Yves. "It's amazing what a few well-placed bribes will get you."

"Who?" Yves demanded.

Connor shook his head. "I don't know the name you knew him by, but he'll likely go by his new title: Maestro."

"Maestro?"

"An honor reserved for the court composer," Connor added with a flourish.

Yves licked his lips. "Wait, I can tell you more than whatever you heard from that slug. None of them know the location. They've never been to Alethia; I have. I can give you what you need, more than they can." All velvet was stripped from his voice, and an entitled self-assurance with an underlying current of desperation took its place.

"I suggest you talk quickly, Yves," Jacs said over her shoulder.

"Alethia, the underground city. You can reach it through the catacombs. I can show you the way."

"And how can I trust you not to betray us?"

"You can't, but I won't. If the brotherhood has seen fit to betray me, then I have no allegiance to them."

"Good. Be ready to leave in a quarter hour. I will collect you shortly." She did not wait for a reply, just stepped out the door and felt the rush of air as it slammed shut behind her.

Connor's broad grin met her on the other side before it was obscured as he swept her into a tight hug.

"That was lucky," she whispered in his ear. "He wasn't even close to cracking."

"I know, we could hear." He pointed to a cupped listening contraption affixed to the wall. "It's lucky he believed me," he said mischievously.

Jacs pulled back and looked at him. "What do you mean?"

"I was bluffing. He was very quick to turn cloaks though, wasn't he? We'd better keep our eyes on him regardle—"

She caught the rest of his sentence on her lips. Phillip cleared his throat to her left and she pulled away. "You are brilliant," she said to Connor.

Turning to the others, she said, "Has anyone heard of Alethia before?"

The guardpair shook their heads almost in unison. Phillip looked away, and Connor said, "That's the place from the myth, isn't it? Where the attercoppe takes bad little boys. Kind of like the Eternal Realms though, not a real place."

Phillip shifted his feet and said, "I thought that too, that's what every boy grows up hearing: *Control your fire, or the attercoppe will take you away*. Ma was never into those stories, but you heard about it regardless. Then when the hoods started seeking me out, they mentioned that name too. They called it their Kingdom. Said it was free from the Queen's oppression. Said a lot of things about that actually." He looked at Jacs apologetically. "They were quick to feed any resentment I held toward the crown, and if I hadn't known you personally, I'd likely have started to believe them."

Jacs couldn't take offense; she was deep in thought. If this group had been twisting the minds and hearts of vulnerable men against the Queen for decades, they must have a sizable army. She still couldn't believe this had gone unnoticed for so long. Hidden in plain sight by a myth used to make little boys behave and a twirling troupe of dancers.

She thought of the missing boys. The little book of names had a few Upper Realm entries, sure, but the bulk had been from the Lower Realm. Lowrians were much more disillusioned than Upperites when it came to the Queen, and men were much more jaded than women in a matriarchal society. In a power-structure system with a strict hierarchy for both realm-birth and gender, Lowrian men were leagues below the rest on the pecking order. They were the perfect group to radicalize against the crown. She thought of Mal, beaten and broken on the riverbank all those months ago. If someone had offered him an alternative life, one free of guardpair patrols and interrogations, one where he was made to feel like he was worth something, she couldn't blame him for taking it.

"Okay," she said slowly, still piecing her plan together, "we are potentially up against a massive organization that has little love for the crown. Appealing to reason likely will not work if their hearts have been poisoned against me. We really don't know the extent of it all, so I'm hesitant to stage a full-bore attack. I think more subtle means might work best. Sneak in, free the captives, sneak out, and with the information we glean from that trip, we can plan our next moves."

Scanning her small audience for their reactions, she saw that they all appeared to be in various stages of agreement. Phillip scratched his jaw and asked, "How do we sneak in?"

Jacs turned to Flent. "Do you know if the guardpairs caught any of the hoods?"

Flent shook her head.

"We'll likely need disguises. Luckily for us, their hoods offer complete coverage, so as long as we keep our faces covered, we should be fine. Especially you two." She indicated Phillip and Connor. "They'll likely only get suspicious if they find out some of us are women."

"But where are we going to get purple hoods if we didn't catch any?" Connor asked.

The last part of the plan clicked into place and Jacs found herself feeling giddy. "Summon Master Moira, tell her to bring as much purple fabric as she can. We have an order for her."

26

BLIND AND BOUND

Why did it have to be both dark *and* damp? One would have been dreary enough, but both just seemed like overkill. Not to mention the smell. Wet rock and cold steel. That special combination of metallic moisture that somehow makes one think of decay when, logically, it should smell clean.

Amber's eyes had been covered with coarse fabric, and her mouth filled with something that tasted like mildew, though it didn't quite mask the tang of whatever they had used to knock her out—another factor that greatly detracted from her experience. In some sense though, she was glad she had these moments to herself. A stretch of time in her own thoughts. Most of all, an excuse to avoid talking about how completely she had failed her Queen. The only positive was at least they were all captured together. She was still *technically* protecting

Jacqueline, even if she was bound, gagged, blindfolded, and wasn't exactly sure where the hoods had stashed the Queen. These were minor details to be sorted out in due course.

But she could use this time to think it over. Examine the situation from every possible angle. Review the events as they happened outside of the moment's heat. Her footwork, her reaction time, her strategy. Where had she gone wrong? Their formation was not ideal, they were greatly outnumbered, and the lighting—*the baselow lighting*, she thought fiercely. Everything is so much harder in the dark, but she expected to have landed a few blows at least, gained even an inch of ground. Her pride shriveled uncomfortably inside her. She had not been beaten this completely since she first trained as a guard. Even their failure at Wrenstrom still held enough moments of success to be proud of.

Next steps, she thought with determination. She needed to get free and find help; failing that, she needed to make it so others could find her. She struggled against her bonds. Her wrists were bound tightly behind her back and her feet were shackled. A glimmer of pride returned that the hoods thought this was the only degree of restraint she required.

Focus, she told herself. *Step one: Where are we?*

With her eyes covered, she had to rely on her other senses for information. The warmth of a body on one side of her told her she was with at least one of the others. The smell was partially tainted by the nasty old rag in her mouth, but they were likely somewhere cold and damp, somewhere that didn't get much sun to chase away the dankness in the air. The sounds while she had been carried had an eerie, echoey quality and had consisted of dripping water, boots on stone, the scrunch of gravel, and some cursing when a hood slipped on the terrain. Underground maybe?

Now, however, she was most definitely in a boat. The wooden boards pressed against her shoulder blades and cut painfully into her contorted arms. Water lapped against the gently rocking hull and a steady rhythm of oar strokes sang over the perpetual *drip, drop, plink.* An underground lake?

A hand gently clasped her wrist. The questing fingers were soft, cold, and firm. Amber stayed very still as a warm sweat-slick piece of sharp metal was pressed into her palm. Hope surged in her chest.

With a few practiced movements, she aligned her bonds with the blade and set to work.

Step two, she thought.

27

A WHIRLWIND OF HOODS AND HORSES

It took a total of one hour from the time Jacs made the order to the time that she, Connor, Phillip, Yves, Flent, Chiv. Fayworth, and Masterchiv Rathbone were standing in floor-length purple hooded cloaks receiving the finishing touches from Master Moira and her team of seamstresses.

"And my dear, to be pulled from that wonderful gala and put to work, why I don't think I have ever felt so honored as I do right at this very minute. Didn't I say so, Juliana? I said, 'It's one thing to attend a gala surrounded by your own designs, but it's quite another to be enlisted to outfit a top-secret mission.' Of course, you can count on me to keep my lips sealed. I'm the picture of secrecy, isn't that right Juliana? Dependable as a stone vault, yes indeed. Why, just the other day Yasna over there mentioned she was planning to ask her beau to marry her, and I haven't told a soul, have I, Yasna? No, you can depend on me without a doubt."

Jacs shared a look with Connor and quickly said, "Master Moira, we, of course, trust you beyond measure; however, for your safety, may I offer lodgings in the palace and guardpair protection for the next day or so? As our honored guest, of course."

Master Moira's ringed fingers flew to hover near her throat, and she took a few elaborately staggered steps backward. "An invitation to stay at the royal palace. Why, I would be most honored, Your Majesty. Yes, I will feel much safer knowing I was within these mighty walls. While I assure you, not a word about your covert mission will pass these lips of mine, I feel it will be much easier to talk of other things while housed in the palace. Preferably facing east, I do so love watching the sunrise. It *quiets* me like nothing else." The seamstress stood back to appraise her work and made a severe tutting sound. "The hems are nonexistent, and the fastenings are inconsistent. If you gave me a few more hours to work my magic, my dear, I could make these rocks shine!"

"Master Moira, we really have to go, this will pass in the dark, and that's all we need," Jacs said quickly.

Master Moira pursed her lips and said, "Then you will do me the honor, Your Majesty, of omitting my name when someone asks who designed your look."

"Of course, not a word."

With a reluctant sigh, she snapped her fingers, and her team quickly removed the last of the pins from the cloaks. "Then best of luck to you. At least I have done your calves justice, yes that I did do."

Bowing deeply, she took her leave, flashes of color peeking out of her pleated skirts. A trail of gray-gowned seamstresses followed in her wake like cygnets after a swan. With one hand poised on the door frame, Master Moira paused and turned to look at Jacs. Her lively cadence was now suddenly serious. "Your Majesty, if you find the rats that took our dear Lena from us, be sure to give them a hearty kick from me."

Jacs nodded curtly, and an expression of grim satisfaction creased Master Moira's mien.

The group rushed through the palace toward the stables. Like a fragment from another life, the gala was still in full swing, and snippets of music, laughter, and boastful conversations spilled from open windows and doors. Partygoers, engrossed in their own merriment, barely spared a moment's notice as the Queen and her entourage moved through the halls. By the time a head thought to turn in their direction, they had already disappeared around a corner or through another passageway.

Jacs saw no sign of the Council and suspected they were safely holed up in their chambers by now. She sent a silent *thank-you* to Adaine for that. There was also no hint that a hoard of purple cloaks had infiltrated the palace. Guardpairs and serving staff scurried around to return order to the gala's uproar.

With each second bleeding out, Jacs's nerves were wound tighter. Thankfully, Connor had sent word to the stables to saddle seven horses when he summoned Master Moira, so a small herd awaited them in the stable yard. Peggy's ears perked forward happily at the sight of Jacs, a welcome warmth.

After everyone had identified their mount, Yves strode over to the spare horse boldly. With shoulders back, chest puffed, and a rolling grace to each step, he reached his mount and floated up into the saddle with one easy movement. Hand resting casually on the saddle pommel, he surveyed the courtyard possessively.

The light of confidence in his posture was snuffed out suddenly as Masterchiv Rathbone snapped a lead rope to his mare's bridle and attached it to her saddle.

"Looks like you're my shadow tonight, Lightfoot," she said bluntly. "Try to stay upright, I doubt anyone here will catch you if you fall."

Saddled, mounted, and paired, the group set off into the twilight heading for the Catacombs of Lethe. The underground labyrinth had been the location of the second task. Jacs wished it were harder to believe those caves concealed the secrets of Alethia, and she shivered despite the cloak and the warm evening air. She had felt it during the second task. Felt that the caves held something more than just wet stone and glowworms. They contained something that infiltrated the mind like a fog. Now that she knew the truth, she didn't relish the idea of returning to the darkness.

The moon lit the path like an ethereal guide. What had taken the contestants most of a morning to cover at a gentle pace took Jacs's crew half that time. They flew across roads and fields, wind whipping hair and cloaks in swirling banners behind them. The journey passed quickly, and Jacs barely touched the saddle.

Their pace only slowed once they reached the forest. Here, the moonlight left them as they crossed the threshold into the gloom of the trees. Sounds were muted, and riders spoke in whispers. Each time they had to stop to untangle a bramble or double back to find a clearer path, Jacs felt a knife twist in her gut. She just hoped they had made some time back with their mad dash across the plains. Likely with six or more unconscious bodies, the hoods would have had to slow their pace and work harder to avoid detection.

Jacs could only hope.

All too soon, and not soon enough, they reached the grassy basin in the middle of the woods. Yawning caves mocked them in the still night, beckoning them closer. The party dismounted in silence but stayed in the fringe of trees for a moment. Each was hesitant to step out into the open glade. In the seclusion of the trees, they were free to talk.

"So," Connor whispered. "What's the plan?"

Jacs felt six pairs of eyes on her. She turned to Yves. "You will lead the way, what does the path entail?"

Yves scrunched up his nose to think, the effect disarmingly endearing. "We need to follow a certain path, I know which one of course, to an underground lake. There we will find a number of wooden boats—well hidden, but I know where to look—and from there we take the boats to the banks of Alethia. There's a main gate that we will do our best to avoid. I happen to know of a more secret entrance. It will involve us getting wet though. I hope you can all swim." He smiled winningly at the stone-faced group.

"Is that all?" Jacs asked.

"The brunt of it, yes, my Queen."

"Excellent. Flent, take this," she held out a spare strip of purple fabric, "and gag him. We don't want him giving away our position."

Yves spluttered indignantly, "Your Majesty, I wouldn't dream of—"

"Then the gag will not be an issue," she said firmly and watched as Flent followed orders. "Bind his hands in front. Be sure they're concealed under his cloak." She handed a second strip of fabric to Flent.

Yves's brow furrowed and he made a muffled sound against his gag that did not take much imagination to decipher.

"We will unbind you when I feel we have nothing to fear from you," Jacs said simply.

Yves glowered at her, then slowly inclined his head in defeat. When he rose, his showman's mask was firmly in place, and he even had the audacity to wink at her.

Jacs wrinkled her nose and turned to the others. "So, with Yves kindly leading the way, we will infiltrate Alethia. Ours is a rescue mission only. Avoid confrontation as much as possible. Our goal is to find the six women who were abducted: Lena, Anya, Andromeda, Amber, Jaenheir, and Cervah."

At the mention of Amber's name, Flent stood straighter.

Jacs pressed on. "If we are successful and find our friends, the secondary part of the mission will be to find where they are keeping my mother and Master Leschi." Phillip nodded around the group and met Connor's gaze defiantly. "However, I have reason to believe that we will find dozens of missing boys as well. Likely they will be against us, but they are not our enemy, so restrain and contain wherever possible."

Masterchiv Rathbone stepped forward. "Your Majesty, having experience in these sorts of missions already, may I offer some suggestions?"

Jacs felt relief bloom in her chest. "Of course."

"Missions like these with multiple tiers can often lead to failure if the risk of continuing is not properly appraised. We must keep in mind that a bird in the hand is worth two in the bush. If we have to leave with only a few rescued people, that is better than getting us all captured. Better to retreat to fight another day, than die for nothing." She rested her hand lightly on the pommel of her sword as she spoke. With solemn eyes she turned to Jacs and added, "Forgive me, but Your Majesty I must insist you stay behind. You are putting your life in very real danger. If you are caught, they will ransom you. If you are killed, all you have achieved will be for nothing. Please."

Jacs looked around at the faces peering at her in the gloom. Concern was etched into all features except Yves's. She thought about the months spent dancing to the Council's tune, about how useless she felt behind the palace walls. In a rush, she remembered the feeling of flight with the Court, how her heart had sung to be actively doing something for her people. Again she experienced the joy that had followed her all the way back to the palace, and the satisfaction of seeing the wagons filled with scry crystals days later. The echo of action thrummed in her veins, and she yearned for more.

To Masterchiv Rathbone's obvious dismay, she shook her head.

"While I appreciate the concern, Masterchiv, and highly value the advice, I cannot be a Queen who sits by and does nothing. Calloused hands mean a job gets done, and I know I can help in this."

Silence stole over the clearing, and no one appeared to know what to say. Connor fidgeted uncomfortably but did not speak out against Jacs's decision. Phillip had a proud smile on his face and rocked backwards and forwards a little on the balls of his feet. Flent simply looked impatient to go, and Jacs couldn't blame her.

With a clap of her hands, Jacs said, "Right, everyone has a lantern, it's probably better we don't use the glowworms unless we have to." She looked to Yves, who confirmed with a bob of the head. "Let's go."

28

RECLAIMED HONOR

Amber felt the boat slide onto the bank and shudder to a stop. Staying motionless, wrists still crossed behind her back, she strained her ears to locate their captors. They said very little and walked around on silent feet, so it was a challenge to determine their number, but not impossible. The scrunch of the rocky beach underfoot betrayed at least half a dozen pairs of boots. There had been nine hoods in the gallery, and while some may have stayed behind, she thought that was unlikely. It was just a question of whether more had joined them on their escape. The difference between six and a dozen was significant, after all.

She was pretty sure they were still underground. Every noise had an echoey quality and the sound of dripping was constant. Wherever they were, it was dreary, to say the least. Several times over the course of the blindfolded journey, a dark thought had tried to enter her mind. She was quick to quash it, but it was not often she had to work so hard to stay out of a spiral.

A phantom voice would whisper to her: *I'm not enough to fight this.* And she would counter it dismissively. "That's ridiculous. I've overcome worse."

We're outnumbered. "That never stopped me before."

No one's coming for us. "Of course they will. I'm a Soterian knight captured with two Courtiers and the Queen."

I let the Queen down, just like I let my battalion down in Wrenstrom. "I learned from those mistakes; I'll learn from these too."

I'm going *to die down here.* "Not a chance, I need to see things through with Flent first," she said to herself with a wry grin.

It almost became a game. A volley of blows within her own mind. Not the most fun, but it occupied the time.

A new voice interrupted her musings. "Get them up."

She felt hands under her armpits, and she was lifted from the boat. Keeping her hands firmly clasped behind her so as to avoid early detection, she thrashed in the man's arms. A swift kick hit home, and he dropped her painfully on the stony bank. Her hands came up to rip the blindfold and gag free and she took in several things at once.

The area was lit dimly by some form of flameless ghostly white luminescence. She'd knocked the wind out of her captor, who was doubled over in pain a short distance off. A wagon sat waiting farther up the bank. Five other blindfolded women accompanied her, one less than was in the gallery. Each was in the arms or over the shoulders of hooded figures, and Jacqueline's telltale auburn hair was decidedly missing. The hoods had let their guard down; their formation was sloppy.

"Now!" she roared.

Suddenly the shore was a flurry of movement as each woman, hands free, twisted, clawed, punched, and tore herself away from the hood holding her. The techniques were more polished in the guards and knights' maneuvers, but the Courtiers' were just as effective. Amber dashed over to her fallen assailant and with two swift moves had him face down and hogtied with her blindfold. Next, she jumped at the hood wrestling with Lena. He landed a blow and Lena doubled over, gasping for air before Amber reached her. One, two, and Lena's three sent him sprawling.

"You can restrain him?" Amber asked.

"Yes," Lena wheezed. Her face was pale and sweat beaded her brow, but she looked determined.

"Good." Amber was off toward the hood holding tight to Anya's wrist. Andromeda materialized beside her and together they took four more hoods down. Shifting through stances like dancers through steps, they fought seamlessly. The thrum in Amber's veins spurred her on. Andromeda's blows and parries harmonized perfectly with her own and they moved as one. Grunts and shouts nearby told her that the guardpair Jaenheir and Cervah were just as successful.

Amber surveyed the hooded bodies scattered across the shoreline and lowered her fists. "That's more like it," she said to Andromeda, feeling balance return and honor restored.

"Any sign of Jacqueline?" Andromeda asked.

Amber shook her head and a chorus of no's came from the other women.

"Why would they leave her behind?" she asked.

Andromeda shrugged. "To scare her? To warn her? Maybe she escaped." Slowly, Andromeda walked over to the nearest unconscious figure and flicked back their hood with the toe of her boot. It was a young man with sandy brown hair and peach-fuzz cheeks still rounded with puppy fat. She rubbed her jawline pensively. "These are just kids," she said softly.

Systematically they threw back each hood. The oldest boy looked to be slightly younger than Amber's two and twenty years. The youngest could have been twelve.

"What do we do with them?" Anya said, walking over with her arm around Lena. The Dame was walking slightly hunched over and held tight to Anya for support.

Amber cast her gaze over them to check that they were unharmed. Anya seemed fine, Lena was pale, and her hands shook slightly as she brushed hair away from her face. No blood, possible bruising, potential for shock. Stripping the cloak from the nearest hood, Amber handed it to her without a word. Lena took it and Anya helped her place it around her shoulders. The latter shared a look with Amber who understood its meaning immediately. They needed to get Lena out of there.

Now that she realized where they were, Amber's struggle with intrusive thoughts from before made sense. They were in the catacombs. Deep, deep within the catacombs. Much deeper than they had been during the Contest, she could feel it like a weight in the air. These caves did something to the mind—of that there was no question, but Amber had found Lena catatonic down here during the second task. For whatever reason, they seemed to affect her more than the others.

A faraway look stole into Lena's eyes and Anya gave her a little shake. "Lee," she said softly. "Are you all right?"

She nodded.

"I'm fine. One punched me here." She pointed to a spot on her stomach. "Just have to get my breath back. Nothing's broken, it's just sore. I'm fine." Anya looked unconvinced, and her eyes kept darting back to Lena's face. Her arm remained protectively around her shoulders.

"Status?" Amber said to Cervah, who was returning from inspecting the wagon.

"Empty except for some manacles, rope, a couple lanterns, and this." She waved a bottle of dark liquid at them. "Which, by the smell, is either celebratory or used to grease the axles."

Amber did a quick count of the bodies. "There's nine of them, there were six of us. We need to interrogate them, we also should investigate what's down here, and we need to find Jacqueline and let her know what happened."

She folded her arms in front of her.

"Okay, here's a plan. We separate into two teams. Team one goes back to the palace. We load three hoods into the boat. You four"—she indicated the guardpair and the Courtiers—"take them to the palace. Hopefully, the Queen's still there. If that's the case, you can fill her in. She can interrogate them for more information.

"Team two investigates whatever this organization is. Chiv. Turner and I will don a couple of hoods and take the remaining six bodies in the wagon. We'll chain them up, cover them with the rest of the hoods, and pretend to be delivering captives. Once we're in, we can use our disguises to blend in and get answers. What do we think?"

She looked around the group. Andromeda looked resolved, Lena looked relieved, Anya looked worried, and the guardpair looked ready to obey. It was as close to a yes as she cared to wait for.

"Everyone, grab a body. Let's go," she ordered.

Before they all piled into one of the boats, Amber handed Lena one of the lanterns they had retrieved from the wagon. She lingered a moment, unsure what to say or how to help. In the light of the flickering flame, Lena was now white as a sheet.

"Stay safe," Amber said. Lena's mouth quirked up at the corners in an attempted smile.

Next, Amber turned to Anya and grasped her forearm, pulling her close and causing the taller woman to stoop slightly. "Keep an eye on her," Amber muttered in her ear. Anya gave her arm a squeeze to show she understood.

Once Lena and Anya were seated around the three unconscious bodies, Amber turned to Jaenheir and Cervah. They tapped crossed wrists together in salute.

"Keep them safe," she ordered briskly.

"And don't let your guard down," Andromeda added, motioning to the men.

With a hearty shove, the knights launched the boat into the black lake, sending it off to safety. As the lantern grew smaller across the water, Amber felt she could breathe a little easier. A running jump saw her up into the driver's seat of the wagon with a cloaked Andromeda. She pulled her own hood low over her forehead. Her partner gathered the reins, and with a gentle flick, the wagon lurched into motion.

The two black horses pulling the cart seemed unaffected by the commotion, the caves, and entirely unconcerned by the change of ownership. They wore blinders and their tails and manes had been cut short. Black canvas sacs were secured tightly around each hoof, and once the wagon had cleared the rocky shore to join a broken cobbled road, it became clear these were to mute the hooves' clatter. The wagon shuddered to a halt as Andromeda drew them up short in the shadow of the structure that rose from the gloom.

A solid wall, woman made, not naturally formed, cut the shoreline off from whatever lay beyond, and a single tunnel marked the way through. Its toothless maw gaped open, waiting for its next meal. Amber shivered. As if on cue, a cold rush of air escaped the tunnel. The horses pricked their ears forward and awaited instruction.

"I hate this place," Andromeda said softly.

"Don't let it get to you," Amber said. "It's just a hole in the ground, don't let it mess with your head."

"I know. I can still hate it," Andromeda said humorlessly.

"Yeah, I hate it too," Amber said after a time. "Did you see Lena?"

"Yes. It's good she's getting out of here."

Amber cast a sidelong look at Andromeda. What thoughts was this place dragging into her mind? She couldn't see her face, shadowed as it was by the hood, but she noted her hunched shoulders and tight white grip on the reins.

"You doing okay?" she tried to ask casually.

Andromeda grunted, noncommittal. "Let's just find what we're looking for and get out of here," she mumbled and flicked the reins again. The horses stepped forward, drawing them over the threshold. Their lone lantern hung from a hook above Andromeda's head. Its light was an impossibly small sphere against the void.

29

RELAPSE

Lena thought she had beaten him. She thought she was free of him. Free of his grasping, smothering weight. Like the monster in the closet, she had locked him up, trapped him behind fortified walls and thrown away the key. But she'd only ever been struck like that once before and the sharp blow to her stomach had sent a shock through her system. The pain had lowered her defenses for a moment, had stripped the walls from her mind for half a heartbeat. Seizing its chance, the darkness rushed in and the memories returned in full force.

To cover rot with fresh flowers only dooms the flowers.

She hated him. And in the dark and damp of the catacombs, she hated herself. She hated the small ball he rolled her into, and she hated that she had been foolish enough to think she was stronger now.

Now?

No.

Nothing had changed.

Bitter resignation dragged at her bones.

She sank deeper.

30

SKIRTING THE VOID

Yves paced the shoreline. He would have cut a more imposing figure, but his bound hands forced him into more of a duck waddle than a march, and after a labyrinth's worth of stumbles, he had stopped trying to avoid them. With every catch of the toe or snag of the heel, he rolled into the fall and popped up again like a gopher from its hole. This was made much more impressive in the narrow and jagged terrain of the caves. Jacs had to give him credit: He was talented. And his little hop as he popped back up put a smile on her face each time.

The group watched him pace. The inky black lake stretched away into the darkness like a smooth slab of obsidian. His brow furrowed in frustration, he finally approached Jacs. With a smooth incline of his head, he gestured for her to remove his gag. Jacs hesitated. He made an impatient sound and glowered at her. Drawing herself up, she met his ferocity with a steady eye, and after a moment, he lowered his gaze. Only then did she remove his gag.

"The boats are missing, Your Majesty," he said humbly.

Phillip swore. "What are we supposed to do now?" he hissed, fidgeting where he stood. The deeper they had walked into the caves, the jumpier and more irritated he had become. Jacs had felt it too. It was just like during the second task: A heavy fog toyed at the edges of her mind, fingers creeping into the folds and corners of her thoughts. Whispers echoed in the steady *drip-drip-plink* of the catacombs. First her father's voice, then her mother's; but she ignored them. Logic told her it was an illusion, a trick of the mind. She fought to keep the darkness at bay, but it seemed to grow stronger the deeper they moved into the catacombs.

Connor had been very quiet the whole trudge in. Once he had whispered, more to himself, "I can't believe I sent you all down here with only a lantern."

"A lantern that wasn't meant to last," Jacs teased to lighten the mood. But in the dark and damp of the tunnels, it came out barbed and Connor fell silent.

"There's supposed to be at least one boat right here," Yves asserted, snapping Jacs out of her reverie.

"Well, there's not. So, what do we do now?" Masterchiv Rathbone, ever the pragmatist, asked, addressing Jacs.

Jacs bit her lip, thankful for the darkness to hide her uncertainty. She didn't trust their resolve to swim that far, but it seemed like an act of defeat to turn back. The possibilities unraveled before her, each creating a path that steered away from their goal.

"What's that?" Flent asked in a small voice. She stepped forward down the shoreline, pointing out across the lake.

They all moved closer to peer at whatever had caught her attention. Any plan, no matter how small, was better than no plan at all.

Jacs squinted in the gloom. Almost too small to see, a little spot of gold glittered in the sea of black. A pinprick star in the void. It bobbed and shivered in the expansive darkness.

The party on the shoreline stared in wonder as it came closer and closer. Connor finally saw sense and whispered, "We should hide, it could be more hoods."

"Right," Jacs said.

They all scurried toward the overhanging rocks that Yves said typically concealed the small fleet. From there, they watched, hardly daring to breathe, as the light grew larger and larger.

The soft dip and splash of steady oar strokes soon reached their ears. *Just the one boat then,* Jacs thought. *That's good odds.*

The scrunch of wood on stones told them the boat had found land. Whispered voices gave orders and two figures splashed into the water to pull the boat farther up the shore.

"Someone help me with Lena," a familiar voice said. Anya.

"Honestly, I'm fine." Lena's thin voice wavered.

Jacs turned to the others in relief, "It's them," and raising her voice a little, but keeping it gentle so as not to startle them, she called, "Anya! It's Jacqueline. I've brought reinforcements."

Scrambling out from her hiding spot, Jacs ran to embrace first Anya, then Lena.

She looked around their group and said sharply, "Where are Chivilras Everstar and Turner?"

One of the guards, Miera Jaenheir, stepped forward. She reported what had happened in staccato points and related their instructions. Masterchiv Rathbone moved over to inspect the three unconscious men in the bottom of the boat. They were bound and gagged, but one had started to stir. She dealt with him swiftly and he returned to stillness.

"They went into Alethia," Jacs said in disbelief. "Did you see the city? Did you see what it looked like?" Four heads shook no.

"I could tell you what it looks like, Your Majesty," Yves said smugly.

Jacs regarded him coldly, but realized he had a point. "That would be useful, Yves. Maybe in the boat?"

He winked at her and, despite his bound hands, sunk into a bow. "It would be my pleasure."

Not wanting to lose any more time, Jacs quickly split the group into those who would be sailing in the wooden boat with her and those who would take the captives back to the palace. She was alarmed to see how pale Lena looked in the lantern light, but her question died on her tongue at a severe shake of the head from Anya.

After a brief discussion, it was decided that Lena, Anya, Jaenheir, Cervah, and Chiv. Fayworth were to take some of their horses and the hoods to the palace while Jacs, Connor, Phillip, Masterchiv Rathbone, and Dyna Flent would go after the knights. Flent had been surprisingly adamant about accompanying them. In a place as bleak as this, Jacs admired the guard's enthusiasm.

As everyone readied themselves, Anya supporting Lena and the two guards and Chiv. Fayworth claiming their deadweight, Jacs pulled Connor aside.

"Listen," she said quietly. "Maybe it's best you head back with the others." He balked at her words, and she pressed on before he could refute them, "Seriously, it might be dangerous, and this way I know someone with their head on properly will be able to carry on without me. I have notebooks of ideas, our ideas from all those years of letters, for a better Queendom. They're in my study. Without someone to carry them out, they'll just gather dust."

Connor shook his head. "Then why don't you go back? I have no real power as a man. I can't enact even a fragment of those plans."

"You can guide the next Queen; you can make sure Lowrians are included in the next Contest. You don't give yourself enough credit. You could make real change."

"That may be, but Jacs, you *are* Queen."

"In name, sure," she said bitterly and felt the fog gain ground in her mind. She heard how pathetic she sounded but couldn't help feeling in her heart it was true. She cleared her throat and stood up straighter, ignoring the slivers of doubt that had taken root in her head.

"Don't do that, look at all you've accomplished so far!" Connor said.

"This is beside the point; you need to head back with the others."

"No."

"What do you mean, no?"

"I won't leave you down here." He gestured to the walls then tapped his temple angrily.

Jacs looked at him more closely. "Connor," she said carefully, "what do you see down here?" She paused. "What do you hear?"

He shook his head and snapped his mouth shut, lips forming a thin line.

In the silence, an echo of her mother's voice floated around the back of her skull, prickling behind her ears, *Hello, Plum.* But it was just the dripping water. It couldn't be real. Her mother was locked away.

Connor's eyes widened slightly, and a slight shift in tension stretched along his jaw.

"Connor, please," she whispered. "I can't lose you too. If you go back, then at least I'll know you're safe."

"You might, but I won't," he said, crossing his arms.

"I'll be fine," she said, trying to inject a confidence she did not feel into her voice.

"You don't know that." With a sigh, he scrubbed his face. "Jacs, this is not a debate. If you're going, I'm coming with you."

He brushed a hand across her cheek, and she closed her eyes briefly against the sensation. Everything had happened so quickly; she hadn't allowed herself to think too hard about any of it. The carrot dangling ahead just out of reach had consumed her focus. Thoughts of finally rescuing Master Leschi and her mother had spurred her on, but now she was on the doorstep of a secret organization that hated the crown. It wasn't like her to charge into danger with a half-baked, barely researched plan.

"We're ready, Your Majesty." Masterchiv Rathbone's voice cut across her thoughts, and Jacs opened her eyes. Sharing a look of resolve with Connor, she took the first step.

Farewells were brief, but Jacs had a chance to give Lena a tight hug. Jacs couldn't imagine what was happening behind Lena's eyes but, considering how they had found her in the second task, knew it was likely a feat of incredible strength that she was upright. As they pulled apart, Anya gently wrapped an arm around Lena's waist to keep her steady and clasped Jacs's hand with her free one.

Settling herself in the bow of the boat, she watched as the others found their places. Nerves sealed her voice in her throat, so she smiled encouragingly at them all. Yves had convinced them to unbind his hands and even offered to row. Jacs had to admit that it would look suspicious if one of them was found tied up, but she wished there were a better fail-safe in place.

The darkness slipped past them. If not for the lantern, Jacs could imagine they had fallen into a starless sky. The light became a grounding rod, evidence that they were still real. It didn't illuminate much, but every once in a while, it lit up a stalactite hanging from the ceiling. Yves appeared to be using these markers to guide his course, as Jacs frequently saw him looking up and adjusting the boat beneath the dripping spikes.

After what seemed like a lifetime, a faint white luminescence smudged the horizon and grew larger with each oar stroke. As they approached the bank, the boat crunched home, and Masterchiv Rathbone and Flent splashed into the shallows to pull the vessel higher onto the shore. Jacs gaped at the expansive stone wall and ominous tunnel that greeted them. Somehow, the smoky white light made it appear almost alive. The walls seemed to breathe and shift like the coils of an enormous gray snake.

"Are we going in there?" she whispered to Yves. He stacked the oars inside the boat, sprang onto the rocky shore, and held out his hand to her in assistance. She hesitated before accepting.

"No, Your Majesty," he said smoothly. "That would be far too obvious, as that tunnel leads to the gates, which are carefully guarded, and all those coming in and out are expected and accounted for. We will be taking a different entrance. One a touch less glamorous, I'm afraid."

As easy as breathing, he shifted position so he was no longer in front of her but standing beside her. His hand was now a perch for hers to rest on, his other respectfully behind his back. She felt as if they were stepping into a ballroom, not toward an underground city. "Although I've found glamour is less in the attire and more in the attitude, wouldn't you agree, Your Majesty?" he said, his head bowed low as he spoke softly in her ear.

Suddenly they were coconspirators exchanging court gossip rather than a Queen and her prisoner on a dangerous covert mission. Jacs was in no mood for banter. She simply nodded and allowed him to steer her up the bank. Masterchiv Rathbone and Flent fell into protective step behind her, but she had the feeling that the threat Yves posed was of a different nature from what they were used to. She felt Connor's eyes on them and dropped her hand.

"So," she said briskly, "where to next, Yves?"

Yves crossed his arms and tapped his chin thoughtfully. "Your Majesty, my brothers did not hesitate to betray me. I am here to right their wrong. However, I am also in a unique position in that I am your only hope of getting into Alethia undetected."

Jacs arched an eyebrow. "What is your point?"

"Well, before I give away all my hard-earned secrets, I need assurance the exchange will be well worth my time," he said smugly.

"You rat!" Connor hissed.

"I've been called worse, Your Grace, and name-calling gets us nowhere."

Jacs considered this for a moment. "What are your demands?"

A crooked smile spread across Yves's face, and he began ticking items off his fingers as he spoke. "I want an estate on the coast that makes enough revenue to live off comfortably, a holiday in my name, and invitations to every grand event at the palace until I tire of them."

Jacs looked to Connor doubtfully, he shook his head a fraction and she countered, "Would you settle for a cottage on the coast, a concert hall named in your honor, and invitations to at least one gala a year that I host at the palace?"

Yves barked a laugh and stuck out his hand. "Make it two galas a year—one each to showcase my summer and winter wardrobes, put the concert hall in Basileia, and it's a deal."

Jacs hesitated and smothered a smirk as an idea struck her. She placed her hand in his and said, "It'll be in Hesperida. Lord Claustrom is well known for her love of music, and I have a mind to show my support of her interest."

Yves conceded, the deal was made, and the dancer proceeded to jaunt as if springs had been inserted in the heels of his boots.

Phillip, who was busy pulling the boat up beside the other vessel on the beach, looked over at the group. In the moment of distraction, he lost his grip and dropped the boat painfully on his foot. Swearing loudly, he hopped in place, then kicked the offending hull which prompted another round of profanities.

Yves surveyed the spectacle with the cool air of a displeased aristocrat. Once Phillip settled down and joined the group, he said coldly, "Silence is key."

It was hard to tell in the misty white glow of the luminescence whether it was from embarrassment or anger, but Phillip's cheeks darkened. He pulled his cloak about his throat and studied his poor toes moodily.

"Everything echoes terribly in the walled city, so we want to be as muted as possible. Think butterfly alighting on a dandelion rather than"—Yves paused and pursed his lips delicately at Phillip—"whatever *that* was."

With an elaborate sweep of his arm, Yves beckoned the group to follow him. As one, they put their hoods up. Scrunching along the stony shore, they walked parallel to the looming wall. Jacs's neck prickled, and she fought the impulse to keep checking over her shoulder.

Connor sidled up beside her. "You sure we shouldn't have gagged him again?" he murmured, the half jest almost making her smile.

"I haven't ruled it out." Her hand found his in the gloom.

"This place is awful," Phillip muttered to her left.

"How are you holding up?" she asked quietly.

Phillip shook his head. "I swear I keep hearing voices in the dripping." He coughed a humorless laugh. "Only been down here an hour and I'm already losing it."

Jacs felt a squeeze from Connor's hand and returned the pressure.

"It's not just you," Connor said quietly, "I hear it. Seeing things in the dark too. I imagine anyone spending any length of time down here doesn't last long."

As if he had screamed at them, both Jacs and Phillip's necks snapped around to look at him.

Connor, realizing his mistake with wide eyes, said quickly, "That's not what I . . . No, I meant the hoods, I'm sure your mothers are . . . I mean they're strong."

A shushing sound came from Yves up ahead, forcing the three into a prickly silence. They had begun to follow a bend along the shore and came across a river running away from the lake. Jacs saw Yves point to where the river snaked into a small hole cut into the wall. If she hadn't known where to look, she would not have been able to discern it from the surrounding darkness. The domed arch opening above the surface of the water was just big enough for a person to crawl through. However, Jacs did not know how deep the river was beneath.

Yves spun around to face them all and said with forced cheer, "Now we must get wet, my friends." He hoisted his cloak up to gather around his middle, then thought better of it and removed it, folding it carefully into a small, tight bundle. With a wink at the group, Yves stepped into the river. A sharp intake of breath marked the temperature.

Jacs followed suit, holding her tightly folded cloak above her head. She hesitated at the bank. With the muffled quality of whispers through a pillow, Master Leschi's voice flittered from the left to her right ear. She shook her head and stepped into the river. Water rose up and spilled over the lips of her high boots, rushing down her legs to pool around her toes. The ice cold assaulted her feet, her ankles, her calves, but she did not flinch. Focusing on keeping her cloak high and dry, she waded behind Yves.

The current of the river tugged her toward the little opening. Like tiny hands pulling and pushing her onwards; she struggled to remain upright against their force. Somewhere behind her, Flent slipped and Masterchiv Rathbone caught her by the elbow to stop her from going under. At the mouth of the opening, Yves held his hand up to halt their progress. The rush of water was louder here, echoing in the tunnel.

"Now," he said in a stage whisper, "the tunnel is tight, and some spots are deep. You'll likely get up to your chest in some areas. Keep your cloaks dry if you can, they'll be a much-needed warmth on the other side. The river drops off quite severely a few meters after the exit point, so don't miss that or you'll be wishing you learned how to fly. Keep hold of the side at all times, don't let yourself get swept away, and stay quiet. Any voices you hear in the tunnel are phantoms trying to lead you astray; don't listen to them." He glanced meaningfully around the group. "And as soon as we enter the city, consider any word you say as heard, and any move you make as seen. As long as we don't look suspicious, we will be fine. Any questions?"

They all shook their heads and he beamed.

"Marvelous, let's go then, shall we? I can't feel my nethers as it is."

With a playful wink at Jacs, he stepped into the tunnel. Inch by inch, the shadows swallowed him up. Bowing his head, he stooped low and pressed his hand with the cloak against the ceiling. His other hand was anchored firmly to the wall, fingers trailing along the stone. Jacs followed close behind. The sound of running water buffeted her ears and her own breaths took on a metallic echo. The walls and ceiling were smooth and slick. She felt as if she were walking through the neck of a glass bottle as someone poured out its liquid.

The group walked on, mute and blind. The darkness pressed in on Jacs's eyeballs like a tangible weight, and the reverberated rushing of water made her already foggy brain feel heavy. Dark images outlined in a smoke gray danced across her vision. Distorted memories and half-forgotten fears swirled around her like the eddies in her wake. She kept her mind focused on the next steps of their plan and forced herself to ignore the faces that floated before her in the dark.

There was something so familiar about the experience. Of course, she had felt this before in the second task, but something about the sensation reminded her of the visions Altus Thenya showed her what seemed like a lifetime ago. The only difference was that this was perverse, weaponized.

A wild muttering came from behind her. Phillip had begun talking to himself. "They know we're here; they can see us. Always watching, lurking in the dark. They know why we're here and they won't let us win. We're never getting out. I'll never find her. I should have joined them. They would protect me. Alone in the dark. No one will know. I didn't know. I couldn't stop it. Stop it. Stop!"

Jacs turned in the direction his voice was coming from, tricky as it was in the echo chamber, and felt around in the dark for him. "Phillip?"

she said softly. "Phillip, it's Jacqueline. I'm here with you. Where are you? Take my hand. We're almost through, but you have to stay with me. I'm real." She felt a hand against the stone and grasped it firmly. "See?" she said in that same soothing tone. "We'll get through together. Don't let go, okay?"

His shuddered gasp at her touch turned into a sob and Jacs's heart went out to him.

"We'll be out of the dark soon," she said. His large hand enveloped hers and clamped on with fear-fueled force. She winced but held tight, now trusting her cloak-filled hand to guide her through the rest of the tunnel.

After what seemed like an age, a fog-white glow appeared in the distance: a silvery, smokey bubble suspended in the blackness that grew steadily larger as they approached. Yves, now a black silhouette outlined in white, stopped and shifted so that Jacs could see his profile.

"Before we get to the edge, we'll climb out to the left. If you reach the open air before pulling yourself out, you've gone too far." An unmistakable mirth colored his last words. The levity of his tone jarred against the weight on Jacs's mind and Phillip's grip of her hand.

With a flourish and a bound, Yves had stepped forward two paces to stand in the shadow of the tunnel's arched ceiling then floated up and out to the left. In a blink, he was gone. Jacs bit off a yell of shock and a moment later, saw his head swing into view around the lip of the entrance. He swept an offered hand toward her. She pried her fingers from Phillip's grasp. Touching his cheek, she saw recognition steal into his clouded eyes, and he looked at her properly. Lips pressed into a tight line and a small nod of the head were the only indication he gave her that he would be fine. She lingered a moment, looking over the white faces of Connor, Masterchiv Rathbone, and Flent, then pivoted to Yves and took his hand.

He grasped her forearm and swung her up and out of the tunnel. The water sucked at her boots and threatened to pull them both in, but Yves was strong and saw her safely to the stone ledge. He paused, her arm pulled in close to his chest, the length of his body aligned with hers, their faces inches apart, breathing heavily. In the dim white light, his eyes looked almost black, but this was the first time Jacs had noticed the delicate golden spiderweb that laced his irises.

With as much dignity as she could muster in her shivering state, she dropped his hand and stepped back, motioning for him to help the others up. It was only once he had his back to her that she fully understood what peril lay at the end of the tunnel.

The ground simply vanished. Water tumbled over the edge in an inky ribbon and cascaded into the dark abyss leagues below. She stood on a narrow stone ledge that skirted the cylindrical void. Squinting in the dim silvered light that came from the same luminescence that had coated the outer wall, she could just make out a grand stone-hewn bridge to her right, cutting a path across the darkness. To her left, a number of much more modest bridges spanned the gap. Their destination: a monstrous stone stalactite piercing the abyss.

The jagged cone structure was ringed with stone roads and pockmarked with tunnels and doorways. It plunged into the darkness below, and as Jacs peered over the edge, she saw a network of stone bridges linking it to the rest of the cave system. It was unclear whether these bridges acted as support as well as access, or whether the stone city was connected to the ground at the top. Or would that be its base?

Her head started to spin, and she took a step back from the edge. They had found it, the secret city of Alethia. A slate thorn in the Queendom's side. A poisonous rot in their foundation.

Jacs strained her eyes in the gloom and saw dozens of tiny figures scurrying around the stone city like ants swarming around a nest. All dressed in purple, and she imagined, though she could not see from this distance, all hooded. A fire ignited in her belly, and she clenched her fists, nails biting into flesh. *Finally*, she thought to herself.

She was so close.

31

TWO WOLVES

He would have pulled *himself* out of that blasted tunnel, but his limbs were cold, and he couldn't get the image of his mother's last moments out of his head long enough to see straight. His mind perseverated on the scene in a maddening loop: the arrow's fletched shaft protruding from the center of a growing red target. Wide-eyed and terrified, she had reached for him, and he hadn't been able to do a damned thing but hold her hand as the life left her. So, he accepted Yves's hand without comment and was grateful the dancer refrained from any chitchat.

It wasn't until he stood beside Jacs on the narrow stone path emptying the water from his boots and adjusting his hooded cloak around his shoulders that he forced himself to actually look. The dark of the tunnel had pulled his eye inward, but he could see now. Looking past his mind's eye he gasped as Alethia's spiraled stone city came into focus before him. The chasm it pierced was impossibly black. The kind of black that seemed to draw you into its depths. A black that denoted absence, a void, something that was missing. It wasn't space, it was a lack thereof.

Jacs reached for his shoulder and drew him away from the edge. He hadn't realized he had been so close to it.

"Incredible, isn't it?" she said quietly. "This has been here all along and nobody knew about it."

Connor shook his head in disbelief. "Nobody knew," he repeated absently.

Phillip moved to stand next to them, a faraway look in his eyes. "Who'd choose to live down here?" he grumbled.

"Maybe they didn't think they had a choice," said Jacs.

"They always have a choice, Your Majesty," Yves said with a grunt as he pulled Dyna Flent out of the tunnel. "This was the lesser of two evils."

"How—" she began.

"When you have nothing, or worse, when everything's been taken from you, and someone offers you protection, a home, and something close to a family, you'll put up with the cave's whispers and the cold air. You'll put up with most anything, actually," Yves said, face serious. With one last heave, he pulled Masterchiv Rathbone from the tunnel and instructed, "Everyone don your hoods. From here on in, you're all loyal Sons of Celos. Heads down and let me do the talking."

Jacs shot him a warning look. "Yves, don't forget your place in all of this. I'm trusting you to see us through safely. If you betray us—"

"Your Majesty, I have already started decorating the interior of my seaside cottage. Do not for one moment think that I would betray that for what this place offers." He gestured at the silvered city with an air of disdain. Connor had seen a similar look on Edith's face after she ran a finger along his mantel and found it dusty.

Yves looked around the group and took in their pale and drawn faces. His face fell and his brow creased beneath his dark curls. "Listen, this place feeds on your darkest thoughts and memories. Don't ask me why, it just does. If you dwell too long in the darkness, it won't let you go. Trust me on that."

"How—" Flent's voice cracked, so she coughed and tried again. "How do we avoid . . . you know . . . dwelling?"

Yves shrugged. "I think of something I like," he said simply. "My favorite song usually keeps the beasties out." He tapped his temple with his forefinger. "Whatever you choose to think about, just make sure you're feeding the light. The darkness is always hungry," he said, lowering his voice to a menacing growl, attenuated by the mischievous glint in his eyes.

Startling everyone, he adopted a dancer's pose, weight on his back foot, front foot pointed, one hand resting on the small of his back, the other outstretched, and recited:

Two wolves clash claws inside my head,
The victor wins my heart
One wolf of darkness, one of light,
Fierce fangs rend each apart.
Both starve, though one draws strength from me
To fell her eternal foe.
As one wolf thrives, her sister wanes
My choice feeds joy or woe.

He looked around in the stunned silence that followed his recitation and performed a little half bow.

"That choice," he said as he righted himself, "the wolf you decide to feed, the wolf that wins, is yours to make." With a dramatic swish of his cloak, he spun on the spot and began walking along the stone pathway that circled the chasm.

Flent scoffed but looked down self-consciously and shifted her weight between her feet. Connor resisted the urge to roll his eyes, but what Yves had said lifted some of the weight from his mind. He would never have admitted it, of course.

As they made their way along the stone pathway to the nearest bridge on their left, Connor found himself imagining two wolves dancing around each other in his mind. *Feed the light,* he thought. His gaze shifted to his right, drawn to the abyss. *Harder to do in the dark.*

Warmth spread from fingertips to palm as Jacs slipped her hand in his. He looked down and met her gaze, nudging her shoulder with his playfully. She smiled up at him, the same smile from all those months ago when he'd fished her out of the river by the Cliff. The first time they met, before they realized they had already known each other for years.

Harder in the dark . . . but not impossible, he thought with the shadow of a smile dancing on his lips. Placing one foot in front of the other, he moved forward through the darkness.

32

THE DOE IN THE DEN

Anya's arms were warm and solid around Lena's waist. The night air brushed her hair from her face and cooled her feverish brow. With each hoofbeat on the forest floor, Lena felt the pieces within her shift back into place until, by the time they had reached the castle, she felt almost whole again. Almost. A bitterness swept through her.

Bounding down from where she had sat behind her in the saddle, Anya helped her from the horse and crouched to peer into her eyes.

Lena blinked and looked away. "Flower girl, I promise I'm fine," she said. The fog in her mind retreated, the numbness lifted, and with it came a deep sense of shame. Heat flared in her cheeks as she recalled again how absolutely useless she had been in the caves. Without the others, she'd likely still be stuck there. They hardly needed another dead weight dragging them down.

Anya gently cupped her chin with her fingertips and tilted her head left and right, unconvinced.

"Your pupils are massive, Lee," she said softly. "Let's get Master Epione, just to be safe."

Lena pulled away. "It's dark, that's all. I'm honestly fine," she said, still avoiding Anya's gaze. "Nothing that needs any more fuss. I'd hate to bother Master Epione. Besides," she cast her gaze around at the knight and guardpair and their unconscious prizes, "we have much more important things to attend to." Clearing her throat, she lifted her chin defiantly. "We should alert the Council at once."

Anya studied her carefully and sighed. "Fine."

"Courtiers," Chiv. Fayworth said in the still night air, "we'll take these dregs to the prisons. I imagine the Queen will have questions for them upon her return."

"Thank you, Chivilra Fayworth," Anya said, and offered Lena her arm.

Thankfully, she made no comment about the tightness of Lena's grip, nor the degree of support she required. She merely guided her around any unevenness in the cobbles and slowed her pace as they ascended the stone steps to the palace.

Once the horses had been handed over to a wide-eyed stable boy, the knight and guardpair hoisted their loads up and half carried, half dragged them until more guards could be summoned to help escort the unconscious men to their cells.

While the palace appeared sleepy and still from the outside, the moment they entered the halls, Lena and Anya were buffeted with sound and movement. Staff scurried around them with head-down determination. Their strides were as close to running as was appropriate for a member of the palace staff, and instructions were passed between them in low and hurried tones. Ready smiles turned to grimaces as soon as they were sure a guest was not looking.

The gala, it appeared, was in various states of winding down.

Without the Queen, or anyone of status to direct the evening's entertainment, guests had continued to drink, eat, and be merry into the early hours of the morning. Weary musicians were coaxed into their sixth and seventh encore, and dancers swayed with giddy discoordination.

Lena and Anya picked their way through the mess. Wilted flowers, spilled champagne, a sobbing Lordson receiving much-needed encouragement from a bleary-eyed companion. Members of gentry interlocked in alcoves and dark corners, and Lena even saw Dame Shane Adella demanding a handsome server hand-feed her chocolate truffles.

Anya's arm slid protectively around Lena's waist, and they spoke very little the whole way to the Councilors' chambers.

Two guards flanked the doorway, and one of the women nodded in acknowledgment of the two Courtiers.

"Good evening, Your Elegance," she said, addressing Lena and with a look of concern adding, "Are you well?"

Lena drew herself up and smiled benevolently. "Good evening. Tell the Council that Courtierdame Lena Glowra and Courtier Anya Bishop request an audience."

"Your Elegance," the guard said respectfully, "unfortunately, they are currently holding an audience with Lord Claustrom. May I suggest you wait here? I'm sure—"

The door creaked open, cutting the rest of her sentence off, and a serving man appeared. Seeing the guards and Courtiers on the doorstep, he bowed his head and hurried off, leaving the door behind him slightly ajar. Voices from within the chamber spilled into the hallway before the guards had the chance to close the door.

"Need I remind you that my mother is no longer Lord and should hold no further sway in decisions concerning Hesperida *or* Alethia's resources!" Hera's piercing tone held the warmth of a frosted blade and cut just as keenly. "I did not consent to this madness! Her mother would be livid to discover that we were responsible for—and now we've lost the Queen! She could be dead, for all we know! And what would that solve? What would that do for our Queendom? My mother did not have the authority to fulfil such a—"

The door slammed shut. Five fingers splayed firmly against the heavy wood and held there for a moment to be sure. Tentatively, the guard who had spoken to Lena removed her hand. Not a sound could be heard from the room beyond. The four women in the hall exchanged glances, all with equal expressions of shock, but Lena doubted it was for the same reasons.

"May I recommend waiting in a window box?" the guard suggested, pointing farther down the hall where a few empty window seats held plump velvet cushions. Soft lamplight could be seen from the gardens beyond through the dark windows.

"Excellent idea," Anya replied and firmly guided Lena away.

They selected a window seat that was beyond earshot of the guardpair. Lena leaned back and rested her head on the cool marble behind her, grateful for the soft pillow she sat upon. It was a welcome change from the hard wooden hull of the boat and the jolting of the saddle.

Anya sat next to her, knee to knee, hip to hip, although Lena's knees fell a touch short against Anya's longer leg.

"I've never known Hera to raise her voice like that. She was talking about tonight like it was their fault," Lena said softly, looking out the dark window.

"Lee, she mentioned Alethia. That's the name Jacqueline used for the underground city," Anya said quietly near her ear.

Lena hid her surprise; she was uncertain how interested the guardpair were in observing them, but she didn't want to draw any unwanted attention.

"How would she know about it?" whispered Lena.

"And that means the Council knows too," Anya added. "They were talking about Alethia's resources. Do you think that means the hoods?"

Several pieces fell into place in Lena's mind, and she reeled. Feeling like a doe in a wolf's den that realized its mistake too late, she gripped Anya's arm. "Anya," she said hurriedly. "We shouldn't be here. They think we were captured. How do we explain why we're back and Jacqueline isn't? They're going to know she's still out there!"

"And if they're on the same side . . ." Anya said slowly, her own realization dawning.

"Then they can warn the hoods!" Lena finished in a low hiss.

"Your Elegance," a guard announced as she approached the two women at the window. "The Council will see you now."

Lena looked at Anya's concerned face and smoothed her own features. Rising slowly, she said pointedly, "Wonderful. Courtier Bishop, thank you for the company, but I will no longer be needing it this evening. Do enjoy the rest of the gala. Or, as it's winding down, head to my chamber. I will meet you there later." While her mind was still catching up with the new information, she held on to one fact firmly. If this was a trap, it was better that only one of them was ensnared in it.

Anya struggled to hide her shock and spluttered, "But surely, it's no trouble, I don't mind accompanying . . . The matter concerns—"

"Myself alone, but thank you for being a listening ear through all this. I will see you soon, it has been a trying night for everyone," Lena finished smoothly. She held Anya's hand in hers and gave it the briefest of squeezes before rising on tiptoe to kiss her cheek.

Panic fluttered like a sparrow within her rib cage, but she would not let the others hear the traitorous bird's song. Wishing she could say more but feeling the guard's eyes on her, she smiled tightly at Anya and turned toward the Council's chambers.

Anya rose quickly and blocked her path, placing a hand on the small of her back. Lena's gaze snapped upward and she took in the mixture of irritation, confusion, and concern warring across Anya's face. After a moment's hesitation, Anya's fingers traced around Lena's back to her hip, and Lena felt a small object slip into her concealed pocket just below her ribs. With her back to the guard, Anya used her other hand to lift Lena's hand toward her lips. Winking, she placed a light kiss on her knuckles and said, "I will see you soon, Your Elegance."

33

ONE OF DARKNESS

Jacs was under no delusions. She knew death came for everyone in the end, but never before had she felt its presence so keenly, and never had she considered that it could be so persuasive. She had assumed it was a passive entity, waiting patiently to claim those whose time had come, not an active being with the ability to entice its victims closer.

Suspended high above the abyss, Jacs could have sworn the being was perched at the bottom calling sweetly to her. The void had an eerie, compelling presence that seemed to draw Jacs to it, and any wandered thought or absent step led Jacs closer to the edge of the narrow slab spanning the darkness. The bridge was hewn of stone and had no handrails. The neatly cut slabs rose subtly in the middle and tapered off toward the edges, likely for drainage purposes—not that it could ever rain down here. If one wasn't careful, a foot could follow the droplets of condensation right into Death's beckoning arms.

Jacs forced herself to keep her gaze locked on the stalactite city looming across from her as they crossed the narrow bridge to Alethia. Up close, it resembled a wasps' nest she had once seen in the eaves of her farmhouse. Layers of stone wrapped in overlapping rings, appearing paper thin at their jagged edges. Deep, merlot-tinged water stains, pockmarks of abandoned tunnels, twisting alleys, and black, yawning doorways leading into the depths of the hive peppered the expansive surface. In the unnatural pure white light, it was monstrous. The constant, almost synchronized movement of hoods along the outer alleyways and the absolute silence of their footfalls made the whole structure appear to be a living, breathing entity. The blots of purple stood out as the one splash of color in an otherwise colorless scene.

Yves almost danced across the narrow bridge, and the others, with one hand outstretched to clasp the hand of the person in front, and the other reaching back to offer the same favor, walked solemnly behind him. Before stepping out across the chasm, Yves had warned them all again to stay silent. Jacs pulled her cloak tighter around her still-damp form and suppressed a shiver.

One by one, their feet left the bridge to land on solid stone. Smooth steps spiraled around the stalactite down to their left and up to their right. Yves, with a quick check over his shoulder to make sure nobody had fallen over the side, tucked his hands into his opposing sleeves and bowed his head slightly before turning right and walking up the steps. His feet made not a sound on the stone; the hem of his cloak slithered over the lip of each stair.

Their group was less silent, and Jacs noted a tightening of Yves's shoulders anytime a foot fell too heavily. But they all mirrored his movement as best they could and passed by other groups of hoods walking the opposite direction without incident. To Jacs it all felt like a surreal nightmare. Her mind was steel-edge focused on the tasks at hand, desperately vigilant against attacks. Any moment of weakness, any lowering of her mental walls allowed the darkness to gain ground, and she frankly didn't have time for that. It was as Yves said, and she would not feed the depths.

A large part of her mind worried about Phillip and Connor. Both were struggling with their demons in this place, she knew. Luckily, Phillip had quieted his muttering once they had left the river, and Connor had even attempted humor once or twice.

The Queensguard maintained a stoic front, but if this place fed on the darker thoughts and memories within the mind, then she hated to imagine the horrors two women in the military were forced to relive. She noticed Masterchiv Rathbone's hand floating above the hilt of her sword, a movement the knight seemed unaware of. Everyone knew that a knight's skill was measured by how little they needed to unsheathe their blade. It was rumored that Masterchiv Rathbone had only ever done so twice in her career. With dread, Jacs wondered what was causing the knight's hand to wander so often to her pommel.

They climbed, calves burning, until, without more than a half-second pause, Yves made a sharp left and led them into the heart of the city. The thick stone walls enveloped their group, and the already chilly temperature plummeted. Where the catacombs had smelled of damp and mildew, the hive smelled clean and slightly metallic. It was unnerving, the lack of odor, offensive or otherwise.

In the narrow confines of the alley, light came from sporadic patches of the same ghostly white luminescence. All she could really see of the others were their silhouettes outlined in silver. Her feet trusted the smooth stone beneath her and followed the now downward-sloping path. The dotted doorways to their left and right were ignored, and passing hoods were not acknowledged. They moved through the streets like specters.

Ragged breathing was increasing steadily in rate and volume behind her. Phillip. She reached her hand back and fumbled for his, but either he didn't notice, or wouldn't take it. Yves's shoulders rose with every new gasp and Jacs could almost feel the tension radiating from the dancer.

Finally, at a stifled sob from Phillip, Yves whirled around and shot past Jacs with surprising speed. He reached Phillip, clapped a hand across his mouth and shoved him through the nearest archway, pressing his back against the wall, away from the patches of silvery glow. The motion was so fluid, Jacs could have missed it with a mistimed blink. The group stopped on either side of the opening and Jacs heard Yves hiss, "Silence is key, brother. If you can't keep it together, you risk us all."

Another whimper from Phillip.

To Jacs's surprise, Yves's tone gentled, and he said, "I don't know the nightmare within you, but I do know it can't hurt you unless you give it power. Your strength becomes its strength if you let it."

Jacs saw a group of five hoods gliding toward them in the gloom and hurried to stand in front of the alleyway, concealing Phillip as best she could. Connor followed her lead.

Yves said to Phillip in a low voice, "Answer me honestly, can you fight this?"

The hoods moved closer. Jacs couldn't think of a way to alert Yves without giving them all away. Her heart rose in her throat. Phillip whimpered again behind her. They were abreast of Flent now. Jacs's group kept their heads bowed and hands clasped in front of them, backs to the wall obscuring the alley beyond. The new hoods held the same posture and moved on silent feet. Two had drawn level with Jacs.

Then a desperate, "No. I can't!" broke from Phillip, and five hooded heads snapped up and swiveled toward the mouth of the alley. Phillip slumped to the floor behind Jacs.

In a flash Masterchiv Rathbone and Flent contained the two nearest them. Precise jabs and punches sent the first to his knees, and a swift blow to the temple felled the second. The third turned too late to dodge a sweeping kick from Flent and crumpled without a squeak of protest.

Jacs jerked into motion as the fifth broke into a run and caught his cloak before he could flee. She spun him into the wall and heard an oof as the air left his lungs. Number four ducked behind Connor to avoid Masterchiv Rathbone's next attack, but Flent kicked off the opposing wall and landed on his other side to send the hood reeling with a punch to the gut and retching with a kick slightly lower.

Jacs struggled with the fifth against the wall. He twisted in her grasp. Suddenly, his calloused fingers encircled her throat and she clawed at his hands to break free. The five-banded pressure tightened around her windpipe. Stars burst in front of her eyes. In an act of desperation, she flicked the blade free from her holster and drove it into his wrist. He screamed, clutched his hand, and dropped her, gasping, on the ground.

Masterchiv Rathbone twisted the man's cloak around his mouth and tied him within the folds of the fabric in the three heartbeats that followed, but the damage was done.

Already Jacs could hear the scream reverberate within the silent passages like an alarm. It shot down both ends of the passage faster than any scout could have run. Jacs resheathed the blade and looked at the others in horror.

A large hand grasped her wrist; she looked down at it and up at Yves's stricken features.

"Run!" he commanded and darted ahead of her down the corridor.

Connor grabbed her hand and pulled her to follow Yves as he sprinted away in the dark. Jacs turned to find Phillip, but too late, Masterchiv Rathbone and Flent pushed her squarely between the shoulders and kept her moving.

Phillip's hoarse, "Wait!" followed them down the passage and she heard him scramble to his feet. The stomp of his boots thundering behind them. "Don't leave me here!"

They ducked into doorways, twisted through side alleys, climbed winding stairwells, and dove deeper into the city, all the while dodging the groups of purple hoods in their path. The thud of Phillip's boots became quieter and quieter. He cried out several times, but each time sounded farther away.

"We have to get Phillip!" Jacs panted when she realized they were losing him.

"Your Majesty, keep moving, he will be fine," Masterchiv Rathbone said coldly. Jacs pulled up short and spun around. The whole group stuttered to a stop. "No, we have to—"

Without warning, a wad of fabric was forced between her teeth and at a finger snap and sharp order from Masterchiv Rathbone, she was hoisted off her feet and onto Yves's shoulders. "Apologies, Your Majesty," she said. "This is for your safety."

Jacs screamed into the fabric as she was torn away from Phillip. She caught Connor's eye, and he looked away hurriedly and kept running apace. The group left the shouting, panting, crashing Phillip farther and farther behind. Squirming in Yves's grip did her no good as he was obviously used to handling people much heavier and much stronger than herself. Defeated, she allowed her head to slump forward over Yves's back.

Her mother's barely perceived whisper, *Hello, Plum*, echoed in her ears.

34

TWO OF LIGHT

The hoods obviously never dreamed of anyone infiltrating their city. Not only was Alethia deep within the heart of the Upper Realm, but to get there was to venture deeper into the catacombs than even the treacherous second task had required, across a vast underground lake, and farther. With faces concealed, and reciting the overheard and much-repeated phrase *Praise be Celos* in deep voices, Amber and Andromeda had a golden ticket to the place; although much of it was spent waiting for an impossibly heavy stone doorway to open. Apparently, the men turning the crank had needed to wait for a new wooden handle before they could open it for the wagon.

The only concern the men had shown was if there were any stowaways under the wagon. They had apparently expected the interior to be full of captives, so they barely glanced inside. Amber would have smiled, but it seemed out of place down here, so she decided to save it for the surface.

Once the doors had opened, their wagon had trundled through the long, narrow tunnel, then emerged to cross a grandiose stone bridge over a nasty-looking chasm. Then it was through the city gates, and *boom*, they were being led to the prisons by a hood who had met them at the bridge.

They passed through a relatively dark corridor.

"Much farther?" Andromeda asked the hood gruffly, signaling to Amber behind his back. "I've gotta see a lass about a horse."

"No, we've got two lefts, then you're there," the hood grumbled without turning around.

"Good," she said, and he didn't realize Amber was behind him until he was blinking up at her, bound, gagged, and in the back of the wagon with his colleagues several moments later.

Amber took his place and walked on at the front of the wagon.

Two lefts, then they were there. The stone walls looked much like the ones they had passed through, but the bars were new. Andromeda pulled the horses up at a hand gesture from Amber as soon as the prison came into view. Down at the end of the long stone avenue, it loomed. Black, twisted iron bars guarded the entrance, not that they were needed. Escaping this labyrinth was a feat unto itself.

Slowly, Amber signaled to approach. They had discussed their plan in the wagon, but now that it was time to see it through, it seemed much less straightforward. A lone guard stood at the entrance. Despite the cloak, his posture revealed he was alert but relaxed. He leaned casually against the black stone wall and picked at his teeth beneath the hood.

Seeing the wagon, he stood to attention.

"Praise be Celos," Amber said in a deep voice by way of greeting.

"Praise be." The guard nodded. His features were obscured, but a break in his voice betrayed him. He had only just hit puberty. It was likely he wasn't even taking his silphium resin yet—the monthly resin all men of Frea took to halt their ability to father children until they and their partner decided they were ready. Amber, obviously, had never had to try it, but apparently it was nasty stuff. She smirked beneath her hood.

"Come for the traitors," she said.

The boy stood up straighter. "The what?" he squeaked.

"Don't make me repeat myself, boy." Amber added a growl to her tone. Dealing with new recruits was one thing, dealing with a pup like this was child's play. "The traitors. A group of hoods were found plotting against Celos. Praise be."

"Praise be," the boy said automatically.

"Orders to take them and the other traitors to a new location."

"Where?"

"Well, if you weren't told, I won't tell you. I didn't ask questions, and neither should you." The boy deflated a little under his cloak, and Amber pressed on. "We're told to pick up two women. From the Lower. The ones with the balloon."

The boy's head snapped up and Amber caught a glimpse of a long, thin nose and freckles in the dim, smoky light. "But they're—"

"Traitors. Yes. Now hop to." Amber felt sweat prickle her brow. She knew she was making a lot of assumptions and just hoped his youth would bend him to her authority.

"But that's not . . . I think I need to get—" A clatter from halfway down the alley cut him off, and he reached for his waist. Amber didn't give him a chance to retrieve whatever was there. She pounced, with a quick jab to the throat and another to the base of the skull. The boy collapsed without a sound. Amber spun and crouched low over his body, squinting in the gloom to see what new threat had entered the street.

With one hand, she retrieved the ring of keys from his belt and the whistle he had been reaching for.

A lone hood barreled into the street and skidded to a halt. This struck Amber as odd, considering all the other hoods she had passed had been silent and almost painfully slow. The hood froze, staring at the wagon. The narrowness of the street meant the bulk of the wagon blocked anyone in front of it from his view. Amber signaled to Andromeda to take care of the crumpled hood while she crept around the side to get a better look at the intruder. His hood had fallen back, and she could make out a face she recognized.

"Traitor," she growled.

It appeared to be the Lowrian boy, Phillip. Suddenly it all made sense: Of course he was a hood. The Sons of Celos used his connection to Jacqueline to get into the palace, to infiltrate the gala, to get to the Queen.

"You're one of them!" she snarled, stepping out from behind the wagon. The worm stumbled backward and bolted down the alley. Amber considered following, but a few moments later, Andromeda materialized beside her with the young hood's body, and together they added him to their purple-cloaked collection in the back of the wagon.

"That Leschi boy is working with the hoods," Amber muttered to Andromeda.

Andromeda gave a start. "Are you sure it's him?"

Amber nodded.

"But Jacqueline trusted him. They've been friends for years."

"Basemutt betrayed her," Amber spat.

Andromeda's face darkened. "Let's go. Before he has a chance to raise an alarm." She glanced at the wagon and back at Amber. "Do you think he suspects—"

"Not sure. What I said spooked him though," Amber replied and scratched her knuckle along her jawline.

"Come on," Andromeda said.

With a jingle of keys and a scraping of metal, they entered the prison. The horses snorted, mist rising from their nostrils.

The knights abandoned the wagon in the entrance yard, which was eerily empty.

"Where is everyone?" Amber whispered.

Andromeda shrugged and bowed her head, clasped her hands in front then walked purposefully down the corridor to her right. She was following the sounds of gibberish, moaning, and muttering coming from that direction. Amber mirrored her posture and followed, ears tuned to any sound beyond her own breath. She hated how the hood cut off her peripheral vision.

No wonder these loons were so easy to bring down, she thought as she turned her head slightly to the right. The hood obscured her vision completely.

A soft gasp from Andromeda drew her attention. She had drawn level with a gap in the wall and taken three hurried steps backward. In a moment, Amber understood why. They had arrived at the first "cell," if you could call it that. There were no bars. The corridor, walled to the left and open to the void to the right, cut away completely. Amber peered over the lip of the corridor and saw an open-air three-walled room one story down. Where the fourth wall should have been was a gaping hole leading to the abyss. If she laid on her stomach and reached her hand down into the cell, and the person below had stretched on tiptoe toward her, she imagined they could touch fingertips.

Andromeda said softly, "Rope." and darted back to the wagon to retrieve a long length of rope from the back. Amber watched the prisoner in the cell below rocking violently back and forth, hands pressed over their ears as if they wanted to press their palms right through their skull.

Andromeda returned. They shared a look of apprehension and pressed on. The stream of sound became increasingly louder with every cell they passed. Each time they peered down into one, they saw prisoners in various states of disarray and filth. Most were pressed into the wall closest to the elevated walkway, as far away from the void as possible, but Amber saw two who were right next to the edge. One stood, toes hanging over the lip of the cell floor, arms outstretched, and head thrown back, with a gleeful grin on his face. The other lay along the edge, stroking the empty air lovingly and cooing softly to the void.

"This is horrific," Andromeda said quietly.

"Beyond horrific," Amber agreed.

Andromeda looked at the rope and then over at yet another huddled prisoner.

"Listen," she said, "we're running out of time. We know where they're keeping the prisoners. We can assume Jacqueline's mother is one of them, why don't we leave and come back with reinforcements? This place is giving me the creeps, and I can't help but feel we're pushing our luck the longer we're here," she said it all in a rush, and Amber caught the plea in her tone.

That more than anything made her pause.

A strangled voice came from the cell ahead of them, rising above the babble. "Jacqueline? My girl, my brave girl, my Plum. Is she here?"

The knights hurried over and peered down into the cell. A woman with a mess of long, dark, white-streaked hair sat with knees pulled tight to her chest, facing the corner of her small cell. She looked directly at the walls in front of her and said airily, "She is my only child, you know. Francis and I tried for more, but my heart could only break so many times before we decided to stop. He was a wonderful man, Francis. Wonderful men can still break your heart though. Not that he meant to of course. But this is the shape. See? Now my heart is shattered and look! There are all the pieces." She giggled in a girlish manner that made Amber's skin crawl. With an extended forefinger, Amber watched her calmly trace various shapes onto the wall.

"Ms. Tabart?" Amber whispered softly down to her. The woman didn't hear her at first, as she was still deep in conversation with the wall. Amber tried again, louder this time. "Ms. Tabart?"

Her chatter stopped, her finger fell from the stone, and she looked up.

"Someone come for tea?" she asked. "Let's sit under the apple tree. Francis would like that. He made the chairs himself." She looked down at her hands and at her blood- and filth-stained dress as if seeing them for the first time. "But I can't have guests today, I'm not ready. No, this will not do."

"We can't leave her here," Andromeda said quietly. Amber agreed. She was surprised the woman had lasted this long in this place. If they waited to come back, who knows what state they'd find her in?

She looked helplessly at Andromeda, who had already begun fastening the rope around an iron ring set into the stone wall. Amber noticed similar rings set in intervals down the corridor opposite each cell. Likely they were used as anchors for the hoods or for lowering prisoners.

"I doubt she'll take the rope," Andromeda said bluntly. "And if she does, she won't have the strength to pull herself up."

Amber nodded and met Andromeda's pointed gaze. "What?" Amber asked.

Andromeda raised her eyebrows and handed her the loose end of the rope.

Understanding her meaning, she sighed. "Fine."

Holding tight to the coarse fibers, she lowered herself into the cell. "Hi, Ms. Tabart," she said softly as she landed.

The woman stiffened and fell silent but didn't turn around.

"My name is Amber. I'm a friend of your daughter's."

Maria turned her head and curled tighter into the corner. "Not going to trick me this time. Purple beasts," she muttered angrily. Amber looked down at her purple cloak and could have kicked herself.

Pulling her hood back, and throwing the cloak over her shoulders, she said, "Ms. Tabart, this is a disguise. I'm one of the knights who protect your daughter, Jacqueline."

"Jacqueline? My Plum is here?" The hope in her voice quickly shifted to horror. "She can't be here! It's not safe! We need to get her out!" Maria turned with raw fear in her eyes. Amber caught a glimpse of her face for the first time and suppressed a gasp. Her eyes were sunken into their sockets, cheekbones sharp, almost piercing through her paper-thin skin. A dark bruise spanned from eye to jawbone in various shades of color that blended to black in the smoky light. Dried blood was crusted under her nose and across her chapped lips. With hair wild and a tunic covered in bloodstains, she looked fresh from a crypt.

Amber held her hands up and lowered to her knees. "She's safe. Ms. Tabart, I've come to take you to her. I'm here to rescue you."

Her eyes darted to Amber and around the cell, purposefully avoiding the gaping hole of the void. "Rescue?" She whispered the word like a prayer.

"Yes."

Maria covered her mouth with a trembling, bloodied hand. Amber noted one finger looked broken, and two had bloodied messes where the nails used to be.

Andromeda cleared her throat from above, and Amber shuffled forward. "Ms. Tabart, I know you're hurt, but we're going to get you some help. May I touch you? I need to help you out of here."

Maria, tears in her eyes and a hand still covering her mouth, nodded and rose. Amber kept her face neutral but felt her stomach tighten to see the full extent of her wounds. Amber approached her slowly.

"Tell me if something hurts, or if I'm holding too tightly, okay?" she said as she gingerly wrapped a hand around her waist and walked with her to stand below Andromeda's waiting arms.

Maria nodded.

"Now, I'm going to lift you up, and my partner Andromeda up there, see she's wearing a disguise too, no we're not with the purple hoods. We're friends of your daughter. We're friends of Jacqueline.

Yes, there we go. Okay, I'm going to lift you up and Andromeda will pull you out. It will hurt your hands, but we need to be as quiet as possible."

Maria nodded and mimed buttoning up her lips.

Amber looked up at Andromeda to see she was in position. "Okay, here we go, Ms. Tabart. Careful now. One. Two. There we are." And with a final grunt of effort, she lifted the paper-light woman up until she felt Andromeda pull her weight from above. Shifting position, she pushed Maria from below. Unable to find a handhold that was not bloodied or bruised, she endeavored to be as gentle as possible. Despite her buttoned lips, Maria gasped and stifled several cries of pain. Her muffled moans simply added to the cacophony of gibberish coming from the other prisoners.

In a moment, she was up and over the edge of the cell, and Amber followed her up the rope.

"Where is she? Where is my Plum?" Maria asked, she was crouched over, protectively cradling her hands, but her eyes searched the empty corridor.

"She's safe in the palace, Ms. Tabart," Andromeda said gently while Amber untied their rope.

"Let's go and see her, shall we?" Amber said.

"Yes. Yes, I would like that very much," Maria agreed and allowed the knights to steer her toward the wagon.

They crept along the passage in a single file. Andromeda at the helm, and Amber guarding the rear. Her eyes scanned the half-lit stone ahead and behind them.

Suddenly, a metallic creak and deafening crash reverberated down the passage. That had to be the prison gates. The prisoners below fell silent. Andromeda froze, threw an arm out, and drew Maria behind her against the wall. The calm that came before every fight stole over Amber, and she settled into a stance as Andromeda unconsciously did the same.

Slowly, slowly, Andromeda signaled for them to keep moving. Maria started to hum nervously in long, tuneless notes. She turned to look at Amber when the latter touched her gently on the elbow, pressed a finger to her own lips, and shook her head. The battered woman mimed buttoning her lips again, this time with shaking fingers, and her humming died away.

Reaching the end of the corridor, Andromeda stopped them again and peered around the corner into the entrance yard. Amber heard Maria's hitched breathing and strained her ears to pick up anything that was happening beyond.

"The gates are closed. No movement," Andromeda muttered softly.

The back of Amber's neck prickled. Andromeda waved them forward. They crept into the yard. Again, it struck Amber as odd that it was so quiet in the prison. No guards, wardens, or even food bearers to be seen. She supposed a prison like this needed very little surveillance. If a prisoner did manage to crawl out of their pit, they'd still have to navigate the city, the lake, and the catacombs to properly escape. However, it just seemed wrong that there was no one there.

Andromeda reached the horses first and began untying the nearest one. Leaving Maria to pat the other, Amber hurried to the back of the wagon to check on the hoods. They lay prone and unmoving next to each other, cloaks cast around them like blankets. It almost looked cozy. Amber tugged at the nearest cloak and pulled it free of its host, then tucked it under her arm to give to Maria.

Jacqueline's mother swayed gently back and forth as she stroked the nose of the pitch-black stallion. She didn't seem to notice when Amber draped the purple fabric over her shoulders, nor did she react when she fastened the clasp under her chin.

"Such a pretty horse," Maria said softly.

Amber helped Andromeda boost Maria onto the back of a horse once they were unhitched. She was about to swing herself up behind Maria in the saddle when a movement caught her eye.

"Turner," she hissed, too late. Two hoods stepped out of the shadows on either side of the gate to bar their path. Amber wheeled around, three more had materialized to block the corridors leading away from the yard.

"It appears you have lost your way," a soft male voice rose from one and somehow all of the surrounding hoods. "May Celos guide you in the darkness." They took a step forward. There was a metallic slither as the men unsheathed their swords.

35

THE THORN IN ONE'S SIDE

Strength is a creature with many forms. Lena had never considered herself strong by any means. Her mother had always been stronger. While Lord Glowra had never called her daughter weak outright, it was by comparison that Lena had deduced over many years that she must be. The weak Dame, hiding behind her strong Lord's skirts. Head down and flinching through life, she had been the picture of obedience. Under her mother's strength, she hadn't needed her own.

That is, until she had met Anya. That was when her strength took shape. It was not a strength of physical power, or one with an intimidating presence. No, in her world, that form would have been quickly quashed by those more powerful and more intimidating. Her strength was a by-product of living under her mother's will for so long. A result of the accidental training that took place between the moments of her mother's might. The strength to navigate the honeyed tongues of those in power. The strength of the Dame's mask.

Feeling Anya's hand slip from her waist as she walked to the Councilors' chambers alone, Lena drew herself up. She may need to lean on others to climb a mountain or to escape those horrid caves, but here in the palace, she stood tall. Here, she could support the weight of those around her. Just as she had grown up protecting Anya within her mother's tangled web of policy, etiquette, and protocol, so too could she protect her and their Lowrian Queen in whatever web the Council had spun.

She could do this. She *would* do this. Heat pulsed through her veins.

The guard listened to Lena's whispered order, led her through the door and hurried away as she stepped into the center of the room. Four throne-like chairs rose away from her like points on a compass. A Councilor occupied each one. Hera stood in the center of the room and turned as Lena entered.

"Thank you for your time," Hera said to the Councilors, her tone frosty, and turned to leave.

"Wait," Lena said quickly, "Lord Claustrom, if you have no urgent matters calling you away, I would like you to attend this meeting also."

Like a cloying perfume, Hera had lingered around the palace for the past few weeks, and it would have been a breath of fresh air to have her leave; however, Lena couldn't deny that it would be helpful to have a witness to what was about to happen.

After a moment's hesitation, Hera inclined her head in agreement and moved to stand beneath Cllr. Perda's seat.

"Courtierdame Glowra, we are so pleased to see you are safe and returned to us!" Cllr. Stewart squeaked to Lena's left. "You must be exhausted; do you need any refreshments? Would you like to sit down?"

Lena shook her head and replied, "No, thank you for your concern, Your Eminence, but I am fine. This matter is important and needs immediate addressing."

"Oh?" Cllr. Dilmont said. She sat behind Lena.

"But where is our young Queen?" Cllr. Perda said from her seat directly opposite Cllr. Dilmont. "She set out to find you; where is she?"

Weighing her words, Lena said carefully, "We met her on the road, she sent us ahead on the faster horses to deliver her message. She is following behind with the others."

Cllr. Perda's face split into a relieved smile a moment too late. "That is wonderful news."

"And her message?" Cllr. Dilmont asked. To keep from being disoriented, Lena did not turn to look at her but remained facing Cllr. Perda.

"That she is safe. She also sent hostage hoods with us for questioning. They will tell us more about their secret organization."

"Then I would call that a successful venture," Cllr. Fengar said from Lena's right.

"Indeed," Lena agreed. "It has been an incredibly long night."

"You must be exhausted," Cllr. Stewart said.

"I noticed you did not attend the gala," Lena said neutrally.

"We were detained by business," Cllr. Stewart replied.

"You missed quite the show. The Sons of Celos were wonderful. Had you seen them before?" she asked, again keeping her tone light.

"No, they—" Cllr. Stewart began.

"Oh interesting, so how did you hear of them?" Lena cut across her. The Councilor flinched as if she had been slapped, and Cllr. Perda narrowed her eyes.

"W-well, it was a glowing recommendation from Lady Sybil Claustrom," Cllr. Stewart stuttered.

Hera shifted uncomfortably.

"Ah, and she's well acquainted with their work?" asked Lena.

Cllr. Stewart cleared her throat and Cllr. Fengar piped up. "I assume she must have seen them once before. She may have—"

"If it was a glowing recommendation, I would imagine she was more than fleetingly acquainted with them, especially to suggest them for the Queen," Lena pressed on.

Cllr. Perda held up a hand, and the room froze for a breath. "You will do well not to interrupt members of the Council, child," she said coldly. "Your relationship with our young queen has made you bold but, I trust, not disrespectful."

Lena bowed her head, fists clenched within the folds of her skirts. "My apologies, Your Eminence."

"That's quite all right. You've had a trying night after all," Cllr. Stewart said with an apprehensive look at Cllr. Perda.

"As we all have," Cllr. Dilmont began. "So, if you would be so kind, what is your purpose for this audience?"

Lifting her chin, she leveled her gaze to Cllr. Perda's glittering black eyes. The Councilor sat leisurely in her chair, drawing the chain of a necklace through her fingers. The long, slender ruby pendant hit the fleshy base of her thumb each time before she let the chain slip loose, only to pull it through her fingers again. The pendant was a little longer than her palm and tapered to a sharp point at one end.

"Now, social decorum dictates that you, the hosts of the event, are present, especially when the event is in honor of our matriarch," Lena began. "I find it odd, Councilors, that you hired a troupe you knew nothing about for a gala you did not attend. I find it interesting that, while you were absent, the hooded men infiltrated the palace and kidnapped the Queen's entourage. I find it curious that the troupe leader was able to lead the Queen directly to the hoods' underground city. And I find it too much of a coincidence that all of this is unconnected and that none of it happened without your hand."

"As Cllr. Stewart mentioned, we were detained. We couldn't possibly have been implicated in this evening's events," Cllr. Dilmont said quickly.

"And yet, here you sit. Attending late-night meetings with Lord Claustrom and myself. You must have completed this business in good time, so why could it not have waited? What was so pressing that it prevented you from fulfilling your role as hosts? Since you were not at the gala, where were you?" Lena drove the question home, all light evaporated from her voice.

"We were—" Cllr. Fengar offered.

"Likely helping the hooded men into the palace, how else would they have conveniently known the escape route the Queen would take? It can't have been a coincidence," Lena said swiftly.

"What are you implying, that we—"

"My apologies, I meant to be direct. You hired the dancing troupe that led the hooded kidnappers right to the Queen." Lena laid the accusation before them neatly as though presenting a new way to fold napkins to her servants.

"That is the final time you interrupt a member of the Council, child," Cllr. Perda said, her voice dripping with venom.

"And this is the final night you sit as Councilor, *ma'am*," Lena said with a flourish, brandishing the last word like a whip.

Cllr. Perda snatched her necklace into her fist with a snap and leaned forward in her seat. "How *dare* you—" she began, low and threatening.

"All this is speculation," Cllr. Dilmont said dismissively.

"And no one would take your word on any of this regardless," Cllr. Fengar said with a nervous laugh.

"That's where you're wrong," Lena said softly.

The Councilors waited, Cllr. Perda arched a questioning eyebrow, and Cllr. Stewart fidgeted nervously with her shawl. Lena took a breath. With steady hands, she withdrew a folded piece of parchment from within her embroidered bodice and unfurled it carefully. She had kept it close to her heart ever since Jacqueline slipped it into her palm on the balcony.

The Queen's seal weighed the bottom corner down and she brandished it high.

"By order of the Queen, I am to act in her stead during her absence. I have here a royal decree signed and sealed by Her Majesty."

"That's not—" Cllr. Perda began.

"And as such, I hereby charge you all with treason. Guards!" The doors burst open, and the two uniformed women who stood at the door, as well as almost a dozen more guards, flooded the room. "Seize them. The Council of Four are charged with high treason and will be tried upon the Queen's return to answer for their crimes against the crown and our fair Queendom."

"And Lord Claustrom, Your Elegance?" one of the guards asked, spying the Lord at the base of Cllr. Perda's raised dais. Hera had held her hands up in surrender the moment the doors opened.

"I have evidence against these traitors," Hera said quickly.

"You!" Cllr. Dilmont snarled.

"And will happily testify," Hera finished defiantly.

Lena noticed that a few of the guards stormed forward to secure the exits and apprehend the Councilors, but the majority wavered, looking expectantly at Cllr. Perda.

"What are you waiting for?" Lena snapped at those who seemed hesitant.

Again, their eyes flickered to Cllr. Perda, who smirked and sat back in her chair.

"They are waiting for my orders," she said simply.

"But my orders—" Lena began, feeling the color drain from her face. Adrenaline cooled in her veins, allowing tendrils of dread to take its place.

"Are in the name of a queen who has a shaky foothold on her throne at best. No, pet. She has no power here, and Lord Claustrom, I am disappointed in the speed with which you turned your cloak." Cllr. Perda tsked. "Your mother would be ashamed."

Hera opened her mouth to respond, but nothing came out.

"No, here's what will happen. Guards, escort Lord Claustrom back to her chambers. Cllr. Dilmont will deal with her there. One rash slipup need not spoil a long and fruitful relationship. The rest of you, wait outside. I wish to speak with Courtierdame Glowra alone." The concerned parties, including the other three Councilors, rose to follow her command. Hera looked uncertain but allowed herself to be led away with a half glance back at Lena.

The empty room expanded around Lena, where she stood at its center. She suddenly felt like a fly awaiting an approaching spider.

"You," Cllr. Perda said, rising slowly from her throne and descending the steps until she stood right in front of Lena. "You are more of a thorn than your mother gave you credit for." She placed a hand lightly on Lena's shoulder. "She will be sorry to hear of your accident in the catacombs."

"What acci—" Lena's eyes widened in shock, and her words died in a shuddered gasp as white-hot pain lanced up her side. It plunged deep, with thin, sharp teeth that bit into her flesh hungrily. Cllr. Perda jerked her wrist free and withdrew the now dripping blood-red ruby pendant from below Lena's ribs.

"Tragic really. You made it all the way back to the safety of the palace, only to bleed out from your wounds. Driven by duty and blind to your own pain, you ignored our pleas to seek out Master Epione and in doing so, doomed yourself. A shame. You had such potential." Cllr. Perda looked down at her coldly, as Lena sank to her knees, one hand clutching her side, the other grasping at Cllr. Perda for purchase. The Councilor's eyes bore into her. There was no emotion behind them, just two drops of obsidian reflecting Lena's own look of horror.

Lena's bloodied fingers fumbled over her wound, warm and wet. She willed the gash closed, her fingertips brushing against a lump that had deflected the pendant's deadly course. She fell forward, landing heavily on her other wrist.

"It won't be long now," Cllr. Perda said, crouching low, her voice reaching Lena's ears from far away. She twirled the bloodied pendant between her fingers triumphantly. Making an exaggerated show of it, she looked around the empty chamber with mock surprise plastered across her face. "And it looks like no one is here to help you."

Lena felt the blood slip over her fingers and knew the Councilor was right. She was alone, staring into the eyes of a woman happy to watch the light leave her. No one was coming for her. She had even sent Anya away because she thought she was strong enough to do this one thing by herself.

But Anya hadn't left her completely alone. In a flash she recalled the slight shift in weight as Anya had slipped something into her bodice, remembered her comforting wink before her hand left Lena's hip and she let her go.

Realization sparked through her. It was her knife.

Lena's hand fumbled at her side, searching for the concealed blade. She was sick of feeling powerless. Sick of being the victim. She let the fury consume her. Gritting her teeth against the pain, she gripped the hilt and lunged. A snarl escaped her lips as she pushed up from the ground and threw herself at the Councilor. With a startled cry, Cllr. Perda toppled over and Lena pressed her blade against the quivering pulse at the woman's throat. Her knees and free hand pinned her to the ground beneath. She felt power surge through her behind the blade.

She would show them.

Her vision flickered; the searing pain in her side screamed. Why was there so much blood? She pushed that concern away. Here, she was in control. Liquid fire coursed through her veins. Life and death bowed to her. She would show them all she was no one's victim. She pressed the blade into Cllr. Perda's neck and saw a thin rivulet of the Councilor's blood well up and around it, trickling down her knuckles. The richness of the red surprised her; she had expected black.

At the blade's touch, the Councilor froze, eyes wide and searching. Her gaze flicked across Lena's face and down to the streaming wound in her side. Cllr. Perda took short shallow breaths in the silence.

Watching.

Waiting.

A knowing smile played around the Councilor's lips.

36

LOST AND FOUND

"This way, hurry!" Yves's hushed whisper echoed too loudly around them as they raced through the labyrinth of side streets and alleyways. They had been running steadily downhill for what seemed like an age. Jacs imagined a marble swirling around and around a funnel and just hoped they weren't about to drop out of the pointed tip of the stalactite-shaped city.

Suddenly he stopped short, and Connor had to hop sideways to avoid crashing into him. Panting and clutching at his side, Yves peered around them, a finger to his lips. Connor doubled over, hands on his knees, breathing heavily. Seizing her opportunity, Jacs, who had ridden on Yves's bouncing shoulders limply, twisted violently in his arms. Thrown off balance, Yves struggled to hold her still, but dropped her to save his own footing instead.

She landed painfully on the rough stone ground and glared up at him. Reaching up with her now free hand, she ripped the fabric away from her mouth. "You left him behind," she said in a low voice. Rage had left her cold.

"Your Highness, he was a liability. Our mission came first," Masterchiv Rathbone said flatly. "Your safety comes above all else, and he not only put you but all of us in danger."

"You *left him behind*," she repeated. Silence radiated from her words. No one quite knew what to say next.

"Yes," Masterchiv Rathbone answered simply.

"How cou—"

"And *you* brought him down here. Knowing how this place affects people, you allowed him to come. Did you even warn the boy?" Masterchiv Rathbone's words held no judgment, but Jacs felt the sting like a slap.

"I didn't know it would—"

"You brought him down here, you brought us all down here. I'm trying to get us out. Forgive me, Your Highness, for not disregarding the safety of all for the sake of one."

Jacs was ashamed to feel a lump form in her throat and tears threaten the corners of her eyes. She saw Phillip's frightened face flash before her, and blinked to see the pale, drawn faces of the others. They had all been battling some degree of demon down here for far too long, and it was all her fault.

"I'm sorry," she said softly, a dull ache in her temples. "You're right, I lost sight of the goal. I just . . . I didn't expect we would have to leave *anyone* down here. I hadn't prepared myself for that outcome."

"No," Masterchiv Rathbone agreed.

"Good news," Yves said with forced cheer. The others turned to him. "We're lost."

"How in Queen's name is that good news?" Flent asked incredulously.

"Because if we're lost, I doubt my brothers will be able to find us either," he said with a winning smile.

"So, what do we do?" Connor asked.

Yves shrugged. "Keep moving forward? You've seen this place—at some point we'll reach the edge and then we just turn around and try a different way."

The group stared at him.

"That's your plan?" Flent spluttered.

"Pretty much. That's how I managed the first few months living here," he said. "The prison's on the edge, so we'll find it eventually."

He spun on his heel and strode off down the narrow street. Without a better plan, the rest of the group followed him. Jacs hugged her arms around her middle. A new voice whispered inside her, *Wait! Don't leave me here!*

Waves of panic rolled through her, just under the surface. Not enough to hitch her breathing—it left her no outward sign to show to the world—but she felt it heavy and hot on her chest. Pulsing through her heart like the purr of a satisfied cat.

With every step they moved downward, she was painfully aware of the vast weight of rock over their heads, and the nightmare maze that served as an exit. Colder and colder it grew, until their breaths rose in mist around their heads. The silence was peppered with shivers, and Jacs cursed their damp clothes.

They walked for what seemed like hours. Down and down and down. They had stopped running into other hoods and the passageway was eerily quiet. The kind of quiet that smothers any sound that dares intrude. Yves halted again and turned with wide eyes. "Okay friends, I . . . I honestly have never seen this part of Alethia before. I think we should turn back. This doesn't feel ri—"

The rest of his sentence was engulfed by a sound like thunder. Jacs clapped her hands over her ears. It was coming as though from right beside her. From inside her. A lion's roar harmonized with an eagle's cry. She knew that sound. Her heart pounded in her chest, and she looked around wildly. She *knew* that sound. But what was it doing down here?

"Was that—?" Connor began.

"Griffins," Jacs breathed.

"They're close," Masterchiv Rathbone said.

"We should leave," Yves said hurriedly. "This is all wrong, we shouldn't be here."

"Why are there Griffins down here, Yves?" Jacs asked forcefully.

"I . . . well, I honestly don't know. I didn't know. I'd heard stories about an Undercourt but never actually believed . . . I mean, they were merely stories. Tales we'd whisper to each other in the dark with no more substance in them than in the shadows from which they arose," he replied, his words slowing as theatrics bled into his tone.

Her feet started moving toward the sound before her mind could process the ramifications. She reached the end of the corridor, the pressure in her temples increasing all the while. A massive wrought-iron door barred their path. The panel inlays beneath the twisted iron design shone with that same silver glow that peppered the walls.

Jacs looked at the others, their faces reflecting the ghostly glow behind her as well as her uncertainty. *Keep moving forward*, Yves's words and her curiosity compelled her to lift her hand to the talon-shaped handle and push. The door was unlocked. Obviously, the fear of intruders this deep in the city was nonexistent. With an unqueenly grunt, she threw her weight into the door, and it eased open.

A low growl emanated from behind the door and echoed in the recesses of her mind. She felt a tug, an impatient pull on her thoughts and the memory of her mother, battered hands clasped around the prison bars, returned to her in a flash.

Hello, Plum, the memory whispered. She shook her head and entered the room beyond, the others silently following behind. Smothering her gasp behind her hands, she stared, horrified, at the scene unfolding before her. The door opened to an upper landing with a waist-high banister running around the outer perimeter of the cylindrical room. Long purple crystals of different lengths hung from the ceiling and lined the walls like sconces. Unlike the hazy white luminescence that covered the walls, these did not omit any light of their own.

Scry crystals, Jacs thought in horror. Growing from the ceiling and walls like a sinister inverted forest.

The first thing her eyes landed on was a silver-tinged pure white Griffin, flying at eye level in the vast cathedral of a room. It's beak and neck were wrapped in a cruel iron bridle, and it flapped its wings desperately against the thick iron chain pulling it back to the floor below. Dark streaks of what must have been blood striped its haunches and the feathers around its beak and neck. Through its muzzle, it roared again, an angry human shout came from the end of the chain beneath it.

Standing near the edge of the balcony, she glanced down. Dozens of Griffins, feathers reflecting the ghostly light around them, were shackled in iron and chained in the hall below. Hoods hurried among them, holding onto chains, brandishing whips, and barking orders. Some Griffins were flying at the ends of their chains, only to be ripped from the air at the whim of their master. Others were huddled in groups around moldy bales of hay or cowering in the corners. A larger portion of Griffins were protectively guarding a vast nest filled with golden eggs.

The golden orbs cast a warm glow into the cold white light around them. The nest looked damp and was built of moss and scraps of cloaks. It was a sorry imitation of the grand nest atop Court's Mountain.

The Undercourt appeared to have no power against the hoods. No way to prevent a hood from plucking a precious egg from their nest. Jacs watched in horror as the circle of protective Griffins parted submissively at a hood's snarled order. He reached into the nest, withdrew a golden egg, and taunted the nearest Griffins with it. Feigning to drop it on the stones and laughing at their cries of outrage. Jacs stared up at the Griffin, still flying in front of her. She met its eyes, shining black pits speckled with golden stars. The moment was suspended between them. She stepped forward and lowered her hood, not realizing what she did.

Another roar ripped from the Griffin's throat as it was torn down to the earth by a hood wrenching on the chain. Jacs felt an equal wrenching in her mind, and her vision was forced inward.

Get to the bank! Her father's voice called from behind her. Her eyes clouded and she saw the ice settle over top of her, almost felt the weight of her new winter coat pulling her down into the depths of a lake she was nowhere near. Pain lanced through her knees, and she registered as though from far away that she had fallen to the ground.

Wait! Phillip's voice screamed in her ears. His stricken face, hand reaching for her, grew smaller and fainter as he fell further behind.

I'm so very proud of you. Master Leschi's words sent an icy blow through her heart. *They'll write songs about you one day.* They were in her mentor's living room, books stacked up to their ears, cups of tea warming their palms.

She wanted nothing more than to sink and keep sinking, curl into the pains of the past. To stay down was so much easier. To rise took a strength she was not sure she possessed. But her father's voice whispered in her ears, *Despair is a pit that goes nowhere.* She had to fight this.

Focusing on the minute shift of the muscles around her eyes, Jacs blinked and looked around. She was on her hands and knees; Connor had sunk down the wall to curl into a ball on the floor. Dyna Flent, her hands firmly over her ears, was muttering, "Not real, not real, not real." Masterchiv Rathbone, her eyes glazed, had halfway drawn her sword, and Yves stood panting, one hand on the door frame, looking as though he had run a mile. She had to get them out.

Pushing off her hands and sitting back on her heels, she shook her head as if to clear water from her ears. A second growl rolled from down below and again Jacs felt something seize her mind. The sensation mirrored the judgment of Altus Thenya on the mountaintop. Only here it was barbed, cold, and perverse. Where Altus Thenya had gently led her to the memories deep within her mind, this was a twisted, forceful ripping of her darkest thoughts to the surface.

She bowed forward with a groan, willing the memories, the nightmares away. Flames flickered behind her closed eyelids, and she watched her clocktower burn. Bodies lay like discarded toys around the base of the town fountain as the King intoned their fate. She unclenched her fists and felt the stones beneath her palms. *Get up.*

"It's them," she said out loud. "It's the Griffins."

Stumbling to her feet, she reached Masterchiv Rathbone first and shook her shoulders roughly. Focus returned to her gaze. She looked down at her half-drawn sword and hurriedly shoved it back into its sheath. Sharp eyes taking in the situation, she asked with gritted teeth, "What do you mean?"

"They're doing this to our minds," Jacs whispered, grounding Masterchiv Rathbone with heavy hands on her shoulders. The knight's gaze kept slipping in and out of focus, but Jacs could tell she was fighting to remain with her. She hurried to explain. "The Court can do it through touch. I've experienced it firsthand. But this is different somehow. Broken. And stronger." Jacs winced and doubled over. "So much stronger."

"How do we stop it?"

Jacs shook her head, desperate to clear it. Underlying her own pain, she felt something deeper, more brutal. An all-consuming agony. Pure torment. A vision that was not hers forced its way into her mind and a sharp stench of mildew and rot washed over her. She saw a baby bird deep in a black pit, hopping fruitlessly toward a distant light high above its head. It cheeped feebly, flapping two bloodied stumps for wings. The wounds bled freely. Rich crimson streaked its torn feathers and trickled down its twisted clawed feet. She blinked the image away.

"I don't know, but we have to get out of here." Stumbling toward Connor, she grabbed his arm and hoisted him to his feet. His cheeks were streaked with tears, and he had the same faraway look in his eyes she'd seen in Lena and Phillip. Yves materialized on his other side to help support his weight, but Connor pushed him away. Masterchiv Rathbone quickly replaced Yves and helped Connor stay upright. Yves, unperturbed by the rejection, offered his arm to Jacs. With Connor supported, Jacs accepted Yves's arm and pulled Flent up with her free hand.

Each point of contact helped ground Jacs in the moment and kept her out of her own head. Flent clung to her with the desperation of a drowning woman, and Yves began to tremble.

They turned back to the iron doors, and Masterchiv Rathbone let out a low hiss. Two hoods stood in their way.

"Praise be Celos," one muttered. "What are you doing down—" he cut off as he saw Jacs's uncovered face.

"Intruders!" the other spat like a curse.

"Run!" Yves cried and sprang forward. Quicker than the hoods had time to react, he pulled Jacs and Flent back through the door, knocking the men aside as if they were flies, and barreled along the passageway.

Desperate roars and snarls followed them out of the chamber. Jacs focused on the weight of her arm in Yves's and the sound of Flent panting along beside her as they raced away. Jacs couldn't hear the hoods pursuing them, but she assumed her heart pounding in her ears was drowning them out.

It was a while before they stopped hearing the Griffins calling to them. It was longer before they dared speak. Finally, Yves pulled them into an alcove, and they doubled over to catch their breaths.

"I promise. I didn't know. About the Griffins," Yves panted.

Jacs shook her head, a metallic taste in her mouth. "Is everyone all right?" She looked up.

Flent and Yves stood beside her. The alcove was empty. Her heart shuddered in her chest.

"Where's Connor?" she asked.

"Where's Masterchiv Rathbone?" Flent asked at the same time.

Yves scratched his jawline and peered out of the alcove, back the way they had come. "I think," he paused, considering. "When I said *run*, we went one way, but I swear I heard them running farther into the Griffin chamber."

Jacs gaped at him.

"That probably explains why my brothers followed them and not us."

"We have to go back!" Jacs exclaimed. Flent bit at her thumbnail, and Yves frowned.

"Your Majesty," he said softly, "that is the last thing we should do. Masterchiv Rathbone is more than capable of taking care of herself, and we would only make it worse by going in after her. That's a wasps' nest down there. Did you see how many of my brothers were milling about? Not to mention, now they're expecting us. No." He shook his head.

Flent spoke up, "Your Majesty. Our plan was clear, and we failed. Yves is right. We need to retreat. Your safety is our priority."

Jacs looked helplessly from one to the other. First Phillip, now Connor, and they had come all this way only to leave empty-handed. Not just empty-handed, but worse off than when they started. She felt her heart splinter inside her. "We have to help them," she said stubbornly.

"And we will. We can bring a force here on a different day. Masterchiv Rathbone said that a battle might be lost today but won tomorrow. We can win this, but we will lose if we attempt it now," Flent said gently.

She looked from Yves to Flent and back again. She hated that their logic made sense. Hated that their plan was the better one, and most of all, hated that she could not reason her way out of this without admitting she had to leave Connor behind.

"Fine," she said hoarsely. Like a prisoner in irons, she let the others lead her to the surface.

37

THE MUMMA-BEAR INSTINCT

A calm had washed over Amber's mind the moment she saw they were surrounded. She knew this calm well. It allowed her to think clearly and quickly in a fight, and it gave her time. In the heat of emotion, time slips away rapidly. In the midst of calm, time lingers. With a call to Maria to head toward the gates, Amber and Andromeda didn't wait for the hoods to make the first move. Leaping into action, Amber swept low, Andromeda struck high, and in an instant, one of the hoods crumpled.

It was trickier in the open courtyard; the hoods were spread out and harder to pin down. Amber flew toward the second hood. Andromeda accommodated her sudden change of course seamlessly and kept pace. The hood brandished his sword and stepped toward Amber. She dropped to the ground, rolled behind him, popped back up, and with two well-placed blows along the spine, dropped him at her feet. His sword clattered to the ground, and she kicked it away, spinning to face their next assailant.

Andromeda darted forward and Amber, as natural as breathing, joined her in step and they met the third hood, felling him easily. A satisfied smirk spread across Amber's face. *Child's play*, she thought.

The fourth and fifth approached from the gate, giving Maria an opening to move closer to the exit. The hoods made a beeline for the knights, paying Maria no mind.

Back-to-back, the knights faced the hoods and kept one eye on Maria. Moving through their steps, constantly shifting position, they attacked. Amber deflected a sword thrust and stepped in, placing an upward blow to the hood's abdomen. A rush of air escaped his lungs and he fought to draw his next breath. She heard the second hood cry out from Andromeda's swift kick. With a spin and a shove, Amber pushed the last hood into Andromeda's fist. He hit the ground before Andromeda settled back into her stance.

They shared a nod and ran toward Maria where she stood with the two horses near the gate. Just before they reached them, Amber felt a shift. She didn't hear the hoods approaching, but the air changed in the way it does when people enter an empty space. One moment she and Andromeda were alone in the courtyard, the next moment they weren't. It was as simple as that. She turned mid stride and saw ten, twenty more hoods filing into the courtyard and upper balcony from the surrounding corridors. The upper balcony she had not noticed before. They approached on silent feet, some brandishing shortswords, others holding bows. There was a tight spiraling creak as the bowmen drew back their arrows.

The knights were so close to the open gate. Maria had found the opening mechanism and sat on her horse next to the open gates with her hands clasped. She smiled like a child who had done something clever.

"Go!" Andromeda called to her. Maria's smile vanished and she dug her heels into the horse's flanks. With a muffled clatter of cushioned hooves, Maria raced through the gates. The bowmen loosed a round of arrows and Amber ducked, swerving erratically as she made for the opening. She heard a cry and for a moment thought it had come from Maria's lips, but it was Andromeda who stumbled.

An arrow protruded from her back, below her left shoulder. Her knees buckled, and Amber caught her before she hit the ground. Crouching under her weight, she propelled them forward, their run nothing more than a hobble, toward the second horse. Arm outstretched, she fumbled for the reins and swung Andromeda close to the stirrups.

Another flurry of arrows followed them, and the horse whinnied as one glanced off its flank. Its skin twitched along its haunches and Amber held the reins firmly, steadying the beast. A few more clanged off the stone pillars or metal bars, but Amber heard the sickening sound of metal on bone and Andromeda cried out again. Her right leg buckled beneath her. Amber almost fell on top of her as she dropped suddenly to one knee.

"Get *up*," Amber snarled through gritted teeth, forcing her partner to her feet.

The hoods on the ground floor had stayed below the protection of the upper balcony while the archers loosed their volley, but now began to move forward.

"Get on the horse," Amber ordered Andromeda. She crouched beside the black beast and cupped her hands as a foothold for Andromeda to use.

Her partner, balancing on one foot, one arm curled at her side, the other clutching her chest to ensure the arrow hadn't passed all the way through, looked down at her and shook her head.

"No, you have to get Ms. Tabart out of here." Andromeda coughed and winced as if the movement pained her. The arrow must have punctured a lung. "I can't pull myself up there, and I can't protect her like this." She gestured to the arrows with a grimace.

"Don't be stupid, you won't stand a chance," Amber snapped, gesturing again with her cupped hands.

"I might," Andromeda said with forced humor.

"I can't leave you here," said Amber.

"You have to. You need to get her out. I'll be fine," Andromeda said with a weak smile.

"Turner, I can't just—"

"You will."

"No."

"It's been an honor, Everstar."

"No!"

Amber's mind raced, the calm evaporated and was replaced with panic. She needed to get Andromeda on the horse. She couldn't leave her, but she couldn't lift her, and she certainly couldn't carry her. Turner wouldn't last three minutes against the hoods alone, and together they wouldn't last ten. They needed to get out, needed to protect Maria. The arrows were buried deep. Turner was so pale. She couldn't leave her. She couldn't leave her. She couldn't just leave her. Something snapped inside Amber's mind, and she acted on impulse.

"Self-sacrificing pain in my—" she growled and caught Andromeda roughly by the arm as she took a step toward the hoods. She felt something more than adrenaline course through her bloodstream. Something more than grit, more than muscle, something that rose from a heightened protective instinct. With a strength she did not know she possessed, she swept Andromeda over her shoulder, and hoisted her up onto the horse's back. Her muscles screamed and she felt a pop in her shoulder, but Andromeda flew into the saddle behind the force of Amber's shove.

With a snarl, Amber pulled herself up behind Andromeda and dug her heels into the horse's sides. Clutching Andromeda around the middle, and careful to avoid the fletched arrow protruding from her shoulder, Amber held her partner firmly in place as their horse sprinted through the gates. The hoods shouted after them, and the archers fired another round of arrows as the men on the ground floor gave chase.

Muted hoofbeats thundered in time with the beating of Amber's heart. A rumbling sound met her ears, and it took her a moment to realize it was coming from Andromeda. The knight was laughing. It was a jolted, staccato sound, humorless and interrupted with every thumping gallop of the horse, but a laugh, nonetheless.

"You stubborn, crazy—" Andromeda muttered.

"Shut it, I need to focus." Panting, she gripped the reins and peered around Andromeda's uninjured shoulder to steer the stallion through the labyrinth after Maria's steed. She could see the other horse's tail whip around the corner ahead. Almost there. Maria must have heard them, because in the next moment, Amber realized the horse in front had stopped and was waiting for them. She pulled up short.

"Didn't know . . . you had that . . . in you . . . Everstar." Andromeda's words were stilted as she paused to catch her breath. She inhaled deeply, or tried to. Her eyes widened as she tried and failed to draw in more air, and she doubled over in pain. Her breath now came in short, shallow bursts. "Thanks," she said, voice thick with emotion.

Amber patted her gingerly on the back. "Well," she said with an attempt at bravado, "you can't leave me yet. I mean, I need *someone* to keep me in line. Especially since Flent made a pass at me the other night."

"She what?!" Andromeda attempted to spin around in the saddle, but Amber pushed her to face forward, narrowly avoiding an arrow in the eye.

"Watch it!" she yelped. "You're still a pin cushion!"

Andromeda bent over the horse's neck as if to stave off dizziness, her breathing shallow and splintered.

"I obviously still need you around," Amber said, thankful Andromeda appeared too focused on her pain to hear the worry that betrayed her tone.

"Get them out." Andromeda panted, jerking her head toward the arrow in her back.

The sound of the oncoming hoods was still a way off, but they were losing time. Amber hesitated.

"Now!" Andromeda ordered, one palm braced against the saddle horn, the other curled at her chest.

Amber's stomach clenched as she awkwardly leaned away from her and scooched backward to look Andromeda over. Horseback was not the best place to perform a medical exam. Luckily, the arrow in her leg hadn't hit an artery. But the one in her back was a worry. Even without the small amount of medic training she had, Amber would have known arrows didn't belong near lungs. With mounting dread, Amber saw the blood fizz and bubble around the arrowhead. A definite puncture, then. Amber had encountered this kind of wound several times in the field, it rarely ended favorably without immediate medical attention.

"We'll do it once we're clear, the leg one's probably okay, but the one in your back . . . if I rip it out and we don't seal it right, your lung might collapse, or at the very least the wound will start sucking in more air."

Andromeda nodded. She was putting on a brave face, but she looked rough. Her breathing came in short gasps and her face was pale and clammy. "Okay," Andromeda said quietly, considering their options. "Let's"—she swallowed and licked her lips—"get Maria . . . out of here." She paused to clear her throat. Amber rested a hand on her shoulder encouragingly, and Andromeda waved it off. She had never been one for coddling. Painfully, she finished: "Make a break for . . . the bridge . . . and head for the boats."

Amber nodded. Maria began humming again.

"Ms. Tabart?" Amber called softly. "You get to follow our horse now. Okay?"

"Okay," Maria said dreamily. "You know where to go, I know because you know."

"Great," Amber muttered. She spurred the horse onward.

38

RETREAT

Jacs's mind had become a blank slate. Numbness flooded her thoughts and stretched to her fingers and toes until she felt like a hollow husk. Her feet moved automatically, and she followed the others without complaint, but her heart had remained far below in the belly of Alethia.

They had stumbled onto the shoreline outside the cursed city after an hour of retracing their steps. Their disguises and Yves's knowledge of how to interact with the other hoods had been enough to ensure their swift exit. It felt cheap, laughable, that they had encountered so few obstacles on the way out.

Her boots scrunched along the pebbles and shale as they left the river tunnel. Water dripped down her calves and pooled around her ankles. *Where was Connor?* She was looking forward to being dry again.

Was he okay? They rounded the bend to where she knew the boats waited. *It was her fault.* Jacs didn't notice Flent throw out her arm to stop her until she walked painfully into it. Looking up, she saw what had caused their sudden halt.

Three hoods were climbing from midnight-black horses and walking toward one of the boats. The first swayed a little as though dancing a waltz and the second supported the third who was hunched over his left side and hobbled on a wounded leg. The latter two kept checking the tunnel over their shoulders.

Jacs, Yves, and Flent froze, unsure what to do. The hoods hadn't noticed them yet, but it wouldn't take long. Jacs squinted in the gloom and saw the second hood, who was much shorter than the third, stop and inspect what Jacs now saw was an arrow jutting from their brother's shoulder. After a moment's hushed conversation, the lanced hood drew the shorter into a rough embrace. Yves looked at Jacs and said, "That's very unorthodox."

"What do you mean?" Jacs whispered. They had all lowered to a crouch to observe the scene unfolding before them.

"We don't hug," Yves said bluntly.

Jacs peered closer at the figures, ears straining to catch their whispered exchange. As they pulled apart, the shorter figure's hood fell back, and Jacs caught Amber's face in the silver light. Relief washed over her so forcefully, she almost laughed out loud. Standing, she threw back her own hood and waved to them.

Amber caught sight of her past Andromeda's shoulder and her face broke into a crooked grin. Letting go, she ran to Jacs and the others, Andromeda turned and limped after her. A hysterical relief claimed the group as they reunited. All careful to keep their voices down, all just so happy to see the others safe. Jacs noticed Flent rush to embrace Amber, think better of it, and share a stoic guard salute instead.

The third, waltzing hood drifted around the bow of one of the boats, oblivious to the commotion behind them, and dancing their fingers along the wooden hull instead. Amber followed Jacs's gaze, and her own expression sobered.

"Jacqueline," she said seriously, taking Jacs's hand. "I want you to be prepared. She's badly hurt, and her mind's not right."

Jacs cocked her head to the side, throat constricting. "Who?"

"Please don't be alarmed," Amber continued, "but we found your mother." She pointed to the hood at the boats.

Jacs looked from Amber's face to the figure on the shore in shock. Too scared to hope, she croaked, "My—"

Amber nodded, confirming. Jacs felt her limbs move first. She dropped Amber's hands and ran to where her mother stood.

"Mum!" she cried. The hooded figure turned and sank to her knees, cowering on the bank, hands rising to shield her face. Jacs slowed, dread forming in the pit of her stomach, and knelt down in front of her.

"Mum," she said softly, "it's me."

Her mother flinched.

"It's Jacqueline," Jacs said even quieter. Carefully, she lifted a hand and pushed her mother's hood back. Her hair was matted, and her face was hidden behind bruised and bloodied hands. "It's okay," Jacs cooed, forcing herself to stay calm.

Her mother's damaged hands lowered to reveal the gaunt shadow of her face. "No, just tricking me again," she mumbled, not meeting Jacs's gaze.

"Mum," Jacs repeated, "it's me, it's really me. I'm here."

Her mother looked at her then. Something lurked in the depths of her eyes that had not been there before, and Jacs swallowed the lump in her throat. Squinting at Jacs, her mother's expression cleared. Recognition washed her apprehension away and she gasped. Gingerly, she lifted a battered hand to Jacs's cheek, wiping a tear that trembled there.

"Hello, Plum," she said, eyes creasing at the edges. "My sweet Plum." She giggled and patted Jacs's cheek clumsily.

Her hands were dry and brittle, but they were real.

Kneeling together on the jagged rocks that lined the shoreline, leagues under the earth, hovering between Upper and Lower Realms, mother and daughter reunited. Jacs laughed a sob and gently drew her mother into a hug, treating her as though she were made of glass.

"Hi, Mum," she breathed, throat tight with emotion. "Let's go home."

39

THE STRENGTH TO STRIKE OR SHEATHE

Lena pressed the blade into the Councilor's neck, marveling at the way the skin bowed under her force. It would be so easy, just a little more pressure and she would have done it. No wonder the Councilor had been able to stab her so swiftly, skin was hardly a barrier to a blade.

"Why are you doing this?" she asked Cllr. Perda. Her vision was blurred around the edges, and she was having a hard time focusing on the woman's face. "You're meant to fight *for* the throne, not against it."

Cllr. Perda's eyes flicked over Lena's ashy features and dilated pupils. She licked the corners of her lips and said slowly, "I will do what has to be done to protect the Queendom, even if it means defying the crown. A dog is no more a Dame than that Lowrian is a Queen."

Lena's hand began to shake, but she did not let up. It would be so easy. This woman deserved it. She needed to be stopped, and this was the quickest way to do it. Just a flick of the wrist. A bit of pressure. She could just let gravity do most of the work and lean forward. So, what was stopping her? She wasn't weak. She wasn't. She would show them she wasn't.

Sweat beaded her forehead and she blinked her eyes in an attempt to clear her vision. *Just do it,* a tiny voice whispered. *It's a matter of millimeters.*

Off to her left, the chamber doors creaked open. It was now or never; she was running out of time.

"Lee!" Anya called from the door; her feet slapped against the chamber floor as she ran to her side. Lena's head shot up and the speed of movement caused it to spin nauseatingly. Seizing Lena's moment of distraction, the Councilor cried out, "Help! Dame Glowra's lost her mind! Get her off of me! Guards!"

Lena turned back to her prey and dug the blade into her neck in warning. Cllr. Perda's shouts stuttered into silence.

Anya approached cautiously. "Lee—"

"She stabbed me."

"She stabbed—" Anya began in alarm.

"Lies!" cried the Councilor. "The woman is delirious."

"She overthrew my orders; she defied the Queen's rule. She's working against Jacqueline. She's behind the hoods," Lena said vehemently.

"Lee—"

"She deserves to—"

"Lee!" Anya's frightened tone cut across Lena's ramblings. Lena was breathing rapidly now, the fire in her side spread to her chest. She could feel the flames licking through her, flushing her cheeks, and making the veins in her eyes glow red. Blood continued to flow from her side, pooling beneath her.

"Lee, give me the knife," Anya said softly, her shaking hand outstretched.

Lena looked down at where her blade had drawn a trickle of blood from the Councilor's throat. She saw her own white, bloodstained knuckles wrapped around its hilt. No longer the unblemished hands of a Dame, she could almost believe they belonged to someone else.

She turned to look at Anya. Her Anya. With her hand outstretched and a plea in her voice. A perverse echo. Slowly, Anya knelt beside Lena.

"Let me do this," Lena snarled. "I can do this!"

"Lee, please—"

"I can do this at least," she muttered, eyes snapping back to the woman beneath her.

"Lee," Anya said in a whisper, "you're not a killer."

"She's a monster," Lena spat. "They're all monsters."

"If you do this, you'll become one too," Anya pleaded.

Lena's hand shook, the hilt tattooed a pattern in her palm. "I can—" Lena's eyes widened, muscle and sinew tensed, poised for the final blow. Cllr. Perda lay very still, shallow breaths shifting her collarbones. Her dark eyes reflected Lena's pain-warped features and, Lena realized, nothing else. There was nothing. Cllr. Perda meant nothing; she was nothing. This action would make her everything to Lena.

"Let it go, Lee. She's not worth your pain," Anya said gently.

Lena pressed the blade a hair deeper and saw the Councilor flinch. It would be so easy. A knight would have done it by now; Chiv. Everstar would have done it by now.

No, the thought made her pause.

Amber wouldn't. None of the knights would have. Their blades remained sheathed until there were no options left.

It *would* be so easy, she thought, but weakness took the easy route. Brutality was not strength; it was merely weakness's armor. True strength lay in sheathing the blade. The idea spread through her mind like a balm, cooling the fire that raged behind her eyes. With horror, she realized she'd almost let it consume her.

"No," Lena whispered, and withdrew the knife from Cllr. Perda's throat. Staring down at her bloodied and bloodless fingers, a wave of disgust rushed through her. In one swift movement, she tossed the blade across the room. The fury that had fueled her vanished and left her empty. Her vision wavered. She collapsed into Anya's arms.

The Councilor seized her chance and threw Lena off, scrambling free. Lena felt Anya's arms tighten around her. The pain in her side flared, swallowing her whole, and her vision flickered out like a snuffed candle flame. The sound of retreating footsteps and Anya calling her name were the last things Lena heard before everything went black.

40

THE DOWNWARD SPIRAL

R*un!* Yves had yelled.

That was something Connor could do. It didn't take much thought, and Alti knew that he had no more space in his head for another thought. One foot in front of the other. The rhythmic pounding of boots on stone was a steady comfort. Anything that drew his thoughts away from the nightmare playing on a loop in his mind. He felt Masterchiv Rathbone's hand in his and trusted her to know the way. She had a head for these things after all. He had a head for policy. He had once had a head for adventure, although given how this one was going, he'd gladly take on another puzzle related to the golden egg count than whatever this had devolved into.

They sprinted around the balcony of the cavernous chamber, the tortured screeches of the Undercourt following them through a side door and long after they were out of sight. Deeper and deeper they ran, further and further into the heart of the stalactite city. How had he not known of this place's existence?

How long had it thrived in the dark undetected? How long had they been stealing the young boys of the realms to fill its corridors? And where had the Griffins come from?

How dare they defy the divine order and imprison them underground like this?

In a flash he recalled the nest with the Undercourt's hoard of golden eggs and could have laughed, his mind giddy, detached, and grasping for an anchor. *Mystery solved*, he thought mirthlessly. More Griffins would mean more eggs. However, why the Undercourt's eggshells ended up in the Queendom's treasury every year didn't bear thinking about. Not now.

He was dimly aware of the few hoods Masterchiv Rathbone felled as they ran. Their groans followed them through the labyrinth. At times he was thrown back while she dealt several swift blows to the oncomers, who were clearly unprepared and outmatched for an opponent of her rank. Not once did her hand hover near her sword. A good sign. He tried to shake the haze free of his mind. The farther they ran from the Undercourt, the clearer his thoughts became, and it wasn't until they stopped in a quiet side passage that he felt the cobwebs finally dissolve.

"Where," he panted, "where do you think we are? Where are the others?"

Masterchiv Rathbone straightened and looked around. "They went a different way. The hoods followed us, so we successfully drew the assailants away from the Queen."

Connor, head between his knees, lifted his chin. "What do you mean? They're not . . ." The quiet and empty passage answered his question. Panic gripped him, and he took a few steps back the way they had come.

Masterchiv Rathbone grabbed him roughly by the arm. "Stop," she commanded. "We can't just go barreling back up there."

"But—"

"Flent has her orders; if we were to become separated, she knew to get the Queen to safety. It's likely they are now heading for the exit. The best we can do is get ourselves out and aim to meet them at the palace."

"So, they're—"

"Not coming back for us, and we won't be going back for them. Our mission now is to get out."

"How can you be so callous?" Connor whispered.

Masterchiv Rathbone rounded on him. "Your Grace, I am doing my duty. This plan put both the Queen and the Royal Advisor directly in harm's way, and it is my job to make sure one, if not both, are returned to the palace safely. You can punish me for insolence once we're there, but until that time, if you want to see daylight again, I suggest you do exactly as I say. We have no time for moping." She rubbed her temples, making the blonde tufts of hair along her hairline stand up at odd angles.

Connor scratched the back of his neck. "You're right."

Masterchiv Rathbone nodded and then paused to listen. "Do you hear that?"

Connor strained his ears and noticed the sound of running water farther down the passage. "Water?"

Masterchiv Rathbone, with a curious expression on her face, indicated for him to follow and walked cautiously down the dark passage. The patches of misty luminescence were noticeably sparser down here. Connor only saw the vague outline of the knight in the dim light, and as a result stubbed his toe painfully once or twice on the uneven ground. Each time, he received a sharp reprimand to remain quiet.

The passageway ended abruptly. The stone wall rose severely in front of them with no side corridor to continue along. Connor's shoulders slumped and he prepared to turn around, when Masterchiv Rathbone stepped closer to the wall and her boots clattered on wood instead of stone. She froze, mid inspection, and crouched down. With a sharp rap of her knuckles, she found what appeared to be a wooden trapdoor at the end of the corridor. Connor approached and bent down. Wiping his hands across the surface, his fingers brushed against an iron ring set into the wood.

"There's a handle," he whispered.

Masterchiv Rathbone crept to the side of the door and both of them clutched the large iron ring. On the count of three, they each heaved on the handle and felt the large heavy door shift. Its rusted hinges protested the sudden movement but finally relented. A metallic whine set Connor's teeth on edge, but at last the door swung open, revealing a spiral stone staircase. The sound of rushing water was louder now.

They looked at each other. Masterchiv Rathbone whispered, "By now the hoods will know there are intruders in the city. I'd much rather keep going forward than have to fight our way back through whatever barricades the hoods will have likely put in our way. Agreed?"

Connor nodded in the gloom, quietly relieved they wouldn't have to pass the Griffins again, and hurried to clarify. "Yes."

"I'll go first and let you know if the coast is clear. If something happens to me—"

"It won't," Connor said earnestly.

"Your Grace, save your sugarcoating, it might," Masterchiv Rathbone asserted. "If something happens to me, you'll have no choice but to go back the way we came. Keep your head down and don't draw attention to yourself. And for Queen's sake, don't lose your head."

"Okay," Connor agreed.

Masterchiv Rathbone took a breath, then descended the stairs. Her head disappeared beneath the lip of the trapdoor, and Connor peered into the gloom to follow her progress as long as possible. He saw her pause, then look back up at him and motion for him to follow. Connor hurried to comply, lowering the trapdoor closed above them.

It took Connor a second to realize what was different down here. There was no ghostly white light. The light here was a pure, crisp blue coming from the doorway at the bottom of the spiral stone staircase. With one hand on the center post guiding him around the tight turns, he landed at the bottom only slightly dizzy.

Masterchiv Rathbone flanked one side of the doorway, and Connor took up position on the other. Together, they peeked into the room. The sound of water was much louder here. Compared to the musty dank smell from the Undercourt's chamber and the deeper part of the labyrinth, in this room the air was cold and smelled fresh.

Allowing a moment for his eyes to adjust to the new blue light, Connor's jaw dropped. Inside this chamber was an immense underground waterfall. The towering rock it cascaded over was entirely made of ice-blue crystal, glowing with a light of its own. Connor shared a look of disbelief with Masterchiv Rathbone, and together they stepped into the room.

His eyes were fixed on the waterfall, while hers scanned the perimeter and she peeked around boulders and into alcoves to ensure they concealed no one. High above their heads, the black void stretched up and away like a starless sky.

Giant jagged chunks of blue, glowing crystal rose around the base of the waterfall, like a splash flash-frozen in ice, and were scattered around the edges of the pool at the waterfall's base.

"What is this place?" Connor whispered. His words echoed around the chamber, adding to the waterfall's melody, then were unnaturally stifled, as though absorbed by the water. In fact, the sound from the waterfall had an odd quality to it too. Where the room should have been filled with its constant roar, the roar itself seemed to stop short, as though each water droplet hitting stone was allowed one solitary note to give the air before stopping abruptly.

"I don't know," Masterchiv Rathbone replied. Her words were also allowed a moment of freedom to dance with the water's percussion before being swiftly swallowed. Despite the beauty of the place, Connor felt unease creep down his spine like a cold finger. He dragged his gaze away from the water and looked around for an exit.

Voicing his thoughts, Masterchiv Rathbone said, "We should keep moving. If we are where I think we are, we have a long road ahead of us."

Connor tilted his head to look at her. "Where do you think we are?"

"In the Lower Realm, or at least level to it. Come on, I think I found the path."

Connor felt his gut clench, and he imagined Jacs and the others miles above them, running to safety.

Walking closer to the pool, he bent and palmed two hand-sized chunks of blue crystal. "Here," he called to Masterchiv Rathbone and tossed one to her.

She caught it without looking at him and passed the crystal between her palms.

"In case we need light," he explained. Even if there were glow worms in the tunnels down this deep, he didn't relish the idea of having to sing their way into the Lower Realm. Masterchiv Rathbone nodded her thanks, and they turned their backs on the waterfall, entering the dark mouth of the tunnel to their left.

"It just keeps going," Connor said into the endless silence, holding his crystal high. Its light didn't extend much farther than a foot in front of him, but he was thankful for it all the same. His voice sounded hollow, as though the cave was absorbing its vibrations moments after they left his lips. They had been walking for what felt like hours. The farther they walked, the more he wished he had taken a drink from the waterfall's pool. His stomach was empty, and his lips were parched. He couldn't help thinking that adventurers in books always seemed well-fed. Amelia the Daring never complained of an empty stomach. As if to prove a point, a rumbling protest erupted near his navel.

Reaching into a small pouch on her belt, Masterchiv Rathbone withdrew a strip of waterlogged jerky and handed it to Connor, retrieving another one for herself. "It's going to be a long walk, so preserve your strength as much as you can."

Connor was too hungry to care much about the sliminess of the jerky and gnawed at it regardless of the texture—or taste. With aching feet and a hollow stomach, he followed the knight further into the dark, the icy blue light casting a deathly pallor across their features.

41

PLAYING THEIR GAME

The group returned to the palace in a sorry state indeed. Andromeda rode with one foot out of the stirrup and a sopping tunic from where Amber had removed the arrow and wrapped the wound on her back with wet leather. Yves rode with her to keep her upright. She had worsened at an alarming rate, and he was the only one strong enough to keep her on the horse. He was also the only one with enough zeal left in him to keep her conscious with bawdy jokes and scandalous anecdotes. Her indignation seemed to fuel her consciousness more than anything else.

Jacs rode with her mother. She forced herself to ignore how frail she had become. With every shift of the horse, she felt her mother's rib cage against her chest, felt the delicate bones in her damaged and swollen fingers grasp her own, and felt her wince from wounds too numerous to count. It would all be okay, she assured herself. Master Epione could work wonders and, she hoped, miracles.

Clattering into the stable yard, they were allowed exactly forty-five seconds of peace before the Queen's return was discovered and the servants were thrown into a frenzy.

"Has Cornelius returned yet?" Jacs asked the nearest stable hand, who paled, seemingly shocked to be directly addressed by the Queen, and quickly shook his head. Disappointment enveloped her, but she shoved it aside. Grooms helped them from their mounts, and stablehands swiftly removed the horses. Adaine appeared with a fleet of servants carrying blankets, warm beverages, and to Jacs's surprise, a stargazer lily.

When asked what the flower was for, Adaine blushed and said quietly, "I panicked. It's customary to give a gift when someone returns from a trip, but this wasn't a normal trip, so I didn't know what was expected. I know you like them, and thought you'd need a reason to smile." To Adaine's marked relief, the bloom had the desired effect, and Jacs accepted it gratefully.

Jacs called for Master Epione, but a few moments after the summons was made, the messenger returned without her. "Sorry, Your Majesty, she's busy with a patient."

"Who?" Jacs asked.

"Courtierdame Glowra," he replied.

Jacs blanched. "Is she okay? Is Courtier Bishop with her?"

The boy fidgeted and answered. "I'm not sure, but that's why she has to stay. Said it was critical. She lost a lot of blood, Your Majesty. Courtier Bishop is with her."

"Blood?" Jacs whispered, with equal parts alarm and confusion. She felt her heart tremble in her chest and looked at Andromeda and her mother, as well as the pale faces of the others. It had all gone so wrong.

She seized her next step.

"Right," she said briskly. "Then summon stretchers for Chiv. Turner and my mother, they are to be taken to the infirmary. See that their wounds are inspected by Master Epione's apprentices in the meantime."

The boy nodded and hurried to obey.

Clutching her cloak around her slim frame, her mother started humming to herself. She looked so small. Jacs moved to stand beside her. "We're going to the infirmary, Mum," she said gently. Maria nodded, her eyes slightly glazed, but Jacs noticed she was less hunched over than she had been in the catacombs.

A small relief at least.

That counted for something, didn't it?

The stretchers arrived, the patients were loaded, and the group followed them to the infirmary. Yves appeared more and more anxious the further into the palace they walked, until Jacs fell into step beside him and said in a low voice, "Yves, you were a great help this evening. Don't worry, you are a guest in these halls."

He turned to her with a dazzling smile and said, "I'm not worried, Your Majesty, no, I'm simply deciding what kind of decor I want in my parlor. If it's overlooking the sea, I don't think this much gold will be tasteful. Too flashy in the morning sun, you see. Maybe I can utilize some darker jewels to avoid the glare."

Jacs conceded, playing along, "Of course, but understated is always more tasteful than overstated, I've heard."

"You've obviously not talked to many performers," he retorted, eyes gleaming. "We tend to have a flair for the dramatic."

"I've noticed," Jacs said. Her gaze drifted to her mother, lying a short distance ahead of them on her stretcher. She was pointing to the ornate ceilings in wonder.

Jacs's face changed, and Yves said sincerely, "She will be all right, you know."

Jacs turned her head to look at him. His face had softened in sympathy.

"How do you know that?" Jacs asked, keeping her voice steady.

"The effects of the tunnels are never long-lasting once you're out. One of the reasons I chose to head the troupe all these years. After a few days, the pain fades away."

"What if it's too late?" she all but whispered.

"It's never too late. No one is ever so lost they can't be found. Besides, you're forgetting her advantage," he said mischievously.

"What advantage?"

"She's your mother. If she has even half your strength, she'll be more than equipped to come back from this."

Jacs, caught off guard, fumbled for an appropriate reply but was saved the hassle when Yves added, "Now, for my garden, what is my budget for peacocks? I think at least four would be sufficient, but my lucky number *is* seven, so I'm torn. I mean, can one have too many peacocks?"

Jacs snorted. She made a mental note to organize a strict budget with Connor later, and to document each and every purchase made for the dancer. The thought sent a ripple of fear, worry, and guilt through her. Where was he? Was he safe? Hurt? Lost? Alone? And most important, a little voice inside her wondered . . . *alive*? Not knowing was the worst part. As politely as she could, she extricated herself from Yves's chatter and moved to walk beside her mother's stretcher, deep in thought. Her mother pointed out the cloud formations and various characters in the ceiling frescoes and did not notice her mood.

"Jacqueline! Thank the Goddess you're safe!" Anya rose from her seat outside the surgery chamber.

She looked haggard, her eyes were bloodshot, and her smile quivered on her lips.

Maria and Andromeda were now safely in the hands of Master Epione's staff, each settled in a crisp white bed in the infirmary. Amber and Flent had insisted on staying with them while Jacs went to find Lena. Jacs had noticed Andromeda roll her eyes when Flent volunteered shortly after Amber.

"Anya, it's so good to see you made it back to the palace. What happened to Lena?" Jacs's words tripped over themselves in her impatience for answers. The two women embraced, and Anya's eyes flickered to the closed door.

"She was stabbed. She's still in surgery," Anya said softly.

"Yes, and she attempted to murder Councilor Perda." Cllr. Fengar's voice came from an alcove to the left of the doorway. Jacs had not noticed her sitting there and almost jumped.

"Councilor! Forgive me, I didn't see you—what do you mean, attempted murder?" Jacs spluttered.

"No, she didn't!" Anya replied heatedly, rounding on the Councilor.

"You said so yourself, child. You found her on top of Cllr. Perda with her knife pressed against her throat. We're just lucky her wound was bad enough to stop her from finishing the act," Cllr. Fengar said calmly.

"That's not what happened. Cllr. Perda stabbed her first. It was self-defense!"

"Nonsense, she was stabbed by one of those dreadful assassins. Cllr. Perda had no weapon on her person when you made these foul accusations. How do you suppose she stabbed Courtierdame Glowra without a weapon? And, while we're at it, *why* would she stab her in the first place?" Cllr. Fengar shifted contentedly in her chair.

Anya started forward, finger pointed in accusation, but Jacs stepped in front of her and stopped her advance. From around Jacs's body, Anya hissed, “Stop lying! Lena would never hurt a fly, not without reason. Before she passed out, she said Cllr. Perda stabbed her. Said she was working against the Queen. She wouldn’t make that up!”

“What do you mean, working against the Queen?” Jacs said with alarm.

“All a fabrication, Your Majesty. This one has convinced herself of these false truths to excuse her betrothed’s behavior. Do not be sucked in by them. Obviously, the Queen and the Queendom have always been the Council’s first priority.”

Jacs looked from the smug Councilor to the earnest Anya and narrowed her eyes at the former’s pretty speech. “Of course,” she said stiffly. “However, if these accusations are true, they will need to be dealt with seriously. Luckily, Master Epione is a skilled surgeon. Courtierdame Glowra can fill us in when she recovers, so we will await her account before we pass judgment.”

Cllr. Fengar bristled but smoothed her complexion swiftly, a slight red blotching on her cheeks the only sign that betrayed her ire. “Most just, Your Majesty. As always, your assessment is fair and magnanimous.”

“Where are the other Councilors?” Jacs asked.

“Councilor Dilmont is with Lord Claustrom—she had quite a scare earlier—Councilor Stewart is in her chambers, and Councilor Perda is, understandably, getting her wound treated in an undisclosed area,” she said with a pointed look at Anya.

Jacs shifted to block Anya as she attempted to bolt around her. Jacs thought quickly; she didn’t know what to do, but she knew she needed more time. Keeping her tone neutral, she said, “We have all had a long night. I need to talk with you all and debrief with my Council, but let’s wait until tomorrow. Hopefully, by that time we will have more information about what transpired between Courtierdame Glowra and Cllr. Perda, and I will have had some time to collect my thoughts about my journey. Cllr. Fengar, you also must need some rest; please send for any refreshments and retire to your chambers. We will discuss everything tomorrow evening. Let's meet in my throne room. Tell the other Councilors," she said.

"But, Your Majesty, my instructions are—"

"To follow the Queen's command above all else, are they not, Beatrice?" Jacs rebuffed her.

Cllr. Fengar hesitated, mouth open, then snapped it shut and nodded. Rising slowly from her chair, she replied, "Of course, my Queen. I will relay your message at once. Although I doubt the throne room will be cleaned from the gala in time. May I suggest our chambers?"

Jacs glanced at the closed door, and after a moment's consideration said, "No, the chill will be too much in there, the throne room will be ready in time. I will send you an updated location if it is not."

Pursing her lips, Cllr. Fengar rose, inclined her head in what could be considered a bow, and left the room.

As soon as she was gone, Anya spun her around to face her. "You can't meet with them, not by yourself," she said urgently. "I promise you I'm telling the truth. Lena went in to talk to them alone. I was supposed to meet her in her chambers later but doubled back to make sure. Next thing I knew, a bunch of guards went in and came out moments later with three of the Councilors and Lord Claustrom, and then by the time I went in to check if Lena was okay, she was straddling Cllr. Perda with a dagger at her throat. She told me just before she fainted that the Councilor stabbed her and was behind the hoods. She wouldn't lie, Jacqueline. And she wouldn't attack anybody unless she had to. I promise you. I would be willing to swear on my life. She's not—"

Jacs held up a hand. "I believe you," she said simply. "But I need to get to the bottom of this, and they'll play along if I do." She caught Anya's hand in hers and felt the golden band around her ring finger. Looking down, she sighed and added softly, "What a mess. I doubt either of you could have imagined spending the day after your engagement like this."

Anya scoffed an almost laugh and squeezed Jacs's fingers. Their eyes met, Jacs's creases of worry, a poor imitation of Anya's chasms.

"Connor's still down there," Jacs said quietly, looking away. Anya squeezed her hand reassuringly, and a panic seized Jacs so suddenly she jerked away.

"I need to hear what happened from Lena's account, so send for me the moment she wakes up. I'm going to have trusted guards watch over you both while I'm gone. Keep her safe and look after yourself."

"Wait, where are you going?" Anya asked.

Jacs bit at the skin around her thumbnail. Next steps. She had so many questions and so few answers. Now she only had a few short hours to find out as much as she could before she confronted the Council.

Meeting Anya's gaze, she replied, "To get more information."

Anya looked uncertain, but Jacs didn't leave room for objection. Her mind whirled against the heavy fog of fear that kept creeping inside, and she forced herself to keep moving, keep acting. With one last check-in on her mother—she would talk with her more after she had had a few hours to rest—and curt orders to the guards and knights in charge of her care, she swept from the room.

She had made mistakes before, but never one as big as this. She had led a team into the catacombs, and not only had they failed in their mission but they also had lost half their number. What was almost funny was that the mission would have been a near complete success without her meddling. Her captured friends had escaped, and her mother had been found.

What had she achieved? Nothing. She'd just made things worse. Oh, and found an Undercourt of Griffins. She clenched her fists, strides lengthening as she headed toward her study, another problem. Alti forbid she actually solve one before finding another.

If she had just stayed put, trusted the others' capabilities, stopped to think for one minute . . .

A mistake is a lesson earned. Master Leschi's words interrupted her compunction, and she missed a step on her way to the second-floor landing, stumbling to a halt.

"And a triumph is a lesson learned," she whispered, finishing her mentor's ditty. With the heel of her hand pressed into her sternum, she forced her breathing to slow, forced her mind to settle, and forced herself to assess the situation. *If I walk into the Council's web without a plan, I've already lost,* she thought bluntly. Approaching the Council head-on had never worked in the past. Why should it work now? No. She needed more than logic—she needed cunning.

She knew the Council; she knew how they could twist events to suit their narrative. They were harder to pin down than a watermelon seed and twice as slippery. But as her mentor had said to her years ago: No one ever sets out to be the villain. She had to believe they were doing what they thought was right. Or, equally likely, what was in their best interest, and what was in their best interest was power.

Suddenly she was transported to the first moment she had met the Council, what had they said to her? *It's all about connections.* A glimmer of hope sparked in her mind, and her next steps led her on a new path, away from her study. She knew whom she had to speak to first.

"Your Highness! I wasn't expecting . . . to what do I owe . . . ? Please sit." Lord Claustrom's hands fluttered like a pair of turtledoves. First, they alighted on her chest, then they hurried up to tuck a few fly-away strands of hair into her updo. She then swept a hand around her to vaguely indicate a nearby chair.

Jacs had never been in her chambers before. Of course she hadn't—when had she ever needed to? Failing that, when would she have wanted to? She hovered on the threshold for a moment, taking in the décor. It had clearly been designed by the Lord herself, and she obviously did not expect to have to explain it to the Queen. Even Yves might have said it was too much. The center of the ceiling was adorned with a large, golden sun-shaped chandelier and acted as the middle point to the billowing, luxurious navy and powder blue silks that extended toward and cascaded down the walls.

The curtains were drawn against the rising sun. Candles safely housed in golden lanterns dotted the room like stars in gilt cages. The bed, directly below the sun in the center of the room, was circular in shape and could have fit half a dozen people comfortably. It was piled high with gold and blue cushions. Hera had been sprawled among the pillows and had almost not managed to get up when Jacs entered.

"I see you're a fan of the royal colors," Jacs mused. Hera blushed and pursed her lips. Jacs felt no pleasure in her discomfort, nor did she care about the décor. If she had been in a better mood, she may have even found it funny, but she had come here with a purpose.

Inclining her head in thanks, Jacs accepted the proffered chair, a golden velvet dome-shaped thing, and sat with her elbows resting on her knees. She took a moment to assemble her thoughts. Hera watched her warily.

"Lord Claustrom, I know you don't respect me. It's likely you resent me, for reasons that are entirely understandable. You, as Lord of Hesperida are, arguably, the most powerful woman in the land, yet you don't get to wear the crown, and you have to bow to me, in your eyes a Lowrian commoner."

Jacs paused and Hera said nothing, her eyes narrowed as if suspecting a trap.

"Am I correct?" Jacs pressed.

"You're not one for small talk, are you?" Hera sniffed.

Jacs shook her head. "Answer me honestly," she continued. "If you were Queen, what would change?"

Hera picked up a nearby pillow and ran the tassel through her fingers. With a sneer, she asked, "What do you want?"

"For you to answer my question."

"And if I refuse?" Hera drawled.

"Then I understand you no more than I do right now," Jacs said softly. "And we stay as we are."

Hera sucked her teeth and tossed the pillow to one side. Leaning back on one hand, she inspected her cuticles on the other. "If I were Queen?" she repeated.

"Exactly, what would change?"

Hera waved her hand with attempted bravado. "I would wear a crown of course, a much better accessory for my hair than yours."

"Diadems are fitting accessories for Lords, and you have worn much more elaborate headpieces than my crown on several occasions. What would change?" Jacs persisted.

"I'd have a title."

"You have a title."

"There are many Lords, but there is only one Queen."

"True, and while the responsibilities of a Lord are great, as Queen, you alone would carry the weight of the people on your shoulders. Is that what you truly want?"

"Yes!"

Jacs raised her eyebrows and waited.

Hera fidgeted under her gaze and looked away. "No, not really."

"Help me understand, Hera," Jacs said softly. "What would change? Why do you want it?"

"Because."

"Because *why*?"

Irritation flushed Hera's cheeks, and she said flippantly, "Because then I'd answer to no one."

Hera sighed, and Jacs noticed the dark rings under her eyes. She looked strained, and much worse than that day in the library.

After a time, Hera finally filled the silence. "If I wore the crown, I wouldn't be Sybil Claustrom's heir. I would be her Queen."

"Ah," Jacs said.

"It sounds petty out loud."

"No, it doesn't," Jacs said gently. "It sounds honest. Although not completely accurate. As Queen you'd still have to answer to the Council."

"Maybe *you* do, but I wouldn't. I'd have the power, the title, the connections, and the crown. I wouldn't need to listen to the Council. Or answer to my mother." She added the last thought bitterly.

"But you're Lord now, you shouldn't be answering to your mother. Unless you still need her help."

"I don't need anyone's help, especially not *hers.* But it's not that simple," Hera snapped. "I was born to rule." The boldness in her manner was marred by the shifting of her eyes, and she added, "Just not like this. Not to be some mouthpiece for a woman who can't let go of the reins. She's relentless. It's hard to enjoy a pie when someone's fingers have been in it."

Jacs nodded. "So, you feel like you're restricted by your mother's demands?"

Hera crossed her arms and said nothing, as though worried she had given too much away. Jacs took her silence as agreement and pressed on. "I can relate," she said quietly. "I've been Queen for around four months now and every decision I've made has either been dictated or denied by the Council." She watched Hera's reaction carefully, but the woman hid her emotions well.

"That Dilmont's a piece of work," Hera said finally. Her voice wavered and she studied her cuticles again. Cllr. Fengar mentioned that Cllr. Dilmont had visited Hera this evening. Jacs wondered mildly what they had discussed. From the look on Hera's face, it had left a bad taste in her mouth.

"They all are," Jacs agreed. "What they've made me realize is that I need help. I cannot hope to rule the way I need to without support."

Hera smirked. "You want my help?"

Jacs nodded. "Without help, I'm just *their* mouthpiece."

The smirk flickered.

"You don't have to like me. I'm not expecting anything more than a business deal," Jacs clarified.

Hera sat forward, mirroring Jacs's posture with elbows resting on her knees.

"What are your demands?" she asked.

Excitement sparked in Jacs's chest, but she kept her face neutral. "Hesperida has many resources and much of the support from the other Lords in the land. Opposed, the crown will accomplish nothing. United, we can work wonders."

"So, nothing will change except I will answer more directly to you, as well as my mother?" Hera said edgily. "I need more than that."

Jacs studied her. "What did you have in mind?"

Without missing a beat, she demanded, "A seat on the Council. With a direct link to the Queen's ear, and the title of Councilor."

Jacs considered, "Okay, but give me a year to appoint you. It will take time to remove the member you will be replacing."

Hera blanched. Jacs watched her expression shift from apprehensive to defiant and she said, "If it helps speed up the process, I have evidence against all of the members of the Council."

Jacs shifted forward in her seat. "What kind of evidence?" she asked.

Hera chewed her lip prettily as she weighed her next words. Jacs stood, held out her hand, and said, "With or without your evidence, we do have a deal. You promise to help me, and I will appoint you Councilor. Your information may simply speed up your appointment."

Hera's gaze shifted between Jacs's face and offered hand. She stood slowly and shook it.

"Done," she said.

"Done," Jacs echoed. "Now, tell me what you know."

Hera told her everything. It was as though the floodgates long kept sealed had opened, and she talked with a fervor that brought color to her cheeks and light to her eyes. She confessed that her mother had only abdicated her title so she could work more closely with Alethia's ruler, Celos, to sabotage Lords that had gotten a little too powerful and ensure that Hesperida continued to be the most influential county in the Upper Realm. Some Lords had been more pliable than others. Lord Witbron of Luxlow had happily complied with the requests Lady Sybil had made.

Others had been less willing. Lord Sierra Lemmington of Newfrea had required significant persuading, and Dame Merina Lemmington still walked with a limp. Lordson Brutus Lemmington had even gone missing for a week, returning with no memories of his time away and an acquired fear of the dark.

Hera shared that she had been oblivious to her mother's dealings and of the existence of Alethia and the Sons of Celos until very recently, when she had discovered her mother had ordered the capture of Jacs's guard and closest friends.

"But why them and not me?" Jacs asked, bewildered.

"Because the Council wanted to isolate you. Apparently, your Advisor was also on the list, but they hadn't anticipated that he wouldn't be with you during the ambush and left him to take those they had managed to subdue."

Jacs felt a tightness in her chest—she had delivered Connor to Alethia herself—but bade Hera to continue. Hera then explained that she had confronted the Council and demanded that they stop listening to her mother's orders as she was no longer Lord of Hesperida.

"They refused, of course," Hera said sourly. "Even when I showed them a letter from my mother exposing her treason."

Hera walked over to a small desk almost hidden in the silk wall hangings and retrieved a letter to hand to Jacs. Jacs accepted it with thanks and pocketed it to read later. She waved Hera on.

"They insisted that my mother's actions aligned with the views of the Council and that her control over Alethia was an asset they would be foolish to dismiss. The Council, of course, never commands Alethia's resources directly, but they work closely enough with my mother that they might as well. This way they keep their hands clean, but their will is enforced.

"Then Courtierdame Glowra barged in with her sword flashing and claimed she had a decree to enact laws in your absence. She demanded the arrest of the Council for matters of high treason. I offered to share evidence of their crimes, but when the guards arrived, they turned against us. I was escorted out and received a stern talking to by Cllr. Dilmont." She winced and tugged her sleeve below her wrist. "And Glowra, I've heard, is now in the infirmary with near fatal wounds." Hera shrugged delicately and met Jacs's gaze with defiance.

Jacs sat back. Air escaped her lips in a low hiss.

"Your Majesty," Hera said tentatively. "You're right. I don't respect you, and until very recently I didn't think you deserved the crown on your head."

Jacs raised an eyebrow and waited, fingers knitted across her abdomen.

"But you risked a lot to save people you care about this evening, and as much as I hate to admit it, you have held your own against the Council's games with a grace I would have never been able to maintain. You have to believe that I did not wish for any of this to happen. I didn't have a hand in the actions of the Sons, and I never would have allowed it if I had known or if I could have stopped it."

Jacs waited.

"If anything"—Hera had the decency to look uncomfortable—"if anything, I just enjoyed causing you discomfort. But I would never dream of doing anything that would put others' lives at risk."

Jacs studied her. "Thank you," she said as Hera shifted in uncomfortable silence. Thinking over what she had heard, Jacs suddenly sat up straighter.

"Just to confirm, you said that the Council instructs Lady Sybil Claustrom to order the Sons of Celos to carry out their wishes."

Hera nodded, looking slightly awkward after her confession.

"And they act only on orders from the Council; they are not hired out by other people at all?"

Hera shook her head. "No, they wouldn't be effective if everyone knew of them. They acted only on orders from my mother, and those orders were taken from the Council."

"And the Sons were responsible for assassinating Queen Ariel," Jacs said softly.

Hera's eyes widened as she realized the implications. "No, my mother wouldn't have . . . she couldn't have . . . she loved Queen Ariel. She . . ."

But Jacs's mind had already moved past this point and was evolving a plan. She was so wrapped up in her own thoughts, she didn't notice Hera's fidgeting subside as she grew very still. Too late, she saw the light of satisfaction shine in her eyes and in the corners of her slow smile. Her next words cut across Jacs's musings and took an extra half second to process.

"It's not enough," Hera said calmly.

"What?"

"I've changed my mind, it's not enough." All apprehension had vanished and she sat before Jacs now composed and confident. A prickling sensation skittered down Jacs's spine.

"What's not enough?" Jacs asked warily.

"I did not realize the value of the information I just shared. A seat on the Council would cover that, but I've decided it does not cover the support of my county and, by extension, the Lords that fall under my influence." Hera studied Jacs with the languid ease of a cat sitting in a particularly delicious sunbeam.

"We shook on it," Jacs said, forcing her temper down. "That was the deal."

"No, the deal was that I help you. We hadn't specified that the help extended beyond my providing you with the evidence you needed to condemn the late Queen's murderers."

Jacs narrowed her eyes. "What do you want?"

Hera plucked a speck of dust from her gown and flicked it away. "Have you met my brother?"

"Your brother? No," Jacs replied, thrown by the question.

"Lordson Theo Claustrom. He's a dear. Currently unattached too."

Jacs felt the claws of a trap nearby but was unsure where to place her next step. "What do you want, Hera?" she demanded.

Hera tsked. "Always so quick to get to the point."

Jacs waited. Sighing prettily, Hera continued, "The resources I have at my disposal, in your hands, will solidify you as Queen of Frea more firmly than any pretty speech you can make. Letters with my seal containing proclamations of loyalty to the crown, your crown, will convince even the crotchetiest old Lord and her Genteel to bend the knee. You will very quickly have most of the Upper Realm under your thumb. My family has spent generations building their wealth, land, and reputation for this purpose. We have never given away our loyalties frivolously, and I am certainly not going to break tradition for the sake of a Lowrian peasant."

"Your point, Hera," Jacs said through gritted teeth.

"This is what will happen. I will write to my brother and insist he visit the palace. I will make the introductions, you will court him, and within the year, you will make him your King."

Jacs felt her heart freeze in her chest.

Hera continued. "You're right. I don't want the burdens of being Queen, but I am done with answering to outdated windbags. This way I will not only be a Councilor, but the Queen's sister. As your sister, of *course* it will be in my best interest to support your rule and ensure others remain loyal throughout your reign. All of Hesperida's resources will be at your disposal. Your position on the throne will be secure, and who knows"—she smiled innocently—"you may even like Theo."

Jacs shook her head. Any and all words danced just out of reach of her tongue.

"That is my deal," Hera stated.

"Surely you don't—"

"I will accept nothing less."

"What if we—"

"That is my deal," Hera repeated.

Jacs's thoughts reeled. Her heart screamed a defiant *no*, but, though she hated to admit it, there was logic in Hera's offer. That thought lodged like a barbed splinter in her mind. A marriage between her and Lordson Claustrom would finally give her the power she needed to help her people, to enact change in the Queendom. But what about Connor? She couldn't imagine her life without him. She couldn't imagine ruling the Queendom with another man in his place. They were supposed to do this together. If Theo wore his crown, where would that leave him?

Could he bear it? Could she?

Hera rose slowly and held out her hand to shake.

"I—" Jacs stalled for time. She couldn't accept it. There had to be another way to get Hera's support and keep Connor.

As if reading her thoughts, Hera said softly, "Love is a luxury reserved for the poor and powerless. If you wish to be neither, you will take this opportunity before I change my mind again."

"I—" Unbidden, Connor's words came back to her, *I have always been yours, Jacs*. He was hers and she was his. That was a fact as certain as gravity. But she had been fooling herself. She did not belong to Connor alone. Her life was forfeit to the Queendom, to her people. Hera was right, she did not have the luxury to marry for love. Not at the expense of power.

Hera gave her hand a little shake.

This is the only way. As though climbing the steps to the hangman's noose, Jacs felt herself rise from her chair. Her hand lifted inch by excruciating inch from her side to meet Hera's in the space between them. Fingers clenched, palms touched, hands shook.

A heart broke.

"Done," Hera said triumphantly, sealing her fate.

Done. Jacs felt the word like a blade through her ribs.

She cleared her throat, desperately trying to regain her composure. "I look forward to meeting your brother and will be honored to call you sister." She forced a smile while the rest of her shattered.

Hera beamed. "As will I, Your Majesty."

Still scrambling for control, Jacs said, "I will be confronting the Council tomorrow evening. It will be the perfect opportunity for you to demonstrate the power of your influence over the realm's Lords. Can I count on your support?"

Hera bowed low. "Of course, sister. And when will you be announcing your engagement?"

Jacs's mouth went dry, thinking fast, she said, "These matters require appropriate occasion and celebration. Once he arrives and I have met him, I will court him for the appropriate amount of time, then make the announcement to the Queendom."

"Then I shall write to him directly. I wouldn't want to keep you waiting," Hera said with a voice of honey. "I wonder if Her Majesty has a token I may send to assure him of your intent. A ring is customary, I believe."

Jacs clenched her left hand into a fist and felt the band of Connor's ring bite the base of her finger. Not that one. Never. Instead, she lifted her right hand and worked a gold ring dotted with sapphires from her pointer finger. "Please send this as a token of my . . ."

"Affection?" Hera supplied.

"Intention," Jacs finished.

Hera pinched the ring delicately between thumb and forefinger and inclined her head.

"Of course, Your Majesty. I look forward to witnessing the fruits borne from the union of our families."

42

CHECKMATE

The following day passed in a haze. Jacs had not slept since the night before the gala and fought against the weariness in her bones with the vigor of someone who knew they were inches from their destination. She kept reassuring herself that the alliance was necessary, crucial in fact. Besides, she had time. Time to find another solution. Time to tell Connor. *Connor.* Her heart stuttered.

He still had not returned. On top of the search patrols she sent to scour the distance between the palace and the banks of the underground lake—she would not make a move on Alethia itself before she had more time to concoct a proper plan—she now had the palace scryers tasked to check for him every quarter hour in their mirrors, and she received an update every half hour. These updates were always the same, "No sightings, Your Majesty, and the mirror handle keeps buzzing erratically when we check for him." On top of the disappointment each report brought, the buzzing was a worry. What if it meant the magic was faulty?

The minutes leading up to each half hour filled her with hope, and each empty report added another weight to her chest. A selfish part of her now loathed her insistence to remove all scry crystals from both realms. There were so few left in the Queendom, but she reminded herself that she would at least know the moment he was in range of one.

She had spent most of the morning with her mother, talking with her in a low voice and watching shreds of Maria knit themselves back together before her eyes. The fits of humming had subsided, and the focus was slowly returning to her gaze. Yves had said the effects of the catacombs wouldn't be long-lasting, and Jacs hoped he was right.

Lena was out of surgery but still had not woken up, and Jacs had ensured that no Councilor or any guardpair she did not personally trust was allowed access to the infirmary. Anya barely left Lena's side, and the times she did, she made sure Westly was there to take her place. The portly valet spoke in a wavering voice to Lena about happy moments from her past and refused to look at the heavy bandages wrapped around her ribs.

Andromeda had insisted Amber and Flent rotate with another guardpair, and when they finally relented and left her in the care of their replacements, she said to Jacs quietly, "If I'm honest, Your Majesty, I couldn't handle another moment of their flirting."

Jacs, not used to Andromeda saying anything that wasn't factual and of a serious nature, was surprised by the smile the comment conjured. She asked, "Since when have they . . .?"

"They're not," Andromeda said. "But if Everstar doesn't shut it down, they will be." She shook her head. "She knows better, but Flent's persistent." As Jacs left Andromeda to rest, she wondered how she could have missed something apparently so obvious.

She kept moving, kept talking with people, kept planning. To stop was to feel, and to feel was torment. Never before had it been so hard to listen to her head over the screaming in her heart. Emotion, so easily restrained by logic, now refused to sit quietly within her chest. She ached. She was betrothed to a man she did not love and had completely failed the people she loved most. She couldn't allow herself to spare a thought for Connor, Master Leschi, Phillip, or Masterchiv Rathbone, yet in the moments between thoughts and the space between breaths, she felt their absence cut her to ribbons. Her loss. Her failure. Her fault.

A messenger from the palace scryers approached. Her heart lifted.

"Any news?"

He shook his head and she fought to keep her face composed as he relayed the same information he had half an hour ago.

Resolve was key, and she needed all her mental energy for her confrontation with the Council. For want of a better solution, she wrestled all her pain into a tiny box within her mind, locking it securely until she was ready to open it. She just hoped it would stay there.

Finally, it was time. Adaine dressed her with a constant stream of chatter at Jacs's insistence. She talked about the most efficient way to launder linen while pinning Jacs's hair in place and smoothing the lines of her gown. Jacs wore a high-necked sleeveless sheer navy bodice embroidered heavily with gold lace that dropped low in the back. Split navy silk skirts shone and flowed from her waist. They were cut above the knee in the front and below the ankle in the back. An intricate gold pattern edged the fabric and could be seen on the inside of the back panels. At first glance the pattern seemed to depict vines, but upon closer inspection, it became obvious that it consisted of embroidered interlocking cogs and gears. As she walked and her train fanned out behind her, they appeared to move. On her feet, she wore golden-heeled boots. The last thing to don was her crown, and Adaine placed it on her plaited auburn tresses reverentially.

"Thank you," Jacs said to her. She was ready.

Jacs watched from her throne as one by one the Councilors filed into the hall. First came Cllr. Stewart with her white, wispy hair tamed into an elegant swirl around her head. She wore a humble cream-colored outfit that she had obviously owned for many years but had mended and maintained beautifully. What Jacs had originally perceived to be skirts were instead wide-legged trousers cinched neatly at the waist.

Next came Cllr. Dilmont and Cllr. Fengar. The former strode toward the throne with her chin high. She wore an outfit that was reminiscent of the knights' formal wear, tailored dress tunic, dark leggings, and high boots. Her red painted lips did not smile at the Queen as she approached. Cllr. Fengar, in contrast, wore her usual silver fringed gown. Her neck, wrists, and earlobes dripped with jewels, and her thick, brown, wavy hair was twisted in a chignon at the base of her skull.

Last to arrive was Cllr. Perda. She wore a dark burgundy velvet bodice with long sleeves ending in points that tied around her middle fingers. Her velvet skirts rippled around her as she walked, the hems edged with onyx beading.

They assembled in a line at the bottom of the dais and bowed low. Jacs pushed down her nerves and welcomed them warmly.

"Councilors," she began. "You have upheld your positions and served my Queendom for many years. Your influence has shaped rulers before me, and enacted policies that propel our Queendom down the path you deem right and true."

Jacs balanced her next words carefully.

"I have recently learned of a secret organization that actively works against our Queendom's efforts for peace, equality, and justice. I have learned that this organization has enslaved a Court of Griffins and recruited the young, vulnerable men of Frea to twist their minds and actions against the Realms. I have also learned that this very Council not only knew of this organization but helped guide their activities."

Shock registered on the three Councilors' faces, although Cllr. Perda remained impassive.

Jacs waited a beat before continuing. "Now I ask you this simple question, and I want you to consider your answers carefully: Why? Because I cannot believe that you know the extent of their evil if you are willing to work with them."

Cllr. Stewart looked to Cllr. Perda, Cllr. Dilmont stared defiantly at Jacs, and Cllr. Fengar studied her toes. The room itself held its breath. A muffled thud and a clatter could be heard off to the left from the antechamber, but Jacs pointedly ignored it and the Councilors did not appear to notice.

"It's as I said on your first day as Queen, Your Majesty," Cllr. Perda said softly. "It is our duty to uphold the Queendom's traditions, policy, and cultural heritage. We act for the well-being of the realms and do what must be done to ensure its continued prosperity, whatever that may be, and regardless of the brutal nature it may require."

"All this is well and good, Councilor. I would even agree with some of your decisions and sympathize with your desire to contain and control a new Queen like myself. After all, I am from the Lower Realm. All of my experience I earned half a Queendom away. However, you took it too far, and you chose blackmail and shady dealings to get your way. We could have worked together. I was so eager to work alongside you all, but you wrestled me into submission before you knew more than one thing about me."

"Your Majesty, your ideas threaten to change the very way of life we have fought so hard to preserve all these years. We cannot let you jeopardize the Queendom's integrity," Cllr. Perda replied. Her marble expression cracked; tiny fissures betrayed her rising temper.

"With all due respect, Councilor," Jacs replied coolly, "if your way alienates and oppresses over half of our people, then the only logical conclusion is that we are on the wrong path. Don't you see that? Obviously, we can never appease everyone with every decision we make, but there is a difference between a law that is unpopular and a law that strips citizens of their basic rights. A Frean citizen should *never* have to feel watched in their own home. A young Lowrian man should *never* feel like his ruler has abandoned him. He should *never* have to choose a hooded life underground over a life in his hometown."

Cllr. Perda pursed her lips. "How *dare* you," she hissed. "You lay these accusations at our feet and don't for one minute acknowledge the necessity behind these so-called evils. A Queendom can only thrive if its ruler is able to make hard decisions. The greater good should always outweigh the plight of the individual."

Jacs saw anger's fire flicker in the Councilor's eyes. Finding the pressure point, she dug in and said, "So the greater good requires sacrificing the privacy of an entire realm? The greater good requires pushing hundreds of young men into the arms of an organization that preys on their weaknesses and deepest fears? The greater good requires looking the other way when that organization enslaves an entire Court? If it causes the suffering of thousands, how can you still claim your actions are for the greater good?"

"You know nothing, child," Cllr. Perda snarled.

Cllrs. Stewart and Fengar stared with wide eyes and open mouths. Cllr. Dilmont stood beside the fuming Cllr. Perda, nodding encouragingly from time to time and glaring at Jacs.

"These acts were necessary. Without an organization like the Sons of Celos, we wouldn't have the means to carry out the more brutal, yes, but necessary acts. Without the sacrifice of a few, we would never maintain order," Cllr. Perda said.

Jacs narrowed her eyes and replied, "Is that how you justified Queen Ariel's assassination?"

Cllr. Perda opened her mouth to retort, but no sound came out. Cllr. Dilmont jumped in. "You have no proof. How dare you accuse the Council of such a heinous act!"

Jacs rose to her feet and walked to the edge of the dais. "You admitted to commanding the Sons of Celos. I have evidence of your connection to the group via Lady Sybil Claustrom, both documented and in her daughter's testimony. But even without that, I was there that day. I saw the Sons and I saw what they did to my predecessor. You may not have fired the arrow, but you murdered the late Queen, and you will pay for your crimes."

She snapped her fingers and the antechamber door to the left of her swung open. All four Councilors' heads turned to see a host of women flood into the throne room. True to her word, Hera had rallied the Lords to stand behind her, to stand behind Jacs. At Jacs's instruction, they'd waited in the antechamber to listen to the Council's confessions and act as witnesses.

First came Lord Hera Claustrom herself, looking resolved and glowing with self-satisfied pride. She caught Jacs's eye and indicated those behind her with an arched brow. Dames Shane Adella, Danielle Hart, and Fawn Lupine came next, then Lord Lucia Barnaby, Lord Sierra Lemmington with her Genteel Ariana and their daughter-heir, Dame Merina. A few more Lords, Genteels, and twice as many Dames followed, their faces shifting and lost in the crowd.

As the smaller room emptied into the large one, the remaining—and unscathed—knights of the Queensguard emerged last—Chivilras Everstar, Ryder, Pamheir, Fayworth—along with three guards: Dyna Flent, Miera Jaenheir, and Faline Cervah. All wore grim expressions on their faces. Seeing her niece, Cllr. Fengar called to Flent, but she only once made eye contact and quickly looked away.

"Now wait just a minute, it's not what it sounded like. My Lords, Your Elegances, there has been a grave misunderstanding," Cllr. Stewart said, panic staining her words.

"We have been framed by this Lowrian pretender to the throne! You cannot take her word over ours!" Cllr. Fengar cried.

Jacs descended the steps slowly. "As long as I have breath in my lungs and blood in my veins I will fight for the rights of my people. Corruption will always be brought to light, and you four have abused your power long enough. You are henceforth stripped of your titles and will live out the remainder of your days with only each other for company."

"You cannot—" Cllr. Perda stammered, seething with rage.

"Oh," Jacs said, "of course I can." With another snap of her fingers, the knights and guards apprehended the Council of Four and marched them out of the throne room. Cllr. Stewart began to splutter, tears spilling down her cheeks, while Cllr. Fengar called again for Flent and swore her innocence. As for Cllr. Dilmont and Cllr. Perda, the former stared straight ahead and marched silently toward the open door, while the latter glared at Jacs over her shoulder until Chiv. Everstar roughly thrust her head forward.

"Enjoy the weight of that crown, Your Majesty," she called, just before Chiv. Everstar shoved her through the doors. Ignoring the weight of Hera's eyes on her, Jacs watched them disappear down the corridor.

She had won.

EPILOGUE

The chill had long since gone unnoticed and even without the measures available to him, his mind had long been fortified against the whisperings of the Undercourt. He strode with the practiced air of one who knew the exact edge of a step, the precise limit of each muscle. He knew how to keep his footsteps silent, and he knew how much pressure was required to make them ring out. At this time, he kept them muted. He passed through the narrow silver halls like a shadow.

His hair was so white as to appear translucent and remained colorless in the silver glow of Alethia. Tall and with features that could have been cut from glass, he wore a layered cloak. Black, not purple. His sons wore purple. It was appropriate, they were derivatives of the source. His source. And as the source he must be pure, incorruptible.

The very essence of darkness. It was light that wavered. Light distorted the shadows and allowed perception to mar the truth. Light brought forth shades of gray.

He entered his chamber and pressed a fraction more firmly into his toes. The gentle rap of his feet on stone echoed around the circular room.

An assortment of sculptures and trophies hung on the wall. Most sculptures were distorted rock formations placed at intervals around the room's perimeter. Their faceted surfaces were marred with threads of quartz and pockmarked with holes. He liked the way different rocks and minerals warped and twisted through even the densest slate. Even stones could be corrupted. A reminder for him when temptation beckoned. One trophy stood out against the others. This one was the most important. The preserved body of Altus Hadierna; the last ruling matriarch of the Undercourt. Its front knee was bent, and its head sunk low over it in a deep, reverential bow. A gesture it had refused in life, now preserved forever in death.

Celos had long since discovered that working alongside the Griffins was a waste of energy. Like any beast of the field, they were merely tools, and tools needed a firm hand to guide them. To his delight, Altus Hadierna had been a more useful tool than he had even dared to imagine. The power of the Undercourt was a dangerous force when left unchecked. The skill to reach into the deepest recesses of the mind and pull forth the darkness that lay there had the potential to shape realms. All Griffins had this power, but the matriarch alone had the ability to control it, channel it, and (he discovered) pass it on to another. To one with a greater vision for its use.

He walked confidently around the chamber and stepped around a table to sit in his wingback chair. Without looking at it, he located the thick satin rope hanging near his right ear, and he reached up to give it a tug. A bell sounded somewhere beyond the walls, and it took ninety seconds for a son to respond.

The door creaked open. Celos could see the sliver of silver light widen across the room's diameter.

"Send them in," he commanded.

His son knew a simple bow was all that was necessary to show he understood. He departed. This time the wait was longer, four minutes and seventeen seconds until his first guest arrived. The door opened, ushering in both light and sound. Celos bristled.

"Father," the voice, deep, coarse, and not yet muted by time spent in Alethia, echoed around the room. "Thank you for seeing me," the buffoon said as he inched uncertainly into the room. He was a newborn. Eager to please, quick to succumb to the Undercourt's power, and full of potential.

Celos did not raise his voice, but it entered the room with the force of a slap and silenced his new son. "Mallard," he said. "Welcome. I trust you are adjusting to the city?"

"Yes, F-Father," the boy stammered.

"Good."

"I was wondering when I would see my brother?" his son asked.

Insolent. It was not his fault; he had yet to learn. Celos had not asked a question, so there was no reason for Mallard to speak. With practiced calm, he opened a drawer to his left and retrieved a bright reddish-gold ring. It had been forged by mixing the golden shell of Altus Hadierna's last egg with a gilded feather from its brow, and the final drop of its lifeblood, squeezed from its stuttering heart by Celos personally.

Placing it carefully on his finger, he turned his gaze toward Mallard and clenched his fist.

The boy gasped and crumpled to the floor, hands clutching his head as he groaned, struggling with the demons that rose within his mind.

"You will remain silent unless a question is asked of you," Celos said calmly.

"Yes F—" a twist of Celos's wrist brought forth another groan, and finally, the boy was quiet. He was learning. Celos opened his fingers and rested them lightly on the desk. Mallard pushed himself up with shuddering breaths. The point had been made; the lesson learned.

"Good." Celos observed the boy. "I am helping my sons to thrive in a world that stifles them, and I can't do that when surrounded by unnecessary chatter, now can I?"

A pause. "No, Father," his son answered.

"Exactly. Wait here, we have two more coming."

Mallard rose shakily to his feet and fidgeted where he stood, face ashen. Celos could see his internal struggle as if he had stepped into the boy's mind. Fear was present in a healthy dose, but also defiance, pride, and anger.

The door creaked open again, and a woman entered.

"For the last time, I won't do it," she cried. "You can do what you want to me, but I would rather spend the rest of my wretched days in this dank, depressing tomb than lift one finger for your cause." Her voice was hoarse as though from screaming, and her tone bordered on delirium. She chuckled to herself. "You absolute threadless screw of a man. Soon you'll realize you can only spin in place so long before it gets tedious."

Celos had long learned that this particular woman needed more than a few bad memories to shut her up. To his surprise, Mallard turned and addressed her first.

"Master Leschi?" he said hesitantly.

Celos shifted forward in his seat to lean on one elbow, his chin resting lightly on a crooked finger. This was a surprise.

The woman turned to the boy, eyes squinting in the gloom.

"It's Mal, Mal Wetler. Shyna and Gordon's so—" He cut off with a shuddered gasp as Celos pointed his ringed finger at him. Mallard clutched at his head desperately as if that could stop the memories from entering.

Celos lowered his fist. "Master Bruna Leschi, may I introduce my son, Mallard," he said smoothly.

Master Leschi looked from Mallard to Celos and back again. In a horrified whisper, she said, "Oh Mal, my dear boy. What have you done?"

The door opened a third time, and a son pushed a bound and gagged man through. It closed behind him with a hollow *clunk*, and he screamed against his gag in panic. Eyes wild, he stumbled clumsily toward the two figures in the center of the room. With a clatter, he tripped and lay sprawled in a heap at Master Leschi's feet.

With fingertips tented against the desk, Celos allowed himself a slow smile in anticipation for what was to come. Master Leschi reached for the man and with a piercing look in Celos's direction, crouched down next to him. He was completely shrouded by a ragged purple cloak. Kneeling on the floor, she tentatively touched his shoulder. He looked up sharply and several things happened at once. Master Leschi pulled her hand back as if burned and gasped, hands covering her mouth. With a wild sob, she flung her arms around the man while simultaneously attempting to remove his gag and hood.

Clutching his face in her hands, she cried, "Phillip! What are . . . how did . . . You're okay!"

The man struggled, pulling the fabric covering his mouth the rest of the way down and said, "Ma! You're—"

"That's enough of that," Celos said coldly. This time he clenched his fist and glared at both of them. Master Leschi froze as her eyes glazed over, and Phillip curled in on himself, moaning as if he'd been struck. Celos relaxed his hand, and the reuniting pair fell silent. Master Leschi clutched her son and shifted to position her body in front of his. Touching.

"What do you want?" Master Leschi fired at Celos.

He tsked and tapped his forefinger against the desk, sending a wave of the Undercourt's power toward Phillip. Phillip's supporting arm buckled, and he squeezed his eyes shut tight. “Get out of my head,” he growled.

“Master Leschi, I admire your aggression and continued defiance of my rules. I like to think you know me well enough now as a man of my word. Let me be clear: I promise every sound you make I will tally in his mind with every black thought and dark memory he possesses. Unless I ask you a question, I only want to hear you breathing,” Celos said.

The silence rippled around them, and he folded his fingers delicately.

“Good.” He let the moments tiptoe by before speaking again. “You’re all here because you have a mutual acquaintance. The Queen.”

Master Leschi balled her fists and opened her mouth to retort, but when she looked at Phillip, she shut it with a snap.

Celos continued. “Up to this point, I have had orders to house her mother and mentor”—he indicated Master Leschi—“and to isolate her from her allies. All this was under the assumption she knew nothing of my city. In return for my efforts, those who did know of its existence were to help keep it secret.”

He cleared his throat.

“It has come to my attention that the Queen not only knows of my city but has visited it and has discovered an even deeper secret in the process. So naturally there has been a change of allegiance and a change of plan. Since Hesperida’s protection is null and void, we no longer have to answer to Lord Claustrom nor the Council. Given we will likely no longer be able to exist in peace, my sons and I must act first and finally spread our wings. You three will tell me everything you know about our little Queen. Then, Master Leschi, you will ready the fleet.”

Master Leschi hesitated before answering. “I. Will. Not.”

Celos sighed and shot another wave at Phillip. He groaned and reached for his mother’s hand, holding it tightly as he cowered. Master Leschi gathered him into her arms and looked back at Celos in horror.

"You will, Master Leschi. Your Phillip is a grown man. He's lived a full life. No one moves through this life unscathed, and everyone has a breaking point. I wonder how much his mind can take before it embraces the sanctuary of madness. I wonder how deep his despair goes. You are a woman of science. Shall we experiment?" He squeezed his fist on the desk and watched Phillip curl further into himself.

Master Leschi looked from Phillip to Celos and back again. Her face betrayed the turmoil within, and she faltered.

"Oh dear," Celos said calmly. "What about . . ."

Phillip screamed as Celos extended his ringed finger toward him, knuckles still resting on the desk.

"Ma, don't." Phillip gasped and struggled to push himself away from Bruna, away from Celos. He closed around himself, shrinking inward.

Celos relaxed his hand and allowed Phillip a moment of peace. The boy shuddered and drooped like a puppet with its strings cut. "I'm sure we can go deeper," Celos said calmly, pointing at Phillip again.

"I won't help you," Master Leschi snarled as she clung to the now shuddering form of her son.

"Even deeper," he whispered and was pleased to see Phillip flinch before he sent the next wave.

In a flash, every muscle along the boy's back tensed and he covered his head with his arms. A low moan tore from his throat that ended in a whimper.

"I'm sure we can do better than that," Celos purred.

His next wave ripped a scream from Phillip as if he'd been stabbed. Master Leschi whispered words of comfort in her son's ear and rocked him in her arms.

"Comply," Celos demanded.

"Never," Master Leschi spat.

"So be it." Celos snapped his fingers before pointing his ringed forefinger at the crumpled figure in Master Leschi's arms.

Phillip screamed in anguish, shuddering sobs raking his body as he cried, "No, no more, no more, not like this, please. Stop, I'll do anything! No more. Please!"

"Stop!" Master Leschi commanded. "Stop, please, just stop."

Celos paused, hand relaxed, fingers curling gently inward. "How soon before I have my fleet ready to load?" he asked softly.

"S-six weeks, Celos."

Celos drummed his thin fingers along the tabletop.

"Yes. Six weeks at least," she breathed.

"For the sake of your son, make it four," he commanded. Master Leschi began to protest but stopped suddenly at another roar of pain from Phillip.

"End it!" Phillip screamed. Clutching at his mother's hand like a man drowning, he stared at her with wild, pleading eyes. "End me," he whispered, "please." Master Leschi paled.

"Four is fine, Celos," she said hurriedly.

"Good." He relaxed his hand, and the boy collapsed without any further fuss. Celos adjusted the ring on his finger. "Now, what do you know about our little Queen?"

The
FREAN CHRONICLES

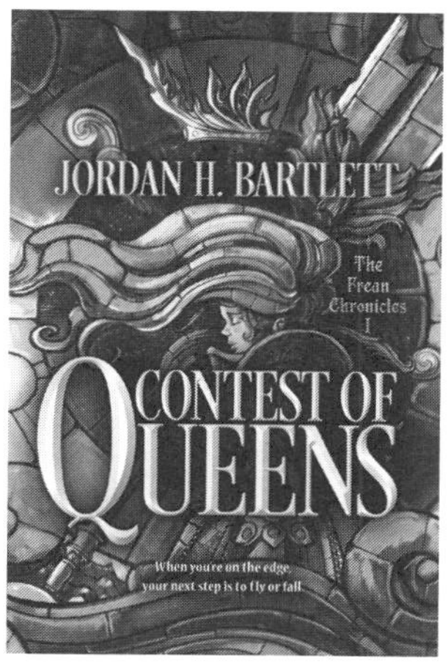

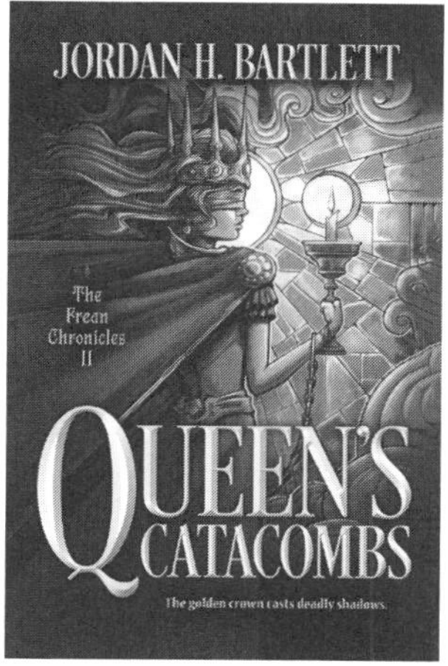

Coming 2024:
QUEENDOM COME

ACKNOWLEDGMENTS

To write and publish *Contest of Queens* felt like standing on top of a mountain, whooping into the air. Now with *Queen's Catacombs* sitting pretty right next to it on my bookshelf, I am awestruck that there was an even more satisfying mountain from which to whoop.

There are a few key people that helped make this sequel a reality, and I know that no words on paper are going to be sufficient to thank them enough, but here's to trying.

First and foremost, thank you to Sue and the CamCat team for continuing to have faith in me and my world. Bridget, my dream editor, thank you for your spark, your enthusiasm, and your spice-level wisdom. Thank you, Maryann, for outdoing yourself with this gorgeous cover, and all the other behind-the-scene superstars who helped get this book out into the big wide world.

To my incredibly supportive family. Cathy, Tim, and Josh. Mum and Dad, you planted the seeds that have become my stories. With your encouragement and endless patience, you gave me the space to give them a voice. Josh, I'm forever in awe of your wisdom and outlook on life. You truly have the makings of greatness in you. To the incredible family I have in New Zealand, England, and Canada—the Bartletts, Highleys, Birds, Hollands, Archers, Jones, and Nashes—I feel so lucky to have a support system that spans hemispheres.

A huge thank you to my beta readers, your passion for these characters helped bring them to life: Nikki, for your help finding Connor's backbone, you are the definition of slay and are an arched brow queen. I hope we never tire of Austen re-reads. Sarah, for your help finding Lena's power, and the great dilemma that is Theo. Thank you for spooking up my life, I used to be so confident not believing in ghosts.

To my dear friends: Katie, I like you, have a cupcake. No words can describe the place you hold in my heart, but know that I'd travel the world with you in an instant. Thank you for everything. Andrew, for drawing borders around Frea, and for the fairytales filled with marigolds and rose petals, you are a constant inspiration. Kate (and Squid), for being a sunflower among weeds, thank you for our chats. Syd, for showing me the strength it can take to feed the right wolf, I hope you know the brilliance with which you shine. Dr. Jessie, you have the elegance, dignity, and intellect of a literal elven queen. Thank you for your concern about Brindle (and so much more) and for talking medically accurate gore with me to make these stab wounds sting! Sonya, every moment spent with you is an adventure, thank you for showing me roots can grow anywhere, and for your endless optimism.

To my incredible Kula: Erin, Colemen, Larissa, Em, Michelle, Teale, and so many others. You all are candles in the dark and have helped me through my own Lethe. Thank you. To my friends across the world who hold pieces of my heart: The flawless Angelica; Jamie,

Angelina (and Pippa), endlessly creative and kind and who always have time for me; Erin (and Percy) who adds melody to my life; Billie (and Jasper) with your incredible eye for beauty; Joe and Sammy, you help me believe in modern day true love; Riley with your flair and ability to hold space while we hold mimosas; Laura, wise grandmamma Sibyl! your kindness is endless; Dana, my new author friend who I feel I've known for years; Josh, a fellow world builder and inspiration; Karli, a fellow queen; Lara, Kayla, Hilary, and Kelsie my goodest willed fellows; Asha, Julie, and Sarah, my inspiration for an elite team of girlbosses; Jo Annie and Olive, you two bring magic to my life; Nathalie (and Jack), my guardian angels and fellow star-gazing Austen fans; Matt who brought music to my realm-crossing love story; Sara, a true mentor and friend; and so many more. You are all jewels in this crown of life.

To those who feel lost in the dark, know that light is always within you. To those with the strength to get back up and to those who are still trying, know that we fall to rise again stronger. This life is hard, but it is also so incredibly beautiful—and it is undeniably a much better place with you in it.

And finally, to you, dearest reader. Oh Nelly. I want to thank you from the bottom of my heart for every page you turned and every word you read. For all the reviews and feedback, for the kind words and the critiques. This world I've created comes alive in your eyes, so thank you for seeing it. Thank you for living in it for a short time. I hope it gave you comfort, I hope it brought you joy, and most of all, I hope it made you think.

ABOUT THE AUTHOR

New Zealand-born Canadian Jordan H. Bartlett has lived on islands and surrounded by mountains, has fallen asleep to the sound of waves and train whistles. Growing up, home was the label given to family, not places, and stories of adventure kept her reaching toward the horizon. She grew up reading books about boys for boys and struggled to find that strong female heroine she could relate to. While empowering female characters are more prevalent in recent literature, they are often found in worlds dominated by men. Bartlett wrote *Contest of Queens* and *Queen's Catacombs* to create a world asking: What if female was the default gender?

Bartlett has studied the areas of children's literature and the role of women in literature throughout history. It is this affinity for fairy tales mixed with her desire to breathe life into compelling, unique, and ultimately flawed female characters in a world where they have not been tethered that she hopes to flip fantasy tropes and challenge gendered expectations in young adult readers—while keeping the levity of a fairy tale.

Bartlett typically resides in Banff, Alberta, where she works as a Speech Language Pathologist and is a certified yoga instructor. However, at the time of publishing *Queen's Catacombs*, she embarked on an adventure of her own to travel the United Kingdom. She is currently working on finishing the Frean Chronicles in the land of castles and Queens. She has devoured literature all her life and is honored to add to the world's library.

Find other works, author interviews,
and much more information at
https://jordanhbartlett.com

If you liked
Jordan H. Bartlett's *Queen's Catacombs*,
you'll also like
Kristi McManus's *Our Vengeful Souls.*

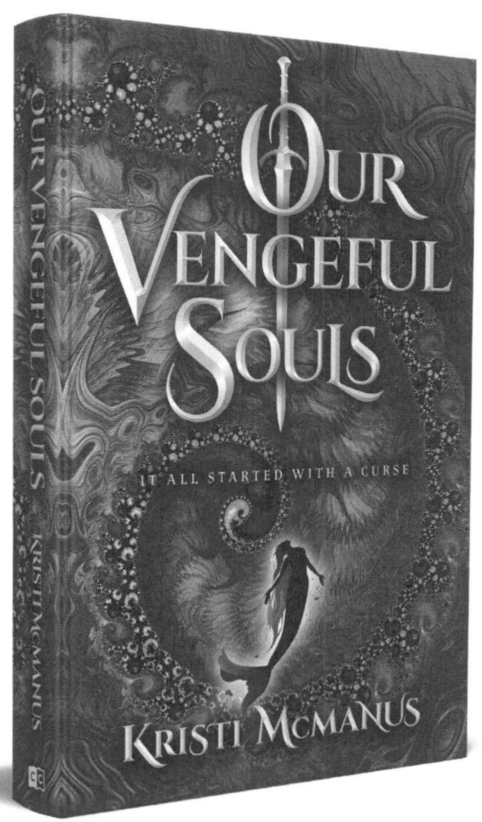

CHAPTER ONE

Our swords collide with a deafening crash, sparks sizzling and dying in the water as the blades strain against each other. The moment they touch, they break apart again like opposing magnets never able to resist each other, yet never able to truly connect.

I pivot quickly, narrowly missing Triton's next strike as the blade swings by my cheek. The disturbed water brushes softly against my skin like a caress, but warning sings in my veins of how close he came to spilling my blood.

Spinning to face him again, I clutch my weapon with both hands, fingers tightening along the hilt as I eye my prey. His tail is curved, coiled like an eel preparing to strike as he takes inventory of me just as I am of him. His cerulean-blue eyes are narrowed, lips parted, muscles tense. His chest heaves, panting breath escaping through clenched teeth, evidence that he is winded. The longer we face off, the angrier he becomes. Not at me, necessarily, but at himself for taking so long to defeat me.

We've been at this for hours, with barely a moment to rest. Not that either of us would admit to needing one. To require rest would be to admit weakness, that the other is skilled enough to push us to our limits.

Such a concession is unacceptable. Beyond our teachings of strength and focus, our endless hours in this ring, our pride is the strongest factor in our stamina.

We never back down from each other.

He surges forward through the water without warning, blade poised overhead in his iron grip, ready to hand out a match-ending strike, but I am faster, lithe, and swift, bringing my sword up to block the impact inches from my face.

Rather than retreat again, continuing our dance, he remains poised above me, his superior height blocking the few rays of light piercing through the water until he is little more than a silhouette before my eyes. His blade presses against my own, metal grinding in protest, neither of us relenting.

My muscles quiver at the effort it takes to keep him at bay. They burn with an exquisite pain, reminding me that I am alive, that I am powerful. My teeth grind, lips curling back as I stand my ground. I see a glint of light reflect off the steel in my hands, shaking as I resist the possibility of defeat.

His full lips curve into a grin, teeth grinding despite the playful, goading gesture. Golden hair spills from the tie at the nape of his neck, dancing around his face, catching the light from the surface. The sharp jaw and angular features that cause the other mermaids to swoon are tense with the effort of our fight.

"Tired, sister?" he asks coolly. Despite his attempt to appear indifferent, the lines of his face are hard, his jaw tense. He is struggling.

Weakening. The realization causes my lips to quirk into a smile to match his own.

"Not at all, dear brother." I bring my face closer to his, and in turn, closer to our connected blades, and magic prickles beneath my skin. Strands of my white-blonde hair wave around me like a crown under the influence of the sea, my green eyes burning into his. "I will endure as long as you require. I wouldn't want to bow down too soon, thus not giving our precious heir a suitable sparring partner."

My taunt does as I hope: his teeth snap as a growl erupts deep in the back of his throat. The moment I feel the pressure of his sword weaken, I strike, swiping my tail outward and knocking him off balance. He hits the sea floor with a thunderous impact, sand and stone billowing out from around his prone form. Pride sings through my muscles, burning away the exhaustion. Putting Triton to the ground never ceases to thrill me, no matter how many times I best him.

A gasp ripples from those around us, the select permitted to watch us train. A few of the maids present, hovering in the corner to gawk and swoon over my brother, cover their mouths in horror. His muscular frame lies sprawled across the floor, hair once smooth and controlled now wild and loose in the gentle current. No longer does he look so pristine and perfect, now that I have cracked his confidence.

This area of the palace is restricted for most. Beyond the coral halls and glistening stone floors of the living quarters, banquet halls, and meeting rooms rests the arena in which we barter our worth. Sand floors and towering stone walls breaking to an oculus ceiling high above allow the remaining reach of the day's sun to breach to our depth. An expanse of weapons covers every wall—blades and staffs, all with the singular purpose of training the royals.

Casting a glance to the outskirts of the hall, I find my parents lingering in the shadows. Their scales glitter, catching the light like precious gems, brighter than those around them. Even without their crowns they exude regal poise. Something I have yet to master.

Looking their way is a mistake, of course. A weakness I repeatedly chastise myself for, as it never provides the assurance I hope. And yet, every time I force Triton to his knees, I cannot help but look for a sign of approval.

My mother watches with keen green eyes, with the kind of look that makes you feel as though she is cutting right through your soul. Her hair, the same white blonde as my own, plaited down her back, is contrasted against the deep greens of her sea lace top. Long sleeves adorned with pearls cling to her slender, enviable frame, the neck high to her jaw. Her skin shimmers as if diamonds are embedded in it, a symbol of our kind, luminous and beckoning. She is stunning, her mere presence demanding attention and respect. And her hypnotizing gaze is locked on me, a proud smile toying with the corners of her coral lips.

Against my better judgment, I allow myself a glance at my father. He is as I expect to find him: jaw tight and teeth clenched, his deep blue eyes locked on the shape of his eldest son and heir pushing up from the ground. Displeasure radiates off his form, causing the water around him to ripple against his power. When his eyes turn to me, I do not see pride. I see fury, barely concealed.

He isn't proud that his daughter is a skilled fighter. No more than he is proud that my magic exceeds that of my brother. He is angry that I dare embarrass him by putting Triton on his back.

My confidence wavers under his stare, my grip weakening on the hilt of my sword.

The momentary distraction is all Triton needs. I feel the water move before I see him from the corner of my eye. By the time I tighten my hands around my sword, steady my stance, he collides with me, knocking the air from my lungs. His massive weight knocks me back, forcing me to drop my blade rather than end up on the ground. I backflip out of the fall, landing coiled and ready to respond to his next attack, but he doesn't retreat or pause his pursuit, satisfied with disarming me. Instead, his large hand grips my throat, throwing my body to the floor painfully, his blade poised above my heart. Breath knocks from my lungs at the impact of the ground at my back, bones aching in protest and muscles burning.

My hands grapple at his arm, body writhing against the weight pinning me, but it is no use. He has won.

A smile curves his lips as he loosens his hold on my neck. "Always so easily distracted," he taunts, running the blade along my cheek like a lover's touch. "Well done, baby sister."

I growl, unable to form words, as he pushes up and releases me. Soft applause fills the hall as he swims away, arms raised above his head, relishing his victory, the muscles of his back flexing with each flick of his tail. The maids in the corner of the arena titter as he comes their way, running their fingers through their hair, their tails swaying seductively.

I lay on the floor a moment longer, my eyes trained skyward, through the oculus to where the sun dances beyond the surface of the water. Its brightness is muted at this depth, battling against the power of the sea. The sand is soft at my back, like a gentle touch consoling my loss. From where I lay, I cannot see the walls of the arena for the open ceiling, the ombre blues of the ocean leading to a world beyond this one. From here, I can almost pretend I am somewhere else.

Rubbing my face with my hands, I exhale a long breath before pushing up and accepting my defeat.

I don't look their way, but in my peripheral vision I can see my father clapping Triton on the back, congratulating him for his win. My jaw clicks against the force of my teeth biting together. It doesn't matter that I had him on the ground, or that I could have ended the match in my favor more than once. All that matters is, in the end, that Triton was victorious. That is all that ever matters to him.

Swimming off the floor, I head toward the exit, desperate to make it back to my quarters. All I want now is quiet, solace, to collect myself and my pride. Fury ignites the spark within me, and I can feel my magic simmer under my skin. Flexing my fingers, it crackles as it comes alive, whispering consolation and reminders of where my true power lies.

Before I can escape, I am met by my mother at the edge of the hall.

"You did wonderfully, Sereia." Her hands reach out to tuck a lock of my hair behind my ear. She usually scolds me for allowing my hair to be loose, reminding me of the expectation that it be tied and tamed rather than left wild and free. Today it would seem she recognizes the dent to my pride and holds her tongue.

"I lost, Mother." The words are bitter on my tongue. I run my fingers over the scales of my tail, feeling each ridge, watching the iridescent colors change from blue to green to purple. I lose myself in the tactile sensation, grounding myself and my body.

I am powerful, I remind myself silently, a chanting prayer to sooth my honor. *I am strong. I have magic beyond his wildest dreams.*

"Only because you allowed yourself to be distracted," Mother says gently, pulling me from my thoughts. "You lost focus, allowing Triton to take advantage. If you had remained in the ring, both mind and body, I have no doubt—"

"No doubt that Father would have continued the match until I was weakened, exhausted and breathless, so Triton could use his strength to win."

Her lips curve downward, the green of her eyes darkening. "Never allow yourself to dwell, Sereia. Whether Triton is meant to be victorious is irrelevant. It does not diminish your skill or your worth."

Looking up from under my lashes, I find my brother and father conversing with a member of the council. No doubt already deep in conversation about kingdom matters. Things that my sister and I are not privy to. I cannot help but wonder what my father would have done if I had been the firstborn. If rather than a son born in his likeness, a daughter, bright and powerful, were his heir? Would he still dismiss me? Think me nothing more than breeding stock to his line?

Following my gaze, my mother purses her lips.

"Your brother may be superior in strength, my daughter," her voice breaks me away from the sight. "But you harness the most potent magic of us all. While he excels in the ring, through your gifts, you strike fear and power in a way no one else in our history ever has. Never doubt yourself, Sereia."

I nod in silent agreement, ready to change the subject as my eyes skim the room.

"Where is Asherah?" I ask, pulling my shoulders back to straighten my spine. I refuse to appear defeated, for others to see me cower, even if my soul wishes to escape and lick my wounds.

Mother's lips twitch. "Off on another adventure, I'm sure."

A single laugh escapes me. "If Triton or I ran off so frequently, we would have been dealt the whip," I remind her with a quirked brow.

Mother waves her hand dismissively. "You seem to forget all the trouble your brother and you got into when you were her age. Just because you are of age now, don't fool yourself to think you were never as tenacious as her. You were hardly obedient or cautious."

I snort in response, but don't bother arguing. It would be pointless. Memories of breaching the boundaries of the kingdom, venturing into the darkest depths of the sea were still fresh in my mind. With Triton at my side, I was fearless. Unshakable. Just as he stood taller knowing I had his back, that nothing could defeat us when together.

It felt like a century ago. When our childhood was still filled with freedom and possibility, and the expectations of our birthrights felt like a far-off dream. Before we were pitted against each other, the heir versus the girl who grudgingly held the position of spare.

"You let her run wild like a hellion," I point out gently, earning myself a soft look of warning from my mother. I smile innocently but continue. "She's still a princess. Anything could happen—"

My words are cut off by a flurry of raised voices, the swishing of tails in a corner of the arena. Breaking my gaze from my mother, I watch as a group of guards approaches my father, their faces hard. Their golden armor catches the dying rays of sun from the surface, the dark obsidian scales of their tails marking their rank imposing in contrast.

General Aenon, the leader of the guard, reaches my father first, removing his helmet in respect. His face is all sharp angles and rough skin, a scar leading from the corner of his lip to his eye. An unfortunate encounter with a human hook as a child that marred him for life but added a sense of strength when coupled with his rank. With a small, almost imperceptible bow, he brings his lips to Father's ear, whispering rapidly. From where I stand, I cannot hear their words, but I don't need to. I can read my father's face like the pages of a book, and as his eyes widen and skin flushes, I know there's trouble.

"What's going on?" I whisper, my voice barely audible despite the deathly silence of the room.

"I don't know," Mother admits, taking my hand and pulling me toward the group.

My initial instinct is to pull away, to remind her that I have no place in their gathering. Despite my blood, as second born and female, I am still excluded from all form of kingdom matters. But my mother's grip is firm, whether in fear or assurance, I cannot tell. I do not refuse her, hoping if nothing else that my presence gives her strength.

Drawing up to Triton's flank, I wait silently.

"I told her not to go there," Father growls, the ground quivering against his rising rage. The walls of the arena shake, groaning in protest against his power. Sand and stone fall, dripping from the walls like blood. "I swear, the girl is careless."

"We have sent a group after her," General Aenon replies, assuring him as he casts a glance to my mother's worried face. "You have my word, Your Majesty. We will bring Asherah home."

With a nod, the general turns to his troops, quiet mutterings of plans and tactics already spilling from his lips.

"What happened?" My mother asks, her hands falling on my father's thick forearm.

For as harsh and cold as he is to me, he is soft and loving to her. The way he looks at her, cherishes her, is the source of legends throughout our land. It is the only proof to me that he has a heart at all.

"Asherah," he sighs, shaking his head. "She escaped her guard detail. Again. They've gone after her along the edge of the Blue Hole, since she tends to frequent the places she is forbidden." He pauses, his eyes turning soft, and I know he is considering holding the next statement back. But he never refuses my mother, and he knows she will ask if he does not offer everything he knows. "They saw humans in the area. Several ships, poaching from our waters without limit or remorse."

A gasp catches in my mother's throat, her delicate hand coming to her lips. "Poseidon—"

Turning away from the Court, from the guards, and even from my brother, he brings his hands to her arms. In this moment, I know no one else is present to him. He sees only her. My heart aches at the unwavering adoration in his gaze.

"We will bring her home, Amphitrite. I swear to you, I will bring our daughter home."

As he pulls my mother against his broad chest, tears burn at my eyes. Fear for my sister grapples against the jealousy I fight to ignore, the pain of the affection he has never shown me, like powerful seahorses pulling me in two directions at once, threatening to tear me in two.

My father releases her before turning to Triton, all softness fading like the dying light of day. "Be ready to leave in five minutes," he barks, calm leached from his voice. "We will need all the help we can get to find her."

Triton nods once, pulling his shoulders back in pride. This is the first time my father has allowed him to take part in such tasks, and the thrill of the opportunity flickers through the deep azure of his eyes. The chance to prove himself worthy of the throne, and the trident which would amplify his power and solidify the right to rule.

The trident is all Triton has thought about since first truly understanding what his birthright entails.

Of the power, the amplified magic it would bestow him, unmatched by any other weapon remaining in the world since its twin disappeared more than a millennia ago. Where the lost trident has faded to legend and myth, the remaining is all my brother now covets.

Before they can step away, my mother reaches out, grasping my father's arm. "Wait." She clutches my hand, pulling me forward. "Take Sereia with you."

Shock and disgust drips over my father's features, making my stomach turn. The way his eyes widen in surprise before narrowing in defiance at the mere suggestion causes my gaze to fall to the floor. His lips pull back, revealing his white teeth.

"Amphitrite, this is not a training exercise. We—"

My mother cuts him off with an angry glare, her voice as sharp as coral. "Sereia is the most powerful sea summoner we have, and you know it. If you wish to control the sea, to prevent the humans' escape if they dare have Asherah, she is the only one powerful enough. This is not a game. This is our daughter's life!"

Tension pours from my brother like lava escaping an underwater volcano, heating the water around us. I don't look his way. I don't dare. I am not foolish enough to miss the insult thrown his way, as Mother reminds everyone around us of my power.

A level of power my brother does not possess.

Swallowing a bitter retort, my father lifts his chin. "Very well."

Turning to me, his eyes harden. "Keep up. If you fall behind, we will not wait for you, nor will we go in search of you if you become lost. Don't embarrass me by becoming a liability."

I am not given a chance to respond before he spins away, tail thrashing through the water, toward the armory. The guards follow without a word or glance, churning the water violently in their haste.

My mother's beautiful face comes into my eyeline. Reaching a hand to my cheek, she swipes her thumb along the skin under my eye. Her silent way of wishing me well, before she, too, retreats to her chambers to wait. Her mermaids-in-waiting follow, each with head bowed, until I am alone with my brother.

The water is heavy all around me, crushing me under its weight the longer neither of us speaks. I can feel the burning heat of his gaze at the side of my face, hear the crack of his knuckles as his fists clench. In this moment, I am certain he wishes he had plunged that blade through my heart while he had the chance.

Ignoring the frantic beating of my heart, the uncertainty coursing through my veins like ichor, I take a deep breath. The corners of my lips threaten to turn upward, but I refuse them. A smile now would be asking for a fight. But I cannot ignore the pride that runs through me, erasing the fear and shame.

Finally, I can show him what I can do. If I succeed, he can no longer ignore me, casting me to the side.

Slowly wiggling my fingers, my magic courses through me like a silent predator.

I am powerful. I am the master of waves and swells. I am descended from the Gods.

Risking a glance toward Triton, I find him staring at me.

Fire licks behind his eyes, sparks igniting at his fingertips. I wait for him to speak, whether to assure me that we will save our sister, or to damn me for daring to intrude on his moment to prove himself, but he says nothing. He merely glares at me, his silence almost as bad as any harsh word or scathing insult.

Our father returns, an army at his back, and neither Triton nor I have moved. Hovering at the entrance to the hall, he is adorned in steel-and-gold armor, an ornate helmet taming his long golden hair. The family crest, a Trident overlaid upon a triangle, is embossed on his chest, marking him as King. The Trident is in his grip, shining and terrifying.

While he shouts for both of us, he only looks to Triton.

"Come, we need to move. Now!"